W9-CAH-784

"Susan Krinard has set the standard for today's fantasy romance."
— *Affaire de Coeur*

"The reading world would be a happier place if more paranormal romance writers wrote as well as Krinard."
— *Contra Costa Sunday Times*

"A master of atmosphere and description."
— *Library Journal*

PRAISE FOR
Secret of the Wolf

"The third book in Krinard's saga of the loup-garou Forster siblings, an artful combination of heartfelt romance, psychiatric historical detail, and werewolf lore, will elicit howls of delight from her ever-growing following."
— *Booklist*

"A fascinating story, skillfully told, *Secret of the Wolf* may very well be Susan Krinard's best book to date. Always a powerful storyteller, Susan Krinard offers another complex, richly textured tale . . . It may also be her most successfully realized romance."
— *The Romance Reader*

"This is by far Ms. Krinard's deepest, most intense book ever!"
— *Rendezvous*

"An excellent story . . . Ms. Krinard's characters are up to her usual high standards . . . A wonderful read! I can't wait to add it to my 'keeper' shelf."
— *Old Book Barn Gazette*

"With riveting dialogue and passionate characters, Ms. Krinard exemplifies her exceptional knack for creating an extraordinary story of love, strength, courage, and compassion."
— *Romantic Times*

continued . . .

The
FOREST LORD

Susan Krinard

BERKLEY BOOKS, NEW YORK

This is a work of fiction. Names, characters, places, and incidents either are the product of the author's imagination or are used fictitiously, and any resemblance to actual persons, living or dead, business establishments, events, or locales is entirely coincidental.

THE FOREST LORD

A Berkley Book / published by arrangement with the author

PRINTING HISTORY
Berkley edition / November 2002

Copyright © 2002 by Susan Krinard.
Cover design George Long.
Cover art by Franco Accornero.

ISBN: 0-425-18686-5

BERKLEY®
Berkley Books are published by The Berkley Publishing Group,
a division of Penguin Putnam Inc.,
375 Hudson Street, New York, New York 10014.
BERKLEY and the "B" design
are trademarks belonging to Penguin Putnam Inc.

PRINTED IN THE UNITED STATES OF AMERICA

10 9 8 7 6 5 4

This book is respectfully dedicated to the wonderful authors who first introduced me to the delights of Regency romance: Jane Austen, Georgette Heyer, Rosemary Edghill, Elizabeth Thornton, Mary Balogh, and so many others.

Special thanks to Margaret Evans Porter and the members of the Regency Loop, whose expertise enabled me to navigate the sometimes treacherous waters of Regency life and history. Any errors are my own, and in no way reflect upon the talents of these generous individuals.

Prologue

*O*nce upon a time, there was a great and mysterious
   forest at the heart of Westmorland in the north of England — a place where few mortal men dared trespass.
This forest lay on the estates of the Flemings, men of
wealth and property, who long ago had sworn an oath to
protect the forest and all its inhabitants from the ravages
of mankind. In exchange, the Flemings and their kin
should never suffer want or ill fortune.

   The ruler of this enchanted wood was not of human
blood, but of the Faerie, or Fane, an ancient race of near-
immortal magical beings. He had lived among mortals for
millennia, wearing many names and guises, and had become one of the last of the Elder Race to remain in the
realm of man. But he wearied of his exile from the Blessed
Land of his own people — Tir-na-nog in the language of
the men of Eire — and sought to leave behind the forest he
had guarded.

   The Fane had grown few in number, and their blood
was thin. To save the race from extinction, each Fane stole
or sired a half-human child to increase their numbers. The
Forest Lord alone had not provided his people with such a

child, and so the queen of the Fane commanded that he should not enter Tir-na-nog until he returned with an heir of his making.

Despising mankind, the Forest Lord withdrew to his wood. He watched, and waited, and kept his oath with the human masters of Hartsmere.

The Flemings flourished beyond their wildest dreams. The king granted an earldom, and the Fleming lands grew. Hartsmere became only one estate of many, and the age-old pact was all but forgotten.

So it was that one day the oath was broken. Cyrus Fleming, the Earl of Bradwell, did not believe the stories of the bargain that kept his pockets filled and his lands prosperous. He had almost everything a man could desire, including a beautiful daughter and the leisure to pursue his passion for hunting the beasts of the earth and the birds of the sky.

One autumn day, he traveled to Hartsmere in search of prey and followed his baying hounds across the fells and dales and to the very edge of the forest. There he glimpsed the most magnificent creature he had ever beheld: a stag of immense size and nobility, waiting as if to invite his shot.

Lord Bradwell fired at the beast and pursued it as it fled into the forest. But he found himself alone. His hounds had vanished, and even the trees seemed to bend down with twisted arms to catch and hold him.

In the place of the stag stood a man such as he had never seen: tall, handsome, and dressed in skins and rough cloth. Upon his head he wore a crown of antlers woven with holly and mistletoe.

"You have trespassed upon my realm," the man said in a voice of thunder. "You have sought the life of one of my own and broken the pact. For that you must be punished."

Lord Bradwell realized at once that the stories were true: This man — if man he could be called — was the guardian spirit of the forest, deathless and merciless, a creature of fey power beyond the ken of mortals. Struck mute, Lord Bradwell had no defense to make as the Forest

Lord raised his hand to strike. All at once the ground about his feet swarmed and danced with a hundred woodland creatures.

"Should I let my brothers and sisters decide your fate?" cried the Forest Lord.

"Mercy," Lord Bradwell whispered.

"As you have shown mercy to those so much weaker than yourself?" He stroked the head of a fox that crept up to lick his hand. "I could take away all the bounty and fortune you and your lands have enjoyed. You would be left with nothing but your life." His smile chilled Lord Bradwell's blood. "Death might be more merciful. But I will grant you both life and continued prosperity in exchange for one small thing.

"You will give me your daughter."

Horrified, Lord Bradwell thought of the girl who waited for him far to the south — girl no longer, for she had just turned eighteen. Eden, her beauty pure and untouched, her innocence unsullied, had been groomed all her life for marriage to a man of consequence and title.

"I will never give my daughter to a monster," he cried. But even as he spoke, he felt his legs grow numb. When he looked down upon them, he found them brown and covered in bark and rooted deep into the earth.

"I have guarded this land for many of your centuries," said the Forest Lord, "and I grow weary. It is time to rejoin those who have gone before me to the Land of the Young. But I must bring an heir of my body to replenish our race. Your daughter will bear him for me."

"Eden is too young," Lord Bradwell begged. "Do not ask this of me." He felt the numbness rise to his waist, and the beasts of the wood drew closer. He knew then that he had no choice but to agree.

"I will do as you demand," he said, "but only if you present yourself to my daughter as an honorable man of stature and court her as a mortal man would do. If she is seen to be with child and has no husband, she will be ruined."

"I have no wish to harm her," said the Forest Lord, frowning with terrible wrath. "I will wed your daughter for the time the child grows in her body. I will appear in any guise necessary to protect that virtue which you mortals so value. But after the child is born, I will take him and leave your world forever."

Lord Bradwell bent his head. "You are without pity."

"What do mortals know of pity? The pain your daughter suffers will be small, and she will be rich for the rest of her life."

Gathering his courage, Lord Bradwell looked into the Forest Lord's cold eyes. "I have one final condition. You must win my daughter's love. Nothing can be taken by force or trickery or fey magic. She must give herself willingly."

"I agree to your conditions." The Forest Lord waved his hand, and Lord Bradwell felt his legs again. "Now, go. Do what you must to prepare my way, and come to me when all is ready. But do not dally, or I will send my brothers to remind you of our bargain."

With shrieks and cries, the beasts of the forest drove Lord Bradwell from the wood as he had driven the hare and the stag. But when the earl sent for his daughter and looked upon her face, he knew what he had truly done.

Today is my wedding day.

Eden woke to the sounds of hooves and carriage wheels on the cobbles outside the open window. The morning air was cool and moist with the promise of a spring storm, yet she didn't mind. The rain-laden breeze carried all the freshness of life and hope and a shining future.

She stretched in the unfamiliar bed, and her fingertips brushed the warm body beside her.

My husband, she thought. Cornelius.

She closed her eyes and trembled with sheer happiness. The very core of her being was still imprinted with his form, his scent, his masculine strength. She had not guessed that to lie with a man could be so wonderful. And to think they had almost waited — waited until Gretna.

She was glad they had not. Gretna Green was a mere five miles away. By day's end, they would truly be husband and wife, with a lifetime of such nights to look forward to.

"Cornelius," she murmured, snuggling against his chest. "It is morning."

He stirred but did not open his eyes. She spent the glorious minutes studying his face. Any woman who saw him now would be stung with envy at her good fortune. Surely no man had ever been so beautiful and yet so strong. She allowed herself the liberty of tracing her finger around the curve of his jaw, over the firm set of his lips, across the straight, dark brows.

Six months ago he had been a stranger, a distant cousin come from India, and of little interest to her. After all, she did not intend to remain in country exile forever; the tedious winters she spent with her father eventually ended. With the coming of each spring, she returned to London, where she had spent so much of her childhood under Aunt Claudia's fashionable wing.

Aunt Claudia had made it clear that when Eden married, it must be to a young man of good standing in the *ton,* who enjoyed high rank, a generous income, and the many pleasures of Society.

Cornelius Fleming was merely a curiosity, a distraction from the dull sameness of country days and the awful pall of loneliness. Hartsmere was the original Fleming estate, least of the earl's many holdings. Eden hated it above all the others, remote as it was from London and her friends. Her father was casually affectionate and otherwise ignored her — she, who dreaded solitude more than anything in the world.

Cornelius had paid attention to her. And, gradually, she had seen him as the perfect subject upon whom to practice her growing skills at beguiling the male sex. "You must allow men to believe they are in control but never lose it yourself," Aunt Claudia had taught her. How could she lose control with a dull fish like Cornelius Fleming?

How odd and vexing she'd thought him at first, with his haughty airs and long silences. He had an irksome propensity to wander off into the fells like any foolish tourist who came to gape in wonder at peaks and lakes and crags. His utter lack of interest in Society might have put her off entirely, if not for his god's looks and the sense of power that he wore like a cloak.

"Be kind to him, Eden," her father had said in one of his rare conversations with her. "He has been long in India, unfamiliar with our ways. Should my brother and nephew die, he may very well inherit the title when I am gone."

She'd laughed and dismissed his uncharacteristically sober words. But she could not dismiss Cornelius. She found his gaze following her wherever she went, and his glances heated her blood. Behind his reticence lay unexpected tenderness. Every day he brought miraculous gifts of exotic perfumes and fine silks. At the New Year, he presented her with a diamond of amazing size and brilliance. Little by little, against all her best intentions, she found herself in love.

Aunt Claudia had not approved. She had actually come from her apartments in London to observe this dubious suitor. But though Lady Claudia Raines had ruled her niece since childhood, Eden was no longer a child. When Cornelius asked her to elope, she hadn't hesitated for a moment.

Now he was *hers*. She would teach him as Claudia taught her, mold him to become the perfect Society beau. He already possessed a Corinthian's muscle and a remarkable way with horses. In time, he would come to love fashionable London as much as she did, and they'd nevermore return to the icy, echoing, desolate halls of Hartsmere.

First they must find a perfect London town house. Then she would tease Aunt Claudia into presenting them, making all the necessary introductions, and smoothing any awkwardness resulting from the elopement. Once Lady Claudia recognized all the advantages of the match, she must relent.

The *ton* would come to know, as Eden did, that Cornelius's arrogance and retiring nature concealed boundless generosity, excellent taste, and an elegance that was natural rather than taught.

No one but she would know his more intimate skills. . . .

Somewhere within the inn a door slammed. A stray raindrop blew through the window to kiss Eden's cheek. Cornelius sat up, the sheets cascading from his bare chest.

"Cornelius?" Eden touched his shoulder, gripped by sudden desire. "Good morning. I hope I didn't wake you —"

He stared at the door. "Get dressed, Eden."

It was not the greeting she expected. She wanted him to kiss her, draw her into his arms, whisper endearments as he had last night.

A chill slipped down the collar of her night rail. She hugged herself, wanting to close the window but afraid to leave the warm sanctuary of the bed.

Afraid of what? This was only the beginning of her life. Of their lives together.

Cornelius swung his feet to the floor and went to the chair where he had laid his clothing. He dressed swiftly and efficiently, barely hesitating to glance in her direction.

"Clothe yourself," he said. "We may need to leave quickly."

"What is wrong, Cornelius?" She could hear raised voices downstairs. "Is something —"

"We will speak of it later." He snatched her fine white muslin carriage dress from the clothespress and tossed it onto the bed as if it were made of sackcloth.

She smoothed her hand over the skirts of her gown. "It is sadly creased," she murmured. But he was not listening. He finished tying his neckcloth and strode to the door.

"Remain here until I come for you," he said. He paused

at the door and attempted a smile. "Do not worry. I will return." The door closed with ominous finality behind him.

Something was wrong. Very wrong. Cornelius had not treated her with such negligence since their first meeting. And after last night . . .

I am not a child, she told the tears gathering at the corners of her eyes. She picked up her dress and resolved to put it on without asking the help of one of the maids. But the tapes defied her best attempts to tie them. She should never have left Hartsmere without Tilly.

Another door slammed, and the voices moved under her feet. One of them was her husband's. The other . . . was Papa's. He had come after them. But why? He had encouraged the match, and he was no high-stickler. He was himself impetuous enough to understand why she had not wished to wait for a formal wedding.

She threw her pelisse over the half-buttoned frock. Obedience might be a wife's duty, but she was not a wife just yet. She would not expect Cornelius to face her father alone. She slipped through the door and descended the stairs, following the voices and holding her head high in defiance of any curious stares she might encounter.

The door to the private dining room off the entrance hall was firmly closed. With utmost concentration, Eden eased it open the merest crack.

"You agreed to the bargain," Cornelius said, his voice more harsh than she had ever heard it. A stranger's voice. "You knew the penalty for breaking it."

"Yes." If Cornelius spoke severely, her father was the very soul of weary despair. "Yes, I know. I was wrong to agree. A coward." His ragged breathing was that of a frightened old man. "I wished to save myself at my daughter's expense. She deserves far more than the sorrow you will give her. She loves you."

"Is that not what you asked, that I win her love?"

"But you do not love her. You cannot." He made a sound terribly like weeping. "I ask — I beg — that you let Eden go. I shall accept whatever punishment you choose."

"It is too late." Cornelius's boot heels drummed across the floor. "The choice is yours no longer. Last night I got her with child."

Eden felt her throat close up, as if to strangle a scream she was too distressed to utter. Raindrops began to patter on the roof overhead. She leaned her forehead against the door.

"You swore to marry her —"

"And so I shall, this very day. As we agreed. And all the rest will proceed as we agreed. You will not interfere."

Eden knew that the voices continued, but she no longer heard them. Her heart had swelled into a great, aching lump in her chest. *Is that not what you asked, that I win her love?*

A bargain. Her father and Cornelius had made a bargain with her as the spoils. For what? Not for money or title or land. Cornelius cared nothing for such things. Or had he deliberately led her to believe he didn't? He spoke of her as if she were a . . . a horse or a fine Herdwick ewe.

I got her with child. Eden touched the smooth plane beneath her breasts. Was that what he had wanted? Aunt Claudia had hinted of men who might rob a lady of her virtue, but Cornelius still planned to marry her.

Marry a woman he could not love.

The ache in her chest grew bigger and bigger until it threatened to burst.

"Very well," her father said. "I cannot hope to stand against you. But I ask you to drink with me, one last time, to prove your good faith." Footsteps, and the tinkle of liquid pouring into a glass. "Drink to my daughter, and to her happiness."

Silence followed — one heartbeat, two, three. And then came the brittle shattering of glass upon the floor.

Eden burst through the door. Her father half crouched against the far wall, an untouched glass of dark liquid in his hand. The other glass lay smashed in a pool of spilled liquor at his feet.

The man who had broken that glass raised his hand, and her father dropped to all fours.

Something was happening to Cornelius's face, his hands — something that made Eden betray herself with a cry of horror.

Her father's tormentor turned sharply to Eden, and she froze in midstep.

Her husband-to-be had vanished. In his place stood a creature with his face but dressed in animal skins and rags. From his brow grew a crown of antlers that nearly scraped the low ceiling.

He had become a monster.

She covered her mouth with her hand. The creature with Cornelius's face opened his mouth to speak, and took a single step toward her with one brown hand outstretched.

The blood rushing in her ears drowned out the steady drum of rain and her own gasping breaths. She stumbled back, feeling for the door behind her.

And she ran. Blindly, with no purpose other than escape. She passed a handful of servants and the innkeeper, following the cool, wet draft of air that meant freedom. The inn's door stood ajar, admitting a sodden pair of travelers. Eden pushed past them without a word.

The dirty cobbles of the stable yard were already slick with mud. She dodged the horses and hostlers and dashed for the gate. In a matter of minutes, her dress was soaked through and her pelisse half fallen from her shoulders.

Still she ran, until the roar of thunder muffled even the hammering of her heart. When she could go no farther, she stopped and turned her face up to the sky. Her hair hung in knotted ropes down her back. One of her shoes was lost. *She* was lost.

She laughed. Her mouth filled with water, and she swallowed it, wishing to be drowned. She fell to her knees and rocked back and forth, shivering, while raindrops played the role of tears that would not come.

Today is my wedding day.

Today her life was over.

Chapter 1

"My lady, Mr. Winstowe is asking for you."
Lady Eden Winstowe turned from her bleak view of Brook Street and acknowledged the butler's hushed summons with a nod. "Thank you, Bailey. I shall go up presently." She glanced out the window again, through the splattered raindrops that drowned the world on this dark November morning.

So the time had come. How strange that it should fall at a season when most of the *ton* had left for their estates to enjoy hunting and holidays, family and friends.

Her throat tightened with the memory of grief. Spencer had been lost to her long ago, before his final illness had drained the life from his body. She had known for years that he wanted to be rid of her, free to marry some fresh young woman with a larger and more reliable income — though it seemed increasingly unlikely that any woman would accept the debauched, unbalanced man he had become. She would gladly have given him that freedom rather than see it end like this, in such pain and bitterness.

Once she'd hated him. Now she felt only pity and helplessness. Lady Eden Winstowe could flout anyone except Death.

"The fire has gone out, my lady. I will send a maid to light it again."

Eden glanced at the coals in the grate, aware of the chill for the first time in hours. "It is quite unnecessary, Bailey. As long as the fire is adequate in Mr. Winstowe's chamber —"

"It is, my lady. The doctor is still with him, and Mr. Reynolds. Is there anything more I can do for you?"

The poor man had little enough to do now that they had taken the knocker from the door and closed the house to visitors. "I shall see Mr. Winstowe now, Bailey."

He bowed and retreated from the room, leaving her to face the stairs alone. The stairs that led to yet another ending.

The doctor looked up as she entered, his eyes telling her everything she needed to know. Mr. Reynolds never paused in his silent reading of his Bible, straining to make out the words in the light of the fire. The room stank of the chamber pot, but it was a smell with which Eden had become most familiar.

"Eden."

Spencer lay propped up among his pillows, his sallow face gaunt as a skull. The once-handsome dandy was withered and wasted, but she could still see mockery through the swelling of his faded gray eyes and feel his barely veiled contempt. It only made her pity him the more.

"Spencer," she said, knowing that formality was pointless. She sat in the chair beside the bed and took his hand. "You wished to see me."

"My gay, beautiful Eden," he said. His voice was reduced to a husky rasp. "How it must appall you to be trapped here with me."

"No, Spencer." She struggled for words. Their marriage had never included much conversation and far less sympathy. "I only wish —"

"That I'd gone sooner? All these . . . dreadful weeks of

nursing me —" He tried to sit up and coughed, a deep, racking sound followed by a wheeze as he fought to breathe. Dr. Jones placed a gentle hand on his shoulder and eased him back down.

I wish that we might have made a real peace before this, Eden thought. There was still time. One last chance.

"I wish that I had been a better wife to you," she said. "I wish that I could have made you happy."

He laughed. "Oh, you did . . . for a while, lovely Eden. As long as the money lasted." His breath rattled, but he summoned up his strength and continued. "Unfortunately, your father did me the great discourtesy of losing his wealth and most of his land. After all I sacrificed to marry such —" He closed his eyes and shuddered. "But that would be most indelicate of me, would it not?"

Eden well knew what he'd been about to say. With the bribe of a steady and generous income, her father had arranged her expeditious marriage, five years ago, to an impoverished but well-placed viscount's son. Spencer Winstowe, practiced rake and gamester, had known she was not a virgin.

He had not known about the child who had died. Papa had taken great pains to hide that scandal from both Society and the local folk of Hartsmere. But he could not silence the rumors of an elopement, and Spencer had never let Eden forget that he had been "forced" to marry her.

Even when he began to be ill after the first year of their marriage, he would not accept her concern or solicitude. He openly preferred his bits of muslin and gaming hells to her company. His increasing ill health did not slow him but drove him to even greater extremes in a mad quest for every sort of dissipation available to a man with connections, money, and no restraint.

He and Eden went their separate ways, like so many couples of the *ton*. Aunt Claudia's instruction in the ways of Society had saved Eden. She had learned how to pretend that nothing was wrong, that sorrow could not touch her.

Even when the money stopped coming, and Spencer cursed her to hell.

But nothing had taught her to look upon death as she had come to view all the other exigencies of life with her husband. This was no joke to be laughed away with a mask of cynical indifference.

"However," Spencer said, cutting into her thoughts, "we have no more leisure for delicacy." He turned his head on the pillow to catch the doctor's eye. "What I have to say to my wife is not for your ears. Get out."

The doctor and clergyman exchanged wary glances. "Mr. Winstowe," the physician said. "I strongly feel that —"

"Get out, I tell you — if you want your fees paid!" Spencer began to cough again, and both men reluctantly sidled out the door.

"I suggest you . . . make certain that the door is closed," Spencer said hoarsely. "You will not wish what I have to tell you to become fodder for the gossip mill . . . at least . . . not yet. It may be too much even for your band of aristocratic wantons."

Eden checked the door and returned to stand by the chair, gripping it for support. Spencer would not go to such elaborate lengths unless what he had to tell her was bad indeed. And he had nothing to lose.

"You should not upset yourself, Spencer," she said. "Can we not make peace —"

"Peace? I shall be quite at peace soon enough, provided there are whores and card games aplenty in hell." He wheezed a laugh. "But you, my dear, shall have your reckoning here in this world." His thin, pale hands moved restlessly over his sunken chest. "Blast it, where is that letter? No matter. You . . . sit, my loving wife. I would not have you swoon."

Eden's fingers pushed deep into the padding of the chair. "Please, Spencer."

"Very well." He turned his head slowly, until he could look into her eyes. "A most interesting piece of information came my way not long ago. I debated for some time whether or not to tell you . . . but it would be cruel to take it with me to my grave." He smiled. "You had a son, Eden. One you and your father failed to mention."

Eden had mastered the *ton*nish art of hiding her true feelings. Denial was pointless. "You knew when you married me that I was not untouched."

"Oh, yes. You were no weeping virgin, more's the pity. But I did not know of the child."

"The child —" *My son.* "It would have made no difference. The child did not survive."

"Oh, but he did. Your son is very much alive."

All at once the rejected chair seemed essential if she wished to remain upright. "Alive?"

"Indeed. It seems that he has been —" He sucked in air, as if it were becoming harder and harder to fill his lungs. "He's been living all these years with peasants in some . . . filthy hovel."

"But how —" She closed her mouth and struggled for control. *How can that be?*

"You're an . . . excellent actress, Eden, but I can see through you. How can a . . . a child's own mother not know he is alive?"

Because Papa told me. And I believed.

"Lies . . . and . . . deceptions —" Spencer broke into a fit of coughing that became dry, barking heaves, though he could not have anything left in his stomach to bring up. She hadn't been able to make him eat in days. She knelt by his side and held him until the fit passed, but it seemed to have torn something inside, letting all the force of his life leak out of his body.

"How . . . tender you are," he said. "You want more. But I . . . have no more to give."

"Spencer," she said, leaning close. "I beg you. Where is my son?"

His laugh became a rattle. Eden sprang to her feet and stumbled to the door.

"Doctor," she cried. "Mr. Reynolds. My husband —"

The two men, who had been waiting at the end of the

landing, hurried to join her. The doctor swept past her into the room, but the clergyman paused to take her hand.

"Be not troubled, my lady," he said. "He is in God's hands."

She murmured the appropriate response and stood aside to let him follow the doctor. Spencer's breathing was too labored to permit speech. The drone of Mr. Reynolds's voice drifted through the door, extolling the joys of life everlasting.

Eden composed herself and went to her husband for the last time. She knelt and tried to pray — for Spencer, for herself, and for the son she had never known. Most of all for her son. But the prayers were ashes in her mouth, with nothing behind them but convention and the lost faith of childhood.

"My lady."

She looked up at the brush of Mr. Reynolds's hand on her shoulder. "It is over. Your husband is at rest. His pain is ended."

Convention saved her. "Thank you, Mr. Reynolds. I am grateful for the comfort you have given to us." She accepted the clergyman's arm and rose, staring blindly across the landing. Yes, Spencer's pain was ended. She was glad for that measure of mercy.

But my son. Oh, Spencer, where is my son?

The child she had borne but never knew. Never held in her arms. Never rocked to sleep. The son who had left her womb an aching void.

She started downstairs in a daze. Bailey and several of the maids and footmen stood at the bottom, pale and anxious.

Eden did not begrudge them their concerns. They had not only lost a master this day but likely their positions as well. As long as Winstowe lived, they had all been able to maintain the fiction that wealth and plenty were endless, money a concern unbefitting such well-placed members of the *ton*.

That fable had reached its inevitable conclusion.

The front door opened before Bailey could perform the service. Aunt Claudia stood on the threshold, rain dripping from her pelisse. She removed it and handed it to the footman, fingers already busy with the ties of her bonnet.

"I came as quickly as I could," she said. "The messenger —" She broke off as she met Eden's eyes. "Oh, my dear." She opened her arms, and Eden walked into them as she had done so many times for as long as she could remember.

Claudia drew her into the morning room and pressed her into the chaise longue. "When?"

It was so like her aunt to drive to the heart of the matter. There was something deeply comforting in such practicality. "Only moments ago," Eden said. "I was with him."

"I am sorry," Claudia said. But Eden knew that all her pity was for the living, not the dead.

"Whatever he may have done — whatever you may have thought of him — he did not deserve any of this. Nor did you. You cared for him with no thought for yourself during this past month, and you are worn to a nub. There is nothing more you could have done."

"No thought for myself?" Eden rose and moved with aimless steps toward the marble mantelpiece. "When did I ever do anything with no thought for myself?" She stopped before the ornate mirror hung over the mantel, hardly recognizing the sunken-eyed, brittle creature in the reflection. "We all pay for our follies, do we not?"

"You have paid for your husband's. Now you are free of him."

Claudia's merciless judgment left Eden cold to the bone. Had this not been her beloved aunt, the woman who was dearer than a mother to her . . .

The woman whose unsentimental pragmatism was so very reassuring. Who spoke aloud what Eden thought and despised herself for thinking.

She took a careful breath. "There is at least one folly that is mine alone. One that Spencer had no part of." She turned to face her aunt. "He had a farewell gift for me, a final declaration.

"He gave me back my son."

Claudia did not allow her face to show so much as a flicker of astonishment. She had been the one to teach Eden how to confront the world as if nothing mattered, as if every little trouble could be cast aside with a casual wave of a well-gloved hand and a satirical laugh.

But this she had not expected. The young woman who stood before her was more than merely exhausted and distressed by the long weeks of Spencer's illness and her own preposterous sense of guilt. The drastic changes in the niece Claudia knew — the niece who had most of the *ton* wrapped around her smallest finger — should not have lasted long beyond Spencer's death. Claudia had counted on Eden's natural resilience.

Now she knew that Spencer had found a way to poison Eden's life even from beyond the grave. For Eden's eyes were filled not with returning sanity but with tears of hope.

Ruinous hope.

"Your son?" Claudia said, rising quickly. She hurried to Eden's side and took her hand. It felt terribly thin and fragile, as if it might snap with the slightest of pressure. "I do not understand. How could Spencer claim to know such a thing? How could even he be so cruel?"

Eden shook her head. "I do not care why he told me or how he discovered it. He said that my son is alive, in the countryside, living with some family —" Her desolate gaze took on the first real brilliance it had shown since Spencer's illness. "My son, dear Aunt. You and Papa told me he had died."

There was as yet no accusation in her voice. No suspicion, only bewilderment and hesitant joy.

Curse Spencer Winstowe to hell. He'd had the last laugh, it seemed. But he was dead, and Claudia was very much in control. As she had always been, and always would be.

Denying Spencer's claim would be most unwise. Eden was confused at the moment, but she had never been dull.

"Sit down, my dear," she said, guiding Eden back to the chaise. "I see that I must explain what I had hoped to spare you."

Eden had not been an innocent for many years. All of Society saw her as sophisticated and up to every rig and row. She had survived disappointment and the destruction of each callow, youthful dream, and replaced them with more immediate pleasures.

But she had not grown quite impervious enough. She was still capable of feeling betrayed.

"You knew?" she asked in a whisper.

"No. I only suspected." Claudia gazed down at her hands as if reluctant to speak. "I know you do not remember much of what happened during the child's birth. You were delirious, and it was not going well. My brother — your father — insisted upon employing the services of a local midwife rather than a physician. The woman sent me from the room when the child was born, despite all my pleas to stay by your side." She looked up, allowing sorrow to shadow her eyes. "Afterward your father came to tell me that he had spoken to the woman, and that the child . . . had not survived." She reached for Eden's hand. "I could not bring myself to doubt him, though deception . . . had occurred to me. I never saw the child — or the midwife — again."

Eden's profile was bleak. "My father?"

"If he deceived you, my sweet child, it was for the best. You were . . . very ill before and after the child's birth. You wanted nothing to do with its father. And Lord Bradwell himself was . . . not well."

She saw that point strike home. Eden never showed that she missed her father. He had been half mad ever since that night at the inn on the way to Gretna Green.

In the year after Eden's marriage to Winstowe, Lord

Bradwell had gambled and caroused his way through his fortune and all his unentailed lands. Claudia remembered how he'd deteriorated, driven by guilt and shame, only to disappear from sight and cut off all contact with his only child. He was rumored to be dead, or living in exile on the continent. Even Lord Bradwell's solicitor had no news of him. Eden had stopped inquiring years ago.

"He gave my son away," Eden said. "That changes nothing. I must find him."

"Find your son?" *Or your father? Thank God that either will be nearly impossible.* "Did Spencer tell you where to look for him?"

"No. It does not matter. I shall find him."

"But why, Eden?" Claudia leaned close, filling her voice with sympathetic persuasion. "Think of the child. Surely he is better off wherever he is, among those who raised him. Whatever his reasons, your father would have seen to it that he went to a good and decent family, with means enough to raise him properly. He does not know you —"

"I am his *mother.*"

"And who was his father?"

Stricken, Eden closed her eyes. "You think I could not love him because —" She shook her head. "You are wrong." She opened her eyes again and held Claudia's gaze, her elegantly curved brows drawn in an expression that was almost savage. "Can you think that I am the same naive girl who came to London five years ago? After all you have taught me?"

Claudia could not mistake the edge of mockery in her voice. The cynicism of lost innocence underlay everything Lady Eden did, everything she was.

Except in the matter of her resurrected child.

"You know nothing of children," Claudia said with deliberate coldness. "You never behaved as if you wanted any."

"There are still things you do not know about me, Aunt."

But I know that in five years of marriage, Spencer never gave you a child. I believe I know why. Yet none of the lovers did, either.

God knew that she had taught Eden to be careful.

"A woman alone," she said, "left as Spencer has left you —"

"Nearly penniless?"

So Eden was not unaware of the state of her finances, though she had lived as though the money would last forever. Claudia admitted she bore some of the blame for that; she had indulged the girl too much. But she could also supply the remedy — once she had put an end to this madness about Eden's son.

"Spencer left many large debts of long standing," she said. "The creditors will be sending in their bills now that he is dead."

"Yes. But I suspect that is not your greatest concern, Aunt. Can it be that you fear for my reputation?" She laughed, the throaty, musical sound that drew men to her like bees to a blossom. "That I shall somehow ruin myself by suddenly producing a son who is not my husband's?" Her smile held a wild, irrational edge. "Everyone knows that Lady Eden Winstowe is almost beyond redemption. Why should the *ton* be shocked?"

"Even a liberal society has its limits," Claudia said firmly. "You have always taken my advice before, and I give it to you in all familial affection. Your position may be more precarious than you will admit, now that your income is so vastly reduced. Do you wish to be ostracized by the *ton*?"

Eden lost her smile. That point, too, hit its mark. "I have friends —"

And have you not learned how little such friendships can mean? "In this last year, Spencer was more intemperate than ever before. You know that he was not right in the mind. He accumulated the sorts of debts, and reputation, that caused much ill will among those who were once his friends. The *ton* was already beginning to cut him, Eden.

You were simply too involved in your own affairs to notice, but it would have affected you soon enough. And now . . . think, my dear. You must have time to consider carefully. This is no time for rash action."

She gestured about the room, at the fine furnishings and rare antiques. "You can no longer bear the expense of running such an extravagant household. Your father's investments have failed. The income from your marriage settlement has fallen to a trickle, and not enough remains to pay your debts and continue in any fashion that would maintain your place in Society. Nor can I help, for my own jointure . . ." She paused delicately.

"I know, Aunt. I have done my best to repay you for all you have done, but now . . . I do not know how I shall help you to maintain your own establishment."

"That is of no moment, dear Niece. But how can you consider bringing an innocent child, raised by simple folk, into this questionable situation?"

Eden's face had grown unreadable once more. "We shall sell this house and the furnishings and move to more modest lodgings."

"Where? In Hans Town, perhaps? Would you really care to receive your fashionable friends draped in dull mourning garb, no longer able to join in their scandalous conversation and too impoverished to charm them with expensive entertainments?"

Eden stood again, her swift movements belying her apparent calm. "I am well aware of the necessities. I will reduce the staff as well, though it grieves me. We must sell Spencer's horses and three of the carriages. That alone will settle many of Spencer's debts, those that cannot wait."

"And what of your own?"

"What do you suggest, Aunt? If we cannot afford to live as we have become accustomed to do, and we are in such danger of being cut by the *ton,* then where are we to go? I can think of but one place that remains mine without encumbrance."

Claudia tried not to shudder. There was, indeed, one

sanctuary open to Eden, a place to which she had sworn she would never return. One Claudia dreaded with equal fervency.

Hartsmere.

Not that Lord Bradwell had believed his daughter would return. He had come to hate the place as much as his sister and daughter had. But he had been determined to give Eden some refuge of her own in the event of dire need. Hartsmere was unentailed, and had become part of the marriage settlement; Spencer had only its income while he lived. Income that had rapidly diminished to nothing.

"Surely you cannot be serious," Claudia said.

Eden closed her eyes. "Have we any choice? Papa made certain that it would come to me upon my husband's death, and it cannot be touched by our creditors."

"Spencer had no experience or interest in management, and never put a penny back into that estate. It must be in ruins. I will not allow you to make such a sacrifice when there is a far more sensible solution."

"Pray tell me, Aunt. If there is another way —"

"The Marquess of Rushborough."

Eden blinked, as if the thought had never entered her mind. Perhaps it hadn't. She'd broken with the marquess as soon as Spencer became ill.

Claudia was not so imprudent. "Do you think that the marquess has forgotten you in one short month? He was very much in love with you, Eden — and do not pretend that you were indifferent to him. He was not your usual flirt. I have no doubt that, if you were to approach him —"

"Spencer has just died," Eden interrupted, her voice unsteady. "I am in mourning. You say that you are afraid of my scandalizing the *ton* by finding my son, but begging support from Rushborough is acceptable?"

"The marquess can be most discreet. And it is not his mistress he would be supporting, but his future wife."

Eden gazed unseeing about the room. "What has Rushborough told you of his intentions?"

"His actions are more eloquent than any words could be. Naturally you must maintain a show of mourning your husband. But I have every confidence that if you provide the smallest encouragement, Rushborough will propose — and marry you as soon as you put away your widow's weeds. Until then, he will not allow his beloved to live in disgrace or poverty."

Eden's expression relaxed, and Claudia was certain she had won. Everything she had said was true. "You see how this solves all our problems. You will have the life you deserve, with no fear of debt. As a marchioness, you shall be —"

"No. I am sorry, Aunt, but it is too soon. I cannot ask so much of Rushborough. And before I see him again, I must find my son."

"I thought we had discussed the folly of such a scheme."

Eden's expression took on the willful, reckless look that Claudia had seen more and more frequently. "It is no scheme, Aunt. It is my firm resolve."

Claudia kept a tight rein on her temper. Once, six years ago, she had forcefully tried to dissuade a young girl from throwing her life away, and her protestations had only driven Eden into her lover's arms. The same thing might happen again if she pressed too hard.

But once Eden returned to Hartsmere, she would not be able to bear the place for long. Soon she would be desperate to take her aunt's advice, as she had done for the past five years, and accept the marquess's generosity.

And Eden's hopes of finding the boy were slim. She might search for years and never locate him. By one means or another, Claudia would steer Eden's thoughts away from this lunacy.

This incalculable danger.

"Very well," Claudia said. "If it is your wish to go to Hartsmere, there is much to be done, many preparations to be made — funeral arrangements and lawyers to consult. We must write the steward at Hartsmere to inform him of your return." She took Eden's arm. "Leave it all to me, my dear. You need rest."

As if to give the truth to her words, Eden swayed on her feet. The fight had gone out of her, now that she believed she had her way.

"You will not wish to go upstairs quite yet. Sit quietly and reflect, and Bailey will bring you a soothing glass of wine."

With a faint murmur of thanks, Eden assented. Bailey hastened to do Claudia's bidding; he knew who had taken the reins of authority in this household.

Once Eden was well settled, Claudia went into the study and unlocked Spencer's desk with the duplicate key she had obtained during his illness. It wasn't difficult to find the letter; Spencer had not been a particularly clever man nor a very imaginative blackmailer. She still did not know when or how Spencer had come by the missive. He had made good on his threat to tell Eden of her son, but he was quite unable to savor his victory in hell.

Claudia folded the paper tightly and pocketed it among her skirts. She had a letter of her own to write, and its recipients had best be wiser than Spencer Winstowe.

Chapter 2

Eden's *first glimpse of the estate was a view from the* bumpy unpaved road that descended into the little valley from the rolling fells surrounding it. The coachman reined in his team, taking the slope at an easy pace. Everywhere the world was white with recent snow, and the sun showed no signs of emerging to melt it away.

One expected winter to be a time of quiet waiting, especially here in the rugged north. But as dull and bleak as Eden's last winter here had been, she did not remember such an atmosphere of ruin and decline. It was as if spring would never come again.

Trees lining the road — coppices of pollard oak, ash, and elm — were bent in weariness under their burdens of snow. No few looked wasted and dead, as if struck by lightning or eaten from within by disease. And though the fields and pastures were no more than stubbled quilts of brown and white, even they seemed shadowed by death. Like Eden herself, the whole countryside wore mourning clothes.

The stone cottages and farmhouses on the fellsides seemed to cling there stubbornly like the remnants of a vanished race. Huddled sheep shifted like dirty wads of wool on the inbye pastures near the farmhouses. Eden didn't see a single dalesman tending the animals nor a sign of smoke from the chimneys. She heard no sound, not even the bark of a dog.

"I do not remember feeling quite so cold in the north," Aunt Claudia remarked, pulling her fur-lined cloak more tightly about her. She had endured the long journey from London with her usual stoicism, though the ancient berline, oldest and most practical of Spencer's carriages, was neither swift nor comfortable.

During the five-day journey, Eden had had much time to prepare herself for what lay ahead. She, like Claudia, had heard the solicitor's grim forecast. The elderly steward of Hartsmere had been ill for some time, and Spencer hadn't bothered to replace him or answer his pleas for assistance. All her husband had cared about was the income . . . for as long as it had lasted.

Now Eden was to reap the harvest of his neglect and her own willful ignorance.

"Do you remember," Eden said, "the stories you told me as a child? Hartsmere was at the very end of the world . . . a dreadful place that anyone of sense would avoid. There were monsters in the wood and ghosts in the house." She shivered, and not with the cold. Even Claudia did not know just how real the "monsters" were. She hadn't been there that night at the inn.

The fearsome night of which they had never spoken.

"I made no secret of my dislike," Claudia admitted.

Eden forgot her own fears and covered her aunt's hand. "I know that your memories of Hartsmere are not happy ones. The viscount —"

"Raines's accident was before your birth, and long ago. It is not for myself I fear."

No. You have always looked out for me, dear Aunt. But the one you warned me against is gone. Surely he is gone forever.

"You do not look happy, my dear. Have you second thoughts after all?"

"No second thoughts, Aunt." She spoke the lie with perfect aplomb. She would not increase her aunt's anxiety, or her own, with exaggerated fancies or sorrowful memories. She would not spend her time at Hartsmere looking over her shoulder.

The past was as dead as Spencer. She had come in search of her living son.

She tried to imagine what it would be like to be a mother. Her coterie of fashionable, fast-living matrons spent little time with their offspring, and she had avoided thinking about children. To do so brought forth too many painful emotions.

She could not remember grieving for her lost child; the days just before and after his birth had vanished from her memory. But even the possibility of getting him back dissolved the years, and the loss felt as fresh as yesterday.

How could I ever have believed you were dead?

She gazed out the window, seeking distraction in the landscape. Hartsmere itself had come into view, still half a mile distant. It lay nestled at the foot of a fell, almost at the end of the valley where the beck came tumbling over the rocks and made its way to the tiny lake — the mere of Hartsmere's name.

Behind the house, halfway up the fell, rose the thick patch of wood that spread like a menacing cloud over the land. Eden had been to Hartsmere only a few times in her life, yet she had feared that forest for as long as she could remember. It was almost as if it contained all the despair and loneliness she had known in this place.

She wrenched her thoughts from the past and turned her attention to the house itself. Well she remembered its cold stone halls hung with threadbare tapestries, fires constantly burning to take off the damp chill at all times of the year except high summer.

As if infected by the same pall that had settled over the dale, Hartsmere's gray stones and chimneys leaned upon one another like ancient ruins near crumbling. Eden knew that her vision was only illusion, but the great Elizabethan pile was anything but welcoming.

And did you expect a welcome? she asked herself and laughed under her breath. *You, who cursed this place and vowed never to return?*

"You find something amusing?" Claudia asked. "Pray, share it with me. I would be most grateful."

"I was only thinking that the house is in perfect keeping with our carriage and what little we have left to us. You know that I am a terrible housekeeper, dreadful with servants, and if you do not keep the household accounts, I do not know where we shall be by summer."

Claudia shook her head with a faint smile. "You do yourself an injustice, Niece. But of course I will help you — however long we remain."

Her aunt had not given up on the idea of leaving Hartsmere as soon as the mourning period was over and Eden was free to accept Rushborough's attentions. The matter of Eden's son had hardly come up between them since the discussion two months ago. It was as if Claudia had forgotten.

She had not forgotten. Eden was certain of that. But for the past five years, Eden had lived as if tomorrow did not exist. Until she found her son, she intended to continue living by that philosophy.

The berline made its creaking way down the winding road and into the dale. The beck was a mere trickle, and ice covered the lake. The frozen reeds, usually a haven for water birds, looked as sharp and uninviting as lances.

Now the village of Birkdale came into view. The cottages, like those on the small fell farms, appeared tumbledown and in need of new roofing. For the first time, Eden caught a glimpse of the inhabitants of the dale: a child in ragged clothing and an old man limping down the sodden lane with the help of a gnarled branch.

Eden prepared to signal the coachman, thinking to stop and speak to the child. No sooner had she made the decision than the boy — or was it a girl?— vanished, she could not tell where. No curious faces poked out of the cottage doorways.

Troubled, Eden stared at the village until the road passed around a low hill. That child had not looked well fed, and certainly not well clothed. Six years ago, when she had reluctantly come for the winter at her father's request, Birkdale had seemed a happy village, its inhabitants less burdened by poverty than many of the dalesmen in Westmorland.

With a sinking feeling, she realized that the solicitor had not exaggerated. The dale *had* prospered . . . until everything had passed into Spencer's keeping as part of her marriage settlement.

She closed her eyes, trying to remember how it had been at the beginning of the events that had changed her life. Pictures rose in her mind: of days that seemed sunnier than anywhere else in the country, of endless flocks of handsome Herdwicks, of boisterous shepherds and farmers enjoying a hearty feast after days of hard autumn labor.

None of which she had appreciated during her time spent at Hartsmere.

"I do not believe that managing the household will be my only concern here, Aunt," Eden said quietly. Speaking it aloud made it real: She would be, for at least a little while, mistress and lady of this place. She would have duties and responsibilities to her tenants and servants and laborers. Duties that had been sorely neglected — by Spencer and her — for half a decade.

"If you refer to the poor state of the cottages," Claudia said, "we know that your father's steward failed in his charge. Spencer should have replaced him. You cannot expect to undo five years of inadequate management in a few months."

But Papa gave this estate to me and I should have known. I should have made it my business to know.

Just as I should have realized the truth about my son.

The carriage passed through the gate and over the graveled drive that crossed the park. In Eden's imagination, the trees held naked limbs skyward in a prayer for salvation.

Hartsmere loomed above them as the berline drew around the sweep in front of the porch. The house was deceptively plain, for a former Fleming had attempted to modernize the Elizabethan hulk with an eighteenth-century facade. But that effort could not conceal what waited inside: the vast, cold hall, dark paneled wood, narrow passages, a confusion of chambers in the two wings, and a complete lack of modern conveniences.

A handful of servants waited before the porch, barely suppressing their shivers. They wore dusty, ill-fitting livery and well-worn dresses. Could this be the entire remaining staff?

"Only a pair of maids," Claudia remarked. "I suppose that gray-haired woman is your housekeeper. As for the men, none has sufficient presence for a butler, though the one in livery must be a footman. And that pair of ruffians must be gardeners or stablemen." She shook her head. "This is much worse than the solicitor led us to expect."

"Surely some of the servants must be inside," Eden said, trying to lighten both their moods. "At least we have a welcome of sorts, after this dismal journey."

Claudia arched her brow but made no further comment.

When the berline came to a stop, the lanky footman loped up to open the door and offer his hand to Claudia. She took it and stepped down, surreptitiously brushing off her skirts. Eden followed. Her nostrils were immediately assaulted by the smell of dampness, mold, and decay.

The two maids curtsied, and the housekeeper came forward, her hands folded over her waist.

"Lady Eden," she said. "Praise be that you've come safely to Hartsmere." She bowed her head, but her gray eyes were shrewd and sharp in the mild, wrinkled face. Her words held more than the trace of an accent.

Irish, Eden thought. *I do not remember her.*

"My name is Byrne, my lady. Mrs. Nuala Byrne. I'm sorry for this poor greeting, but there are few of us here now. The cook, Mrs. Beaton, is inside making up something for your dinner, and a pot of tea to take the chill off."

Claudia regarded Mrs. Byrne with a calculated stare that always put upstarts and mushrooms in their places. "I trust that you have rooms made up for us, Mrs. Byrne?"

"Aye, indeed, my lady. I hope they'll be to your satisfaction." Her gaze shifted to Eden. "I hadn't the honor of meeting Lord Bradwell. Mr. Brown, the steward, took me on when Mrs. Outhwaite left three months ago."

Eden felt as if she were being examined from head to toe. If Claudia had hoped to cow this woman's boldness, she hadn't succeeded. But Papa had always said that the folk of the dales — like the Irish — were too independent and proud to bow and scrape to any "outcomer" lady or lord. They waited to be impressed.

"I am pleased to meet you, Mrs. Byrne," Eden said. On impulse, she decided to try informality. She would need loyal servants at Hartsmere. "I'm sure we shall rub along very well together."

Mrs. Byrne hesitated, and then a cautious smile touched her lips. "Aye, my lady. Armstrong will carry up your luggage, and Nancy will wait upon you. Hester will serve you, Lady Claudia."

Eden recognized none of these people and was greatly relieved. No reason to fear that they remembered her elopement with her mysterious cousin. Papa had tried to confine the gossip; any vague tattle that might have followed her to London had died out once she was respectably married to Spencer Winstowe. Whether it was still alive in the dale remained to be seen.

She glanced doubtfully at Nancy. The girl was shaking in her shoes. Eden had dismissed her own expensive and experienced Abigail, hoping that she'd find a suitable girl at Hartsmere. She smiled, but Nancy would not meet her eyes.

"Pray go upstairs, Aunt," Eden said. "I shall follow directly."

Claudia hesitated and followed Hester up the stairs.

Armstrong bounded up behind, juggling a pair of the lighter trunks. The two outdoor servants had gone to help the coachman unharness the horses. The driver's duty was done, and now he could leave Hartsmere in search of more lucrative employment.

"Mrs. Byrne," Eden said. "You said that there are few of you here now. Are there other servants within besides the cook?"

"Not many, my lady. It's been hard to keep good servants, or pay them. Besides Mrs. Beaton, we've the one man in the stables, Dalziel, and three others who see to what needs doing outside — Grubb, Hindle, and Starkie. For other needs, we hire by the day. No visitors here."

Eden could well believe it. There was hardly a dale in Westmorland more isolated.

"And where is Mr. Brown?"

"He took very ill just a few days ago and went to stay with his sister in Penrith. We've no steward at the moment. But now that your ladyship is here . . ." She let the statement drift off into a question.

"I could not help but notice the state of the farms and villages as we entered the dale," Eden said. "Are matters truly as unfortunate as they appear?

The Irishwoman's face showed an instant of surprise. "Begging your pardon, my lady, but I didn't expect you to be so . . . so . . ."

"Frank? I shall be quite honest with you, Mrs. Byrne. I did not wish to come here, but circumstances required it. I seek your help in making improvements for the benefit of us all. May I trust you?"

"Aye, my lady," she said slowly. "That you may." Her eyes took on a real measure of warmth. "I'll help in any way I can."

"I fear there is a great deal amiss at Hartsmere."

Mrs. Byrne sighed. "We've had much misfortune, my lady. The people of the dale would have it —" She broke off with a frown. "But you've journeyed so far, and need your rest."

"Pray continue, Mrs. Byrne. What do they say in the dale?"

"That it's cursed. That long ago the masters of this land struck a bargain with one of the Fair Folk — the Sidhe, as we call them in Ireland — to grant the dale good fortune. They were golden times, with neither want nor sorrow. But somehow the bargain was broken, and the Sidhe lord withdrew his favor. That was near five years ago, they say."

Five years. How was it that Eden had never heard a breath of such tales until today, aside from Aunt Claudia's ghost stories? She had been more than six months in the dale that last time, not including the isolation of her confinement. Had she been deaf as well as blind?

Would she have been prepared if she had known?

"Who broke the bargain, Mrs. Byrne?" she asked.

The housekeeper dropped her gaze. " 'Tis only a tale, my lady."

A tale with the ring of an impossible truth. A curse had indeed come upon this dale, brought by the very family who should have protected and preserved the land and its people.

"Do they say it was my father?" she demanded.

"Aye, my lady."

Eden let her breath escape in a rush. "And what do they say of me?"

The older woman met her gaze. "It will keep. Take some rest, Lady Eden. We'll talk again."

Eden agreed, but only because she had a task of her own to carry out. The housekeeper was admirably cautious but clearly knowledgeable for all her brief tenure at Hartsmere. Eden had won a true ally with a few direct words and a willingness to trust.

The *ton* did not encourage such openness and faith in one's fellow man. Eden had spent the past five years pretending to herself that trust was unnecessary. But she had little left to lose and much to learn if she was to survive at Hartsmere and prepare it for her son.

If necessary, she would make a personal friend of every

servant and farmer in the dale, no matter how strenuously Aunt Claudia objected.

"Please continue about your business, Mrs. Byrne," Eden said. "I wish to walk a little before I sample Mrs. Beaton's cooking."

"It's late, my lady. I smell snow in the air."

"I won't be long." She turned away before Mrs. Byrne could protest further.

Her half boots, sturdy and plain, were well suited for the outdoors. In London she'd seldom walked, but here she expected to do a great deal of it. This would be only the first of many excursions.

From this spot she could see the distant parsonage. Beside the curate's house lay a small grove of limes and the family cemetery, enclosed by a wrought iron fence. There her newborn son had been buried . . . except that it was not he who had been placed in the hallowed ground but something or someone else. Eden had not witnessed the burial — her father and Aunt Claudia had kept her away — but she had wept. Wept so long and hard that they had sent for the doctor.

Her vision blurred. *You are not there. You are coming home to me.* The grieving was over. But there was one other visit to make before she returned. She set off at a brisk walk to the rear of the house.

Behind Hartsmere rose the fell with its snow-shrouded mantle of woodland. Outside the park were pastures fenced with stone, and just beyond that stood a natural escarpment of rock over which the beck tumbled and whispered amid the ice and snow.

On the other side of the rocky wall lay the forest. Eden stopped, struck with panic. How often *he* had wanted to take her there during his fraudulent courtship, tried to convince her that there was some redeeming quality to such a blighted wilderness.

But *he* was gone. *He* had fled back to whatever realm had spawned him. A chill caught her unaware, and she tugged at the collar of her cloak though it was already drawn tight up about her neck.

What will my son be? She'd pushed away that thought every time it had entered her head. Would he be . . . normal? Or something other than human?

It didn't matter. He was her son, no matter what he was.

With every step, the escarpment loomed closer. Each time she paused to catch her breath, she urged herself on again. Climbing over the rocks would not be easy in this dress; once there'd been a rough wooden ladder, but it was gone now, like so much else.

That was merely one more excuse to turn back. She clenched her teeth and charged the wall like a knight hurling himself at the ramparts of a castle.

A streak of red, bright against the drab grays and browns of snow and dead grasses, flashed at the edge of her vision. She turned to see a fox, the only other living creature with whom she shared the pasture. It paused in its flight, one paw lifted, to regard her through button-bright eyes.

She smiled at the unexpected beauty of the creature and at a sudden welling of fellow feeling. Life did exist here, after all. It survived under even the harshest conditions.

"Be at ease," she said. "There is no one here to hunt you."

The fox cocked its head almost as if it understood her, flicked its brush, and executed a graceful spin to run directly toward the forest. Eden found her courage on more solid footing with the fox playing vanguard. But once again her progress was interrupted by movement. This time it was human.

A boy.

At first Eden thought it might be the same ragged child she had seen in the village, but he could not have run so far. His clothes were worn but not yet threadbare. As little as she knew of children, she guessed him to be five or six years old. His shock of unkempt hair was the rich brown of good English farmland.

Like the fox, the boy stopped to stare at her. He had been intent on following the fox's trail, after the fashion of little boys the world over.

A completely baseless hope seized her heart. "Good day!" she called.

The boy looked as if he might bolt after his quarry. She began walking toward him, speaking softly all the while.

"Are you a stranger here? I am. Well, not quite a stranger. I lived here once, you see. A long time ago."

The boy bent his head warily but did not move. She could have sworn that he sniffed the air like any wild creature.

"My name is Eden," she went on. "It's an odd sort of name, I know. My mother chose it for me."

"Mother?"

The boy's voice shot through her like an invisible bolt. It held the lilt of an accent she had heard a very short time ago.

"Yes," she said, drawing close. "My mother, Lady Bradwell. Where is your mother?"

She could smell him now — a clean, almost sweet scent that hinted of spring. His face was handsome even in unformed childhood, his eyes bright green in a freckled face.

Leaf-green eyes, like Cornelius Fleming's.

"Are you my *máthair*?" the boy asked.

Her heart stopped. "What is your name?"

He continued to look at her with a solemnity and directness that belied his age. "Donal."

"And where have you come from, Donal?"

He pointed west, toward the Irish Sea.

"You do not live here?"

He shook his head, sending the earth-brown hair cascading over his eyes. "They sent me."

Eden could not ask who. Something inexplicable was happening inside her, as if a great bell had tolled in the depths of her being. She fell to her knees in the mud and snow.

"Donal," she whispered, "did they send you here to be with your mother?"

He nodded. "My real *máthair*." He frowned. "Is it you?"

Yes. The answer was there, solid and strong as the fells themselves. She held out her arms, answering in the only way she could.

Donal backed away.

"No. Donal, it is all right —" She lurched to her feet, but he was already running — away from her, toward the black fortress of the wood. He moved so fast that she knew she had no hope of catching him.

She stood where he had left her for a long time, a biting wind whipping her hair loose from its pins.

"Lady Eden?"

The gruff voice brought her back to herself. In the gathering dusk she could just make out the stubbled face of one of the two men who had been waiting when the carriage arrived. He tilted his head in a gesture of respect and hunched his burly shoulders.

"Beggin' yer pardon," he said. "Missus Byrne sent me up to fetch you. It's comin' on dark."

So it was. "What is your name?" Eden asked.

"Hindle, my lady."

"Hindle, did you see a child run up toward the wood? A little boy of five or six?"

He shuffled his feet, ill at ease. "Nae."

Eden felt an unfamiliar stirring of temper. When was the last time, before learning of her son, that she'd been truly angry? Nothing else had been as important as this.

"Was a boy brought here to Hartsmere recently? From Ireland, perhaps?"

"Missus Byrne knows more about such things, my lady. If you'll come —"

He was lying, or at least not telling the full truth. But it was too dark now to search by herself.

"I shall go to Mrs. Byrne," she said. Hindle offered a

hand to steady her, but she swept past him and strode down the fell in reckless haste.

There was no more time to devise a clever explanation for the presence of her son, if her son he was. She must think clearly, because whatever she said now would affect the boy's future irrevocably, for good or ill.

Mrs. Byrne waited in the stone-paved hall. Her face relaxed when she saw Eden.

"Wisht, Lady Eden, I was that worried —"

"What do you know about Donal?"

Shocked silence fell between them. Eden read the answer in Mrs. Byrne's eyes. The housekeeper caught Hindle's gaze, and he slipped out the door, leaving her alone with Eden.

"Why didn't you tell me?" Eden demanded. "A child is out there in the darkness, all by himself, afraid of — of —" She caught her breath, alarmed to find herself on the verge of tears.

Unashamed, Mrs. Byrne gave her a sympathetic look. "I thought it best to wait, my lady. All unexpected, a man came yesterday from Ireland with the lad. He said that the boy was to be delivered to Lady Eden, and then he disappeared. I didn't know what to make of it, for I'd heard nothing of this from you. I took the lad in and fed him, but he ran off in the night. I sent men after him, of course, but they couldn't get near him. He was like a wild thing."

A wild thing abandoned without explanation at Hartsmere's door. Why here and now? Who had sent him?

"You should have informed me the moment I arrived," Eden said.

"I didn't wish to trouble you, my lady, when you'd just come in from such a long journey. I've had the men looking since he ran away. I'd hoped he'd return on his own soon enough — when he got hungry, as boys do."

"I saw him in the pasture." *And he ran from me. From his mother.* She calmed herself and presented the story she had hastily concocted. "I could not prepare you for the boy's arrival because I did not know he was coming so soon. Donal is the orphaned child of my late cousin, the son of my father's younger brother, who inherited an Irish estate many years ago. When Donal's parents died, my uncle kept him, but he had lately been ill, and asked to send Donal to me and my husband. But Winstowe died, and I forgot —" She paused, bowing her head. "Until today, when I saw him for the very first time.

"It's that sorry I am, indeed," Mrs. Byrne said. "I'll send Armstrong for the other men at once, so that they may search for the child near the forest."

Concealing her anxiety, Eden glanced toward the door. "If he is wary of the men, I must accompany them. I hope that he is not too much afraid of the dark —"

"What is this commotion? Eden, where have you been?"

Claudia's voice carried down the stairs as she descended, and her sharp glance took in Eden and the housekeeper. She lifted her brows at Eden's sodden skirt and the wet tracks she and Hindle had left on the stone floor.

"Donal," Eden said, holding to calm by the barest thread. "The boy we were expecting — my uncle's grandson from Ireland — is already here at Hartsmere."

Claudia stopped with one foot suspended above a step. She gave no hint of what went on in her mind. *Follow my lead,* Eden willed her. *Is it not my reputation you wished to protect?*

"The child is here?" Claudia said, continuing to the bottom of the stairs. "How can that be?"

Eden smiled with relief in spite of her worry. "It is a wonder, after we had not heard from my uncle in so long . . . I do not know how he learned that we would be coming to Hartsmere. He left no letter for us. But speculation must wait. Mrs. Byrne, please gather all the lanterns and torches you have, anything to be used for light —"

"Surely you do not mean to go out again," Claudia said, hurrying to her side. "You are overtired, my dear —"

"I will not argue. A child is out there, alone." She

grasped the door handle. The door began to swing inward, and she stepped back hastily.

Small fingers gripped the handle on the outside. The fingers belonged to Donal, who moved the great door as if he were thrice his age. New-fallen snow mantled his head and shoulders.

"Mother?" he said. "I'm hungry."

Eden dropped to her knees before him, her eyes filling with tears. "Yes, indeed. I will be a mother to you from now on, dear child." She drew him into her arms, and this time he went willingly enough.

How wonderful he felt. How soft was his cheek and how beautiful his face. Eden did not mind that he had obviously not bathed in several days and had become quite muddy. He walked right into her heart and made a home there.

My son. My son.

"Let us play a game," she whispered in his perfect little ear. "It will be our special secret that I am your mother. I will call you Donal, and you must call me Lady Eden except when we are alone together. Can you do that for me?"

He pulled back and frowned at her. "Lady Eden," he repeated. "I know about secrets."

She hugged him again, astonished at his maturity and understanding. Was this miraculous being her child, indeed? Could such happiness be born of fear and sorrow?

"Oh, Donal," she whispered. "I will make you happy."

But as she looked over his thin shoulders, she saw two faces, one elegant and refined, one weathered and wise. In Aunt Claudia's eyes was grave concern, and in Mrs. Byrne's an understanding that Eden knew she would keep to herself.

And so the secret would survive a little longer.

In the very center of the ancient wood, where sunlight almost never reached the ground and Grandfather Oak stood watch, the fox ended his flight.

He stopped at the tangle of gnarled roots thrusting up from the ground and sniffed the loam. Nothing changed here. All was as it had been for a thousand years, the last enchanted place in the land of the Britons.

And the one who slept within was just as changeless.

The fox shook his bright coat and turned about three times. Red pelt became red hair, and fur turned to skin and rough-woven cloth.

Tod wriggled his bare toes into the earth and prepared to face his master.

"My lord," he whispered.

No answer. Of course, no answer; Lord Hern had slept for nearly five human years. The blink of an eye in the time of the Fane, but his sleep was no less profound for all that.

Tod placed his hand against the warm bark, feeling the heart that beat within. He slapped the bark three times, chanting as he did so.

"My lord, awake! She has returned!"

Silence. Then, after a thousand heartbeats, a stirring. Grandfather Oak groaned at being disturbed in his winter slumber, and his guardian shared the sentiment.

But he did not refuse the summoning. Tod snapped back his hand as the bark began to ripple and grow transparent. A figure became visible within, still at one with the ancient tree. Then, with movements stiff and slow, Lord Hern stepped free of his waiting place.

A thousand times had Tod seen the Forest Lord, but still he felt his power. He was tall, so tall, crowned with his rack of antlers, green-eyed, awesome in his strength and dignity. Lord Hern was the last of the High Fane remaining in this part of man's earth, perhaps the last anywhere. Tod didn't know; he was bound to the lord as he was to this dale, unable to leave it except by Lord Hern's command.

"My lord," he said, and bowed. But he could not hold such solemnity for long. He laughed and did a somersault, bounding this way and that. "Oh, Tod has such things to tell you!"

Lord Hern looked down upon him with eyes still glazed by sleep. "Tod. Why did you wake me?"

"Because she has come back!" With an effort, he held himself still. "She, the mortal who betrayed you."

All at once Lord Hern's eyes flashed like emerald fire. He stepped away from the tree, and the branches of Grandfather Oak shuddered and sighed.

Tod knew better than to tease, though the temptation was great. He had been alone so long, with only the beasts for company. Of those few that remained since Lord Hern had taken his grace from the land, most were sluggish or hibernating for the winter.

But now the lord was back.

"When?" Hern demanded. "When did she come?"

"Today, today! Tod saw her. And Tod saw —"

Tod almost remembered too late. He had sworn to himself that he would not speak of the other. Tod feared little, but Lord Hern's wrath was not something he wished to see again, not until another thousand of man's years had passed. The lord would know the truth soon enough without his help.

It was the lady who most needed the warning.

Hern pressed his hand against the trunk of the tree, now solid and firm and silent. "She has come back," he said, as if the words made him believe. "Why?"

Tod felt sorrow for the great lord. And then he laughed at himself. How could the mighty Hern need his pity? They were both of the same Elder Race, old before the coming of man, and never had the Fane been known for soft hearts — or a failure to take vengeance.

Tod rejoiced that his long boredom was at an end.

Hern felt the weight of his antlers as if they were hung with chains of man's deadly Iron. The earth dragged at his feet, crying for mercy; the trees groaned, brittle with the cold. No bird sang nor animal stirred; the silence was more profound than that of an ordinary winter.

Hern felt what the land had become and remembered what had made it so.

He had, with his curses and his wrath. In his deep sleep, he had neither known nor cared. He might have slept a hundred years, until some man dared to enter his sanctuary, or until the very world crumbled around him.

But *she* had come back.

Lady Eden Fleming, the woman who had been his mate. Who had looked upon his true form with loathing and terror. Who had borne him a son — a son stolen from him by mortal treachery, illness, and death.

She'd fled Hartsmere, rejecting him as her father had rejected their bargain. He had not spoken to Eden since that morning at the inn. All he remembered was the look on her face when she had seen him as he was — a look that held no hint of the love she had professed.

Love, which so fascinated the Fane and drew them like stoats to a rabbit warren. Mortal love, which his kin, fearing solitude though they did, could neither feel nor understand. Which *he* had used for his own purposes, only to find it utterly inadequate.

Fane could not love, but they were not without emotion. The great difference between Fane and man lay in intensity and constancy. Fane could feel affection — for a time. They could suffer the pain of betrayal, until they distracted themselves with pleasure or petty acts of vengeance.

And they could hate. Oh, they could hate very well. Woe to the mortal who earned the wrath of a Faerie when his anger was hot — or who fell afoul of the rare Fane who did not choose to forget.

He had hated *her*. And he had not forgotten.

Hern rubbed his hand against Grandfather Oak, sensing the life pulse from root to highest branch. He had been a part of it for so long, and everything within him wished to remain so — unthinking, unfeeling. That was not to be.

He was High Fane, of the race that most resembled humans. On the Isle of Eire, they were known by men as Sidhe, and in other mortal nations they had borne similar names of power. Once he and his kind had roamed the earth freely, treated with awe and respect by mortals, until men pushed the Elder Race to the edge of the western sea.

Yet some Fane remained. The high lords were not as quick as the lesser brethren to lose interest in that which caught their attention, nor were they so easily driven from their earthly homes. They had come to care for the wild places Fane had once ruled and the humble creatures that inhabited them. They resisted the threat of Iron, which could kill in strong doses or at the edge of blade or arrow, retreating instead to lands that the despised humans did not inhabit.

The Forest Lords, who guarded the earth's vanishing woodlands, had been given many names: Cernunnos by the Roman invaders of Albion, Cocidius by the fair-haired Celts, Hu Gadern by the Cymri, Herne by the English to the south, Furbaide in Eire, Pan among the Greeks, Pashupati in the lands of the Hind, and Tapiola in the far, frozen regions of the north. They had donned the shapes of stags and hinds and horned creatures of wood and field, symbols of the hunt, prosperity, and fertility.

Most were gone now. Hern had taken the English name of legend and retreated to this final haven amid the crags and valleys.

He was the last of the last.

In his solitude, he had become strange and lonely. He kept company with neither Fane nor man. And when at last he chose to return home, he knew the coin with which he must buy passage back into Tir-na-nog: a half-mortal child to bring strength to the thinning blood of the Elder Race. *His* child.

The one he had made with Eden Fleming did not survive. She had betrayed him, and doomed him to exile once more. Oh, yes, he had hated her. And that hatred was stirring again. All he need do was give way to it, leave the forest, stride down the fell, and look for her. When he saw her . . .

No plan formed in his mind. He had never imagined

that this moment would come, that she'd dare return. He had expected her to be dead and gone when he woke, in the way of all mortals.

He willed his antlers away and leaned his forehead against the oak. He was weary, so weary, and the only cure was the green fields and endless forests of Tir-na-nog.

"Home?" Tod asked. "Will you make another mortal child, so that we can go home?"

Make another child? Oh, he had thought of it, after Lord Bradwell broke his vow. But to do so would have required a virtual rape, or the seduction of another suitable female, and he had no will to do either. He had preferred sleep, one that might have lasted an eternity, to dealing again with treacherous mortals.

But now?

Hern pushed away from the tree and took in a deep lungful of cold winter air. It was tainted with decay, disease, sorrow. The wreckage of two thousand years on earth.

The taint was within himself. He would be rid of it only in Tir-na-nog.

And there was but one way to return to the Land of the Young.

"We shall see, Tod," he said. "We shall see."

With a single thought, he clothed himself in the garb of a common man and went to find her.

Chapter 3

Their first breakfast at Hartsmere was made up of burned toast, tough ham, and cold tea, but Eden hardly noticed. Even the drafts, cobwebs, and gloom of the low-beamed dining room did nothing to dispel Eden's happiness.

Donal sat at the noticeably wobbling oak table with her and Aunt Claudia, and was given the adult privilege because he had no nurse or governess to look after him. And, most importantly, because Eden didn't want him out of her sight.

She tried not to stare or seek signs of his father in the boy. The green eyes were unavoidable, of course. But she fancied that his chin was a little like her own. And he was a perfectly normal child.

Good God, he had come from *her*. She touched her abdomen in wonder. She was his mother. He had called her that, not once, but twice. And she swung up and down on a seesaw of joy and terror.

How could she become a good mother to this boy? How could she expect him to love her, an utter stranger?

It had taken precisely an instant for her to love him — a

kind of love she had not known before, perhaps the only kind left to her. She grieved for the years they had been separated, the priceless moments that had been lost. And she agonized over what he might have suffered in Ireland with people who had so easily sent him away.

She and Donal hadn't yet discussed his foster parents and how he had come to Hartsmere. He had hardly spoken at all, though he ate with a will. He watched her with that same guarded, thoughtful stare, so far beyond his years. Judging. Deciding, perhaps, if she was worthy.

She would make herself worthy. For the first time in her life, she would stand and fight for what she wanted, something she believed in: her son and his love. She'd make up for the years he lived in poverty, separated from his true family and the life he should have known. And if she must pretend that he was her cousin's child and not her own, at least *she* knew the truth.

She and two others.

She glanced at Claudia across the table. Her aunt had maintained a stony silence all morning. Certainly Claudia had not expected her to find her son so soon, if at all. And Eden's hastily contrived explanation for his existence had not met with her approval.

But Claudia was here at the table, accepting Donal by her very presence. To do otherwise would have been unthinkable. In time, she would grow to love Donal as Eden did.

Eden crumbled a bit of uneaten toast, smiled at Donal, and made another perusal of her mental list. Though she wanted nothing more than to spend the entire day with her son — holding him, learning to laugh and play with him — she knew that such indulgence was not possible.

There was so much to be done at Hartsmere: speaking with each servant individually; consulting Mrs. Byrne about hiring additional servants and a new steward; taking an inventory of furnishings, linens, china, and the other household goods that remained; and determining the need for repairs in the house itself. The rent books must be examined against their solicitor's and the previous steward's accounts. Eden would learn to economize, despite her inexperience with frugality.

What she dreaded most was touring the estate and facing her tenants. The condition of the dale indicated widespread want. She'd seen the need for renovations and improvements to cottages and farms — those still occupied — but had no idea how such necessities were to be paid for. She couldn't guess how the dalesmen and women would regard her, for Mrs. Byrne's tale had not been promising.

She was certain of only one thing: Hope remained because her son was with her.

"We must find a governess for the boy as soon as may be," Claudia said abruptly. She dabbed at lips with her napkin and signaled Armstrong to bring the platter of cold ham. She cast an enigmatic glance at Donal. Intent on cleaning his plate, he refused to look at her.

"Is that necessary, so soon?" Eden asked. "He has just arrived. Can we not wait —"

"A boy must be taken in hand at once, lest he become unmanageable. Any child of quality must have a governess." She cast Eden a very pointed look and smiled. "You would not wish your *cousin's* child to have less than the best, especially after such a haphazard upbringing in Ireland."

"A suitable governess will surely require a salary greater than we can afford."

Claudia's glance reproved Eden for her vulgar talk of money at the dining table. "We shall discuss it later, in the sitting room."

Eden remained silent until Armstrong left to fetch more tea. "It is clear that I cannot restore Hartsmere on my current income. I will have difficulty making it habitable."

Claudia looked askance at a cobweb hanging from the chandelier. "The bedchambers are unacceptable. The servants are undisciplined, and you have not helped matters by treating them with such familiarity."

Eden rose, unaccountably rebellious. "I am sorry that Hartsmere is so unsuitable, Aunt. I shall understand if you . . . prefer to visit friends until the house is in a more civilized state."

Claudia's stare was as cool and regal as a queen's. "If you do not wish my advice, I shall not force it upon you."

Eden did not retreat. "Dear Aunt, I could not manage without you. Now I must rely upon you to be patient."

"But I am concerned for you, child."

"And I must be concerned for Donal. I need you to help me create a good home for him."

They both studied the boy. Donal was no longer eating but stared toward the front of the house, his head lifted.

"Horses!" he said, and was up and out of his chair before Eden could respond.

If Donal had heard a carriage, the sound hadn't reached Eden's ears. She prayed that it was not the local gentry paying their respects.

For once in her life, Eden did not wish to socialize with anyone. Well-bred visitors would surely understand if she did not choose to receive them at home so soon after her bereavement and long journey from town. With luck, they would leave their cards with Mrs. Byrne and be on their way.

She started to follow Donal, but Claudia's voice stayed her. "You do realize," she said, "that the boy can have no decent sort of life here."

"That is the only reason that I shall consider remarriage — when I cease to mourn my husband. For Donal's sake. But only when I am ready. After he knows me, and when I am certain . . . that the man I marry will accept him, and provide him with a proper education, the best of everything."

Claudia crossed the room and drew back the heavy, moth-eaten curtains to gaze out the window. "He may find some place in Society with Rushborough's aid. But the boy must be trained to behave like a member of the *beau monde* rather than an Irish peasant."

"You may say what you will about me and my foolishness, Aunt, but never speak so of Donal." Eden balled her fists and slowly released them. "I will teach him whatever he needs to know. You need not be bothered."

Eden expected a sharp setdown, but instead Claudia sighed and touched her hand to her forehead. "You mistake my meaning," she said in a voice of utter weariness. "I believe I shall lie down for a while."

Struck by remorse, Eden offered to escort her, but Claudia waved her off and went up to her room alone.

Eden stood at the bottom of the stairs, confused by her own decidedly mixed emotions. *I thought I had learned to live day by day and drain every drop of pleasure from each moment.*

But that was before she found purpose again — not in her own social advancement and amusement but for the well-being and happiness of someone else.

Donal. She had meant to go after him, in case the horses he had heard were attached to a carriage. Setting aside other concerns, she hurried from the dining room.

She passed Armstrong in the hall. He blinked at her, the tray of tea balanced in his hands.

"Did Master Donal come this way?" she asked.

Armstrong pointed with his chin toward the rear of the house. "To the stables, my lady," he stammered.

"Thank you. We will not be needing the tea." To save time, she went along the hall to the green baize door leading to the servant's wing and continued down a narrow corridor that smelled of stale cooking. Small, grimy windows let in enough light to reveal a door.

It led to a yard littered with every conceivable sort of debris, from broken crockery to ashes from the stove. In warmer months it would be overgrown with weeds. To the right lay the remains of a formal garden. A gravel path led to a cluster of outbuildings, including the stables, set some distance from the house on a level area at the foot of the fell.

The morning was eerily quiet. Not so much as a raven croaked or bare branch creaked — until the silence was rent by a harrowing yell.

It came from the stables. Eden picked up her skirts and ran as swiftly as her impractical shoes and mourning dress would allow.

She came upon a scene that shocked her speechless. In the muddy stable yard a groom struggled with a fractious horse. The beast pawed the air and bared its teeth, leaping from side to side in an effort to escape the tether that held it captive.

Dangerously close to the battle stood Donal, looking on with fascination. As Eden watched, he took a step toward the horse, one hand outstretched.

No! The scream didn't make it past Eden's throat. She ran straight for Donal at the same moment that the groom yanked the horse out of the boy's path.

The horse gave a high-pitched cry of rage. Hooves lashed out and struck the groom in the shoulder. He fell, groaning, and the horse whirled about in search of new enemies.

It saw Donal. Ears flattened, and the neck arched like a snake about to strike. Donal didn't move, didn't try to run.

"Stop."

The command was so formidable that Eden obeyed, though an instant later she didn't know if it had been aimed at her or the horse. Her vision cleared, and she saw a man — a stranger — standing less than two feet from the horse, as calmly as if he confronted a kitten.

His body was the only barrier between the beast and Donal, but it was enough. The horse quieted instantly at the man's whispered words. The stranger raised his hand level with the horse's muzzle, but the animal did not bite the offered flesh. Its teeth remained closed while its lips brushed lightly over the man's fingertips. Its ears came up, twitching this way and that. The rolling whites of its eyes disappeared.

Donal stared at the stranger as he had stared at the horse, fearless and fascinated. Taking care not to startle the animal, Eden edged behind Donal and prepared to snatch him away.

"He'll be all right," the man said, without turning. "Atlas is no danger."

"No danger?" Eden said, hearing her voice shake. She wrapped her arms around Donal, who squirmed and protested wordlessly. "Atlas?"

"'At's his name." The groom, forgotten on the ground, tried to sit up and groaned in pain. Eden recognized him: Dalziel, who had tended her father's horses. There was something distinctly wrong about the angle of his shoulder, and he had a bloody gash on his forehead. "Damned devil. Should have put him down long ago."

The stranger turned his gaze on the groom, and the injured man fell silent.

Until Spencer's death, the closest thing to a true crisis Eden had dealt with was the accidental seating of two social or political rivals next to each other at a dinner party, or a tear in the flounce of a ball gown. This was quite different.

"May I know whom to thank for this service?" she asked.

"Hartley. Hartley Shaw," he said. His voice was musical, deep, compelling. Still she had not seen his face, but his simple homespun clothing and sturdy frame suggested that he was an itinerant laborer or local farmhand. His hair was thick, the color of rich loam. His shoulders filled his cotton shirt well as those of any Corinthian.

"Shaw," Eden said, collecting herself, "since you have already done so much for us, will you secure Atlas and look after Dalziel while I go to the house for assistance? I shall be happy to speak with you later." She moved sideways, Donal in tow, to catch a glimpse of Shaw's face.

Shaw did not look at her. Instead, he moved so that Atlas blocked her view completely.

"As you wish, my lady," he said.

Eden was not used to being avoided or ignored, least of all by a mere laborer. But there was far more at stake than her pride or curiosity. She bit back unreasonable annoyance and knelt awkwardly beside the stricken groom. She had not so much as a handkerchief to dab at his cut.

"Dalziel," she said, "I shall bring men to carry you down to the house, and see that a doctor is sent for straight-away."

Dalziel's face was red, and Eden had enough experience of men to know that he was holding a long string of oaths in check. The cut on his shoulder did not look deep, but the arm was set at a peculiar angle, and his discomfort was clear. She felt foolish and helpless and very much responsible. That was part and parcel of living at Hartsmere and becoming its mistress, but it was a not a sensation she particularly relished.

"Mrs. Byrne will make up a bed for you so that you may rest comfortably until the doctor arrives," she said.

He nodded stiffly. "I'll . . . be fine, my lady."

She looked impatiently for Shaw. He had secured a much calmer Atlas to a post and was standing directly behind her. She had not even heard him approach.

With a brisk nod of acknowledgment, she took Donal's hand and started for the house. Every step only increased her untoward curiosity about the sudden appearance of Shaw and his remarkable success with Atlas. He certainly showed little enough deference to his betters, but that didn't surprise her. His behavior was not unusual among the Lakeland folk.

What she did find unusual was the compelling timbre of his voice and his quality of confident strength. He hadn't spoken like a common dalesman. His words were surprisingly cultivated and lacked the broad northwestern accent.

Perhaps he had received some education that had encouraged pride above his station. Eden found herself balanced between the inclination to reward and dismiss him immediately, and an overwhelming desire to see his face.

M*y son.*
       Hern leaned his head against the sweaty withers of the stallion and breathed in the homely, mortal scents of hay and dung, not daring to loose his shock and anger.

My son is here. With her.

They had lied to him. Lord Bradwell, his daughter, the aunt who had so disliked him, all their servants — five years ago they had deceived him when they said the child was dead. When they had buried him beneath their lifeless stone. And he, a lord of the Fane, had believed.

The night of the storm, when Eden had fled from the inn, Lord Bradwell had found his daughter and taken her home. The earl had implored Hern to stay away from Hartsmere after he had pursued them there. "She is very ill," Bradwell had warned him. "She may lose the child."

And she refused to see the man she'd known as Cornelius Fleming. She screamed, Lord Bradwell said, whenever his name was mentioned.

So he'd stayed away. If Eden rejected him, so be it. He would claim the child and consider the bargain fulfilled. But even that was denied him.

"Gone," Lord Bradwell had said with feigned sadness when Hern had returned from his nine-month exile in the forest. "The child is dead. I beg you to leave my daughter to recover. I beg you. . . ."

Stricken by unfamiliar grief, Hern had watched them lay the child to rest. Whatever the mortals had buried, with their pious and hypocritical ceremony, had fooled even him. He had smelled and sensed something of himself given to the earth.

But his senses had deluded him. Perhaps he had been so long in mortal lands, surrounded by the taint of mortal emotion, that he had lost the powers he once took for granted.

For the child had survived. He was with his mother, who had returned to Hartsmere with no apparent fear of encountering the boy's father. Had Lord Bradwell told her that the horned creature she so despised had abandoned mortal lands forever?

Warm, soft equine lips brushed his hand where the halter's buckles had burned his flesh. He had grown unused to cold iron while he slept, and now he must develop his ability to withstand its poison all over again.

"Aye, my brother," he said, stroking the great flat cheek. "You know well enough of mortal hypocrisy."

Atlas tossed his head.

"They've called us masters of intrigue, in their legends and stories. But they were adepts of the game from the moment the first of their kind walked this world."

Like Lady Eden Fleming.

He had almost not known her. His memory, like that of all Fane, was nearly perfect, his senses keener than any beast of field or forest. He could remember every tree he had seen grow from sapling to grandfather, each animal that had ever come to his call, and every man or woman he had met in his long life.

How could he have forgotten so much of his mortal bride?

She had changed, as mortals did. Her face was no longer that of a willful child: starry-eyed, ingenuous, and naively certain of what she wanted. Now it bore subtle marks of experience and shrewdness. Lines born of laughter creased the corners of her eyes. Not that her beauty was marred in any way. It had merely been enhanced by the passage of the years.

He was sure that she did not recognize *him*. He had altered something of the appearance he'd assumed as Cornelius Fleming, roughening his features as befitted a servant or commoner, deepening the pitch of his voice. It did not occur to Lady Eden to look for her former lover in a mere laborer, or an inhuman creature in an ordinary man. She, like all mortals, was blind. And that made the situation so much easier for him. Hartley Shaw, as he must be while he remained in the mortal world, was of no possible consequence to so great a lady.

Or to her son.

Our son. He had his father's eyes and hair, but the mouth was Eden's. Hartley didn't know what else he had received from his mother's mortal heritage, or what magical gifts he possessed.

But he was of the Fane. He was the fulfillment of Lord Bradwell's bargain. It was time for all debts to be paid.

"Tod," he whispered, and the menace in his voice caused Atlas to flinch under his hand. He soothed the beast with a touch. "Tod knew. He found it amusing to hide this from me, but he shall atone for his deception."

"Did you . . . speak?"

Dalziel's voice, rough with pain, intruded upon his dark musings. The mortal remained where he had fallen, half supported on his good arm as he endured the wait for assistance.

Hartley left Atlas and went to Dalziel's side. "I spoke only to myself," he said. "Are you in pain?"

Dalziel laughed. "Aye. But I thank ye for saving Master Donal."

For stepping in to protect his own son. *Donal.* It was a good name. Hartley smiled when he remembered the boy's fearlessness in the presence of an angry stallion. Yes, the Fane gift was there. A magical bond had already begun to grow between them.

Hartley knelt and touched Dalziel's damaged shoulder. The man flinched and gasped.

"Be still," Hartley commanded, "or you will suffer more."

Dalziel froze. Hartley turned a small part of his attention to the injury and drew his hand over the bloodied skin and torn shirt. Dalziel released a long breath of relief and amazement.

"The pain . . . it's all but gone," he said, staring at Hartley in amazement.

Hartley got to his feet. " 'Tis but an easing. The arm is back in place, but only time will heal it."

Dalziel stuttered questions and thanks, but Hartley did not answer. He untied Atlas and led him into the stable, took a brush from a rack on the wall, and began to groom the stallion with long, sweeping strokes.

Healing Dalziel, though the effect had somewhat weakened him, proved that his Fane magic had not waned after five years of sleep. The forest remained the source of his power. Even man's Iron, all around him in this place, was an irritant he could endure. He could enchant Donal and whisk him away before Eden realized he was gone.

But where was the challenge in that? Where was the sweet victory over mortals who thought that they could defy a lord of the Fane and go about their lives unscathed?

No. Let his last days on earth purge him of all mortal desires. He'd beat Eden and her father at their own game.

Atlas snorted for emphasis as Hartley picked up his near hoof to examine it for stones. If he was to play mortal again, he must get used to such humble tasks. He would work his way into Eden's life as he'd done before. And when he had taken what he wanted, he would leave her as she had left him.

Alone. Utterly alone.

E*den found Mrs. Byrne in the sitting room. Donal had* run ahead, and he and the housekeeper were chattering away in an almost incomprehensible Irish dialect.

"My lady?" Mrs. Byrne nodded and touched Donal's shoulder. "The boy has told me what happened. Is Dalziel hurt so badly, then?"

"I believe so. He cannot move his arm. The doctor must be sent for immediately."

"The nearest doctor is five miles away, in Ambleside. I'll send Armstrong on our fastest horse, but Dr. Huddleston may not be at home. And with these roads — well, it may take half the day or more."

"Let us hope not. In the meantime, I require men to bring Dalziel down to the house where he may rest comfortably."

"Aye. I've a notion where Hindle and Grubb may be." Mrs. Byrne pulled the bell cord. Armstrong appeared, and she gave him the instructions. Then she summoned Hester and sent her to find the outdoor servants.

Donal came to Eden's side and took her fingers in his small but surprisingly strong hand. "Mo — Lady Eden, will the doctor fix Dalziel?"

She smiled at him. "Yes, he will." She kissed the top of his head, savoring the smell and texture of his thick, clean hair. "You did very well, Donal. I'm proud of you."

"May I go back to the stable and see Hartley Shaw again?"

"Perhaps your ladyship should sit down," Mrs. Byrne said. "You look flushed. Shall I bring you a tisane?"

Eden felt her cheek self-consciously. "I must return to Dalziel."

"Wisht, Dalziel should have sold that brute Atlas long ago, but I understand that Lord Bradwell bought him as a colt and had great hopes for him. You knew Dalziel, my lady?"

"He was with my father six years ago."

"If he's badly hurt, he will not be able to look after the horses."

"One of the men — Grubb perhaps — can take Dalziel's place until he is recovered."

"Grubb is afraid of horses, and Armstrong hasn't the strength, though he can ride well enough. Hindle knows nothing of the beasts."

"Then we shall simply have to hire another groom."

"Aye, my lady." Mrs. Byrne's expression was both sympathetic and guarded, as if she were about to say something she knew her mistress would not like. "It might not be so easy. So many have left the dale, and fewer still would be glad to work at Hartsmere."

"Ah, yes. The local superstitions. I had hoped that the poor condition of the countryside would make the dalesmen glad of steady employment."

"It has been harder to find work and keep the farms since the war ended, to be sure. Less and less of the young folk want to stay in the country."

Mrs. Byrne was dodging Eden's veiled inquiries quite deliberately. Eden's head pounded, and she sincerely wished that she could leave all these decisions to Aunt Claudia.

But that was not to be. Shaw had already proven his skill with horses. If he were in need of work, the immediate problem would be solved. Yet a certain unease attended the thought. Why?

"Be that as it may," Eden said, as much to herself as to the housekeeper, "I must go up the stable and wait with Dalziel until the men come for him. Please watch Donal until I return."

"That I will, my lady. Here, now, let me fetch your pelisse."

"You'll be a good boy for Mrs. Byrne, won't you?" Eden said, straightening a twist in Donal's collar. "I won't be gone long."

"Can't I come?"

She tousled his hair. "Not this time. But we will be together again soon."

With the merino pelisse drawn close about her like a suit of armor, Eden returned to the stable. Much to her surprise, Dalziel was on his feet. Beside him stood Shaw, not touching but somehow lending support, even so.

And she saw his face.

I know this man, she thought. The moment of recognition was brief, but it shook her to the core before she realized that it must be an illusion. She would have remembered such a face.

Hartley Shaw had looks that took her breath away. His were the sort of features one might find in a member of the *ton,* but more sharply cut, bolder, less refined. The chin was dimpled but firm, mouth generous but masculine, nose decisive.

And the eyes . . . the eyes were the verdant green of new spring growth, nestled in the heart of winter. For Shaw's expression was as cold as the land around them.

He met her gaze with not the slightest hint of deference,

and she could have sworn that a mocking smile lifted one corner of his mouth.

"I've seen to your horse," he said, neglecting to add her title.

"Thank you." She forced herself to look away. "Dalziel?"

"I'm better, my lady," he said, holding his shoulder. "It's still not right, but the pain is gone. Shaw helped me."

Eden would have had difficulty imagining Shaw bending enough to help anyone, had he not stepped in to save Donal. He was as unyielding as one of Elgin's Greek statues.

And yet he had moved with grace and suppleness when he had worked with Atlas. Could a laborer be as graceful as if he'd spent years learning to move in expertly cut clothing, and in perfect time to a quadrille at Almack's?

Dalziel cleared his throat. "My lady, by your leave, Shaw here'll help me to my bed."

"You must wait for the doctor at the house," Eden said firmly. "Grubb and Hindle will take you down."

"Very generous, Lady Eden," Shaw said. She had *not* imagined that touch of insolence.

"You know my name?"

"Everyone in the dale knows of your ladyship's arrival."

He flustered her far too much. Though she had a reputation for taking many lovers, no one would expect her to consider any man so far beneath her station. Yet she warmed under Shaw's gaze as if he were a man she might be attracted to.

Such notions should not even enter her head. She was in mourning, and he was a servant.

But there was more than one way to keep uncomfortable thoughts — and people — at a distance. She gave both men her best smile. "I forgot how quickly gossip travels in the country."

"We're all glad to have you back, my lady," Dalziel said.

Her reply was interrupted by the arrival of Grubb, Hindle — and Donal. The boy dashed past her and came to stand directly in front of Shaw.

"Are you going to live here with us?" he demanded.

"Donal —" Eden began. She hadn't the heart to scold him for leaving Mrs. Byrne. She doubted she would ever be able to punish him for any misdeed. For all his solemnity, he was a high-spirited child.

Shaw cast Eden a piercing look and smiled down at Donal. His smile dispelled the coldness of his face, bringing light and warmth to the harshness of his features. There was even something of tenderness there.

"That's to be seen," he said. "Your name is Donal?"

"Aye. Your name is Hartley."

"So it is." He crouched to the boy's level. "How old are you, Donal?"

Donal held up five fingers. "How old are you?"

Shaw laughed. Like his smile, his laugh transformed him. Behind the sound lay the cherished warmth of summer, the smell of new-mown hay, the rush of clear water in the beck.

"Much older than you can count on these," he said, taking the boy's hand. His fingers were remarkably gentle, dwarfing Donal's. Donal rewarded Shaw with one of his own rare smiles.

Eden felt as if they had created an invisible barricade around themselves, a world of their own that she could not enter.

"Donal," she said. "Please come to me."

Reluctantly, the boy pulled his hand from Shaw's. He backed his way to Eden, watching Shaw all the while, and bumped against her legs.

"Grubb, Hindle," she said, "assist Mr. Dalziel to the house, and give him into Mrs. Byrne's care. Shaw —". She tried to smile, but the expression that once came so easily to her face seemed unaccountably frozen. "Our cook will provide you with a meal. It is the least we can do."

Shaw stared at her with absolutely no sense of propriety. "Aye," he said.

Donal's hand in hers, she led the way back to the house. Mrs. Byrne waited by the door.

"I am sorry, my lady. I turned my back just for a moment —"

"Never mind, Mrs. Byrne. The men are coming with Dalziel. Have you prepared a suitable chamber?" At the housekeeper's nod, Eden hesitated, half afraid to speak the stranger's name. "There is another, one Hartley Shaw, who succeeded in calming Atlas. He deserves a good meal, if Cook will provide one. I shall put Donal in my room for a nap, and then I'll look in on Dalziel."

Happy to leave Mrs. Byrne in charge, Eden took Donal into her room and tucked him into the immense four-poster. He moved about restlessly, kicking at the sheets and looking toward the door.

Shaw, she thought, though it made no sense. *How could Donal have formed an attachment so quickly?*

Indeed, how had she come to find him so disturbing?

She stroked Donal's forehead, smoothing back his hair and marveling that she had fallen in love overnight. *I can still love. Not a man — never again — but I have more than enough for my son.*

As much to distract herself as quiet Donal, she reached back in her memory for a lullaby her own nurse had sung to her when she was little.

Her lullaby succeeded. Donal slept deeply in the way of young children, his mouth half open and his thick brown lashes shadowing his cheek. Eden glanced at the mantel clock. Two hours had passed; surely Shaw would be gone. Aunt Claudia must still be in her room.

What *she* would make of Shaw didn't bear thinking of.

Eden checked Donal once more and went downstairs. Hartsmere was as still and empty at midday as it had been at dawn. The small but cheerful fire did little to warm the sitting room. Eden picked up a copy of *La Belle Assemblée* brought from London and leafed through it idly, unable to summon up any interest in the latest fashions.

"Lady Eden, I have good news."

Mrs. Byrne bustled into the sitting room, looking flushed and very pleased with herself.

"Has the doctor come?" Eden asked.

"Not as yet, my lady. But I've found someone able to take Dalziel's place until he's better."

Eden knew who that someone was before Mrs. Byrne could speak the name. A chill spiked through her body. "Shaw," she said.

"Aye. I've been speaking to him in the kitchen. Seems he's quite experienced with horses. More than that, he's a man of all work, able to do whatever is needed around the place — gardening, gamekeeping, repair work." She smiled broadly. "We couldn't ask for better, my lady, and he's a practical lad. His wages won't be dear." She caught herself. "That is, of course, if you approve."

So he has won you over as well, Eden thought. "What do we know of him, Mrs. Byrne?" she asked in a reasonable tone. "Is he from this parish? Can anyone speak for him?"

"I can speak for myself."

Shaw walked into the room as if he made a habit of visiting the homes of his betters. His cap was in his hands, but that was his only concession to her rank. The green eyes held hers with the same insolent directness.

"Would you care to hear my credentials, my lady? Where shall I begin?"

Chapter 4

During countless years of life in the mortal realm, Hartley had learned to read human faces and bodies as mortals read their books, and with far greater comprehension.

Yet he could not read Eden's. He still expected to see in her the vivacious, uninhibited girl he had courted and won.

That Eden was no more. In her rapid journey from child to woman, she had perfected the art of deception. She smiled at him with all the graciousness of an aristocrat to an underling and seated herself in the chair near the fire.

"Ah, Mr. Shaw," she said. "I trust that you have been well looked after in the kitchen?"

Even the music of her voice had changed; it was more resonant but a little satirical, as if she had learned to wield it as mortals used their tools of Iron, to cut and twist.

"Aye, your ladyship," he said. The honorific stuck in his throat, but it was all a part of the game.

"Excellent. We owe you great thanks for your help this morning."

We, she said. But she didn't mean Donal and herself, or even Dalziel. She used words as she used her rank, to keep him at a distance, and that told him that her mask of indifference was as much a deception as anything else.

She still did not recognize him. *That* she could not hide. But he disturbed her. And now, when he was no longer distracted by the shock of finding his son, when they were facing each other with nothing between, he knew why.

His long-dormant senses woke to their full power. He smelled the answer in the air swirling about her body. He heard it in the pounding of her heart. He felt it in his belly like a draught of heady mortal ale.

To Eden Fleming, he was a servant. But he was also a man, and once he had taken her as a man takes a woman. Her body remembered what her mind did not. Her very bones and blood were imprinted with his spirit as her womb had been branded with his seed.

She wanted him. It was the primal dance that had existed since men had worn skins and worshiped the Fane as gods.

Many times, in their millennia upon the earth, Fane had taken willing mortal lovers. Occasionally it was with no thought beyond a moment's pleasure, but more often it was because of the unique enchantment that mortals alone wielded: the magic of their emotions, made vivid and powerful by their brief, fire-bright lives.

How many lovers had Eden taken since their one night together? That she had taken them he had little doubt. Many mortals were as fickle as Fane in their desires. And why should it matter? If she were experienced in the ways of love and eager to have a new man in her bed, he would oblige her.

By Titania's wings, he wanted her. One night had not been enough to purge himself, nor was hatred a barrier to his lust. It urged him to make her suffer, as he had suffered.

Once he had deigned to court a mortal woman. Let her debase herself to love a servant, and realize her mistake too late.

Hartley smiled, making no attempt to hide his thoughts.

Eden's eyelid twitched. One less acute of vision might not have noticed.

Mrs. Byrne moved up beside him, glancing from his face to Eden's. "Well, now. Tell her ladyship what you can do, lad."

Shall I, indeed? Hartley caught the sudden wariness in Eden's eyes. *Remember the part you play. If you step too far beyond your place, she will run before you've caught her.*

He tempered his challenging stance. "I do seek employment, your ladyship," he said. "I can do all that Mrs. Byrne says. I've a way with dogs and horses, I've experience in foresting and gamekeeping, and growing things do well under my hand."

Eden arched a brow. "Quite the paragon — just as you said, Mrs. Byrne." Without relaxing her posture, Eden gave the impression of indolent amusement.

Laughing at him. At the humble mortal he pretended to be.

He glanced deliberately around the threadbare sitting room. "I'd say that you need help here, your ladyship."

"Indeed. Have you a mind to assist our maids, Mr. Shaw? Perhaps our household is not fine enough for your liking."

"I can do whatever is needed," he said. "But you'll find that my talents lie elsewhere."

She chose to ignore his innuendo, if she could recognize it in an itinerant laborer. But he thought she had. He thought she was even more disturbed than before.

"You will have ample opportunity to display your skills," Eden said, rising. "Mrs. Byrne is acting steward at the moment, so you may discuss the terms of your employment with her. She will decide what requires your immediate attention." She glanced at the older woman. "I believe there is a gardener's cottage available —"

"Aye," Mrs. Byrne said. "Old Coddington's cottage."

Hartley shuddered inwardly at the thought of being trapped within man's walls. "I'll sleep in the stable."

Eden smiled. "Mrs. Byrne, I believe that I will have my luncheon now, when you have finished with our man of many talents."

"Aye, my lady." She took Hartley's arm and steered him toward the door. "You're that lucky," she whispered when they were in the hall. "I thought she'd taken you in dislike. You'll wish to watch that saucy tongue of yours, lad. Our mistress is a lady of quality, used to fine London ways, and she'll brook no insolence." She paused just outside the doors to the servant's wing. "Aye, and she's suffered more than a bit, as well. Lost her husband and her London house. Hartsmere is all she has left, so don't make it the harder for her. Leave off your bold glances and remember your place."

Lost her husband.

Hartley stopped in his tracks. Eden had married, then. He had not even considered the possibility, though he knew he should not be surprised. By the customs of men, she would have needed a father for her son, a respectable name to bear into mortal society. She would have sought a husband who did not care if she had lain with another, who would accept her son as his own.

"Who was he?" he demanded.

"Who was who?" Mrs. Byrne peered into his face. "What's wrong, lad? You look as though you've just met your worst enemy."

"Who was her husband?"

"Mr. Spencer Winstowe, younger son of the Viscount Dillamore, and two months dead. Why would that be interesting you, now?"

Why, indeed. Why should he care if she'd chained herself to the first mortal who would take her?

But his vision was red, and behind the scarlet haze he saw her wrapped in this Winstowe's arms — her husband, her mate — taking him into her body, gasping and crying aloud as she had done with her first lover.

Now Winstowe was dead. Mortal mourning was as brief as everything else in their lives. Though Eden wore the black of sorrow, she seemed to dismiss her husband's passing as easily as she'd forgotten Cornelius Fleming.

"Did she love him?" he asked.

"And what business is that of mine, or yours?" Mrs. Byrne narrowed her eyes. "Best banish all such thoughts from that handsome head if you want to stay at Hartsmere."

Hartley clenched his fists, allowing himself to feel the pain of nails biting flesh. "The boy, Donal — is he the lady's only child?"

Mrs. Byrne gave a start. "Donal is not Lady Eden's son. He is the grandson of her uncle, who lives in Ireland and has taken ill. She is caring for him."

Not her son? Was that what she claimed? Yet another lie, and one that only increased Hartley's anger. Was she so ashamed of her own child that she refused to acknowledge him, as if he were some grotesque changeling?

"The family resemblance is striking," he said between his teeth.

"Enough. As her ladyship said, we've the details of your work here to discuss." She opened the servants' door and ushered him through, ending the conversation.

For the time being. Hartley had many questions yet to be answered, and if Mrs. Byrne refused to cooperate, there were others who would. He'd decided to use no enchantment to steal Donal from Hartsmere, but that did not prevent him from putting Tod to work. The hob could listen in on every servant's conversation within the house and never be detected.

As for Lady Eden Winstowe, she was *his*.

A*fter a day in consultation with Mrs. Byrne and an-* other night in her musty bed, Eden determined to begin restoring Hartsmere immediately.

The doctor had come and gone, Claudia remained in her room, Donal was with Nancy — who had younger brothers of her own, and was serving as temporary nursery maid —

and Eden could not imagine herself remaining within these walls another minute. She had planned to wait for the new steward's arrival before venturing out among Hartsmere's tenants and dependents, but it had become clear that finding one might take longer than she had hoped.

With Hester's help, Eden changed into her riding habit and sent Armstrong to the stables to see that her mount was saddled and ready. She and Claudia had each brought one riding horse, the most reliable animals in Spencer's once-grand stables. Her own mare, Juno, would hardly be a challenge for the new groom.

Hartley Shaw. She stopped in the midst of pulling on a glove and wet her lips. Of course it was not the desire to avoid him that made her almost dread seeing him again. Why should she avoid him? His bold green eyes held no power over her, nor his broad shoulders and splendid form the means to impress one who had seen the very finest the *ton* had to offer.

Yet during the interview, when he had gazed at her with that mocking gleam, she had briefly imagined that she knew what he was thinking. She had envisioned herself naked, open to his view, near shameless as only a married woman of Society could be, reveling in his admiration, in being wanted, in sheer masculine lust. He swept her up in his arms and carried her away to the stables, to a bed of clean straw. She watched him undress, removing the plain laborer's clothing as if it were the work of Bond Street's finest tailor, and felt her heart pound with a lust that matched his own.

All that had flashed in her mind in the sitting room while he told her of his many "talents." For years she'd pretended to be exactly what the *ton* judged her: an exciting, audacious woman who skirted the outermost edges of propriety with devil-may-care abandon. Yet never had she been so tempted to scorn the rules as she was now: to accept as lover a total stranger, a man of no rank who dared to cast his eyes above his station.

Spencer had taken her like a beast in rut on their wedding night. Why should she want more of the same?

Because she had known something better, once upon a time. Because she knew it would be better with Hartley Shaw.

Her servant.

If she had lost a great love with Spencer's death, this mourning might have seemed more real. If they had shared more than a name. If she had truly drowned her loneliness in Society's pleasures, as everyone believed . . . as she wished to drown it now.

She closed her eyes and leaned heavily against the chipped Queen Anne dressing table. It was to banish such thoughts that she had been so determined to ride out on this winter's day. Perhaps the bleakness of the countryside would remind her that her mourning was far from over.

She tossed back her head and laughed. Self-pity was dull and frightfully odious. Not at all the thing.

And she had Donal.

She looked in on him before she went downstairs. Nancy scrambled up from the floor as Eden entered the small room they had set aside for the temporary nursery. The maid's face was screwed into an expression of vexation and bewilderment.

"My lady," she said, bobbing a curtsy. She cast a nervous glance toward the window. Donal was perched on a wobbly chair pushed up against the wall, nose and hands pressed to the glass.

"Is something wrong, Nancy?" Eden asked.

"No, my lady." Nancy wiped her hands on her apron and hunched her shoulders. "We was playing right along, my lady, when he just stopped. He pulled the chair to the window, and just keeps staring out — won't listen to me, my lady." The maid bit her lip. "I'm sorry, my lady."

"It's all right, Nancy." Eden stared at Donal's rigid little back. He reminded her of nothing so much as a caged animal dreaming of freedom. She could not bear to see him so.

"He needs fresh air," she said. "I will take him out."

"Thank you, my lady." Nancy curtsied again and began to gather up the few toys Eden had located in a battered chest in the attic.

"Donal," Eden said, moving up behind him. "Would you like to go for a ride?"

He turned about so fast that she feared he would fall. "A ride? On a horse?"

She had no pony suitable for a child of his age — another lack she must remedy. They would have to take the estate's old four-wheeled dog cart, which Mrs. Byrne had assured her was still in working order, used as it was for twice-monthly visits to Ambleside, when weather permitted, and sometimes to the curate's or the smithy.

It would certainly be put to the test now. Eden hoped that she was up to driving it over the rutted, muddy roads.

The other challenge was taking Donal down to the stables and changing her previous instructions.

She tugged at the sleeves of her riding gloves. "Nancy, I shall be gone for an hour or two."

"Shall I dress Master Donal?"

"Thank you. I shall do it myself." Eden picked Donal up and carried him to her room, where his few clothes were kept. His former guardians — she would not call them parents — hadn't seen fit to send him with much in the way of necessities. The tiny village of Birkdale surely had a woman capable of sewing up a child's clothes, but Donal required the kind of wardrobe that could only be found in a larger town such as Ambleside. Another journey to be made.

Unlike most boys his age, Donal was amazingly well behaved as she dressed him and bundled him up in his jacket. He looked a perfect ragamuffin, but she could not have loved him more.

Do you love me, my son? she longed to ask. But she dared not. How could she expect so much after less than a day? It was miracle enough that he'd accepted her nearly upon their first meeting.

But he looked directly into her eyes, and his own held such an expression of trust that she felt dizzy with gratitude. She hugged him, not too close, and took his hand. His fingers curled about hers. She sighed with sheer happiness.

Juno waited, saddled and ready, in front of the house, but her new employee was not in attendance. She pressed her lips together, suspecting some subtle, fresh impertinence.

Donal released her hand and walked up to the mare's head, stroking her velvet nose. She lipped at his fingers. Before Eden could suggest that they take Juno back to the stables, he had already turned down the drive, marching off to the rear of the house with Juno trailing at his heels like an obedient dog.

Eden laughed. Was every child so full of surprises, or was Donal simply different? She sobered immediately, remembering his reckless unconcern in facing Atlas. All the time she had been rushing about Society like a madwoman, Donal had been alone. She knew he had been alone, left to make his own way in learning about the world. Someone must teach him the difference between friendly beasts and dangerous ones.

Shaw could teach him.

Trust Donal with a stranger? Yet Shaw had virtually saved Donal's life, and the boy had taken to him quickly. Donal needed a man to look up to —

What he *needed* was a father. A father — a man to fill a father's role — of blood and rank. Donal could never learn the ways of Society, or of his true place in it, from a servant.

Eden found herself at the stables with no memory of the walk. Donal was perched atop Juno, balanced on Eden's sidesaddle, while Hartley Shaw held him in place with a firm hand. The boy was smiling as he so seldom did, delighted with his position above the rest of the world. Shaw smiled as well, with what Eden judged was genuine warmth.

Her heart clenched. *He likes children. Donal already*

adores him. But as she approached, the smile left Shaw's face.

Even the most formidable dowagers and high-sticklers of the *ton* had not intimidated Eden as this servant did. Not a single one of the most handsome, witty gallants in Town had been capable of making her breathless with a glance.

Hartley Shaw had that power.

Eden faltered, astonished at her instinctive desire to flee. She drew in a steadying breath, reminded herself who she was, and continued on with the same air of confident nonchalance she wore in the finest drawing rooms of London.

"Mr. Shaw," she said briskly, "My son will escort me into the dale. If you would be so good as to prepare the dog cart . . ."

Shaw lifted Donal down from Juno's back, keeping his hand lightly on the boy's shoulder. He glanced up at the overcast sky.

"I would not advise it, your ladyship," he said. "The weather is about to turn, and the roads are bad."

The sky looked no different to her than it had all morning, and Eden was certain it wasn't cold enough to snow. "We will not be going far. When you have finished with the cart, see that Juno gets a little exercise. She expected an outing today."

Shaw's gaze was as sharp as a saber. "You are concerned for the feelings of your horse, Lady Eden?"

She met his appalling insolence with a smile. "I accord my mare at least as much consideration as I do the servant who looks after her."

To her surprise, he neither took the unsubtle hint nor offered up another insult. "Yes," he said. He held out his hand, and Juno rested her muzzle in the cup made of his fingers. "She tells me that you care for her."

Eden laughed at his absurdity. "I am glad to hear that she gives such a favorable character. It seems that she approves of you as well, Mr. Shaw."

"Juno likes Hartley," Donal said. "She told me so."

The amusement drained out of Eden in a rush. "Donal, come to me."

He did as she asked and gazed up at her with that heart-breakingly grave little face. She knelt before him.

"Did you say that the horse spoke to you, Donal?"

"Aye. She tells me all kinds of things."

Eden stanched the panic that flooded her throat. "Is this a game Mr. Shaw taught you?"

Donal glanced back at Shaw with an enigmatic smile. "He didn't teach me. But he can do it, too. He tells me what he hears."

Clutching Donal's thin shoulders in her hands, Eden suppressed the longing to run to Mrs. Byrne and beg for her reassurance that such absurd fancies were normal in a child of Donal's age and background. He had, after all, come from a country where the basest superstition was commonplace. Was it any wonder that he should believe in fairy tales?

Shaw had no such excuse. He had at least some education. And he had no business encouraging such notions in her son.

Surely they *were* mere notions, and not something more sinister. Something having to do with his father . . .

Eden shook her head. She was Donal's mother. What she did not know about motherhood and children she must learn. And, as little as she liked the prospect, she saw that it would be necessary to have a firm talk with Shaw.

Aunt Claudia would have no trouble dealing with him and putting him in his place. She had a natural, irrefutable authority about her that Eden had never tried to match. Perhaps she should explain the situation to Claudia and leave it to her.

But that was the coward's way out. Eden had decided not to do as she had always done and take the easiest, least troublesome path. If she could not be as strong as Claudia, she might at least attempt to hold her ground.

And Claudia would most likely dismiss Shaw at the first sign of contrariness. That would not do — not while

Donal was so attached to him. She wouldn't deprive him of a single thing that gave him happiness. That was reason enough to endure Shaw's presence and her own troubling response to it, in addition to the indisputable fact that he was very skilled with horses, and there was hardly an overabundance of servants to choose from.

She met Shaw's gaze over Donal's head. His stare shot through her like a bolt of summer lightning. She could have sworn that she felt the damp, throbbing heat of an impending storm gather about her, making her clothing stick to her skin and perspiration break out on her brow.

The storm in Hartley Shaw's green eyes was the source of the lightning, of the heat, of the tingling and wetness between her thighs.

Memory crashed about her like thunder. The inn on the border, a girl's hope and joy, the ecstatic pleasure of being known by a man. Not just any man, but the one she adored.

That was how she felt in Shaw's presence, as if she were back in that bed, lost in physical sensation beyond any she had guessed could exist. Pure, animal gratification, made the more miraculous by love.

It was only much later she learned that not all acts between a man and woman were so pleasurable, that the joy was as rare and fleeting as marital fidelity among her own kind.

A mad notion flew into her head. She had experienced a powerful sense of recognition when she first saw Hartley's face. Could it be that he reminded her of Cornelius? They were not much alike, except for the remarkable, terrifying effect both had upon her. Such incredible, erotic allure . . .

No. It was not possible. Eden swallowed and closed her eyes. All at once the wet heat and lightning was gone, and she was chilled through by the sharp winter wind.

"Please fetch the dog cart, Shaw," she said.

For an instant she thought he looked as shaken as she felt. But that must be a trick of the light, or of her addled brain. He turned for the stable, Juno in tow, before she could be certain.

Donal did not try to follow. He took Eden's hand. "What are you afraid of, Mother? I may call you Mother now, mayn't I?"

Was this wise little man a child at all? She squeezed his hand. "Of course you may, but only when we are alone. When you were high up on Juno's back, were you afraid of falling off?"

Boyish scorn flared in Donal's eyes. "Juno is easy," he said. "I want to ride Atlas."

"Oh, no, my lad." She held back from sweeping him up in her arms and kissed his cheek instead. "Not just yet. Perhaps when you're a little older."

"Like Hartley?"

He went from indignant to wistful in the blink of an eye, displaying all the warning signs of true hero worship.

Like Hartley, indeed. She planned to see that Donal rose to heights a man such as Hartley Shaw could not begin to imagine.

As if he were determined not to be out of her thoughts for a second, Shaw promptly drove the dog cart out of the carriage house. The horse, a pretty chestnut gelding, seemed a bit too spirited to draw such a sedate vehicle. Though Eden had driven many a dashing phaeton on Rotten Row, that was a far cry from the hideous roads in Westmorland.

Determined not to show any hesitation, Eden stepped up to the cart. "Thank you, Shaw. Donal —"

Shaw moved so quickly she hardly had time to think. He jumped down from the driver's seat, hoisted Donal onto his shoulders, and carried the boy to the rear-facing seat of the cart.

"Can you hold on here, very tight?" he asked.

Donal nodded enthusiastically and grabbed the rails surrounding the seat. Shaw came to Eden's side, offered his hand, and gave the barest of nods. His meaning was plain: He proposed to drive.

"Perhaps my intent was not clear," Eden said. "I shall be —"

The chestnut chose that moment to lunge in his traces, causing the cart to shudder from side to side. Eden blanched and hurried to make sure that Donal was safe.

He grinned — a full, dazzling grin — as if it were all a marvelous jest for his benefit.

"Copper has not been out in a week," Shaw said in a mild voice. "I would not wish your ladyship or Master Donal to come to any harm."

"Have you no more docile animal?"

"The stables are nearly empty. Juno is not a carriage horse, and Atlas . . ." His eyes actually sparked with amusement, at her expense.

Given the choice between driving out with Shaw and foregoing the excursion, Eden knew what she must do. Disappointing Donal was out of the question, and the tenants must be visited.

"Very well." She avoided his gaze and made a pretense of tucking Donal's scarf more securely about his neck. Only then did she allow Shaw to take her hand and help her to her seat.

The contact, brief as it was, set her senses reeling. Even through the protection of her riding glove, she felt the warmth of his hand, and something more. Something uncanny.

She tried to wrest free, but he didn't let her go until she was well settled on the seat. She caught the look he gave her — speculative, almost puzzled — before he leaped into the driver's position.

The chestnut stood absolutely still for Shaw, craning his head about with an expression of equine innocence. *It is quite too late for apologies now,* Eden told it crossly.

But of course the horse would not understand *her*. Though one might suppose that a man who could speak to animals could arrange to have his four-legged friend kick up a little trouble for his ulterior purposes. . . .

She nearly laughed again but stopped herself. It was no

matter for levity when Donal was involved. And she was all too aware that the seat she and Shaw occupied, while built for two, left not an inch of space between them. The heat of his body engulfed her. Worse, his hip rubbed hers, and several layers of cloth made a very poor barrier. The position was more suitable for lovers than lady and servant.

Far from taking advantage of the situation as she feared he might, Shaw chose to pretend as if he didn't notice her proximity.

"If you're ready, your ladyship," he said. "Hold on tight, Donal."

Without any visible sign of urging, the gelding began to move down the lane at a pleasant trot. Eden turned to watch Donal until she was sure that his seat was secure.

"Do not worry about the boy," Shaw said. "He won't be hurt."

That was a strange way of phrasing it. "He is only five," she said. "I will not have him put at risk."

Shaw's hands tightened on the ribbons. "He'll never come to harm in my company."

His expression revealed nothing, but his voice held the quiet passion of sincerity. He spoke as if Donal's wellbeing were as personal for him as it was for her. How could that be, unless . . .

Insight burst upon her like sunshine. "You have children of your own."

He looked at her sharply. Once more she felt as if she were being examined, turned inside out by those summergreen eyes. "How did you know?"

Eden was beginning to realize that reminding him of her rank and his place was a useless exercise. "I guessed," she said. "It is clear that you have a way with children."

He stared straight ahead again, guiding the cart through the park toward the gate. "My only child — my son — was taken from me."

Though he spoke in a flat tone, Eden sensed deeper emotions layered underneath. Was he angry that she had brought up the subject, or filled with pain at some tragic memory?

She'd been so sure, during their previous encounters, that his thoughts were easy to guess. She was forced to revise that assumption. How could she possibly know what a man like him had experienced, so far beyond anything she could understand? She had been a child of privilege all her life.

And in that life she had seldom been called upon to give comfort. Entertainment, yes, and amusement, and the occasional minor scandal to titillate her fellow members of the *ton*. Only with Spencer's illness had she found herself trying to care for someone who desperately needed her support, even if he had ultimately rejected it.

With Spencer, she had failed. This might be the first among many chances to prove herself worthy of Donal.

Acting on impulse, she touched Shaw's sleeve. "I am sorry. I can guess what it is like . . . to lose a child."

His gaze speared her hand as if she had branded him with a hot poker. Then he lifted his eyes, and all she saw was scorn.

"Can you?"

We have something in common, she reminded herself. *He must have deeply loved his child, as I love mine. If I were to lose Donal again . . .*

She breathed in carefully. "Yes."

"Is that why you treat Donal as if he were your son?"

The baldness of his question jarred her out of the temporary illusion of fellowship. He'd gone far beyond any previous effrontery. Though he seemed to concentrate on his driving, she knew his question was more than an idle rudeness. He was waiting for her answer.

The set-downs she'd devised never passed her lips. "Donal is . . . all I have," she said, listening to her own admission with dazed astonishment. "Take us back, Shaw."

He continued on through the gate as if he hadn't heard her. At long last, he pulled the cart to a stop.

"I'm sorry," he said. "I . . . spoke out of turn, your ladyship."

His apology was right and proper, yet she felt just as much amazement at his contrition as she had during the rest of their unorthodox conversation. He was as proud as any duke, and far more unpredictable.

But even he could admit when he was wrong.

"I accept your apology," she said. They looked at each other, and Eden felt the beginnings of warmth in the pit of her stomach.

If she gave up now, she'd be back where she started with Shaw. She glanced at Donal. He was watching them with that remarkable stillness, too young to understand the nature of the adult conflict but aware of it nevertheless. She must set an example for him. And for herself.

"Very well," she said, smiling at her son. "Shall we go on, then?"

Shaw's answering smile made her heart tumble like a clown in a Sadler's Wells pantomime.

Chapter 5

Winter still gripped the dale, just as it had seized a Fane heart five years ago with claws of ice and hopelessness.

Hartley's last glimpse of this land had been in December, the month of Donal's birth. The snows had fallen heavily on the day that he consigned himself to Grandfather Oak and abandoned his pact with mortal man.

It was as if the storm had never ended.

Copper drew the cart from Hartsmere's heights, over a road long since in need of repair, and down into the dale. Hartley saw the farms he had once known — small, fellside establishments and those that rested alongside the beck — battered by harsh weather and hard times. Dirty, unmelted snow formed icy drifts alongside stone walls and byres, and even the trees looked brittle as twigs.

This was what he had left behind.

Eden sat very quietly beside him, the recent disagreement — and the moment of peace that had followed — already forgotten. It was only her third day at Hartsmere, and for the first time she confronted what years of neglect had wrought of paradise.

His doing. And Eden's.

According to Mrs. Byrne, Eden's father had been absent from Hartsmere for years. He had left employees and servants to manage the estate, farms, and Birkdale village. Their efforts had not been enough. Nothing would be enough as long as the land lay under Lord Hern's curse.

Contradictory emotions churned through him with such violence that he wondered how humans could tolerate the pain.

Hartley glanced at Eden. He did not yet know why she had returned to Hartsmere, but clearly she had not expected this. In her eyes — eyes that had always laughed until that day at the inn — was the bleak weight of sorrow.

She had known sorrow before. He could not guess what that sorrow was, only that she had borne it while he slept in the oak, cursing mortals as he sank into oblivion.

He should have been pleased by her suffering. Was it not what he had wanted, to know that she paid for her betrayal?

But he could still feel her touch, her sympathy when she had claimed to understand how it felt to lose a child. She was not mocking him; how could she, when she didn't know who he was?

Donal, she claimed, was all she had. When she had admitted it, he'd burned with fierce joy that no mortal had planted a seed where his had grown. That was the wild spirit in him, the horned god of ancient times, who lived by the rhythms and tides of Nature.

The shame that came after was something new and unwelcome. And very human. Eden made him *feel,* now as before. She had taught him the extremes of human emotion, violent enough to tear an unguarded Fane apart. Chains of that emotion still held him as winter held the countryside.

He had accompanied Eden on this ride for the sole purpose of testing her attraction to him. It had not lessened; to the contrary, it grew stronger each moment they were together. Soon she would begin to trust him.

The inconvenience of emotion was a small price to pay for his son. What was *she* willing to sacrifice?

"It has changed," she murmured. "It has changed so much." She made a loose, helpless gesture with her hand. "It was beautiful, once."

When had she ever noticed that before? Hartley smiled bitterly, remembering how, when she had known him as Cornelius Fleming, she had spoken constantly of returning to London and introducing him to the *ton*.

"Winters can be harsh in the north," he said, knowing that was not the reason. "Perhaps you have forgotten."

"No. I thought I had, but . . ." She sighed.

Donal clambered over the rear-seat railing and across the top of the carriage into Eden's lap. An expression of pleased surprise crossed her face, and then she gathered him close.

"Lady Eden," Donal said, "why is the land so sad?"

My son, Hartley thought with a deep swell of pride and sadness. *He already knows so much.*

Eden smoothed Donal's hair. "The whole country is sad since the war ended," she said. Her gaze, darting in Hartley's direction, betrayed her guilt. "We'll find a way to make it better."

"Did it ever matter to you, your ladyship, if the land prospered?" he said. "You have not been here for many years."

She looked at him sharply. "How do you know?"

"Servants talk."

Her voice faded to a near whisper. "I did not think it mattered. Now I know that it does."

"And what made you abandon Hartsmere for so long?"

The color left her cheeks. "I will not discuss it. The past is gone. This is my home now. All this is in my care, and I intend to make it right again."

And for that, you must have my help — if I choose to give it. Hartley clucked to the gelding, though he needn't have made a sound. Copper knew what he wanted. As they continued down the slushy lane, Hartley reconsidered the changes in Eden.

She had never shown interest in the responsibilities that came with the control of land in this country. She'd been quick to see the pleasure and merriment in everything, slow to notice what she did not wish to see.

Was he so different? Had it been his intention to punish all of Hartsmere's people in his rage against the Flemings? Or was this the result of the hatred that spread like a sickness within him? His control over nature was confined to this dale, but it was powerful. His merest thought might alter the balance.

When he had held to the pact, the dale had been abundant with life. But he had not wished to see how dependent the folk of the dale had become upon his blessing. He did not know what fortunes of man's world had challenged the people of the dale. Perhaps, like toy dogs bred from wolves to be man's playthings, they had lost the ability to survive the harshness of the outside.

Eden, too, had been like a flower from warmer climes, unable to thrive where snows fell. London had been her hothouse. Now she was thrust into a snowdrift, but she intended to do more than merely survive.

He — yes, he admired her for that, as much as one of his kind could admire any human. And he was grateful for her kindness to his son. Admiration and gratitude, in proper measure, were not too great a peril.

Wetness kissed his cheek. A light snow had begun to fall from the darkening sky. Eden shivered, pulling Donal close to adjust his coat.

Hartley looked up and willed the clouds to thin. The snow stopped, and the edge of cold faded.

"It can be made well again."

Eden's face turned toward him, and he realized that he'd spoken aloud. Hope — another human emotion — transformed her eyes to the color of the lake in summer.

"Hartley —" She hesitated, waging some inner battle. "You are not of this dale, but you know the district. You are clearly a man of some education. Until we employ a new steward, perhaps you can . . . assist me in speaking to the tenants, and learning what they need. They may trust you more than they would —"

A Fleming? It must have taken courage for her to admit that to him, to ask for his help so humbly. She even went so far as to recognize how much she had to learn.

"I'll do all I can to help you, your ladyship," he said with more sincere warmth than he had expected in himself.

"Of course there is nothing to be done about this dreadful weather," Eden said with a short laugh. "We shall muddle along as best we can until spring. Meanwhile, we can determine which of these houses most needs repair, and what may be done to help the poorest tenants. At least they should not lack for wood!"

Indeed, there were coppices aplenty that the dalesmen could visit for fuel, as long as they didn't invade Hartley's own forest. But many of the coppice woods were untouched or sickly.

Guilt and shame returned, closing up his throat. He wouldn't help Eden only to win her trust and liking. He had his own misdeeds to mend, if only to rid himself of this all-too-human burden of conscience.

At long last they drew into Birkdale. It was much like any country village in the north, surrounded by farmhouses scattered across the fells. There was only one road — linked to the neighboring dale — and nearly every building lay along it.

But it was apparent that many houses were empty, and those yet occupied appeared dreary and run down. The alehouse had a board nailed across its door, and the few shops were closed.

"Please stop here, Shaw," Eden said. Her voice was quiet, chastened. "Mind Donal for me."

Hartley felt, absurdly, as if she'd handed him a precious gift. He stopped the cart, jumped down, and offered his hand to her.

She took it and permitted him to help her to the ground.

Her riding boots gave her some protection from the muck and slush, but her skirts dragged no matter how she tried to arrange them. With a shrug, she let them fall and set out for the nearest stone cottage.

Smoke meandered in a thin line from the chimney, the only sign of life. Eden knocked on the poorly fitted door. She waited for several minutes before it opened.

The woman who answered was thin save for an immense belly declaring her expectant state. A stained apron barely covered the expanse. Brown hair hung in straggly clumps about her face, and Hartley could not guess at her age.

Eden greeted the woman, who stared as if she gazed upon a two-headed calf. Eden's small figure, every bit as vulnerable as that of the daleswoman, aroused unwonted pity in Hartley's chest. For a woman so sheltered, this must take great courage.

"Donal, will you hold Copper while I go with your mother?" he asked.

"Copper says that the snow is going to melt soon," Donal said gravely. "He can smell it."

"He's right." Hartley smiled and handed Donal the ribbons. "If he should like to wander to that patch of dry grass there, let him. He won't go far."

"I know." Donal carefully adjusted the ribbons. "I can manage him."

In the boy's voice was all the pride of responsibility. He had not inherited it from the Eden that Hartley had known.

Leaving horse and boy together, Hartley strode to the cottage. The door closed behind the women just as he approached. It was no obstacle to him, for any Fane could eavesdrop on mortal conversation without fear of being seen. He cloaked himself in a glamor of invisibility and eased the door open.

The interior of the cottage was dark, dank, and smoke-filled. Portions of the floor were covered with stone, but others were bare earth. Dirty water dripped from the dilapidated thatch roof, and a rickety ladder led to a loft where the ends of two simple beds could be seen. A few oft-repaired pieces of furniture clung to the sides of the crooked walls.

It was evident that the woman had made efforts to keep the place clean, but she had no hope of success under conditions such as these.

Hartley's stomach knotted in mingled loathing and pity. Far better the sky and the grass and the clean, cool breeze than this horror. Near the small fire, heating a pot of thin gruel, huddled two ragged children and an older girl. Their faces were smudged with soot, and their bodies were as thin as their mother's.

He had often been disgusted with mortal squalor, but not until now had he any reason to feel sympathy. This poor cottager desperately needed all the help Eden could give.

Eden's face was ghostly with dismay. "Mrs. Singleton," she said, clearing her throat. "I —"

"Please sit down, your ladyship," the woman said. She indicated a three legged stool near the fire. Eden almost refused, but at the last she sat, stiff and uneasy in her privilege.

"Forgive my poor hospitality," Mrs. Singleton said, resting her hand at the small of her back. "We have a little tea, if you wish —"

"No, thank you." Eden swallowed. "Mrs. Singleton, I only just arrived two days ago from London. I will be living at Hartsmere, and I intend to do whatever I can to —" She glanced around the room, at a loss for words.

Mrs. Singleton dropped her head so that her hair swung over her face. "I'd heard the house was to be lived in again," she said quietly. "I hope —" She, too, hesitated. "I thank your ladyship for your care."

"Please do not thank me until I have done something to earn it." As soon as she had spoken the words, Eden clamped her lips shut. "What became of your husband?"

"He's gone." Mrs. Singleton gathered her children and gazed at the smoke-stained wall. "He was a bailiff at

Hartsmere until a year ago, my lady. But when they discharged him, he couldn't find work —"

Eden sprang to her feet. "Discharged?"

"Aye." Mrs. Singleton did not look surprised at Eden's ignorance. Her eyes were very old and very wise, mirroring a thousand days of pain. "Mr. Brown said there was no reason to keep him on when so many tenants had left, that he'd collect all the rents himself."

Eden sat down again, looking ill. Hartley almost rushed to her side, but she recovered and folded her hands in her lap.

"I regret what happened, Mrs. Singleton," she said. "Mr. Brown has also left my employ, so . . ." She took a deep breath. "I require a bailiff. Do you know where your husband went?"

The daleswoman shook her head. "Once he sent a little money, but —" She hugged her children closer.

"We shall locate your husband, Mrs. Singleton, I promise you. Upon his return, his job will be waiting for him. In the meantime . . ." She smiled at the children as though her heart would break. "There are several unoccupied cottages on the grounds at Hartsmere. I invite you to live there until Mr. Singleton rejoins you."

Mrs. Singleton's face lit with hope, but she quickly resumed the stoicism of habitual poverty. "Thank you, my lady. But my home is here. I'll stay, if you please."

If she felt disappointment, Eden didn't let it show. "I understand. Then perhaps you will allow me to bring a few blankets for the children, and some clothing, and meat and bread."

The daleswoman's lip trembled. "My lady —"

"For the children."

Mrs. Singleton bowed her head. "Your ladyship is very kind."

The two women could not have been more different, but Eden herself was near tears. She exchanged a few last words with Mrs. Singleton, smiled again at the children, and fled the cottage. Hartley followed, closing the door behind him, and became visible again.

Eden saw him, but not before he witnessed her terrific struggle to calm herself. She blinked rapidly, looked for the dog cart, and almost ran toward it. Once there, she caught Donal in her arms and embraced him, pressing her cheek to his.

"I never knew," she whispered. "I did not realize —"

Hartley didn't think. He moved up behind Eden and held her as she held Donal, warm and secure in his much larger arms. She was so shaken that she failed to object.

"They have hardly anything. Their clothes . . . the food . . . If only I had known."

Hartley touched the wisps of hair that escaped from under her bonnet. "Aren't there similar tragedies in London?"

"I never saw them. I . . . didn't want to." She lifted her head, became aware of his arms about her, and broke free. But he sensed that she was little concerned with the scandalous liberties he took.

"There must be many others — in Birkdale, on the farms — like her. They will all need my help." Her face took on a fevered flush, and she paced back and forth as if the racing of her thoughts would not let her be still. "Yes, we must return to Hartsmere at once and make arrangements. Find some spare garments until more can be bought. And surely these children should be in school — I'm sure there was one, once. The curate will know. I shall see him tomorrow and bring the Singletons what I can collect."

A new energy emanated from Eden. It had nothing to do with the things that had once made up her world, yet it brought such passion to her eyes that Hartley felt a surge of envy. And loss.

When he'd first courted Eden Fleming, he had regarded the effort as an unpleasant duty. But even he, like all Fane, had been drawn to her emotion, the incandescent spark of joy within her human soul. The pulse of creation itself beat in her heart as surely as sap ran in the oaks and singing becks carried the land's lifeblood. Even her dislike of the country had not lessened her allure.

Gradually, his purely selfish interest had changed into something more. It had taken him weeks to realize that what he had begun to experience was not merely the need for the child she could give him, or even fascination with her vivid humanity. He felt affection for her, affection that was but a pale copy of love, yet an uncommon thing among his kind. He learned, from her, what it was to feel with the soul. He had even believed that he could bring her to understand his ways and the ways of the land he guarded.

He'd never had the chance. But some part of that affection endured, reborn as his anger had reawakened in the forest. For the first time in his long life, he was beginning to understand the human trait of compassion.

And he was beginning to wonder if he could steal Donal from this woman he had hated, when his hatred was dying a little more with every moment they shared.

"You care about the woman," he said. "You would give her all these things, yet you do not know her."

Eden turned to him, still suffused with the enormity of her scheme. "Does that surprise you, Shaw? I see that it does. You think me a useless member of Society, good for nothing but balls and routs and visits to the mantuamakers." She smiled broadly, and mischief snapped in her eyes. "Shall we make a wager, you and I? If by summer's end I have not brought about a change for the better, in this town and in all of the dale, I will . . . I will grant you ten acres to do with as you wish, and waive the rent for a year."

Hartley almost laughed. *She* would grant *him* land? The Fane had been here a thousand years before her first primitive ancestors. But it was no mean offer, when landlords clung so dearly to the income they received from their tenants.

"A generous proposal, my lady," he said with an ironic bow.

"And if I succeed, which I will . . ." She tapped her lower lip with a forefinger. "You, Mr. Shaw, will admit that you have been wrong in all your harsh judgments of me — do not deny them — and will most humbly beg my pardon without the least trace of impertinence."

So bright was her mood that he found it impossible not to respond in kind. "Do you care so much for the opinion of a servant?" he asked lightly.

She maintained her smile. "But you are not really a servant, are you, Shaw?"

He grew alert. "And what am I, your ladyship?"

"Perhaps one day you will tell me."

"I am not sure you will believe me."

"Are you the lost heir to some exotic kingdom, then, or a prince in disguise?"

She was treating him as an equal, not a servant. Her disposition was as changeable as spring weather, and he did not trust it any more than he trusted her. But it meant she was, indeed, beginning to trust *him*.

"Alas," he said. "You have found me out."

"You do have a sense of humor after all, Mr. Shaw," she said.

"I often find mankind most amusing — in its many variations."

Her brow arched high. "Mr. Shaw, there are times when I am quite certain that you are no common dalesman. Are you not a part of mankind?"

"Has membership in a society ever prevented astute observation of it?"

She chuckled. "God help anyone who falls under your satirical eye."

"Some sights are more pleasurable than others."

They gazed at each other. Hartley recognized another emotion in his heart that he had almost forgotten could exist.

Happiness. He was . . . happy, here, with the mother of

his son, and Donal close enough to touch. His happiness expanded outward, warming the ground under his feet, reaching up to pierce the sky. A shaft of sunlight struck through the clouds to gild the stray locks of Eden's hair.

Eden turned her face into the light. "How beautiful. The sun is coming out."

A simple statement, yet she filled it with gratitude and real joy, as if someone had given her a priceless jewel. Hartley closed his eyes and set the winds to blowing. Clouds scudded and raced across the sky, clearing a field of blue above the dale. A robin whistled tentatively from a nearby oak.

Donal walked to Hartley's side and took his hand. "You made it better," he said.

Eden's brilliant smile faded. "Donal has a formidable imagination. It should be encouraged in the right ways, by the proper teachers." She reached for Donal. "It's time to go home, Donal. You must be hungry."

Donal glanced back at Hartley but went to his mother willingly enough. His solemn face showed so little of what he was thinking, yet Hartley knew he was torn. Torn between two worlds, one of which he did not even know existed.

If Eden so much as suspected Donal's true nature — if her mind would let her believe — would she run from Hartsmere and never return?

Go with her, my son. The time will come when you no longer need her. No more than do I.

They drove back to Hartsmere in silence, Donal crowded onto Eden's lap. Despite the somber mood, the sun remained bright and warm enough to begin melting the snow on roof and pasture. Almost at the gate to Hartsmere's park, Donal sat up very straight and pointed to a coppice of hazel.

"The fox, mother," he said. "He's my friend."

Tod, of course. Hartley wondered when boy and hob had met.

"I see it, Donal," Eden said. "There must be many

foxes about." She glanced at Hartley. "My father — Lord Bradwell — used to hunt a great deal, but never on this land."

Hartley did not return her look. "Never?"

"Not that I can remember. He hunted on all his other estates —" She broke off.

"Once men hunted out of necessity," he said grimly, "like any other beast, to survive. Now they do it for pleasure. Is that not so?"

She shifted in her seat but didn't answer. Hartley drove the cart through the park and up to the doors of Hartsmere. He helped Eden and Donal down, but she gave him only the barest nod of acknowledgment and took Donal quickly into the house.

Copper received better thanks: a good brushing and a measure of oats. The iron of harness and bridle and carriage bit Hartley's flesh, but he ignored the pain and temporary injury. The day's accomplishments had been considerable, despite the somber note on which it had ended.

When he was finished with the horses, Hartley took on his true form and sought the forest. He slipped in among the vast trees, touching the trunks as he passed and greeting each by its secret name. Healing flowed into his wounded hands. These were his real friends, as mortals could never be. They renewed his spirit and reminded him that the earth held more than the petty handiwork of men.

Tod ran across his path as Hartley reached the domain of Grandfather Oak. The hob changed from fox to boy in the blink of an eye and bowed before him.

"You are pleased, my lord?" he said.

Hartley sat down on the empty shell of a fallen wych elm. "With what? That you made yourself known to my son?"

Tod laughed. "Tod did not tell who he is. But the boy knows. As he knows you."

"He does not know that I am his father."

"But he will." Tod scurried up into the branches of an

ash and hung upside down from his knees. "When will you tell him, my lord?"

"When I am ready." He scowled at the hob. "What news have you brought me?"

"Good news, my lord. Good for you." He sprang to the ground. "The boy has not been with the woman above two days."

"What?"

Tod puffed up with importance. "*She* came to Hartsmere after. He was sent from Eire by the mortals who raised him. Before that, the woman lived in London and never saw the mortal child."

Hartley leaped up from his seat. "Donal was not with her?"

"Nay, my lord. Not since his birthing."

But that made no sense. Agitated, Hartley paced the length of the clearing. Branches rustled above him, echoing the chaos of his thoughts.

He could well believe that Eden had some part in concealing his son's birth from him and keeping the boy away from Hartsmere. But that she would give him to strangers, claim he was another woman's child, and then behave toward him with such devotion and protectiveness . . .

Less than an hour ago he had found himself enjoying Eden's company, softening toward her. Desiring her. His feelings twisted and turned about like a spider's web torn by the wind. It seemed inconceivable that the woman he had seen in the village would cast her son away.

"Is it not good, my lord?" Tod asked, crouching at his feet. "Can you not take him now?"

If what Tod reported were true, Hartley need have no twinges of burdensome conscience at taking the boy away when the time was right. It was to his benefit if the bond between mother and son was weak and of short duration.

And yet, despite all that had come between them, he did not want to discover that Eden had made mockery of his amended judgment. In the past few hours, his image of her had changed completely. He could not despise the woman he'd seen in the village and with Donal. Like the sun breaking through the clouds, his heart had begun to cast off the bands of iron that had bound it.

Suddenly, he was desperate to prove that Tod was wrong.

"I have another task for you," he said to the hob. "Fly to Eire and seek these foster parents. Learn the circumstances of his coming to them."

And find something that will redeem her.

With a joyous yelp, Tod dashed three times around Grandfather Oak. "Tod shall fly!" he cried.

"But only if you come back as soon as your task is done," Hartley warned. "Do not linger."

His tone silenced Tod's rejoicing instantly, and the hob looked up at him with wide brown eyes. "Shall Tod bring the mortals back from Eire?"

"That will not be necessary. Now, go, and return swiftly."

Unable to maintain any kind of solemnity for long, Tod whooped and flung himself into the air. His form contracted in upon itself, growing smaller and smaller until he was the size of a bumblebee. Three times he buzzed about Hartley's head, and then he shot off through the trees to the west.

In the tranquillity of the wood, Hartley had never felt so alone. He closed his eyes and called out to the creatures that had once lived in this sacred place: the red deer, the squirrels, the field mice; stoat, weasel and marten; badgers still asleep in their setts; foxes busy with mating; and all the birds: thrush, tit, robin, sparrow, wren, and the great owls, hawks, and falcons. One and all he summoned them to return and accept his protection.

The answer came from a hundred minds, near and distant; those that were closest cried out in welcome. The birds and beasts did not reproach him for staying so long away. They poured all that they were into every moment of life, with no thought beyond the day itself.

Once Hartley had lived so, for time was nothing to him.

But now time hung like shackles on his body and mind, as it did on every mortal ever born.

In Tir-na-nog, every day was warm and pleasant, caressed by fragrant breezes, filled with amusements and glorious music and fantastical creatures to delight its Fane masters. There was no lasting sorrow, no hunger, or disease, or fear. Reality could be changed with the wave of a hand. Loneliness was impossible.

What Fane would wish to remain in this world of Iron when such awaited him? Was Tir-na-nog not what Hartley wanted above all else, why he endured this turmoil to acquire his son?

Wasn't it?

The fluttering of wings sounded in the branches of Grandfather Oak. A lone wren, plain and brown, flew out of the tree to land on Hartley's shoulder. It whispered to him of coming spring, of the seeds waking under the earth and sun that warmed the feathers and quickened the blood.

"So it will be, little sister," Hartley said, stroking her breast with the tip of his finger. "I can hasten but not alter the march of the seasons. I have no power to do other than slow or speed what will be, or draw what is best or worst from the land. But I will do what I can. Go, and tell your brothers and sisters that I need them. We must make this land healthy again." He launched the wren skyward, and she flew off as swiftly as Tod had done.

Then he was alone again. It would have been easy to sink back into bitterness and distrust, to believe the worst of Eden and of man's world.

But he had seen the worst in himself. Spring was coming, and with it the promise of renewal.

And hope.

S o, *you are returned at last."*
Eden finished unbuttoning her pelisse and helped Donal off with his coat. Only then did she look to Aunt

Claudia, who, in spite of recent disagreements, appeared well rested and fully restored to her usual equanimity.

"I am later than I expected to be," Eden said, pulling off her bonnet, "but I wished to see something of the village and the state of the tenants right away. Donal came with me."

"So I see." She smiled at Donal with more warmth than she had shown thus far. "I trust he behaved himself?"

"Very well indeed."

"Hartley took us," Donal offered, meeting Claudia's gaze with his distinctly unchildlike stare.

"Hartley?"

Eden blushed. She had no reason to do so; Claudia could neither read minds nor guess at her most secret longings.

"Mr. Shaw. A servant I hired as a man of all work."

"Indeed? I had thought that you and I would discuss the needs of the estate before hiring servants."

"I did not seek him, Aunt. He saved Donal from a dangerous horse, and as he was in need of work and showed considerable skill —" She broke off, determined not to justify herself. "He has proven quite able. He drove us in the dog cart to look over the dale and village. Conditions are far worse than I thought. I plan to start improvements at once."

"Most admirable, I am sure, if you truly think —"

Mrs. Byrne appeared in the hall to take Eden's bonnet and pelisse.

"Good afternoon, Mrs. Byrne," Eden said. "How is Dalziel?"

"Much better, my lady. I'll tell him you asked after him."

Claudia signaled to the housekeeper. "Tell Nancy to take Donal up to his room, Mrs. Byrne. He needs his nap before dinner."

Eden almost protested. She resented Claudia's interference with her son; in fact, she felt less provoked when Hartley Shaw behaved like a relation rather than a servant.

But she would not quarrel again. They were both suffering the strain of so many rapid changes. "By all means," she said.

"I'm not tired," Donal said, continuing to gaze at Claudia.

"Donal, it's impolite to stare," Eden said. She recognized within herself a tendency to be overindulgent with Donal, just as she had always indulged herself. It was not a comforting thought. She took his arm and felt the wiry muscles tense under her fingers. "Excuse yourself to your great aunt, and go with Mrs. Byrne."

Donal pulled free with surprising strength, took Mrs. Byrne's hand, and went directly to the stairs without a word. Eden felt the helplessness of inexperience, inadequate in the face of a child's inexplicable moods.

"I fear he dislikes me," Claudia said dryly.

"He just doesn't know you," Eden protested. "He barely knows me. Give him time." *And give me time to learn to be a mother. A proper mother.*

"Of course." Claudia took Eden's arm and led her into the sitting room. "He is ignorant of manners and proper behavior. A good governess and tutor will correct that problem."

I shall not argue, Eden reminded herself. "If you wish to discuss the hiring of servants, we might do it before dinner, when Mrs. Byrne comes down."

Claudia was agreeable, and so they spent a few minutes in casual conversation until Mrs. Byrne joined them. Claudia said little, but Eden knew that she was taking in and absorbing every comment that the housekeeper offered. The more unpleasant discussion of budget and expenditure had yet to come.

An hour before dinner, when the aromas of slightly burned cooking drifted through some ill-sealed cracks in the wall, Claudia went upstairs to dress. Mrs. Byrne lingered.

"All went well today, my lady?" she asked.

Eden sensed that there was more behind her question

than idle curiosity. "As well as can be expected, given the state of the dale." She looked at her hands. "It is every bit as bad as you indicated."

Mrs. Byrne clucked softly. "Never fear, my lady. I've a feeling that things will change for the better now that you're home."

Oddly comforted, Eden smiled up at the housekeeper. "I hope that your faith in me is justified."

"But I do have faith." Mrs. Byrne glanced toward the window. "Do you know what eve this is, my lady?"

"It is the twentieth of January, I believe. Why?"

" 'Tis St. Agnes's Eve. In the old days, young maids were said to dream of the man they would marry if they fasted the day and were sure not to kiss anyone, adult or child."

Eden laughed. "Well, I shall not be among the dreamers this night. I did not fast, and I've kissed Donal at least once today." *And I am most certainly no maid.* Her body had reminded her of that nearly every moment she was with Hartley Shaw.

"As you say, my lady." But Mrs. Byrne had a twist about her mouth that seemed to hide some secret knowledge. "As you say."

That night, after a dinner somewhat improved from that of the evening before, Eden tucked Donal into bed and retired early. She had thought herself exhausted, but her mind would not let her rest. Long into the night she tossed and turned, her thoughts locked into a whirling pattern made up of Donal, the sad state of the dale, and Hartley Shaw.

She only knew she'd slept when she jerked awake, the sheets wrapped about her and her forehead beaded with perspiration. And then she remembered the dream.

She had dreamed, in stunningly erotic detail, of Hartley Shaw.

Chapter 6

"I cannot thank you enough for your generosity, Lady
Eden," Mr. Appleyard said, bowing for the hundredth
time. "The poor of the dale will be equally grateful, I make
no doubt."

Eden smiled, hoping that the nervous curate would exhaust his praises and be on his way. He was a good-hearted
man; not perhaps the most competent to hold his post, but
the vicar who held the living had not made a personal appearance in some time, and Eden didn't intend to displace
him.

"I wish it could be more, Mr. Appleyard," she said.
"You have everything I could gather in so short a time. But
I shall obtain whatever else is needed, as long as you keep
me informed about the parish folk."

"Indeed. Indeed I shall. And your contribution to the repair of the church —"

Before he could begin rhapsodizing about her many
perfections, Eden held up a hand. "It is my pleasure. Two
of my men will help you load the cart and carry the goods
to the parsonage."

Mr. Appleyard performed yet another bow. "I shall make a special visit to Mrs. Singleton, as you asked."

"Thank you, Mr. Appleyard," she said, drawing him toward the door.

"I have taken up far too much of your valuable time. I shall be most honored to join you for dinner on Monday next."

And I shall spend the next few days preparing for another round of copious thanks, she thought wryly. "Good day, Mr. Appleyard."

"Good day. May the Lord's blessings be upon you!" He bowed himself out of the drawing room and was led away by Armstrong, who closed the door quietly behind him.

Eden sighed and sank back in her chair. One more item checked off her mental list. Her brain felt positively befuddled, filled as it was with figures and inventories and accounts, repairs to be made, servants to hire, and tenants to visit. The work to be done seemed endless, and the limited funds at her disposal could not possibly be enough to complete it.

Certainly Aunt Claudia did not approve of her expenditures. Eden had never been thrifty or careful with money; Claudia had reason to doubt her. But Eden was determined to prove that she was not the frivolous scattergood she had been for so much of her life.

And all this had real purpose. In the fortnight since she had arrived at Hartsmere, every minute of every day had been occupied with learning her role and duties as mistress of Hartsmere or discovering the joys and challenges of motherhood. It was hard work, and she had concentrated until her head ached and a thousand minor concerns kept her from sleep.

But she'd never been happier. Every morning she woke to discover some new miracle: one of Donal's rare smiles when she kissed his cheek, the glorious sun melting the last of the snow, each returning bird that appeared unexpectedly in the bare-branched elm by her window. The whole world was about to spring back to life, opening up as if to embrace her.

She tried with minimal success to ignore the other reason for her happiness. Work distracted her, as did aiding the unfortunate. But whenever she saw Hartley Shaw grooming one of the horses until its glossy coat shone like porcelain, or speaking to Donal with such attentive gravity, her heart set up a thundering pulse that left her breathless.

It was almost as if his arrival, not hers, had signaled the changes in the dale. And that was ridiculous; she told herself that repeatedly and tried to avoid being near him. But the household staff was still small, Hartley was in charge of the stables, and his strength and versatility made it necessary to call on him frequently.

Above all, he was good for Donal. In spite of her very mixed feelings, Eden could not deny it. There was enough of culture and education about Shaw that she need have no fear of her son picking up rough ways or compounding his ignorance while in Shaw's company. And every moment Donal was not with her, playing jackstraws, listening to her read from one of the old books in the library, or learning the proper way to eat at the table, he was looking for his new hero.

She could not resent Shaw for that. She suspected that the future governess would have a great deal more trouble confining Donal than she did.

Unable to sit still, Eden got up and went to the glass-paned double doors connecting the drawing room to the garden. The garden spread out before her, no longer an ugly maze of weeds and undergrowth but tamed into something approaching order. There was still a touch of wildness about it, but she found that she liked it that way.

Perhaps her new appreciation went hand in hand with her gradual discovery that the countryside was not Coventry after all. It was not a place to be avoided, a backwater where nothing ever happened. Even the woods seemed to beckon instead of repel. And Hartsmere itself, after a thorough cleaning by a local charwomen and two additional maidservants, revealed the charms she had overlooked as a girl.

Eden heard voices just out of sight, and soon Hartley Shaw came into view, Donal trailing after him. Hartley touched a few of the dormant plants that he had shaped and nurtured with such surprising care, inviting Donal to do the same.

Hartley knelt on a patch of bare earth, his back blocking Eden's view. Two heads, both nearly the same shade of brown, bent together. After a long moment, Hartley looked up. His nostrils flared as if to smell the air. Then he turned to look directly at Eden.

As always, longing and desire roared through Eden like a Lakeland flood. She put out her hand to brace herself against the doorframe.

Hartley did not smile. He did so even less often than Donal — especially since their first visit to Birkdale. When he spoke to her, he didn't show his former impudence; in fact, he was noticeably distant. But instead of helping Eden overcome her impossible attraction to him, his behavior only served to increase it.

She closed her eyes. *Who would have thought that you had such feelings left?*

"Mother?"

She opened her eyes to find Donal with a stalk of tiny white flowers in his hand.

"For you," he said and presented the flower to her. She was charmed far more than if the *ton*'s richest peer had presented her with an expensive jewel, and profoundly touched.

"Thank you, Donal," she said. "What a very nice thing to do." She was smelling its perfume before she realized that it was a lily of the valley, a flower that did not bloom until well into spring. She looked over Donal's head for Hartley Shaw. He was no longer in the garden.

"Donal, where did you find this flower?" she asked.

"Hartley gave it me."

"And where did he find it?"

Donal pointed into the garden. Eden saw only the bare patch of earth where Shaw and her son had knelt a few moments ago.

There was no sense in trying to make Donal explain. His heart was free of deception, though his imagination was quite extraordinary.

"Did you get your breakfast this morning?" she asked Donal with a bright smile.

"With Hartley, before the sun came up." All at once he was contrite. "Do you want me to wait for you next time, Mother?"

He could still surprise her. She hugged him lightly as he preferred. "I am quite the slugabed, am I not? You need not wait on breakfast, as long as you join me for luncheon."

Donal planted a wet kiss on her cheek. "Very well, Mother. May I go help Hartley with the horses now?"

"Off with you, then!" She watched him run through the garden and toward the stables. The flower, almost forgotten, claimed her attention again.

How very odd. The hothouse stoves have not been lit. How could Shaw have come by it?

"What have you there, Niece?"

Eden turned with a guilty start to face Aunt Claudia. "Donal brought me a flower," she said, surprised at the stammer in her words.

"So I see. How lovely." Claudia examined the blossom and touched one tiny white, bell-shaped flower. Eden waited for the obvious questions, but Claudia did not voice them. She glanced through the open doors.

"Donal is with Shaw again," she said.

"Yes." Eden wandered across the room with an air of unconcern. "Have you become acquainted with him, Aunt?"

"I have no desire to, and you should keep your son away from such unwholesome influences."

"Children seem impressed by simple matters such as skill with horses and other mysterious adult knowledge."

"Donal spends as much time with that servant as he does with you."

"You cannot expect me to smother him. He has no other male to —"

"That can be remedied."

Eden picked up a cracked porcelain shepherdess from the mantel, turning it about in her hands. "When my mourning is over."

"I sometimes wonder if you might wish it to last forever."

"I want what is best for my son."

"Then you will be pleased to know that I have employed an experienced governess for Donal. She should be arriving today — in fact, at any moment."

Eden squeezed the shepherdess in her fist until it bit into her palm. *No. Not so soon!* "But we had not yet discussed it."

Claudia sat down in a wing chair by the doors, serene and confident. "You may trust my judgment, Eden. I couldn't trouble you when you were so preoccupied with estate affairs. I wrote to several London friends for advice."

"Did you explain why we required a governess?"

"I gave out the story you have told everyone here: that your cousin's son has come into your care, and you intend to raise him as if he were your own." She waved such concerns aside. "This woman comes highly recommended. Miss Waterson raised both Lady Gilbert's sons and one of her daughters, and received an excellent character from her previous employer. We are extremely lucky that she finds herself between positions at precisely the time we require her services."

A professional governess, no doubt prune-faced and humorless. Eden carefully set the porcelain figurine down on a chiffonier. "I have not even met her. How can you expect —"

"Donal needs discipline, as you yourself have admitted. You have no experience in raising children. You know as well as I that no lady of the *ton* caters to her child's daily needs. Donal must learn independence and his place in the world in order to preserve your fiction."

"I had no governess — not when I lived with my father or with you."

Claudia smiled. "Your father spoiled you. But when you came to me, you were a very quick study. You understood instinctively how to move in Society. You were a pleasure to teach. Donal is entirely different. He is half wild and uneducated. Once he is under Miss Waterson's care, he will no longer be running after servants. He will receive a proper English gentleman's education."

And that he must have. Eden calmed herself and sat opposite her aunt. Claudia was her staunchest ally, her dearest friend. Eden owed her more than she could ever hope to repay.

"I will see her," Eden said.

"That is all I ask."

While Claudia was in a receptive mood, Eden broached another sensitive subject. "I have discussed the matter at length with Mrs. Byrne, and I do wish to go ahead with the tenants' dinner and fair. May Eve seems an ideal date. It will give me time to find a steward and distribute more goods to the tenants and villagers. Mr. Appleyard —"

"You know my opinion on bestowing such excessive generosity on the tenantry and laborers so soon," Claudia said. "They shall come to expect even more indulgence, which you can scarcely afford. And you've already done much." *Too much,* her silence added.

"Only because the estate was so badly neglected. What I have spent thus far is much less than what I have paid for a few gowns in London. I can hardly cavil at expenses now."

Claudia leaned forward, her handsome face filled with concern. "You were not intended for this, Eden. You should have all the joy and pleasures of life, not its burdens. You must return to Society, to your rightful place."

For a moment, Eden tried to imagine such a return,

freed of her widow's weeds and on Rushborough's arm. London seemed a million miles away, Almack's and Rotten Row in another universe.

But I have changed, Aunt, she thought with wonder. *I can see beyond the next visit to the modiste, the next ball, the next foppish beau.*

She saw, instead, Hartley Shaw, his face intent as he instructed her son in the proper way to groom a horse. Hartley Shaw, who would be utterly out of place in the drawing rooms and ballrooms of the *ton,* as confined and incongruous in tight pantaloons and form-fitting coat as a fox in a kennel.

London would never know such a man.

"I am not the woman I was in London," she said quietly. "I cannot enjoy myself while those around me suffer."

Claudia shot from her chair with uncharacteristic violence and strode to the double doors. She placed one elegant hand flat against a glass pane. Slowly her fingers curled into a fist.

"I hate this place," she said. "God, how I hate it."

The baldness of the statement shocked Eden far more than its sentiment. Claudia spoke from the heart, laying it bare, and Eden caught a glimpse of a woman she didn't recognize: an aging woman with her own measure of regret and bitterness, hiding her fears and secrets from the world. A woman who needed Eden more than the reverse. She hurried to Claudia's side but stopped, afraid to touch this brittle stranger.

"I am sorry," she said. "I have been thinking only of myself." She rested her forehead on Claudia's shoulder. "Perhaps you should return to London. You still have your own jointure. You would be happier there."

"And leave you here alone?" Claudia felt for her hand. "No. You need me, Eden, even when you do not realize it." She turned a haunted gaze on Eden. "I must protect you, as your father did not." Her eyes glazed. "Protect you."

Shaken, Eden squeezed her hand. "Come sit down, Aunt, and I will bring you a nice dish of tea."

She made Claudia comfortable and sent Armstrong for refreshments. Half afraid to leave her aunt in such a state, she settled to wait out the afternoon with a bit of needle-work.

She was in the midst of completing a very tedious section of fine stitching on a handkerchief when the footman announced one Miss Waterson, just arrived from London.

Eden set down her work and glanced at Claudia. Her aunt seemed perfectly restored; if anything, it was as if she had never had the lapse at all.

In a moment Miss Waterson, dressed in a severe gown of tobacco brown stuff, entered the drawing room. She gazed about with a completely expressionless face and curtsied to her employers.

"Ah, Miss Waterson," Claudia said with gracious condescension. "I am so pleased that you could come in such good time." She glanced at Eden. "Lady Eden, may I introduce Miss Amelia Waterson."

Miss Waterson curtsied again, with a precision that suggested she recognized and accepted the degree of separation between a governess and an earl's daughter. "Good afternoon, my lady."

Her voice was cultured but without music of any kind, and her mouth, Eden thought, belonged to a person disappointed in life. Considering how often governesses were impoverished gentlewomen, Eden could hardly blame her. She ought to pity the woman.

"I trust your journey was satisfactory?" Claudia asked, gesturing to a chair.

"Indeed, my lady." Miss Waterson took her seat, more erect in posture than the chair back itself. "You were most generous."

"You must be fatigued. Your quarters are near the nursery. As you see, we are still making improvements, but I believe you will find your room acceptable."

"Thank you, Lady Claudia," she said with a humble nod. "May I see the boy?"

Eden flinched. So soon? Was this colorless woman to take charge of her son's life, just like that?

"If you wish," Claudia said. "I had thought, after such a long journey — but I understand and applaud your diligence." She signaled to Armstrong, who lingered just outside the doorway. "Bring Donal to us at once. You may find him at the stables."

"He spends a great deal of time with horses, my lady?" Miss Waterson asked. "I do not ride."

"It is not expected. My nephew has far better things to do with his time than tarry in the stables. As I informed you in my letter, his upbringing to this point was most unconventional, through no fault of Lady Eden, whose uncle in Ireland had the raising of him. He will need a firm hand and a strict schedule."

"I can assure you that he will have both."

Eden sighed, and Claudia cast her a warning glance. In truth, Eden could not object to any specific thing about the governess. As a rule, English governesses were often tyrants and as much hated as loved by their charges — or so she had heard from friends and relatives.

Her dislike of Miss Waterson came from her reluctance to give Donal into a stranger's care. It was irrational and unfair, this fierce maternal jealousy. Miss Waterson must at least be given a chance.

An awkward silence fell as they waited for Armstrong and Donal. But when the footman returned, he came alone.

"Where is Master Donal?" Claudia asked.

"Begging your pardon, your ladyship, but he wouldn't come."

Claudia exchanged glances with Miss Waterson. "You see how much he requires discipline. Is he still at the stables, Armstrong?"

"Yes, your ladyship."

"Then we shall fetch him ourselves."

"I will," Eden offered, hoping to steal a few moments alone with Donal. She rose and hastened for the stables.

Donal was there, with Hartley. They were not doing

anything in particular; in fact, they seemed to be waiting. Hartley watched her come with the wary reserve he had shown since the first ride into Birkdale. She gave him a stiff nod.

"Donal," she said, "Armstrong came to fetch you because you are wanted in the house." She held out her hand. "Come."

Donal folded his hands behind his back and shook his head.

Eden glanced at Hartley, feeling the heat of a flush creep up her neck. "You may return to the stables later, but now there is someone I want you to meet."

"A governess."

Hartley's voice had the same effect on her it always did, though at the moment it was heavy with what she could only assume was disapproval. He must have questioned Armstrong, although why he should take a personal interest in Donal's governess perplexed her. Men of his station did not have governesses and so could not very well develop a dislike of them.

She shook off the conflicting sensations of annoyance and attraction and wrapped herself in her dignity. "Donal, a lady has come all the way from London just for you. She'll teach you many interesting things." The words caught, as if on a lie. "You must come in now."

"I don't want her," Donal said firmly. "I want you and Hartley."

The flush had reached Eden's cheeks. "Hartley may be your friend, but he cannot take care of you."

"You can," Hartley said.

"I'll thank you not to judge what is best for my family, Mr. Shaw," she said. *And this has gone quite far enough.* "Donal, you must do as I ask." She grasped his hand and firmly pulled him toward the house.

His compact body was full of resistance, but he came. He looked back at Hartley in appeal. The man had enough good sense not to follow.

Donal's steps dragged more and more as they approached the sitting room. He came to a full stop in the doorway, his lower lip thrust out.

"I won't like her," he said.

"Oh, Donal." She knelt beside him. "How can you know that, when you haven't even met her yet?"

He looked into her eyes. "I *know.*"

"Did Hartley say something about her, Donal?"

"Ah, there you are." Claudia joined them, and Donal wedged himself behind Eden's skirts. "Come, child," she said with a kind smile. "There is no reason to be afraid."

Eden wanted nothing more than to turn around and take Donal in the opposite direction. Instead, she put her arm around his shoulder and guided him into the room. Miss Waterson stood up.

"And here is Master Donal," Claudia announced.

Donal froze. "No," he said clearly.

Claudia sighed. "Eden, my dear, I think it would be best if you retired. I fear that Donal will only be more upset if you remain."

Eden could see that her presence complicated an already difficult situation, and that her newly awakened maternal impulses were a definite disadvantage. "Donal," she said gently, "I must step out for a little while. I know that you will make Miss Waterson feel welcome."

He stared at her, wide-eyed, until Claudia imposed herself between them. Eden walked out of the room and the house, telling herself that this was for the best. Donal needed to learn to trust adults other than Hartley and his mother. But oh, why did this parting hurt them both so much?

A few steps beyond the garden doors she ran into something solid and warm. The shock of his touch told her who it was even before she looked up into Hartley Shaw's face.

Chapter 7

N *ow that he held her, he didn't want to let her go.*

Hartley's instinct had been to follow his son, regardless of the consequences. He knew he couldn't rush into the house and steal the boy from the woman they'd summoned to imprison him. But there were other ways of dealing with such an intruder. He'd learned enough of modern man to understand the role a governess would play in Donal's life, and he did not intend to let the woman transform him into a well-trained lapdog.

But as he felt the softness of Eden's arms through the muslin of her sleeves, heard the pulse beat so quickly in her graceful neck, his compulsion struck a new course. He saw sadness and confusion in her eyes, and his anger evaporated.

He had never felt so strong an urge to kiss her. Give up the game, claim her in such a way that she would recognize him, surrender, and beg his forgiveness.

"Eden," he said roughly.

She stiffened with affront. "How dare you."

He released her as if she had turned to Iron. Her indignation demanded an apology, but he could match her in outrage. "You gave the boy to another woman," he said.

Her eyes blazed with anger. "You astound me, Shaw. What do you know of governesses, or of the kind of life Donal was meant to lead?"

"I know more than you guess," he said. "I know that your kind give your own children away to be brought up by strangers. And you are deceiving yourself by agreeing to such an arrangement."

She laughed. "Your impertinence has no limits. This is what comes of letting Donal befriend a servant." She backed away. "Well, that has come to an end."

He answered her with a humorless smile of his own. "You will discharge me?"

"You have done your work well enough, and I still owe you a debt. But Donal will be too occupied from now on to follow you about like a . . . like a lost puppy."

"Not quite a puppy. But he has been lost, hasn't he?"

"What . . . what do you mean?"

"Isn't it true that the boy was raised in Ireland, and he came to be with you only a fortnight ago?"

"It is true, and common knowledge," she said. "My uncle sent him —"

"Did he? Are you ashamed of Donal, Eden? Is that why you tell everyone that he is not your son?"

She went stock-still. "What did you say?"

"You are his mother, Lady Eden Winstowe. Do not deny it. He is your son, but he never lived with you in London."

With careful steps she moved back until she reached the garden wall. "How did you . . . find out?" she whispered. "Who told you this?"

"Never fear. It is not general knowledge, and clearly you wish to keep it that way. Why?"

"I cannot explain. Not here."

"Why did you send him to Ireland?"

Her voice shook. "My son's past, and mine, are none of your affair."

Hartley pursued her, positioning himself so that his body formed a second wall to prevent her escape. "It's that simple, is it? You allowed your son to be raised by others, deny he is yours, and now you give him to someone else? Is that what you call love?"

The last thing he expected from her was tears. Indeed, she fought them, but they pooled in her eyes as if she had been holding them back all along.

"You do not know . . ." She averted her face so that all he could see was her profile.

He touched her chin with his fingers, turning her back to him. *"Tell me."*

She seemed beyond further outrage, exhausted by his persistence and her own interior struggle. "You have no claim on my son."

He wanted to shout, *"I am his father!"* He wanted to cry out, *"You are mine."* He did neither.

"I have the claim of affection," he said, showing mercy. "His for me, and mine for him." He let her go. "Why did you send him away?"

She leaned her weight against the wall. "I did not send him away. I did not even know where he was."

Hartley felt a weight being lifted from his shoulders even as a greater heaviness settled in his heart. "How can that be?"

A tear spilled over and trickled inelegantly down the side of her nose. "He was taken from me at birth."

By your father? Did he steal the child from you, as he did from me? Hartley braced his hand on the wall and lowered his head. Eden's face was so close that all he need do was bend another inch to brush her neck with his lips. It would be so easy to comfort her.

For now he understood the veil of sorrow that he had sensed upon their first meeting at the stables. She was not telling the whole truth, but of one part he was certain: She had not willingly given up their son.

The barrier between them had fallen, the one that he had worked to destroy since that encounter. This trust was what he'd hoped to gain. But it gave him no pleasure to see her weeping, to know that she had suffered in a way he hadn't expected.

He had stayed away from her this fortnight because he had felt his own defenses crumbling — the defenses that should not have been necessary against her. Her emotions were spilling over into his own thoughts, his own heart. But a mere two weeks had not purged her influence over him. He wondered if a hundred years would be sufficient.

He could not afford human weakness now. "Who would take a child from his own mother?" he demanded.

She brushed at her face with a show of spirit. "Does it matter? He is with me. He is safe."

"Was he in danger?" He placed his other hand on the wall, caging her in. "Would someone have harmed him?"

"No. But now he can live the life he was meant to have. I will be certain that he never lacks for anything in this world."

"Except for one thing. Why will you not acknowledge him as your son?"

"I have good reason. You may believe that or not as you choose — but . . ." The last of her pride deserted her. "Will you tell me how you learned of this? It is important. . . ."

"Because the truth will shame you? Who was his father? Was it not your husband, Lady Eden?"

Her head jerked up, bringing her mouth a hair's breadth from his. "His father is dead."

"Was it your husband who sent Donal away, because the boy was not his son?"

She avoided his gaze. "If you care for Donal . . . if you care for him at all, you will not speak of this to anyone." Her eyes met his. "You must realize that he will have much more opportunity in life if he is considered legitimate. Please." She reached up as if to touch his face.

He pulled away. If he knew anything of mortal society, Donal's existence would have been hidden from Winstowe as it had been from him. Had it been hidden from Eden as well? Had she believed her own son dead?

How could she forgive the man responsible — the very man who had broken his most solemn vow to the Forest Lord?

"Do not trouble yourself, my lady," he said at last. "I will not reveal your precious secret."

Her shoulders sagged. "Thank you." Once more her fingers brushed his cheek. He expelled his breath and inhaled sharply, taking in her warm, almost floral scent.

"I think I understand why you feel as you do," she said. "You lost your own child. You cannot bear to see it happen again."

He hardened his heart against her tenderness. "There is a condition on my silence; you must dismiss this governess."

She dropped her hand. "She is here for Donal's good. There are so many things I am not qualified to teach him. He barely knows me, and I am not . . . accustomed to children." She swallowed. "I love him too much to provide the discipline a boy requires. I would do him a disservice to smother and overprotect him now."

Hartley knew that he should encourage her separation from Donal. He had been angry with her for casting their son to strangers, yet it would be far more merciful to both her and the child if any attachment between them was weakened.

But she loved Donal. She had not sent him away or been part of the lie of his death. She had rejected Hartley — his real self — with horror, but that did not stop her from loving their child. He could recognize love, even though he could not feel it.

He *could* feel desire. Eden was nearly in his arms. One small motion was all it would take.

She interpreted his silence as more disapproval. "Donal has already lived with many disadvantages," she said earnestly. "He must be brought up like every other child of his class. I do not want him to be different."

Sympathy evaporated like dew on an August morning.

The tender twigs of the rosebush nearest him shriveled at their tips.

"Different?" he said. "What is this difference you fear in him, Eden?"

Real fear woke in her eyes. "Nothing. And I wish to keep it that way."

"You would cage him," he said. "You would make him like the man who took him from you."

"Never." She placed both palms on his chest as if she had the physical strength to push him back. "Never."

He struggled to ignore the mortal magic of her touch. "We made a wager before, Lady Eden. I'll make you a second. Your governess will not remain above a week, and you shall be the one to wish her gone. She and all of her breed."

"I will not," she said. "I will not wager with you again."

"Because you know you'll lose."

She closed her eyes to block the sight of him. "Please. Let me go."

A command he could have refused, but not this quiet request. He might have appeared a monster to her six years ago, but he wouldn't behave like one.

He drew back, giving her the freedom to leave. But she remained where she was. At last she opened her eyes and looked at him, not with anger or fear, but bewilderment.

"I believe that you care for my son," she said. "I believe I can trust you to protect him. For that, I can forgive you . . . anything."

"I may require your forgiveness," he said grimly. He turned on his heel to go, pausing to touch the withered branches of the rosebush. Healing life swelled up from the earth to repair what had been damaged by his anger.

He did not wait to see if Eden witnessed his magic.

From her room in the family wing overlooking the garden, Claudia watched the manservant walk away from

Eden and knew she had suffered a serious lapse in judgment.

Hartley Shaw. When Eden had spoken of him, she had not revealed any dangerous partiality toward him — at least not of the sort that would ordinarily worry Claudia. Why should she be concerned, when he was merely a servant and Eden had been among the *ton*'s most sought-after women?

But Claudia had been observing the man, and what she saw had increasingly disturbed her.

This had been a month of such disturbances. The much-delayed answer to her correspondence to Ireland had finally been forwarded from London. It had been written by a stranger, informing her of the deaths of Donal's original foster parents — those she had chosen so carefully — and the boy's passing to first one family and then another.

Donal's arrival at Hartsmere had been a definite shock. But she understood now why he had appeared in so poor a state . . . why he had been sent back in the first place. The last family to take him in had not wanted him, and had no incentive, in the form of regular payment by Lady Claudia Raines, to keep him.

Claudia was rarely forced to endure the scourge of guilt. But she had felt it when the letter came, and she cursed herself as well as the Irish oafs who had made the boy endure such discomfort.

There was no crying over spilled milk. The boy would never belong in Eden's world, whatever lies she told, however determined she might be to make him fit in. Even to Claudia it was apparent that compelling him to adapt would be unfair to the child as well as to his mother.

It was true that Donal was not what she'd expected. He was neither so wild nor so intractable as she'd led Eden to believe. But he was a threat to Eden's future. Claudia had resolved to make certain, this time, that the boy went to a much better — and more distant — home. Weaning him away from Eden, with Miss Waterson's help, was a first step.

I failed you before, my dear. I did not keep you safe. I agreed to your marriage to Spencer. My carelessness created this situation and now I must be the one to correct it.

As she must correct the matter of Hartley Shaw.

Claudia shook her head, though there was no one to witness the gesture. For all Eden's reputation of taking numerous lovers, they had always been men of her rank. She would not stoop beneath her for companionship. It was not in her nature.

Except that her nature had changed. Claudia had watched it happen ever since their arrival at Hartsmere. At first she had assumed it to be the lingering aftereffects of Winstowe's death, and the ongoing strain of Eden's self-imposed duties. But gradually Claudia had come to see that the alterations in Eden were of a more disquieting complexion.

The devotion to amusement that had been Eden's hallmark in Society was no longer in evidence. And how could it be, in this dismal place? Claudia had dismissed Eden's initial prattle on the responsibilities of landownership as a mere whim, a passing fancy to keep her mind occupied until she regained her usual spirit. But such had not been the case. As if she'd forsaken all hope of returning to her former life, Eden had ignored the limitations of her income and strength. She had worn herself to a shadow, and the worst was yet to come.

Donal's arrival was in large part responsible for awakening this driven aspect of her personality. So was her complete isolation from the *ton*. As things were proceeding, Eden might come to feel a genuine part of Hartsmere. She might — unbelievable as it seemed — wish to remain.

And that brought her back to Hartley Shaw. Could he have influenced these developments? A servant, a laborer, a peasant? Claudia's sensibilities hummed with alarm at the memory of Eden being touched by Hartley Shaw. Caressed by him. Held in his arms.

Claudia paced away from the window, deep in uneasy thought. Though she hadn't heard the words of their conversation, she recognized elemental attraction when she saw it. How or when this had first happened she didn't know, but the relationship was well established.

Oh, Eden made a pretense of holding Shaw at bay. *He made little pretense of respecting her rank or her person. And he is handsome, in a rough sort of way. He could almost pass for well-bred. Is that what makes her vulnerable to him?*

That, and loneliness. Eden had seldom been without male companionship. Men had flocked to her side in London. She could not be expected to survive without such accustomed tribute.

Giving Eden her own way at Hartsmere had been a mistake. But Claudia must be subtle in handling Shaw. She well knew how to bribe — or blackmail — one of his fellow servants into becoming her personal informant.

In all likelihood, Shaw was simply a cunning, clever young man who knew how to manipulate women — as he had done in "saving" Donal — and was arrogant enough to believe that even Hartsmere's mistress was fair game. Claudia had met such servants before. Some could be remarkably intelligent, even extraordinary in their ambitions. But inevitably they found themselves discharged without a character. If he were a scheming servant of the ordinary variety, she could simply offer him a good reason for leaving Hartsmere willingly.

If Shaw proved to be more than he seemed, there were more drastic solutions. Now that Donal was firmly ensconced in Miss Waterson's care, Eden would have less reason to meet Shaw. Claudia would inquire more diligently about additional stable servants and gardeners to assume his work. And she would stay close to Eden, even if it meant accompanying her on visits to the farms and village.

And, of course, Eden must be reminded of her rank — and what she risked by dallying with a servant.

Claudia sat down at her escritoire, one of the few fine

pieces she had brought from her London apartments. She dipped her pen and considered her words with care.

If the matter had not been urgent, she would have hesitated to write so hastily and frankly, and at a time when neither Eden nor her surroundings would be seen in their most favorable light — if Hartsmere could ever be seen as anything but a disreputable ruin.

But the marquess was not a man to judge the woman he loved by such trivial standards. Claudia was certain that he would come with all due haste once he knew of Eden's isolation.

As for Donal, Claudia would make sure that he was nowhere in evidence when the marquess arrived. Miss Waterson already showed admirable talent for her work.

Claudia sealed the missive with satisfaction and took pains to hide it in a safe place until she could post it. That task accomplished, Claudia went downstairs. Eden stood by the window in the sitting room, distress clear on her face.

"My dear, you look troubled," Claudia said. "May I help?"

Eden turned to her with a strained smile. "Oh, I have just been woolgathering, Aunt."

"An apt occupation in these climes," Claudia said dryly. "But take care not to let the rustic odors cling to your person."

Eden started. *Careful,* Claudia warned herself. She must not let on that she'd seen anything of Eden's conversation with Shaw.

"Donal — is he with Miss Waterson?" Eden asked wistfully.

"They are getting better acquainted in the nursery. I'm sure you agree that it is best for Donal to eat his meals there, so that he can become accustomed to his new schedule." She took Eden's arm. "Come. We've had little time to talk, with you so determined to save the local population. I realize that I have neglected my part in the running of this household. I wish to become involved in your projects and make this more of a home for both of us." *Until such time as circumstances free you of your current madness.* "Please, do tell me about your village, and the farmers. Let me know how I can help."

This time Eden's smile was genuine. "I am so glad to hear you ask. I had thought you did not approve."

"It doesn't matter, dear Niece, if it is what you wish to do. I have been harsher than I should have, I daresay. Please forgive me."

"Of course. But there is so very much to improve. . . ."

Lost in her new passion, Eden prattled on about roof repairs and her plans for the tenants' dinner on May Eve. Claudia shuddered to think of it, but she hid her true feelings readily enough and agreed to help Eden with the arrangements.

It might even be possible to use the gathering as a means to emphasize the vast gulf that lay between Eden and the people she wanted to help. A few discouragements, and Eden would be more than willing to abandon this notion of becoming a female country squire.

Or of keeping her plowboy lover.

E*den had not forgotten her quarrel with Hartley, or all* that he knew about her. It lay in the back of her mind all the while she spoke with her aunt, just as the memory of his touch haunted her.

How did he know? Mrs. Byrne would not have talked, and certainly not my aunt. Who?

It was all she could do to behave as if nothing had happened, as if she had nothing to conceal from Claudia. And when her thoughts were not on Hartley, they were with Donal, "caged" in his gloomy nursery with the prim Miss Waterson.

The only happy circumstance of the afternoon lay in Claudia's decision to begin helping her with the charity work and the tenants' fair. It marked a return to the comfortable rapport that had marked their relationship before Spencer's death.

She and Claudia were still in accord when they sat down to dinner, though the table seemed terribly bare without her son. Eden was prepared to summon Donal from the nursery, governess or no governess.

"Your governess will not remain above a week, and you shall be the one to wish her gone." Hartley Shaw was so sure she would surrender to her maternal desires. But the traditions of English society had been created for a reason. Who was Eden to upset such time-honored methods?

So she told herself, again and again, while the meal dissolved to ashes in her mouth.

When the dinner had been cleared away and she and Claudia had retired to the sitting room, Mrs. Byrne and the maids began to bustle about the house on some new, mysterious task. Too distracted to concentrate on her needlework, Eden watched curiously as they carried armfuls of candles of all shapes and sizes. Glancing at Claudia, she slipped from the room and followed the housekeeper.

"Mrs. Byrne," she said, catching up in the drawing room, "tell me — do you expect this particular night to be so much darker than every one that has come before, or are you scheming to burn my house down?" She smiled conspiratorially. "I own that I often think it would be no great loss."

Setting down her current armload on a sofa table, Mrs. Byrne rubbed the small of her back and smiled. "Burn down this great pile? Now, then, I'm not sure it's possible." She selected a candle and held it up to the dim light that spilled from the chandelier. "Wouldn't you be knowing that it's St. Brigit's Eve?"

"Another saint?" Eden asked, touching a blackened candlewick. "Wasn't it St. Agnes's Eve just a fortnight ago?" She concealed a shiver, recalling the dreams that had come to her that night.

"Aye, so it was. But tomorrow is the second of February, which is the day of the blessing of candles. Candle-mas."

"But we are not Catholic."

"The traditions go back much farther than the coming of the priests," Mrs. Byrne said as she began setting out a row of candles along the windowsill. "In ancient days, Brigit was a goddess of Ireland, who presided over the hearth, healing, fertility, and marriage, especially women about to marry. Here in England she was known as Briganta. When she became a saint, there was a women's shrine kept to her in County Kildare — my own home."

"And what will you do with all these candles?"

" 'Tis the tradition to put candles in every window of a dwelling at sundown and burn them until dawn."

"That is hardly frugal."

Mrs. Byrne paused in her work. "Shall I put them away, your ladyship?"

"No. I shall not stand in the way of your charming customs." She helped Mrs. Byrne arrange the candles and cocked her head to study the results. "There is little else to celebrate at this time of year."

"Yet Candlemas also marks a cross-quarter day — halfway between the winter and spring solstice. 'Tis the symbol of spring's promise and of new life."

Eden laughed. "Why, Mrs. Byrne, have you a bit of the pagan in you? Perhaps you are an Irish witch of some sort, or the descendent of an ancient priestess?"

"If I were a woman of such power, would I work as a housekeeper?" She tapped the side of her nose with a mischievous look. "Should I not have a wart about here?"

"I would not wish such a blemish upon you, Mrs. Byrne, for any amount of magical power."

Feeling more at ease with the housekeeper than she did with her aunt, Eden helped Mrs. Byrne place candles in every windowsill, even her bedchamber.

Claudia's room she left alone. Claudia, in fact, was nowhere to be found when Eden returned to the sitting room. Grasping the opportunity, Eden hurried upstairs to the nursery.

Miss Waterson sat at the opposite end of the room from Donal, arms folded and mouth pinched. Donal stared back just as stubbornly, and Eden sensed that the impasse had been going on for quite some time. A tray of food, resting on a rickety table, was untouched.

She stepped into the cramped room and smoothly interposed herself between the combatants.

"Miss Waterson, if Donal has finished his dinner, I would like to talk with him before he retires to bed," she said. "You may spend a little time putting your things in order, and retire early if you wish. You must be very tired."

"My lady . . ." Miss Waterson looked ready to ring a peal — over her head or Donal's, Eden didn't know which — but the governess got herself under control. "Very well, my lady. But it would be best if he does not spend too long downstairs."

"I understand." Eden ushered her son from the room. Donal took her hand and practically carried her down the stairs. She almost asked him what he thought of his new governess, but she knew that would be a mistake. He needed more time to become accustomed to the woman. As she must.

Donal came to a sudden stop at the bottom of the stairs. "What are all the lights for, Mother?"

Eden led him to the window. "You didn't celebrate Candlemas when you lived in Ireland?"

He shook his head, and his lower jaw jutted. Perhaps it was just as well if his past — and hers — simply ceased to exist.

"Come," she said in a sly whisper. "Let's see if we can find something sweet in the kitchen. I'll wager that I can reach it before you!"

With a yelp of joy, Donal dashed pell-mell for the hall. She followed at a more leisurely pace, giving Donal plenty of time to arrive before she did.

The kitchen was redolent of the evening's dinner and

something warm and spicy. The dishes and pots had already been washed and put away. A plate of fresh buns waited on the broad oak table.

"Cook has gone to bed," Eden whispered. "Do we dare?" She reached for a bun, letting her hand hover over the nearest pastry.

Donal grinned with a waggish expression she'd never seen on his face before. As one, they dove on the buns and took warm, sticky bites.

This was how life was supposed to be. This simplicity, this contentment, this happiness.

Miss Waterson and Hartley Shaw could go to the devil.

*C*andlelight filled nearly every window of Hartsmere, upstairs and down.

Drawn to the light, Hartley gazed up at the gray stone walls. This eve had long been celebrated by men as a time of transition. He felt that transition in his very bones: the rebirth of a new season tied, as if by twisting, succulent vines, to his very heart.

The candles hadn't been lit at Hartsmere for centuries. Eden was not responsible; she had no knowledge of such traditions. But something in the warm yellow squares and rectangles, defiant against the darkness, reminded him of her. They gave the house a sense of peace it did not often have.

The horses, and even the returning beasts of field and forest, seemed very poor company tonight. He needed to know how Donal fared. That was excuse enough to make another sally into Eden's fortress.

He started toward the house but paused after a few steps, sensing a hostile presence.

"Mr. Shaw."

Lady Claudia Raines moved with remarkable skill for a mortal woman. Hartley turned to face her, somehow unsurprised to find her seeking him under cover of darkness. He had known her once before.

She stopped, wrapped in her innate air of superiority

over all lesser beings. She was a handsome woman, in her bearing as regal as the most High Fane. Hartley was not impressed.

Six years ago, she had controlled her niece in every way but one, and therefore she had despised the man she knew as Cornelius Fleming. He had sensed then, on several occasions, that she worked to undermine his courtship of Eden.

He had never understood why. He hadn't cared. Lady Claudia had not been worthy of his attention.

He gave it to her now only because of the role he played. Like Eden, she failed to recognize him. Her reasons for approaching Hartley Shaw were not difficult to guess.

"Your ladyship," he said with a slight nod. "How can I be of service?"

She put out her hand. In her palm lay a pouch. She spilled a few coins into her glove, and they shone silver in the moonlight.

"You will leave Hartsmere immediately," she said.

She was used to giving commands, but so was he. The hair along the back of his neck bristled. His foot dug a furrow into the earth of its own volition, as if he were a stag facing a rival during the season of rut. His brow felt weighted with the many-tined antlers of his heritage.

Instinct. Instinct warned him she was his enemy in a way she had not been six years before.

"Why?" he demanded.

He'd expected to shock her with his insolence. She merely smiled.

"I knew you must be beyond bold to trifle so with Lady Eden," she said, closing her hand over the coins. "If you mean to gain wealth or influence by taking advantage of her, you are sadly mistaken. I shall not permit it."

So this woman had either seen him with Eden or suspected their relationship. He was certain that Eden hadn't spoken of their conversations. Even without recognizing him, Lady Claudia Raines was still intent on keeping Eden from an unsuitable partner. Had she set her seal of approval on the man her niece had married?

He laughed. "Trifle with her? I assure you, I do not trifle, madame."

"No. You play a very dangerous game. I have had experience with men such as you. Generally, they may be bought, and I am willing to pay well for your cooperation. However, the alternative would not be pleasant." Her eyes glittered with contempt. "You will never again find work on any estate in England."

"Very generous, your ladyship," he said. His fingers itched to summon every tiny creeping, biting, stinging thing and set it upon her.

"Then you will do as I ask." She offered the pouch again. "Be gone by morning."

He took the pouch and dropped it to the damp ground at his feet. "I will stay."

She didn't even look down. With a twitch of her skirts, she turned to go. "Very well. You have been warned."

And so have you. "You've forgotten something, your ladyship." He picked up the pouch, overturned it, and sent a cascade of coins spilling like stars onto the dark span of earth.

She didn't answer. She left the coins where they lay, as if they meant nothing.

The ache in Hartley's brow was unbearable. He let the antlers burst forth, a welcome burden that reminded him who he was and of his power. He pawed deep grooves in the ground. His lungs worked like bellows.

But there was no one here to challenge.

You mistake me, madame. You think me a mortal and your inferior, but I was once a god. You cannot withstand a god.

And neither could Eden.

He was weary of mortals and their baseless arrogance. It would please him to show Lady Claudia how easily he disposed of her threats.

The moon rose and began to sink again. Night creatures moved cautiously about him, unwilling to disturb his deep and brooding thoughts. Candles guttered in Hartsmere's windows. A predawn breeze brought with it the promise of new growth from garden and woods.

"Look!"

Hartley came to himself at the sound of a feminine voice. Eden stood at the servant's door — Eden and Mrs. Byrne, together as if they were bosom friends.

"We have talked all night." Eden said. "It is nearly morning!" She laughed. The sound floated across the park to wreath Hartley's antlers in ribbons of music.

"Miss Waterson is furious with me. You should have seen her face when I delivered Donal to the nursery." Eden shook her head, tossing golden hair that had come undone sometime during the evening, though she still wore her dinner gown. "But we were having such fun that I forgot the time. If you hadn't found us, I fear we'd still be playing at jackstraws."

"Children must be indulged," Mrs. Byrne said. "They grow up soon enough."

"Yes. I had almost forgotten —" Eden hugged herself, turning her face to the sky. "I think it will rain again. A pity that Candlemas will be more like winter than spring!"

"Not at all, my lady. 'If Candlemas Day be sunny and bright, winter again will show its might. If Candlemas Day be cloudy and gray, winter soon will pass away.'"

"Then I shall not repine." Eden flung her arms wide. "Winter, begone!"

Invisible to her mortal sight, Hartley closed his eyes. The girl he had known was here again, fresh and bright as springtime.

That was illusion. The seasons could not be turned back, not even by his kind. Eden's spring would never come again.

But there might be a way to stave off winter. Perhaps he could leave her with a new life to nurture when Donal was gone, a second blooming to take the sorrow from her loss. His desire might serve some purpose after all.

And perhaps her curses upon him would be that much lighter.

Chapter 8

Mrs. Byrne's folk rhyme about Candlemas Day proved most pleasantly accurate.

Spring had come upon the dale in all its glory, hard on the heels of winter. The good weather that heralded March had continued without ceasing ever since. All the birds and beasts absent upon Eden's arrival at Hartsmere had returned to delight Donal and fill the air with song. Snow had melted, rains fell in modest amounts, seeds and leaves and flowers grew with remarkable swiftness.

Eden had heard rumors that this freakishly fine weather and unusual advancement of spring had not extended to neighboring dales. Until recently, snow had capped the highest fell that lay between Hartsmere and the next valley to the west. One would never know that it had snowed here at all.

On this last day of April, the afternoon of the tenants' feast, Eden celebrated by replacing the unrelieved black of mourning with a gown of ebony-trimmed lavender.

This tenants' fair was her most ambitious attempt to bridge the chasm between her and the people of Hartsmere. Mrs. Byrne had informed her that May Eve was a traditional day for merrymaking, a celebration of new life and fertility and the plenty to come. Beltane, she called it. Such a day, under the trees on the newly green lawn of the park at Hartsmere, seemed the perfect setting for the establishment of goodwill.

She had begun to make significant improvements for her village tenants and farmers: repairing byres and houses and bridges, visiting and supplying the poorest families with necessities such as food and clothing and medical treatment, and hiring a new steward, Mr. Rumbold, to monitor the various activities.

But though the conditions since February had been everything the farmers could desire — with lambs coming thick and fast and healthy on the fells and in the pastures, and the hay growing tall and sweet — her dalesmen could not forget the years of hardship they had endured. Nor could they trust those they held responsible for it: the Flemings, who had brought down the wrath of a Faerie lord. And the only Fleming available to blame was Eden.

Mrs. Singleton was an exception; Eden had called upon her shortly after the birth of her new son and had been made most welcome. But the rest — poor laborers, shepherds, and tenants alike — greeted Eden with a wary, almost frightened resentment, barely hidden behind their cap-tugging and curtsies. Eden hoped that today's festivities would finally win their trust.

She had presented white May Day frocks to the girls in the dale and sent her invitations via Mrs. Appleyard and Mr. Rumbold. She promised prizes and games and a generous feast.

She surveyed the food heaped upon the recently built, flower-bedecked trestle tables, and prayed. It had required considerable expense and trouble to assemble the victuals and decorations. She'd purchased fresh mutton from her own farmers, but she'd had to send to Ambleside for most of what she served.

If only the tenants and villagers will accept this as what it is meant to be: an apology. A promise of better days to come. A pledge that winter is gone for good.

So far, only Mr. Appleyard had arrived, with assurances that he'd visited all the families in the dale to remind them of the date and time.

"Please do not worry, my lady," he said, bowing once or twice. "It is early yet. At this time of year, with lambing season just ending and fields to tend, the farmers have much to do." He rubbed his hands. "Such a change from last year! But I assure you, Lady Eden, that none of the dalesmen would refuse the honor of attending you at Hartsmere."

Eden peered down the drive toward the gate and wished she shared his blithe optimism.

She looked about for her handful of allies. Claudia had declined to come down, mentioning a headache. Mrs. Byrne, in the kitchen, helped Cook prepare beef and mutton, while Armstrong and the maids stocked each row of tables with forks and tankards, bread, cheese, and pitchers of ale. After helping Grubb and Hindle arrange tables and chairs, Hartley Shaw and Mr. Rumbold busied themselves with other errands.

Eden felt Hartley's absence keenly. Donal, his days fully occupied by Miss Waterson, spent very little time with Hartley. As a result, Eden had few excuses to meet Hartley except when she rode Juno or took out the dog cart.

She ought to be grateful that she didn't have to make an effort to avoid Hartley after their last, most disturbing encounter in the garden. And that Hartley had kept his promise not to reveal what he had learned about Donal.

But she felt no gratitude. She found herself thinking of him constantly: where he was, what he was doing, if he missed Donal as much as she did. She was also guilty of keeping Donal away from his hero, for she hoarded every moment she was allowed to spend with her son.

Allowed, as if she were a beggarwoman. But the governess was still here, and Donal did not seem to be suffering. In spite of Eden's reluctance and Hartley's grim predictions, the woman was not breaking Donal's spirit. Eden thought it might be the reverse.

At Claudia's suggestion, Donal would not attend the party except for an hour or so in the evening. Claudia had made an excellent point that he wasn't yet ready to play the role of earl's grandnephew in public. He'd be more apt to behave like one of the farmers' children.

But oh, Eden wanted him here. As she wished, unaccountably, for Hartley.

She glanced up at the angle of the sun. Surely it was past four, the hour when she had expected the earliest arrivals. Even Mr. Appleyard's smile was a bit strained.

"If you wish, my lady, I will go into the dale . . ." He trailed off, pulling at his collar.

Eden flushed. "That is not necessary. I —"

She broke off as a carriage rolled up the drive. She recognized it as her own dog cart, Hartley Shaw at the ribbons. Passengers crowded the seats.

"I do believe it is Mrs. Singleton and her younger children," Mr. Appleyard said. He hurried off to greet the cart as it approached, helping Mrs. Singleton descend with her new baby. Hartley hopped down and swung the children about as he set them on the lawn. He gave Eden a brief salute when he saw her watching. That was enough to drive all the worry from her heart.

Mrs. Singleton and the children were far better dressed and healthier than they had been three months ago. Eden noted with approval that the hollowness was gone from under the woman's eyes. The little girl was dressed in her pretty white frock, and her red locks were laced with wildflowers. The boy's hair was neatly combed. The baby cooed contentedly.

"You are all most welcome," Eden said.

Mrs. Singleton smiled. "We thank you for the invitation, your ladyship, and for all your kindnesses."

"Mr. Appleyard tells me that you have heard from your husband."

"It was due to your generous support that I was able to locate him," Mr. Appleyard said. "He will return to the dale within the fortnight."

And I hope he will be a better husband and father from now on, Eden thought. It seemed to her that Mr. Singleton deserved a good thrashing for abandoning his wife and children, no matter the circumstances.

The children began to fidget, staring wide-eyed at the vast quantities of food on the tables. Eden laughed. "I believe the children are hungry. Let them have whatever they like. As you can see, we are not lacking."

Mrs. Singleton curtsied. "Thank you, my lady." She herded the children toward the tables with the affectionate skill of an efficient sheepdog. Mr. Appleyard trailed after them like an earnest but ineffectual shepherd.

Eden's eyes grew moist. Mrs. Singleton was a wise, courageous mother to her children, and she had no need of governesses. There were many things Eden could learn, even from so humble a woman.

"I thought that Mrs. Singleton and her children would enjoy a ride," Hartley said at her elbow.

It was as if he was back where he belonged, at her side. She smiled behind a concealing hand. "I should have thought of that myself," she said. "It is a rather long walk, is it not?"

"Country folk are used to walking."

"If one has food enough, and warm clothing," she said, watching the Singleton children laugh, their mouths stuffed with pastries and fruit.

"Which you have provided." His voice was warm, so different than it had been in the garden.

"I had hoped to provide even more. Did you pass anyone else on the way?"

"I regret that I did not."

From out of nowhere, a rather large cloud arrived to block the sun. Eden glanced at Hartley's face, and caught him in a frown capable of summoning thunder from a clear sky.

"For weeks you planned this entertainment," he said, "and this is their gratitude."

"Oh, I cannot blame them. Why should they trust me?"

Hartley snorted. He glared toward the park gate. "I shall go down and fetch them."

"Everyone in the dale?" She laughed, though the sound was feeble. "Perhaps I simply asked too much, too soon."

"We shall see." He turned on his heel and strode for the cart. She hurried to catch up with him.

"Let it be, Hartley." She touched his arm, and felt all the muscles bunch up under his sleeve.

He was angry, she thought with surprise — angry on her behalf. His protectiveness was as gratifying as it was unfamiliar.

Spencer had never tried to protect or defend her from anything. Lord Bradwell had been, for the most part, an indulgent but negligent father. In the end, he had not protected her either.

"Please," she said. "Do not be concerned."

He wheeled about, and she thought he might seize her as he had in the garden. She almost anticipated it.

"Do you wish to come?" he asked.

Mrs. Singleton and Mr. Appleyard were engaged in conversation, while the children tumbled about the lawn. They would scarcely notice their hostess's absence. And if she did not go, she was half afraid that Hartley would be too severe upon the delinquent guests.

"Very well," she said.

He nodded and helped her up into the cart. "What of Donal?"

"He is with his governess."

She braced for an argument, but he merely frowned and took the driver's seat.

All the way down the drive, through the park and beyond, where the road hugged sloping fells, Eden saw no sign of the people she had invited. Only when they had advanced into the dale and were approaching the first farm did they meet a fellow traveler.

He was a dour and very elderly shepherd Eden had seen once or twice with a small flock of ewes and lambs. Was he taking them up the fell or bringing them back down? The old fellow scarcely looked as though he could still climb.

Hartley drew the cart to a halt. The sheep milled about, bleating, and the old shepherd leaned on his staff. He studied Eden with one good eye. The other was milky white. After a moment, he nodded a wary greeting.

"Yer ladyship."

"Good day, Mr.—"

"Kirkby."

A man of few words, as many dalesmen were apt to be in her presence. She smiled. "Did you receive your invitation to come to Hartsmere this afternoon, Mr. Kirkby?"

He blinked slowly. "Aye, yer ladyship."

"I would be glad if you would come with us now. We have much fine food and drink prepared."

"Cannot," he said. "T'sheep, yer ladyship."

Eden could not deny that he had a perfect excuse. "So I see. And does your flock . . . prosper, Mr. Kirkby?"

" 'Tis noo."

"I am glad to hear it." She wondered how to phrase the next question without making herself look foolish. "Perhaps you knew my father, Lord Bradwell, and his father."

"Aye."

He was not making this easy. "I realize that the times have been difficult in the past, but—"

"What her ladyship asks," Hartley said, "is why no one from the dale or village attends the party that she has taken such trouble to prepare for all of you."

Kirkby's gaze shifted to Hartley, and Eden thought that real interest sparked in his rheumy eye. "Thoo's an outcomer."

"Not precisely. Now, tell me. Why has she no guests?"

Eden waited for another monosyllabic answer. Kirkby seemed to be weighing Hartley as much as his question, and he reached a favorable conclusion.

"They're afeared," he said. "Yon grand house is t'heart o' t'curse."

Eden closed her eyes.

"Explain this curse," Hartley demanded.

" 'Tis but a legend," Kirkby said with a cautious air. "Once t'dale was blessed. T'sheep were healthy and plentiful, t'grass grew sweet. Nae man wanted for aught. They said t'last of the Auld Ones watched o'er us, granting good fortune. It has al'ays been thus, far back as memory."

"Go on," Hartley said grimly.

"They say Lord Bradwell angered t'Auld One when he entered the ancient forest, where no men go. They say he brought a curse down upon us."

"And what happened then, Kirkby?" Eden asked, prepared for the worst.

"T'land suffered. T'next year the winter was colder, t'lambs sickly. T'hay rotted, and scarce a 'tatie would grow. T'lord went away, but naught changed. T'blessing was gone."

"And this is why they will not come to Hartsmere."

"Aye, yer ladyship."

"It doesn't matter to you that your prosperity has returned?" Hartley asked. His expression was stormy. "The lady herself gives you food and clothing and sends men to repair your homes. She wishes to give you still more." He snorted. "Your gratitude is overwhelming."

Kirkby became very interested in a loose thread on his coat. "T'auld ways die hard," he muttered.

"It is all right, Hartley," Eden murmured.

"It is not." He hadn't touched the ribbons, but Copper tossed his head and rattled his harness.

"If you go about your business and show the lady proper respect," Hartley continued, "your crops and beasts will suffer no harm from any weather, good or ill. This dale will be the envy of all Albion. You will never know want again. But if you do not appreciate what you have been given —"

Thunder rumbled out of the clear sky. The sheep

bunched and bolted. Kirkby followed as quickly as his aged legs would permit.

Copper set off at a trot toward the farm.

Eden stared at Hartley, at a loss to understand his strange words. How could he guarantee the weather or the good fortune of Hartsmere's farmers?

"Perhaps it was unwise to make such promises," she said. "Please take us home. There is nothing to be gained by pursuing this further."

"So easily defeated, my lady?" he asked. "You allow a superstition to undo all your good work? Or is it your pride you're worried about?"

Her throat developed a lump. "My pride is my own concern. Please take us back."

The cart came to a stop. Hartley glared at her. "These people must be taught to respect their betters."

"And you, I suppose, are the one to set a suitable example?" She laughed. "If they are all as respectful as you, I had better accustom myself to a lifetime of disappointment."

"By Titania's wings —" He frowned up at the sky, and then abruptly turned the cart about, avoiding a pothole.

Eden tried to ignore her wounded feelings. "What these people need most is education. I have already discussed a school with Mr. Appleyard. There was one, once, but it is in disrepair."

"And the dalesmen will surely appreciate that, as well."

"Is it your intention to make me feel worse, Hartley Shaw?"

Copper lunged to one side, nearly upsetting the cart. Hartley steadied Eden with a firm hand and did not let go when the horse and cart settled again.

"No," he said in an altered tone. "It is not. But I —" His grip became almost like a caress. "I do not enjoy seeing you sad."

Eden shook her head. One moment she thought she knew this man, and the next he changed yet again. "It is but a temporary reversal," she said. "But thank you for your concern."

They looked at each other, and Eden was swept back to the garden where they had last shared such intimacy. But now they were no longer at odds. They were allies against a world in which both were outsiders. Eden sensed that a man like Hartley would be an outsider wherever he went, belonging nowhere.

That was true loneliness.

"Hartley," she said. "Why do you . . . care so much?"

She regretted the words instantly, when it was far too late to recall them. Her cheeks grew hot. She almost snatched the ribbons from Hartley's hands in hopes of moving again, anything to distract them both from what she had revealed.

"Eden," he said. Only that, but he filled the name with all the lovely melodies of spring: birdsong, the breeze sighing among new leaves, the rush of water from snow melting high on the fells.

And emotion — a whole world's worth.

What was happening? Eden had known scores of men, and yet none of them had so affected her since . . . since the man she had called Cornelius Fleming. Not one among her peers had made her heart hammer and her body thrum with need as Hartley Shaw could do with but a word.

"I do not think —" she began.

He stroked his hand up her arm.

"Hartley."

He pressed his finger to her lips. Without words, he seemed to be telling her that thinking, and speech, and every social impediment between them meant nothing. She looked into his eyes and knew he was about to kiss her. Here, in the middle of the road.

And she was not going to resist.

His fingertip traced a circle about her lips. He cupped her chin in his hand and lifted it gently. She closed her eyes.

Someone cried out from not very far away. Eden

opened her eyes with a start. She drew away from Hartley, searching for the source of the cry.

They had been seen. How was she to explain —

Her gaze fastened on a figure running at breakneck speed down the fellside. The figure resolved into a boy a few years older than Donal. Eden didn't know him. He wore a dalesman's clothing, and his eyes were wide with worry.

He drew up to the cart, panting hard. He tugged his cap to Eden, but his gaze settled on Hartley. "Beggin' your pardon, sir, can ye help me?"

Without so much as a glance at Eden, Hartley swung down from the cart. "What's the trouble, lad?"

" 'Tis our best ewe, sir. She fell between rocks, an' her leg's broke, an' her lamb is birthin'. Can ye come?

"I will." He finally looked at Eden. "If her ladyship can drive back to the house alone."

How was it that he could show such indifference to what had just occurred? Her own face still burned with consternation and thwarted desire. "You may go with the boy, Hartley," she said, "but I shall accompany you."

" 'Tis a hard climb, m'lady," the boy said, studying her with new interest.

In answer, Eden hopped down from the cart and shook out her gown. "What is your name?" she asked the boy.

"Jeb. Jeb Topping, m'lady."

"You needn't worry about me, Jeb." She raised a brow at Hartley. "I wish to see if Mr. Shaw is as good with sheep as he is with horses."

Man and boy exchanged glances and conceded defeat. Jeb started up the fell, while Hartley hung back to assist Eden.

"Don't wait for me," she said, hitching up her skirts. "I shall be with you presently."

He frowned. "If you should fall —"

Her emotions were in such disarray that she chose to ignore them entirely. "I am not likely to break. Go on."

Surely it wasn't her imagination that his eyes warmed

with approval. "Very well. Call if you need me." He set off after the boy, climbing with impressive speed and agility.

Call if you need me. Such simple words, and yet they made her knees quiver like blancmange. She steeled herself, took a deep breath, and followed Hartley's path up the fellside.

Very soon she realized just how impractical were the flimsy slippers she had chosen to match her gown. Dress and shoes would be ruined, and she was apt to have blisters to boot. Her legs, which had but recently become used to vigorous walking, began to cramp and shake. Setting her jaw, she persevered, slipping and sliding on rocks, mud, and grass.

At the top of the fell — just when she was certain that her legs had lost every bone they possessed — she heard the ewe's pitiful bleating. Hartley and the boy had gone to the other side, where a jumble of large rocks had formed a trap for the unwary animal.

All Eden could see was a mass of ivory wool and Hartley's back. Jeb watched anxiously, eager to help. She descended toward them and tumbled onto her rump. No one heeded her mortification. Abandoning all pretense to dignity, Eden slid the rest of the way until a sizable rock provided a landing place.

Hartley's voice, calm and soothing, comforted the ewe as if it were a frightened child. He lifted the sheep in his arms. One of its forelegs hung crooked, and its belly bulged with new life.

Hartley turned to lay the ewe on the slope. He seemed unaware of anything but the wounded animal. Lifting its head, he bent and breathed on the ewe's muzzle.

Jeb rubbed at his face with a dirty sleeve. "Thank you, sir. I know she willna make it, but the lamb will be saved."

"She'll be fine," Hartley murmured. He ran his hand over the distended curve of the animal's belly. The ewe shuddered.

"There are two lambs," Hartley said. "One is turned." He stroked the ewe again, from muzzle to tail.

What happened then was something Eden had never thought to witness. One moment the ewe was heaving and struggling, and the next she had delivered a tiny, wet miniature of herself. Jeb took the new lamb into his arms and began to clean off the delicate nose.

Another lamb followed swiftly. Hartley's concentration was still fixed on the ewe. Without thinking, Eden scooted down to the second newborn and gathered it into her arms. She mimicked Jeb's actions and cleaned the lamb with her skirts. It bleated daintily. She could feel the patter of its heartbeat through her bodice.

All at once Eden felt close, not only to the lamb but to the earth on which she sat and the grass and the wood and the two people who shared this strangely moving experience.

A shadow fell across her. Hartley stood with the ewe in his arms, Jeb at his side with the other lamb.

"You have ruined your gown," Hartley said.

"So I have." She scrambled awkwardly to her feet, hugging the lamb to her breast. "Should a gown matter more to me than a living creature?"

He smiled. It was greater praise than any words could have been. "You learn well, Eden Fleming."

Three months ago she would have taken offense. The way he addressed her, looked at her, could only put unfortunate ideas in young Jeb Topping's head. But Jeb murmured endearments to the lamb, unaware of the provocative undercurrents.

"The ewe must rest," Hartley said. "Have you shelter for her, Jeb?"

"Aye. Is she truly healed?"

"If you care for her well, she'll be walking in a week."

Jeb gazed up at Hartley with the same adoration Eden had so often seen in Donal. "Are you an animal doctor, sir?"

"Let us say that the animals and I understand one another." He met Eden's eyes, as if asking whether such understanding could ever exist between them. "I can carry the lamb as well as the ewe, your ladyship."

"No." She nuzzled the down-soft wool, not even minding the odors of recent birth. "I wish to keep it."

"Very well. Lead us to your home, Jeb."

The three of them descended the fell, Hartley remaining close to Eden as she picked her way down the steep slope. At the bottom, another boy, several years older than Jeb, was waiting for them.

The two boys were alike enough to be brothers, and soon proved their kinship with an excited exchange of questions and explanations about the prized ewe and the newborn lambs. The elder boy ran off down the road to the nearby farmhouse.

When Eden, Hartley, and Jeb arrived, they were greeted at the doorway by an older woman — Jeb's mother, Eden guessed — and two girls of indeterminate age, along with Jeb's elder brother. The three females stared at Eden in dismay.

Reminded of her soiled skirts, Eden set the lamb down and determined to muddle through this untimely meeting.

"Good day," she said. "These are, I believe, your sheep."

Mrs. Topping shuffled a sort of curtsy. "M'lady. My boy told me what you done, saving one of our best ewes and her lambs. We're grateful."

"I cannot take the credit," Eden said. "Mr. Shaw and Jeb did most of the work."

"An' Mr. Shaw healed Josephine!" Jeb put in.

One of the Topping girls tittered, and Mrs. Topping quieted her. "Your pardon, m'lady. Mr. Topping is up on the fells, or he'd thank you himself. Will you come in for a cup of tea?"

Eden got the distinct impression that Mrs. Topping wished her at the devil rather than in her modest home. She was quite certain that she smelled quite odious, and Mrs. Topping was unprepared for her landlady's visit, especially when she had ignored Eden's invitation to Hartsmere.

"Thank you," Eden said, "but I am not dressed for calling, and my own guests are waiting at Hartsmere."

"Lady Eden refers to the people of this dale, whom she invited to dine and make merry at her expense," Hartley said. "The majority seem to be late."

Every gaze turned to him. The Topping girls' eyes grew very big. Even Mrs. Topping appeared to be smitten.

For the first time, Eden saw Hartley through female eyes other than her own. She had never stopped to think how the maids at Hartsmere regarded him, and Mrs. Byrne was too elderly to consider. But the Toppings' reactions made clear just how attractive other women might find him.

She smothered a surge of jealousy. Why should they not admire? Hartley Shaw did not belong to her.

"Her ladyship was concerned that perhaps you did not receive your invitation," Hartley went on. He raked them all with a scathing look. "Surely, if you had, you would be at Hartsmere now. She has already done far more for the dale than save your ewe."

Mrs. Topping twisted her hands in her apron and avoided his eyes. "Well, you see . . ."

"Mr. Shaw, perhaps you would be so good as to fetch my cart," Eden said. She smiled at the Toppings. "We shall talk again at a more convenient time." She turned away before the woman could stammer an excuse.

Hartley took his time about obeying her, lingering with the Toppings while she walked toward the cart. She overheard a snatch of conversation and then a long silence. She was about to remind him when he strode past her in the direction of the cart.

Once they were on their way back to Hartsmere, Eden released the tight rein she had held on her emotions. "It was not necessary for you to berate the Toppings on my behalf," she said tightly. "I shan't beg for the affection of my people, nor do I demand it as a condition of charity."

Hartley glanced at her. The near kiss had been supplanted in her thoughts by more recent events, but now it was if their dalliance had just been interrupted. She half feared that he might stop the cart and finish what he had begun.

Feared, and hoped. God help her.

He set her mind at ease soon enough. "The Toppings did not show it," he said, "but they were impressed by what you were willing to do to save the sheep. It's not every lady who condescends to help in so personal a manner."

"I must have made quite an impression," she said, plucking at her stained skirts. "And to think that I chose this gown so that I would look my best today."

"Do you ever look less than your best?"

"Is that a question or a compliment, Mr. Shaw?"

His mouth turned up at the corners. "I merely observe that it would be difficult for you to be less than beautiful at any time, Lady Eden."

His formality at this late date was wildly incongruous. "I would thank you, kind sir, but you exaggerate, especially when I have made such a close acquaintance with the fell and its woolly inhabitants that I might be one of them myself."

"A sheep? Not you." His lids dropped halfway over his eyes. "I am no longer sure what sort of creature you are, Eden Fleming. You are not so tame as I once believed."

Eden laughed to cover her pique. "How distressing that you ever thought me tame. Had you seen me in London, you would not have made that mistake. No one among the *ton* thought me quite as dull as that."

There — that was a reminder to both of them who she was. But he chuckled, surprising her anew. "I never called you dull."

"I am gratified that you find me entertaining."

"It has been many years since I was last so . . . well entertained."

She flushed. "How fortunate that you found employment at Hartsmere, where life is so diverting."

"Do you seek to put me in my place again, Eden?" The

tone of his voice grew low, intimate. "Isn't it too late for that?"

Eden was spared the need to answer by their approach to Hartsmere. Her handful of guests occupied one of the tables. No one else had come in the hour that she and Hartley had been absent.

Yet Eden felt less discouraged than she had before they left. Helping to save the ewe and lambs had something to do with it. So had Hartley's company. The wild churning of emotions he inspired made her feel more alive than any of her London intrigues.

Reluctant to meet her guests in her current state, both physical and emotional, Eden asked Hartley to tend Copper and entered the house by a side entrance. Claudia intercepted her at the bottom of the stairs.

"Where were you?" she demanded. "I have been looking for you this past —" Her gaze fell to Eden's gown. "I am quite beyond words. Have you any idea how ill you have timed this . . . freakish start of yours?"

"Oh, this? It was in a very good cause, I assure you. Why are you so distressed?"

"Another guest will arrive soon, Niece. One you will not wish to disappoint."

"A member of the local gentry? Surely —"

"Someone far more important than that. It seems he could not forget you, Eden, and has come all the way from London." She smiled with barely veiled triumph. "The Marquess of Rushborough."

Chapter 9

The Toppings arrived at Hartsmere within an hour after Hartley and Eden's return, crowded onto every surface of their wagon.

Hartley had expected them. He nodded to Mrs. Topping as her eldest son helped her down. She seemed uncertain whether to curtsy to him or hurry past with eyes averted.

He had meant to make an impression on the Toppings, and he had succeeded. The small demonstration of magic he had provided for their eyes alone had unsettled them. They feared to offend him, in case his exhibition had not been a simple conjurer's trick.

In case he was the very source of Hartsmere's curse — and its restored good fortune.

The Topping girls, dressed in their white May Day frocks, whispered and giggled nervously as they made their way to the tables. Jeb grinned at him. He smiled in return, pleased that at least one of these humans did not fear him.

Some Fane had enjoyed being feared and worshiped. That had never been his ambition. He had wanted to be left alone, he and his beasts and forest. With Eden's return to Hartsmere, he knew how lonely he had been.

He came out of his musings to the sound of footsteps and hoofbeats and rattling wheels coming up the drive. News of Lady Eden's exploits — and Hartley's private display — had spread quickly. Farmers and villagers left their horses and carts and cautiously approached the tables.

"She can't be cursed," he heard Mrs. Topping tell a new arrival, "not if he helped save our ewe. She came right to our door, all soiled from the birthing. Jeb saw it. And he said . . ." She lowered her voice. "He said her manservant healed the ewe. I saw the beast walk with me own eyes, when Jeb said her leg was broke. And then — you willna believe this, but the servant did sommat that scared me right out of my shoes. . . ."

The two women moved off, and Hartley smiled with satisfaction. It would take little more to convince the dalesmen that Hartsmere's misfortunes were over — and that the change was directly connected to Lady Eden Winstowe.

He glanced toward the house. Eden had gone inside to change, but she still had not emerged to witness her success. He signaled to Armstrong, who had just served a plate of mutton and bread to an elderly woman.

"Find Lady Eden and tell her . . ." He hesitated, realizing that he very much wanted to surprise her. "Tell her that her presence is urgently requested."

Armstrong responded to his air of command without question and went into the house. Hartley circulated among the guests, listening to the talk and noting with approval that the tide was turning in Eden's favor. People were beginning to enjoy themselves, to relax and appreciate what Eden had provided.

Though the day was waning, Hartley held the wind at bay so that the afternoon's warmth lingered even as the sun began its downward journey. When Eden came out of the house, slim and youthful in a simple gown of sprigged muslin, the angled rays turned her into a gilded angel.

Others had seen what he had. Conversation dwindled, and faces turned toward Eden in curiosity and anticipation.

Hartley watched from a distance as she realized what had happened during her absence. A smile, unfashionably wide and quite inelegant, broke across her face.

She glided to the nearest table. "Welcome," she said almost shyly. "Welcome to all of you. I am so glad you came." She beamed at Mrs. Topping and her daughters. "You are enjoying yourselves?"

Voices murmured respectful thanks and agreement. They were still a trifle wary, but they no longer shut her out.

Eden moved among the tables, greeting each man, woman, and child by name. As she passed near Hartley, she met his gaze. Her smile altered subtly, meant not for the crowd but for him alone. Hartley moved as close as he dared without seeming too bold.

"People of the dale," she said, lifting her hand for attention. "This is a day of celebration, the beginning of a new age in our dale. I asked you here in the hope that you will share my belief."

A long silence was broken by a lone male voice crying, "Aye!" Said another, "They ha' nae sheep in London, I hear, but t'lady is mighty handy with the wee beasties!"

Eden blushed, but her eyes glowed with pleasure. "I have heard that May Eve has always been a time for celebration. And so we shall celebrate tonight, with games and music and prizes for the finest dancers."

A few in the crowd cheered. Young men fidgeted on their benches and cast mooncalf glances at pretty young women. The murmur of enthusiastic response swelled and then faded into an expectant silence.

The back of Hartley's neck prickled, and he turned just as the crowd parted to make a path for a new arrival.

The newcomer was no farmer. He paused just behind the outermost table, leaning on a polished, silver-headed cane, beaver hat in hand. He was handsome and dark, hair meticulously coifed, his suit of clothing fitted to his lean frame as if he had been sewn into it.

Hartley had met his like before. Not in this century, as men reckoned the years; when he had courted Eden, they had remained in the country despite all her urgings to the contrary.

But Hartley recognized this man for what he was: one of Eden's kind. A son of privilege brought up, as she had been, to all the pleasures and comforts money and social connections could buy. The sort of polished dandy to whom Eden would naturally be drawn.

She stared at the visitor. He bowed.

"I beg your pardon for intruding upon your celebration, Lady Eden. Perhaps my call is inopportune, and I may come again at a later time?"

"Lord Rushborough?" Eden said. Hartley could hear the speeding of her heartbeat and the hitch in her breath.

Points of fire burned under the skin of Hartley's forehead. The primitive, rutting male — the angry and powerful beast that was his other earthly self — recognized a dangerous rival.

With an act of will, he remembered that he was Fane. That he had but one claim on Eden, and it was not her body or soul.

Certainly not her love.

Like one enchanted, Eden waited while the dandy wound his way among the tables and stopped before her. "Lady Eden," he said, "my deepest condolences upon your loss."

Eden emerged from her spell. She smiled at the intruder and extended her hand.

"Lord Rushborough. This is an unexpected honor."

Rushborough took her hand and kissed the air above her glove. "I do apologize. I had thought that Lady Claudia was aware of my visit to the countryside."

Lady Claudia. Hartley remembered every nuance of his confrontation with the woman. He stared at Rushborough through narrowed eyes.

The dandy ignored him, as he would any servant. And so did Eden.

"You know how slow the mails can be here in the country," Eden said with a lilt in her voice. "I confess that I did not expect to see you so far from London, in the midst of the Season."

"But I had an excellent reason to come, Lady Eden." He took a step back, raised his quizzing glass, and swept the curious gathering with his gaze. "I am not intruding?"

"These are my farmers and tenants. May I introduce you to Mr. Appleyard, our curate?"

"As you wish."

She led the marquess across the lawn, and Hartley trailed behind. Mr. Appleyard looked up from his conversation as they approached.

"Lord Rushborough, Mr. Appleyard."

The curate bowed hastily, quite overwhelmed. "An honor," he said. "A very great honor indeed, my lord."

Lord Rushborough nodded to the curate with casual condescension and looked at Eden as if nothing else around him was of any consequence. She made a random, uneasy movement that heightened Hartley's vigilance.

"You have traveled a great distance, Lord Rushborough," she said. "My aunt will wish to welcome you herself. Where are you staying?"

"I have taken a house in a neighboring dale — though I must say that you enjoy better weather by far. I can only presume that it is your presence here that works such wonders upon nature."

She blushed. "My housekeeper will prepare a private meal for you, Lord Rushborough. We will talk as soon as I am free."

"My poor Lady Eden," he murmured, looking into her eyes. "How dreadfully dull for you, to waste your many talents on unappreciative farmers. I am very glad I came."

Hartley could feel all that they left unsaid, messages shared from a past in which Hartley had no part. But he understood well enough that Lord Rushborough had come with a purpose, and that was Eden herself.

"Shaw," she said, "please see to Lord Rushborough's horse."

Now, indeed, he had been put in his place. He turned on his heel and went to fetch the dandy's overbred hack. Rushborough offered Eden his arm, and the two of them strolled into the house.

Hartley tended the horse, whose mind was too weary to offer more than a sigh of thanks, and returned to the park to wait for Eden, every muscle in his body rigid with anger.

When she emerged, her smile was fixed like that of a painted figurine. Mr. Appleyard promptly intercepted her.

"My lady," the curate said, "what a privilege it is that Lord Rushborough should visit our humble parish. We are blessed with an abundance of riches this day."

"Yes," Eden said, her mind clearly elsewhere.

"An honor. A very great honor. Is it not as I predicted, my lady? Your feast has been a success."

"So it has." Suddenly she noticed Hartley. "I thank you for all your help."

Appleyard was not so oblivious as to mistake a dismissal. He glanced incuriously at Hartley and bowed himself away.

"Hartley," she said, avoiding his eyes. "Thank you for looking after Lord Rushborough's horse."

She was trying to keep him at a distance, and he knew why. "You did not expect this Rushborough, did you?"

"No."

"But you know him."

"Yes. In London. We were . . . friends."

Oh, no. They were much more than that. The definition of friendship among men did not include such glances as the marquess had given Eden.

Yet she had been married until a few months ago. Had she betrayed her husband with this haughty mortal lord?

"Why did he come?" Hartley asked, unable to keep the coldness from his voice.

"I had no idea that he had even left London until Lady Claudia . . ." Hidden memories played behind her eyes. "I am still in mourning, and Rushborough hates the country as much as I —" She stopped.

"As much as you do?" He curled his lip. "Are you glad he came?"

"I have known him for many years, and he is welcome here. He is also a peer of the realm, and you will treat him with respect."

With a few sentences she demolished the closeness that had grown between them and set them back to where they had begun.

"I will treat him as he deserves," he said.

"And have I deserved to be mocked and subjected to such disrespect?" she asked, matching his coldness. "If you disapprove of my guests, you are free to leave at any time." She picked up her skirts and strode purposefully toward the troupe of musicians who had arrived from Ambleside to accompany the dancing.

Hartley did not follow. His thoughts slowed to match the dull, leaden pace of his heartbeat. Even when the music began and Eden called her guests to the first dance, he could not bring himself to walk away. He watched her preside over the first set and the next and the next.

He left the gathering just as the dancing ended and Eden announced the judging for prizes. She, Mr. Rumbold, and Mr. Appleyard consulted, and the crowd waited in a hush of expectation.

Hartley missed the outcome. He strode to the back of the house, unremarked, and entered through the servant's door. He took the stairs two at a time until he reached the nursery.

Had Miss Waterson been there, he would have walked right past her. She was not. Donal lay in his trundle bed in the adjoining room, curled up on the sheets with the blanket tossed aside. In sleep he seemed far younger than his five years.

For a moment Hartley gazed down at his son. It would

be easy to leave now and take the boy to the forest. When the searchers looked in that direction, as they eventually must, he and the boy would be through the gate to Tir-na-nog.

Home.

He closed his eyes and saw Eden's face.

Not yet. Not without giving her . . .

A little more time to spend with the son he would steal away? A chance to recognize who she rejected when she turned her back upon the man she called Hartley Shaw?

Or the thing he had begun to consider when he had seen her with Mrs. Byrne on Candlemas Eve?

The memory of Eden on that night, and the near kiss today, diffused his anger. He no longer wished to hurt her. His desire for Eden, and hers for him, had become too strong to resist. He had ceased to seek revenge; she was on the verge of surrender. When he and Eden lay together, as they inevitably must — marquess or no marquess — he could make sure that their joining left her with a child to replace the one she lost in Donal.

He had the power to assure fertility, as befitted the god men had once called him; he could even make certain that such a child was free of Fane gifts that might mark it out as different and thus unacceptable among men.

He knew Eden would welcome such a child, whatever questions its birth raised in the minds of her own people. She had too much of mortal love to turn her back on any creature that needed her. She would hold the babe from the hour of its birth and never doubt its origins.

Whatever pain he might feel at abandoning a child of his body, it would be no worse than what Eden would suffer when Donal was gone. And he would leave a little of himself behind on this earth, whose creatures he had protected. If Eden married again, she'd give the child a father. . . .

Rushborough. Did he seek Eden as his mate — that popinjay who didn't deserve to kiss her feet?

The twin points on Hartley's forehead began to throb.

He knelt by the bed, stroking Donal's soft hair away from his face.

"Wake up, my son," he said.

Without the normal transition from sleep to waking, Donal opened his eyes. "Hartley?" he murmured. "Is it night?"

"Not yet." Donal held up his arms, and Hartley lifted him. "We are going to a party, Donal. Would you like that?"

"A party?" Donal's eyes brightened. "The one in the park? Will Mother be there?"

"Indeed she will."

Donal performed a perfect imitation of a rooster's crow. Hartley kissed his cheek and set him down. Together they made for escape.

"Where are you taking that child?"

Donal stopped dead, like a rabbit hoping to be ignored by a fox. Miss Waterson stood in the doorway, her hands upon her hips.

"Why are you here?" she demanded, staring at Hartley. "You are not one of the house servants. Leave at once."

Hartley tightened his grip on Donal's hand. "I will leave with the boy."

"You will do no such thing. I shall call her ladyship —"

"I am taking him to her ladyship," he said. "If you are referring to Lady Eden."

Something in her face suggested that she was not. "Did she send for him? I am to know about everything the boy does."

"And do you?" Hartley smiled. "Do you know where he is every minute?"

Her face twisted with suspicion and affront. "Several times I have found him outside the room before dawn, his clothes smelling of dirt and leaves, as if he had been —" her eyes widened. "You. *You* have been taking him at night."

"Kindly step out of my way."

"You have no right! What do you mean by stealing him

away, and you only a stable servant! When her ladyship hears of this—"

"Why don't you tell her yourself?"

"I will. And when I am done, Lady Claudia will have you discharged without a character, and I shall personally see that—"

Her words cut off on a shriek as a mouse ran out of a hole in the wall and skittered between her feet. It reared up on its hind legs, whiskers twitching with savage purpose, and showed its two long front teeth.

Donal giggled.

"You — you hellion child!" Miss Waterson cried. She pressed up against the wall and glared at Hartley. "Kill it! Kill it at once!"

"That, woman, is not in my profession." With a fond glance at Donal, Hartley stepped around Miss Waterson and swept his son from the room. The governess shrieked again behind them.

Once safely on the ground floor, he knelt and turned Donal to face him.

"Did you do that?" he asked. "Did you call the mouse?"

"Yes. He's my friend." He wrinkled his nose. "Miss Waterson is not."

No fool, his son. "Does she realize it was you?"

Donal bit his lip. "I don't know. I've called the mouse before, and a bat from outside." A secret smile crossed his face. "She screamed even louder at the bat."

"She screams rather well, doesn't she?"

"She doesn't like me," Donal confessed. He stared at the floor. "Like the people in Ballinkenny."

It was the first time he'd volunteered anything about his previous life, but Hartley didn't want to force such unpleasant memories on him now.

"It doesn't matter," he said, cupping Donal's chin in his hand. "You are better than she is. Than any of them. Someday you'll know why."

Donal smiled tentatively and grew serious again. "She found out that we go to the forest at night."

"She doesn't know very much. And soon that won't matter, either." He stood up. "Since you can call the mouse and the bat, next time I will teach you how to call other animals, the wild ones that live outside of men's walls."

It never ceased to amaze him how Donal's entire being could shine so brightly at the slightest kindness. Some of that glow came from his Fane heritage, but part was uniquely his own. He was like a lantern that had been wrapped in dark cloth — hidden, but only for a while. Only until the light was truly needed.

He scooped Donal up on his shoulders and raced down the stairs. "Shall we go to the party now?" At Donal's nod, he jogged to the front door and came face-to-face with Lord Rushborough. The man had changed into a green coat and buff pantaloons more appropriate to a *ton*nish drawing room than a rustic outdoors party.

Rushborough lifted his quizzing glass with a bored air. "Shaw, isn't it? I had thought you worked in the stables."

Hartley let Donal slide to the floor. "Your horse is settled," he said. "He doesn't seem to enjoy the countryside any more than you do . . . your lordship."

"All of my cattle have excellent taste," the marquess replied. He could not possibly consider a servant any sort of rival, but he stood squarely in Hartley's path, blocking the way, and his deceptively mild eyes held a challenge of their own.

For all his city-dulled senses, the marquess had not lost his native human instincts. This was no matter of rank and privilege.

"Who is the boy?" he asked. "Does Lady Eden generally allow grooms and children to run tame in her house?"

"She does this one. I am taking him to her."

Rushborough studied Donal more carefully. "I had not thought her particularly fond of children." He let his quizzing glass fall and stepped aside. "Take him. And when you are done, see that my horse gets another measure of oats."

Donal's presence kept Hartley from replying as he

wished. He ushered the boy out the door and across the lawn.

It was rapidly growing dark. Eden stood at the head of a milling group of tenants, who were showing off their prizes and congratulating each other. As he and Donal approached, Eden's glance fell in their direction. She stopped in midspeech. Her expression hovered uneasily between dismay and pleasure. With a final word to her guests, she left them to join Hartley and her son.

"Donal," she said warmly. She didn't bend to kiss him, but her loving attention was a caress in itself. "Did Miss Waterson let you out to play?"

"She didn't say no," Hartley answered for him. "The boy deserves to join in the fun, don't you agree? You surely didn't want him hidden away where no one could see him. He is, after all, a Fleming."

She ignored Hartley and touched Donal's cheek. "How would you like to join the other children? There's a bit of food left. I'm sure I saw a biscuit or two."

Donal looked at the troupes of children chasing each other about the lawn and then up at Hartley. "Do I have to play?"

"Only if you wish." How could he blame his own son for failing to desire human company? "Why don't you show Lady Eden how well you can climb trees?"

Donal's unique inner light blazed to new brightness. "I will. Watch me!" He dashed away toward an oak with a low crotch perfect for climbing. Hartley and Eden were left alone in a pocket of privacy and silence.

"Your Beltane feast appears to be a success," he said softly.

She met his eyes. "Why did you bring Donal out?"

"Are you ashamed to show him to your own people?"

She paced away, clasping her hands. "Lady Claudia suggested that he remain inside today, because he is not yet ready to face so many strangers —"

"Lady Claudia."

She looked at him sharply. "My aunt is just as concerned with Donal's well-being as I am."

"She was the one who hired the governess. Have you made any attempt to learn if Waterson is helping Donal, not harming him?"

"Harm him? I would know. Donal would tell me."

"Didn't he tell you already?"

"Tell you what, my dear Lady Eden?" Lord Rushborough interposed himself smoothly between them and tucked Eden's arm in the crook of his elbow. He turned a lazy glance on Hartley.

"I believe I asked you to give my horse a second measure of oats. Lady Eden, I fear that your servants take advantage of you."

Eden slipped her arm from Rushborough's. "I always left such matters to Winstowe," she said with a distant smile.

Rushborough accepted the mild rebuke. "Are you training a new footboy? Hartsmere certainly requires more servants, and of better quality. Perhaps I may assist you in that regard." He touched her hand. "I wish to help, Lady Eden . . . in every way."

Eden looked toward the tree where Donal had gone. "Donal is not a servant. He is the son of my late cousin — my Uncle Fleming's grandson. I am caring for him while my uncle is indisposed."

Hartley observed her narrowly. She did not enjoy lying to an old friend, a man who had come to court her. Deceiving servants and country folk was one thing; deluding a peer was quite another.

Hartley stared at Eden until she was compelled to meet his gaze. Shame and defiance turned her eyes the color of tarnished silver.

Rushborough was not oblivious to what passed between them. "You are tired, Lady Eden," he said. "Allow me to take you inside. Surely the farmers can spare you."

"Perhaps you are right." She cast another glance at the

oak. "Hartley, please fetch Donal. It is too dark for him to be climbing trees."

"He is well enough," Hartley said.

"Lady Eden," Rushborough said, "with your permission, I shall escort this insolent knave off the premises."

"An excellent notion, my lord." Lady Claudia approached from the house, the governess at her heels like an angry terrier. Armstrong trailed after them.

The two women curtsied to Rushborough. "I beg your pardon, my lord," Claudia said, "but I have an urgent matter to discuss with Lady Eden. Will you forgive us . . . ?"

"Naturally." He stared at Hartley. "I shall see that you are not disturbed."

Hartley stood his ground. The pain surged in his head, and the breath grew hot in his chest. It was not yet time to end his masquerade, but he knew that if Rushborough provoked him further, he must respond. And the marquess was no match for a lord of the Fane.

"You have greatly offended Lady Eden and me," Rushborough said. "Go the stables, gather your belongings, and be off this estate by morning."

Hartley smiled. "I did not hear my lady give the order."

Rushborough returned his smile, all white teeth and no humor. "Then I shall have to speak for her." His hand shot out with surprising speed and grabbed the shoulder of Hartley's coat.

There were any number of ways that Hartley could have used his powers to send Rushborough reeling, but none was as satisfying as the human method. He raised his bunched fist and drew it back to strike.

Chapter 10

N o," *Eden whispered.*
Hartley heard her. He looked from her to the other women's expressions of horror, and lowered his hand. The marquess pushed him away.

"This ruffian has insulted our guests," Lady Claudia said. "He must leave immediately." She signaled to Armstrong. "There is no need to soil your hands, Lord Rushborough. If he is not gone by morning, we shall send for the constable."

A swarm of midges suddenly gathered about the group and lighted in hungry clusters on Lord Rushborough's face. He made a heroic effort not to hop and slap. Miss Waterson gave a cry of disgust.

"Will you not go inside, my lord?" Lady Claudia said, eyeing the midges. "We will join you presently."

The marquess was torn between his own comfort and the demands of chivalry. The former won out. He bowed to the ladies again, threw a biting stare at Hartley, and strode for the house. The insects followed him in a cloud.

Miss Waterson waited until he was out of earshot and then spoke in a rush. "Lady Eden, I affirm what Lady

Claudia says of this man Shaw. He is a danger to Master Donal. I learned today that he steals Master Donal from the nursery every night and takes him — I cannot say where — but the boy returns filthy. These clandestine outings are a gross breach of discipline and propriety. Shaw is insolent beyond words and encourages the boy to even greater rebellion —"

"Rebellion?" Eden repeated. She remembered Hartley's question: *"Have you made any attempt to learn if Miss Waterson is helping Donal, not harming him?"* She looked at Miss Waterson with new attention. "What do you mean?"

"Why, he — he does not obey. He refuses to sit quietly at his lessons. He will not eat and defies me at every turn, with those strange ungodly eyes of his —" She broke off.

"I see," Eden said in an ominously still voice. "You think Donal ungodly, Miss Waterson?"

"No . . . no, of course I do not, my lady. But punishment does not deter him, and it is no wonder when —"

Eden was uncannily calm, the eye of the storm. "You punish him often, Miss Waterson?"

"It is the only way to invoke discipline, of which he is sorely in need. I was given a charge to perform." She jerked up her chin. "I take great pride in my profession, and if you do not wish my services —"

"Miss Waterson —" Claudia began.

Eden felt very close to the end of her tether. Could this be the same respectful, decorously retiring governess Eden had met in the drawing room? Was this the unembellished character of the woman she had allowed to take charge of her son?

"I confess that I have never heard a governess speak quite as you do, Miss Waterson," Eden said. "I would think that you set a very poor example for Donal."

"I? I am sorry to say this, my lady, but if that man" — she pointed at Hartley —"does not leave tonight, I shall be forced to tender my notice."

Eden looked from the governess to Hartley. "Is it true?"

she asked. "Have you been taking Donal from the nursery at night?"

He nodded once, as if it were beneath his dignity to explain.

"You see!" said Miss Waterson. "This cannot be allowed to continue."

In that the governess was correct.

"You have said you will not remain at Hartsmere unless I discharge Mr. Shaw," Eden said bluntly. "Very well, Miss Waterson. We shall be sorry to see you leave us."

"Niece —" Claudia began. Miss Waterson stared at her, disbelieving . . . until the midges appeared to wreathe her face in a buzzing mist.

With a muffled squawk, the governess ran back to the house.

"How very strange," Eden said, "that insects have such a particular fondness for Lord Rushborough and Miss Waterson." She caught Hartley's smile out of the corner of her eye.

"Shaw," she said coolly, "your conduct —"

Donal ran out of the shadows and grabbed her hand. "Did you see me in the tree? I climbed almost all the way to the top!"

"I saw you, Donal." She steered him toward Claudia. "Aunt, will you please return Donal to the nursery? I have deserted my guests too long."

"This will not do, Niece," Claudia said. Her face was expressionless, but Eden could feel her anger. "We discussed the need for a governess. You cannot simply dismiss Miss Waterson on a whim —" Her gaze cut Hartley like a scythe through hay. "*He* must *go.*"

"We will discuss this further, Aunt, but not here. Please take Donal inside."

To her secret amazement, Claudia acquiesced without further argument and reached for Donal. "Come, child. It is time for bed."

Donal danced out of her grasp and wrapped himself

around one of Hartley's long legs. "Hartley and I are going to the forest."

"You are going inside to sleep," Eden said.

He clung all the more firmly to Hartley. "He teaches me things," he said. "Not like the stick lady. Is she gone?"

Eden almost laughed at his name for the governess. She bit down on her lip. "Would you be very glad if she was?"

He gave a decisive nod. Hartley rested his hand on Donal's head and met Eden's gaze. He didn't have to say a word.

Claudia appeared ready to speak, but she, too, contained herself.

"Go inside, Donal," Hartley said. "It's all right."

"I will come to see you later, Donal," Eden added. She nodded to her aunt, who took Donal's hand and hurried him away. Claudia's posture hinted at the discord to come.

All because of Hartley. Or was it?

"I will speak to *you* when my guests have left," she told him.

"I look forward to it." His eyes had the odd habit of glittering in the dark, as if they caught any stray bit of light. "I am proud of you, Eden."

His praise was like a caress over the length of her body, stroking the anger away. Bereft of words, she left him and went to rejoin the dalesmen who were preparing to depart.

The mood among the people was one of peaceful contentment, utterly unlike that with which the day had begun. The curse had lifted; the folk of the dale had begun to accept her.

She waved the last cart down the drive and watched it disappear into the darkness. Armstrong and the maids she dismissed to bed, assuring them that they could clean up in the morning. Hartley was nowhere to be seen. She had little fear that he had left Hartsmere; she wondered if anything could drive him away.

Or if she could bear the thought of his leaving.

In spite of the unpleasantness that lay ahead, the evening's triumph stayed with her for a few precious minutes as she walked back to the house and went upstairs to kiss Donal good night. Claudia stood to the side, waiting grimly for her to finish.

The door had scarcely closed on the nursery when Claudia began. "I have spoken to Miss Waterson, and she is willing to overlook what happened, on the condition that you dismiss Hartley Shaw immediately."

Eden sighed. "I am afraid that is not very likely, Aunt."

"Do you actually mean that you prefer that man to Miss Waterson?" She followed Eden down the stairs. "How is this possible? After all the trouble I took to obtain a governess of such high qualifications —"

"And such unpleasant habits," Eden interrupted. She softened her voice to take the sting from her words. "Truly, Aunt — you saw how she spoke, as if she were the employer rather than the employed. How could you approve? And she admitted to punishing Donal."

"All children require discipline," Claudia said. "And as for Miss Waterson's outspokenness, she addressed matters that required attention. I quite admire her for it."

"But you don't admire the same quality in me."

"Not when it comes as a stubborn refusal to accept what must be!"

Eden stopped at the bottom of the stairs. "I cannot accept that her way of raising a child is what must be, Aunt. I have never been conventional; you used to encourage that in me. Why should a son not be like his mother?"

"But he is *not* like —" Claudia pressed her lips together. "Eden, I do not wish to quarrel."

"Nor do I, Aunt. Especially not with you."

"Then hear me out." She folded her hands and became the wise, dispassionate mentor Eden had always known. "I concede that it is your decision whether or not to retain Miss Waterson. But I have only tried to help you, Eden. I have observed how you've worked yourself to the bone, and it hurts me to see you so."

"But it is what I wish to do. I am not unhappy —"

"So you have convinced yourself. But you were never

meant to be alone." She touched Eden's chin. "That is why I asked the marquess to come to the Lakes."

"You asked — ?"

"Yes."

Eden laughed to cover her vexation. "Shall I trap him in my toils and scheme to win a proposal, even while I wear widow's weeds?"

"You need do no scheming, dear Niece. Lord Rushborough requires only the smallest encouragement to fall at your feet. He still desires you above all other women. He has told me so himself."

Eden took a step back. "I appreciate your concern, Aunt. But I prefer not to be pushed."

"Promise me that you will seriously consider Rushborough's suit when he makes his offer."

"I shall . . . think about it."

"That is all I ask." Claudia took her hand. "You know I wish the best for you, always. And that is why I urge you to discharge Hartley Shaw. It can come to no good."

"I will concede that he is overly presumptuous, but —"

"I do not refer to his manners. This Hartley Shaw has some power over you, Eden. There is no other explanation for your attachment to a man so much inferior to you in rank and in every other quality."

The urge to defend Hartley rose in Eden even as she choked on a denial. "You are quite wrong," Eden said, as if the matter were of no consequence. "Hartley Shaw is nothing to me. I keep him on because Donal is fond of him, and he is good at his work."

Claudia sighed and shook her head. "I fear for you, Eden."

"You fear for me in the company of a man? Any man?" She laughed. "Please do not distress yourself."

"I will not, if you agree to stay away from Shaw."

"You have already demanded one promise of me this evening. But of course that is the real reason why you sent for the marquess, is it not? To divert my attention from my supposed peasant lover?"

"Do not speak so where the servants might hear."

"But they already know, don't they? Have they not reported to you?"

"You have misplaced your judgment, my girl," Claudia said sharply. "And as long as you are so lost to sense, I must think for you."

As she had done for so much of Eden's life. But not this time. "I will not turn the marquess away from Hartsmere, but I shan't allow anyone — not even you — to tell me with whom I may keep company. Good night, Aunt."

Driven by a fury stronger than any she could remember, Eden sought the freedom of the night. It seemed that everyone was intent upon manipulating her, pushing her this way and that: Claudia, the marquess, Miss Waterson . . . and Hartley Shaw. Perhaps him most of all.

The marquess was waiting for her just outside the door. She came to a halt and gathered her composure. "Lord Rushborough. I thought you . . . had gone for the evening."

"Without saying a proper good night?" He seized her hand and kissed it. "I have missed you, Eden. Missed you terribly."

"Lord Rushborough —"

"Francis. Have we not known each other too well for formalities?" He trapped her hands between his. "Forgive my boldness. I know you are still in mourning — but I also know how little affection you held toward your husband. It is right and proper that you should observe the mourning period, but after . . ." He pulled her close. "We were happy together. You know that as well as I."

Eden did not answer. She ought to be feeling flattered and exhilarated that Lord Rushborough — Francis — had traveled the long distance to Westmorland to court her, in spite of her impoverished state and hasty departure from London. She still liked him, even felt affection for him. Her body remembered the attraction they had shared ever since their introduction by Aunt Claudia at Lady Morland's musicale.

But it was no longer there. She felt strangely numb, as if she had been swimming in icy water.

"Lord . . . Francis . . . I am deeply grateful that you came to Hartsmere —"

"Grateful?" He chuckled. "My dear, when your aunt told me of the conditions here in the country and what you were forced to endure, nothing could have kept me away. Now that I see this place, I understand her concern. But once you are in London, where you belong — but I am too hasty. Forgive me. My rashness is merely the result of seeing you again."

Eden managed a smile. "And I am flattered and honored. But —" She lowered her eyes. "My husband has been gone only six months. I have just begun to win the trust of the people here. There have been so many changes —"

He released her. "Of course. Now that I have taken the house at Caldwick, I will be able to come to you whenever you need me."

"But the Season —"

"Can wait. The world can wait for you, Eden."

But it cannot. It cannot. "Oh, Francis. You were always such a good friend."

"And I hope to be so much more to you, my dear." Without warning, he took her arms and kissed her. It was not a deep kiss, but the passion in it was plain.

And utterly absent on Eden's part. Even Francis felt her constraint. He drew back with a puzzled frown and then dipped his head for another attempt.

"No." Eden blocked his lips with her hand and pulled away. "No, Francis."

He studied her face. "What is it, Eden?"

"I . . . I am in mourning, Francis. It is not proper —"

"Proper?" he laughed. "When did propriety ever encumber Lady Eden Winstowe? No . . ." His eyes narrowed. "You have changed."

"Perhaps I have."

"Has it something to do with that ill-mannered servant, Shaw?"

Eden's face grew hot. "How can you speak so?"

"I observed the way he looked at you — and you at him. I simply did not wish to believe it." He took her by the arms again and gave her a light shake. "Is it true, Eden? Can even you have sunk so low —"

She came within an inch of slapping him. Her sudden, aborted movement shocked them both.

"Lord Rushborough," she said, "as happy as I am to see you, I cannot permit you, or anyone else, to presume to dictate my life!" She turned and fled, forgetting to pick up her skirts and barely avoiding a humiliating fall.

Rushborough didn't follow. By the time she had reached the great oak that Donal had climbed but an hour past, she was out of breath and cursing herself for the worst kind of fool.

She considered returning to humbly beg Francis's pardon, but her pride, shredded though it might be, remained largely intact. He had all but accused her of . . . of . . .

Of the very thing she had feared and wished for ever since she'd met Hartley Shaw.

She was so attuned to him that she felt no surprise when he appeared beside her.

"Who has made you weep, Eden?" he asked.

"I am not weeping."

"As you wish." He leaned against the fine old tree and gave it an affectionate pat. "Is it your aunt who has upset you, or Lord Rushborough?"

"I am a little weary of other people attempting to decide what is best for me and my son."

He ran his hand around the curve of the trunk, drawing closer to her. "You do not like to be commanded, do you, Eden? You have always had your own way."

Not always. She shivered. "It is you who seem to get your own way," she said. "An unfortunate habit in a servant."

"But acceptable in a peer such as Lord Rushborough. He, too, is used to getting what he wants, and what he wants at Hartsmere is obvious."

Eden pressed her back to the tree and averted her face. "I told you —"

"That he is only a friend." He laughed, but the laugh cut short. "Do you love him, Eden?"

The question paralyzed her. Hartley was just like the others, pulling her this way and that with questions and demands. But she could not hate him for it. Her heart began to beat a little faster.

"Were you lovers?" Hartley asked.

"No. All the *ton* thought it — even my aunt — but we never . . ." She swallowed. "I ended it when Spencer — my husband — became ill."

Warm fingers brushed her cheek. "You have not answered my first question, Eden."

"I do not answer to you, or Rushborough, or my aunt —"

"Then answer to your heart."

The heart he spoke of had filled her throat, making it impossible for her to reply. His eyes mesmerized her, sent her tumbling into an endless forest of deep green.

"Once all I cared about was myself," she said. "Everything I do now, I do for my son."

"Everything?"

"From the beginning you have questioned my devotion to Donal," she whispered. "You take him out at night without my permission. You behave as if you were his father, and that you cannot be."

"No?" His eyes glittered. "Why don't you ask the boy how he feels?"

"Is it not enough that I discharged his governess on your behalf?"

"It was a beginning." Another swift change, and his face was gentle again. "You knew it was right."

"I do not believe I know what is right anymore."

He brushed his fingers over her lips. An indescribably erotic charge beset her body.

"If you love Donal, you will do what is best for him."

"Always."

He stroked across her lower lip and then the upper. "There is devotion in you, Eden — more than I had thought possible."

She drew back. "You seem to have difficulty in making up your mind about me, Hartley Shaw. Shall I ever meet with your unqualified approval?"

A strange look came over his face, as if she had asked him a painful question. All at once he was vulnerable, a little lost, just as she was.

"Shall I ever meet with yours?" he asked.

They stood so close that they breathed each others' breaths and felt each others' sighs.

"How can I ever understand you?" she asked.

"Perhaps no understanding is necessary." He smiled, that precious gift he so rarely bestowed. "Is this not the eve of Beltane? There was a time when this was a celebration of life in all its meanings. It was the ritual marriage between the horned god and the goddess worshiped at the beginning of our history — a festival when all fears were set aside, and joy was the only purpose."

"Between you and Mrs. Byrne, you seem to know every folk custom that ever existed in this land," she said with a nervous laugh.

"They were more than merely customs. On nights such as this, couples went into the woods and made merry until dawn. Perhaps this very eve, men and maids may create new life."

Eden wanted to move away from the heat of his insinuations, but she was transfixed. "Not our woods up the fell, surely," she murmured. "Everyone knows that they are haunted by a vengeful Faerie spirit."

"Perhaps he was vengeful because men did not respect any life that was not their own. But I think . . . I think that your Faerie Lord is not angry tonight. I think that he may accept a sincere offer of friendship."

Though his words were strange and disquieting, Eden was not afraid. She knew that the moment had come, a second chance at what they had so narrowly missed in the cart on the way to Birkdale.

She remembered Francis's kiss, and how little it had moved her. She remembered Aunt Claudia's stern reproach. She considered, one last time, what she was about to betray.

And she cast it all aside like so many paste jewels.

She stepped in to Hartley and kissed him.

She had kissed many men. Some were rakes, greatly experienced in the arts of seduction; others had been less accomplished but more sincere. Never had she thought to kiss a common servant.

But there had never been a servant like Hartley, and there was nothing common about him. His answering kiss was the final proof.

It began almost gently, meeting her daring with a stillness like the deep, impenetrable center of the lake that gave Hartsmere its name. But his lips were not cold; they burned on hers and gave no pain, only delight.

Her head spun so that she could not tell up from down, night sky from shadowed earth. She had made the first move, but somewhere in the midst of the endless kiss Hartley took control. His arms came about her, lifting her from her feet. Her body seemed to melt into his. In a distant part of her mind she realized that he, too, must have had much experience to kiss with such expertise. This was not the fumbling, crude caress of a laborer or farmer.

It was a kiss such as the mythic gods of love might have bestowed upon those mortal women they chose as lovers.

Hartley parted her lips with his tongue and she let him inside. The lower half of her body had begun to throb in a way she could not mistake. For most of the past five years, she had denied it the satisfaction and completion it craved, testing her will against that of the men the *ton* called her lovers. Never quite surrendering. Saving herself . . . for what, she did not know.

Until now. Until Hartley. *This* was what she had waited for. She admitted it freely, for denial was pointless. He moved his tongue in such a way that she felt as if she lay naked beneath him on the soft grass while he thrust deep between her thighs.

Yes. The image gave her no shame. She wanted him hungrily, greedily, desperately. She was all desire, swept back to the one time when a man had carried her to paradise. She had tasted it and yearned to taste it again. She, Lady Eden Winstowe, whom everyone assumed took a new lover each month, rumored to be deliciously skilled in the arts of love, was hardly more than a virgin.

She perched on the edge of a limitless crevasse, ready to hurl herself beyond the reach of redemption. If she gave herself to Hartley — oh, as she so longed to do — she would not be indulged by Society as she had been in London. She would become an outcast among her own, a traitor to all the *ton* held dear. Her previous life would be truly over.

That she might sacrifice willingly, but not Donal's future. Not everything that was to be, *must* be his.

"Hartley," she murmured. He was using lips and tongue in a hundred delightful ways on her face and neck, finding places she had not known could bring such pleasure. She wedged her hands between them. "Hartley, stop."

He obeyed instantly, with none of the reluctance other men might show. Her skin felt icy where his hot mouth had been. He stepped back, and a wind as bleak as winter rushed between them.

In his eyes was that same coldness, as if he had been expecting her protest. Her rejection.

And hated her for it.

"Hartley," she whispered. "It is . . . it is not what you think."

His mouth curled in a parody of his glorious smile. "Are you not about to tell me that you have decided that this was a mistake? That you have remembered who you are and what I am?"

He mocked her, but she could not fault him for it. She

had started this. She had to make him understand. "I have never forgotten who I am."

"But you cannot admit that I — this rough form you despise — did to you what no other man could."

His arrogance seemed designed to provoke her anger. But he was right; a thousand men could attempt to seduce her, and every one would leave her indifferent from this moment on. Had she been so transparent, so ingenuous?

"Will it help you if I admit it?" she said, lifting her chin. "Is it so important to you that I become your . . . conquest?"

He expelled a harsh breath. "If I had wanted to conquer you, I could have done it with ease, and your petty defenses would be useless."

She laughed. "How gallant of you, Hartley. You make it quite impossible for me to forget your station."

He moved a step closer, crowding her with his body. "Should I play the role of a true blackguard, Eden? Do you want me to force you, so that you need feel no shame at having a common lover?"

She held her ground. For all his quicksilver changes of mood and many contradictions, Hartley would not stoop to rape. Dark he might be, and unpredictable, but at heart he was a good man. Yes . . . a good man who had been wounded, as she had been.

Perhaps that was all they had in common — that, and desire. Lust. Physical attraction that would bind them for a short while until both were sated.

"Hartley." She took his stiff, unresponsive hand in hers. "I am not pushing you away." She flushed, realizing that what she was about to admit could not be recalled. "It is only that . . . that I want you so much that I fear . . . I fear I may hurt my son."

"By sharing your bed with a servant?"

"Yes." She did not look away from his biting stare. "You are no ignorant rustic. You know what others will say if we are seen together as lovers. And Donal will suffer the consequences."

Donal's name was like a magic invocation that had the power to banish Hartley's anger. His mouth relaxed, and the crease between his brows smoothed as if at the touch of a gentle hand.

"Then your world is not for Donal," he said.

"It is the world to which he was born."

"A world that can be yours again if you marry Rushborough."

Eden flinched. "I cannot consider marriage until my period of mourning is done."

"But you are considering it, Eden. Aren't you?"

"That is between me and the marquess."

"Will he not disapprove of what you do here with me?" Testing. He was always testing her, probing for weakness, demanding more than she dared give. "He does not rule my life. Neither do you."

"And you do not want him."

Eden was weary of wordplay and dissent. "Wanting is unimportant. You asked before if I loved him." She smiled with an uneasy mingling of sadness and pride. "I do not believe that I shall ever love any man again."

His jaw set. "Never?"

"I have had enough of what men and women call love. It has been burned out of my soul. Can you understand that, Hartley?"

She thought he was not going to answer, that her blunt declaration had upset him. Had he actually expected her love as well as her surrender?

"Yes," he said at last. He gave her an ironic smile in return. "Much less complicated, is it not?"

"I do not deny the desire I feel for you. But I must be sure that my son's future is protected."

He was silent for a long while, gazing up into the gnarled branches of the oak. "I can arrange it so that no one will see us," he said. "Not even the servants will know."

How strange and utterly unromantic this conversation was, like a negotiation between warring armies. How very pragmatic and responsible she had become, even in the midst of planning a life-altering indiscretion.

"How can you be so sure?" she asked.

He looked at her and smiled again, a genuine smile that held all the sensual delights she had yet to taste. Tiny lights danced in the green depths of his eyes. "Trust me."

Yes. Trust him. He is an utter stranger, yet you have known him all your life.

Let it begin. Let it be tonight.

"There is too much at stake," she said, silencing the cries of her body. "I need time, Hartley. You must give me time to decide."

"Ah." He laughed. "You mortals, who have so little of it, value time no more than you do the earth that gives you life."

"Mortals?" A shiver coursed down her back. "What do you mean?"

She realized how seldom she'd caught him off guard when she saw the look on his face.

"It is merely an expression, from a poem I read once . . . a long time ago."

She relaxed. "You read poetry as well? We don't really know each other, do we?" She sighed. "But it doesn't matter. Not if we are honest in what we want from each other."

"No. It doesn't matter at all."

"Then, until I am sure," she said —*until I find the courage*—"we must not be seen together. Do you agree?"

He made a leg, the sort of courtly bow that was going out of fashion in London. "I am, as always, your servant."

His mockery had become so familiar that it had lost its power. "Shall we shake hands on it, then?" She offered her hand.

He took it gravely. It was the perfect ending for this most peculiar seduction. She expected him to take her in his arms and kiss her once more for good measure, to remind her of what she might lose. He did not. But there was in his lightest touch such potency, in his look such fire and promise, that a kiss would have seemed redundant.

If she remained in his presence another moment all her prudence would go for naught. "Good night," she said hastily. She started for the house, looking back only to find him vanished into the night.

She stopped by Donal's room and spent the better part of an hour simply gazing at him. When she went down to her own room, Aunt Claudia was standing in the hall in her dressing gown, the candle in her hand casting sinister shadows on her face. Eden hurried past without a word.

Her bed was very lonely indeed.

Chapter 11

He had been so close to victory that he could still taste Eden's desire on his lips.

Hartley ran for the forest, his body demanding a substitute for the activity it had been denied. His legs carried him more swiftly than any human's; once he was beyond the park and the pasture behind Hartsmere he let his animal nature take control. A simple thought, and he was a great stag, the Horned One of the ancients, his antlers so heavy and broad that they rivaled the branches of small trees.

The magnificent red deer of this land rutted only in the autumn. Hartley recognized no such boundaries. So he endured the frustration of wanting and not having, pursuing only to find the pursued slipping through his fingers.

Yes, he had made her surrender her pride and her aristocratic principles. She had admitted that she wanted him. She had all but promised that soon she would be his lover.

But not his love. *"I have had enough of what men and women call love. It has been burned out of my soul. Can you understand that, Hartley?"*

Of course. *He* had not loved, could not love. Who better to understand? She became truly his equal, dispensing with any risk of guilt.

How very convenient that emotion need not enter into their liaison.

Hartley gave himself to the night, charging up the fell as if it were a hillock. Rabbits and hares dashed from his path, and a badger put its head out of its sett to observe the commotion. A fox watched him with laughter in its wise and curious eyes.

His subjects, all. They had come to his calling with the spring, repopulating the barren land. The birds and beasts had no mixed loyalties or fears of losing rank and privilege.

Hartley's great lungs strained, giving him the strength to reach the top of the fell without once pausing in his gallop. At the peak, clothed in sedge, moss, and lichen amid the bare, jutting rock, he flung back his head and roared. The echo crashed down into the neighboring dale.

No other creature dared answer, not even the shepherd's dogs. He pawed the stone hard enough to strike sparks. He tossed his head, challenging the stars themselves.

It was all so much posturing, and he knew it.

With a sigh he shed his animal shape and sat on a boulder. After a time the fox and a few rabbits crept up to him, settling at his feet. Faint rustlings told him where the wood mice and short-tailed voles hid among the rocks, too frightened to come out in spite of the truce Hartley's presence invoked.

He sent a gentle thought toward the nearest tiny life. The mouse scurried up the rock, whiskers twitching anxiously, and settled in his palm.

"You see?" he said, stroking its delicate chest. "You are safe. As long as you remain well away from mortal men. As I should have done."

The mouse sat up on Hartley's hand and sniffed the air.

"It was only a kiss," Hartley said. "Among humans, as among my kind, such are given and taken carelessly enough."

Then why did he feel so powerless when Eden kissed him? Why had he been so easily set on the defensive, letting her control the conversation and its conclusion?

The kiss should have been merely a physical thing, a means to an end. Instead, it had strengthened his desire for her, driven him to distraction, and had proven nothing but that he had mastered neither her nor himself.

If he followed the path of those thoughts, he would begin to imagine a life that included Eden as well as Donal. Such a life as could only be lived in the mortal realm, for the time was long past when men were permitted to enter Tir-na-nog.

He did not want that life. He could not make Eden want it, no matter how well he intrigued and seduced her. In her eyes he was either a man far beneath her rank, or he was not a man at all. They were moving inevitably toward a joining that could not last.

Hartley turned his hand and set the mouse down on the boulder. It remained, gazing up at him as if in concern. Even the smallest of nature's creatures recognized his confusion.

So much for the august dignity of the Forest Lord. Hartley laughed and rested his head in his hands.

The cool nose of the fox nudged at his fingers. Absently he reached out to stroke the pointed muzzle, but his hand found skin instead.

Tod sneezed and sank into a crouch beside the boulder, nimble fingers dangling over his knees. "You are sad, my lord?"

Hartley rose to his full height and frowned at the hob. "You have been gone long enough."

Tod ducked his head. "Tod had far to search."

"And Tod no doubt found other diversions. Have you completed the task?"

"Aye, my lord." He shook his head, tumbling unruly red hair into his eyes.

"Speak," Hartley commanded. "What did you learn?"

Tod made himself very small and peered up at Hartley

from under his brows. He began to speak in a rush, scuttling a little farther away from his lord with every sentence.

When Tod had finished, Hartley stood at the center of a storm, lashing rain and wind that matched the violence of his anger. All the other beasts had fled. Only Tod remained at a safe distance at the edge of the wood, huddled against the stinging drops.

This is what it is to be a Fane child among men. Hartley closed his eyes as if he could drive away the images that crowded his mind. Donal constantly mistreated. Donal starved and beaten. Donal mocked because he was different, and driven away at last because he was feared.

"Shall Tod go back?" Tod said in a small voice. "Shall Tod punish these wicked mortals?"

"No." Hartley calmed his own racing heart, and with it the winds and rain. The downpour became a drizzle and then a mist, shrouding the felltop. "There is no changing the nature of man."

Tod didn't answer. Hartley thought of what he had heard, what he knew of Donal, how Eden feared for her son. She would never forgive herself if she knew how Donal had suffered because of her ignorance of his existence.

Donal would go on suffering if Eden bound him to the mortal world. She wished to protect him by any means necessary, unaware that the greatest danger came from her own kind. She must believe that the marquess would accept the boy. He could offer her honorable marriage, and her son a stepfather, in a way completely suitable to her society and station.

And utterly unsuitable for a Fane child.

But that situation would not arise. It was only a matter of time before Hartley got Eden with a child free of Fane gifts and took Donal away — and then let Eden do whatever she wished with her fine human lord.

No. Lightning cracked above Hartley's head. No mortal should have her again. No man should possess what had been his. Rushborough was unworthy of the Forest Lord's bride.

Unworthy of the woman Hartley had hated and sought to manipulate, whose son he intended to steal.

He shook his head wildly, shouting into the thunder. The Fane seldom went mad as men understood the word, but *she* drove him near to it. She and the emotions she aroused in him, however fiercely he fought to reject them.

The storm snarled and blustered until an hour before sunrise. The sun's first rays poured over Hartley like balm, easing the untidy remnants of his anger. He could not have raised the smallest cloud even had he wished.

But his mind was clear. There was always the chance, however remote, that something might go wrong with his plans to take Donal to Tir-na-nog. Eden must be made to understand why Donal was meant for better things than man's cruel world could offer.

"Tod," he called, summoning the hob from his hiding place. "I have another task for you."

For once Eden was not with the boy.

Nor, for that matter, was she with Hartley Shaw. Both were circumstances to be thankful for, and Claudia would not question the generosity of Providence.

For the first few days after Miss Waterson's departure from Hartsmere, Eden had kept Donal constantly by her side with an almost fanatical dedication. Then, conveniently enough, a number of crises had developed among the farmers and villagers in the dale, and Eden had been sufficiently distracted to agree to leave Donal at the house while she dealt with them.

Since the party, the people of Hartsmere seemed unable to do without their mistress. Nancy had become Donal's surrogate governess, while Eden steadfastly avoided discussing a replacement for the unlamented Miss Waterson. She hardly spoke to Claudia at all.

In Miss Waterson's absence, it would be somewhat

more difficult to keep Donal out of Lord Rushborough's
sight when he came to call this afternoon. His first visit
following that disastrous encounter at the tenant's party
must go smoothly, for it would set the tone for all future
meetings.

Claudia walked through the garden, vaguely disturbed
by its overripe lushness. The days had been unseasonably
warm since February, an extraordinary contrast from the
bitter winter that had ended so abruptly. Nothing seemed
quite right at Hartsmere — but then, it never had. She ought
to be used to this constant state of misgiving and fear.

She wondered if Eden would be back from the village
in sufficient time to make ready for Lord Rushborough's
arrival. She showed little inclination to prepare herself
with the care she'd always taken in London when she'd received callers. Her priorities in general had suffered. Nevertheless, she had not outright rejected Francis's courtship,
and as long as she did not, Claudia would press for his suit
and encourage him by any means possible.

He was a gentleman indeed to overlook the offenses
given him by that devil Hartley Shaw.

Aware of an all-too-common prickling at the back of
her neck, Claudia looked for the groom. He seemed to be
everywhere at once, as irksome as flies about a honeypot.
She knew little more about him now than when he had first
arrived; no one at Hartsmere was able to tell her anything
of his background or family. For all her threats, she had
still not found a way to expel him from Hartsmere. And
Eden refused to cooperate.

Driven by the need to confront what most troubled her,
Claudia turned and walked toward the stables. She was not
surprised to find Donal with Shaw; Nancy was away, and
Mrs. Byrne was a very lax and unreliable keeper.

Man and boy were locked in conversation. Donal was
uncommonly silent much of the time, but with Shaw he became animated — another mark of his unnatural birth. The
boy would rather be among the dogs and horses and sheep,
and those of lowly birth, than with people of refinement.

Why would Eden not recognize what he was? How could she bear to have him near when she had so despised his father? It was a puzzle that haunted Claudia nightly.

Another puzzle was Shaw's daily excursions into the forest. Now that Miss Waterson was gone, he no longer stole the boy from the nursery at night. They went openly during the day, and Eden did nothing to stop it.

The pair were headed for the forest now, marching at a fast clip up the fellside. Claudia hesitated. She had reason to hate the place above all others at Hartsmere. But if what she feared lingered there, it had not shown its face.

Gathering her skirts, she waited until Shaw and Donal had reached the edge of the forest and disappeared among the trees. She followed slowly, picking her way around the natural rock wall and avoiding the beck and its miniature force.

Like everything else in the dale, the forest was well progressed in its spring growth. Most of the trees were in leaf and many were flowering. Skylarks, thrushes, and warblers rivaled each other in song. Unpleasant little rodents rustled under Claudia's feet. She swallowed her distaste and continued to the border of the wood.

Ordinary human voices and footsteps were lost in such a place. Claudia wove a path among the trees and the undergrowth of bilberry, wood rush, and holly, listening. Vigilance rewarded her; she found man and boy before she came too close to be heard herself. She hid behind a stately ash to watch.

They knelt upon the earth, studying the ground intently. Claudia saw nothing to account for their interest. Shaw glanced up at the boy, smiled, and passed his hand over the bare patch of dirt in a circular motion, like a conjurer plying his tricks. Donal pressed his nose almost level with the ground.

The patch of dirt heaved as if a hill of ants had been disturbed. But no insects appeared. Instead, a tiny speck of green emerged from the center. It grew larger, and then burst forth to become a stalk with new furled leaves.

Within a minute, it had grown into a seedling — an infant oak to match its fellow monarchs of the forest.

Claudia bit hard on her lip to keep from crying aloud.

"Now you try," Shaw said. He took the boy's hand, uncurled his fingers, and guided it palm down over a similar bare patch of earth.

Nothing happened. Donal's face screwed up in concentration.

"You are trying too hard," Shaw chided. "Let it come naturally. It is your gift. The acorn only awaits your summons."

Donal tried again, with all the urgent determination of a child learning a new skill. Whatever he was meant to do did not occur. His shoulders slumped, and he looked up at Shaw in defeat. A sole tear ran down his face.

Shaw placed both hands on the boy's shoulder. There was something deeply paternal in his touch.

"It does not matter. You will have much time to learn, and when we go —" He stopped himself. "You will learn. You need not be afraid anymore, Donal. No one will ever punish you again."

Donal rocked back on his heels. Claudia experienced another stab of guilt.

I did not know. I did not know.

"Can I try the animals?" Donal asked Shaw.

"Of course. Who would you like to call?"

"The gray fox. Not Tod, but the other one."

"Very well," Shaw said with an indulgent smile. "Call the gray fox."

Donal closed his eyes. His mouth moved silently. A slow murmur began in the surrounding shrubbery, gradually increasing in volume. Small animals burst from hiding. Even a shy red deer calf stepped halfway into the clearing. Claudia dug her fingers into the ash to keep from fleeing in sheer, instinctive terror.

The animals gathered about Shaw and the boy like subjects paying homage to their ruler. A badger nosed its way into Donal's lap. He laughed with delight.

"You see? The animals aren't hard," Donal said.

"Your call is strong but unfocused," Shaw said. "The beasts obey you. But where is the fox? Is he too busy to come?"

"I can't find him," Donal said. "Where is he? Why isn't he with the lady fox now like he was before?"

Shaw's smile faded. He gazed at Donal with an expression of sadness and regret. "There is a season for everything," he said. "Nothing in this mortal world lasts, Donal."

The pensive moment was interrupted by the arrival of a fox — not the dog but the vixen, trailed by her new cubs. The vixen sidled up to Shaw and rubbed herself against him while the cubs scampered to Donal and licked his hands like unruly puppies.

After a few minutes of rough-and-tumble play, Shaw waved the family back into the woods. They led a procession of beasts out of the clearing at various trots, scurries, shuffles, and bounds.

"You said you would show me the stag," Donal said, sitting up on his knees. "You said you could change whenever you wanted. Show me now?"

Claudia put her back to the ash and closed her eyes. Her body shook as if from a palsy. She clenched her fists, her nails drawing blood.

Him. It was *him*. All the things she had felt wrong about Hartley Shaw made a terrible sense. And so did Eden's inexplicable attraction to a common servant.

He had not disappeared as she had dared to believe. He had not gone back to whatever hellish place he came from. He was *here*— the creature who had ruined her life years before he met Eden Fleming.

And he had found Eden and her son.

Hatred returned, blossoming as swiftly as the roses in the garden. It was a heady feeling. It restored her courage as nothing else could. Her courage, and her determination.

Oh, he'd fooled them all, changed his appearance enough that no one who had seen him as Cornelius Flem-

ing would look for him in a laborer. And who would think
to seek his alien nature beneath the human veneer?

That was why it was up to her to save Eden and to exact
revenge at last. Her life, which had lacked purpose since
their exile to Hartsmere, had meaning again. No longer
would she worry about Eden's infatuation with Hartley
Shaw. She would find a way to use it to her own advantage, and for Eden's ultimate good.

As for the boy . . . if not for her hatred of his father, she
might have let Shaw — Cornelius, or whatever he chose to
call himself — take him away as he surely planned to do.
She could only assume he had not done so already because
he had further designs upon Eden. But if Claudia's plans
succeeded, Donal would be in need of a new father and
mother.

The one thing she could not do was tell Eden who Shaw
really was. He might have her bewitched, and she was too
emotionally fragile to face the truth. Eventually she must,
of course. But Shaw didn't suspect what Claudia knew of
him. That gave her an incalculable advantage.

Calm and clearheaded again, Claudia peered around the
ash. Donal and his father — so much alike, now that she
understood — were discussing the wing pattern of an em-
peror moth. It occurred to her to wonder why this creature
was unaware of her presence, and she guessed that he was
completely absorbed with his son. But that could change in
an instant.

With utmost care, Claudia made her way to the edge of
the wood. The pursuit she feared did not come. Once
safely away from the vicinity of the trees, she relaxed her
walk as if she had just come back from a casual stroll.

She settled in the sitting room and sent for a tea tray.
Her hands were completely steady as she poured. The day
would proceed as expected. The marquess would find
nothing amiss. Nothing whatsoever.

Eden returned only an hour before the appointed time.
She looked harried and flustered, her hair straggling about
her neck and her skin sheened with perspiration.

"I am sorry to be so late, Aunt," she said, tugging off her bonnet. Her hair tumbled free as if the bonnet alone had held it in place. Armstrong hurried into the drawing room to take her spencer.

"You are hopelessly disheveled, my dear," Claudia said. She took Eden's arm and solicitously led her to a chair. "What has happened?"

"What has not?" Eden plopped into the chair with unladylike force. "Everything has gone wrong in the dale. Livestock missing, quarrels over boundaries, flooding, Mrs. Topping ill, Mr. Appleyard upset because Mr. Holmes's sheep got into his garden and ate his vegetables — it all seems to be occurring at once!" She blew out her breath, stirring a tendril of hair that lay across her nose. "I cannot understand it."

But I think, now, that I can. If you are busy elsewhere, he *has more time alone with your — his — son.*

How many of these predicaments are his *doing?* Claudia nodded with the right degree of reserved sympathy. "You should not exhaust yourself. You cannot, nor are you expected to, see personally to every problem in the dale. That is Mr. Rumbold's province."

"Yes, yes. You are undoubtedly right, Aunt, but now that they have given their trust to me —" Her eyes lit, as they had once done at the prospect of a new ball gown or handsome beau. "I do not want to let them down. But I must spend so much time away from Donal. It would not be fair to take him on all these errands. Where is he?"

"With that groom, I believe," Claudia answered, not bothering to hide her scorn. The truth was far more effective than any prevarication. "Nancy is off visiting her family today, and Mrs. Byrne is even less reliable at watching the boy. You are aware that Shaw takes Donal to the woods almost every afternoon?"

"Yes." Eden frowned. "I see no harm in it." She bolted from her seat. "I must find Donal before the marquess arrives."

"You needn't worry about anything but preparing yourself for Lord Rushborough's call," Claudia said. "Surely you don't require the boy until after the marquess departs."

"But I do, Aunt." Eden met her gaze. "I intend to tell Francis that Donal is my son."

Claudia hid her dismay. "Why, after all you have done to establish him as your cousin's child, and legitimate?"

Eden's face took on a peculiar, closed expression, and she spoke as if to herself. "Now is not the time for hesitation. I must see this through. And I must do it before . . . before Francis . . ." She trailed off, flushing. "This is how it must be."

Eden's stubbornness had grown to unmanageable proportions. She knew that Donal was Cornelius's son but did not recognize Shaw's true identity. If she knew of Donal's gifts, she had never admitted to it. Was displaying Donal to the marquess, and presenting him as her own son, a test of Rushborough's suitability as a father and husband? Or was this Shaw's work?

Subterfuge, not confrontation, was the only way to handle this situation. "I strongly advise you against it. . . . But if your heart is set, I shall find the boy. Go upstairs and dress."

"Thank you." Eden pressed Claudia's hand and bent to kiss her cheek. Claudia watched her run lightly into the hall and up the stairs.

When the coast was clear, Claudia went through the garden toward the stables. Much to her relief, Donal and Shaw had returned from the forest and were talking to old Dalziel by the carriage house.

Claudia's steps slowed. Now she must speak to Shaw face-to-face, hiding all the while what she knew of him. She drew on her hatred to see her through.

The three saw her approach and lined up in a row to confront her. Shaw folded his arms across his chest. Donal wedged himself between the men, peeping out between two sets of legs.

Dalziel doffed his cap. He still favored the arm he had injured in his accident with Atlas, but he was healing well, according to Mrs. Byrne. Perhaps he would be able to resume his duties once Shaw was gone.

Claudia drew up before them, holding her body very erect. "Donal, Lady Eden wishes you to come to the house."

"She is returned from the dale?" Shaw asked. He stared at her with challenge in his eyes, acknowledging her as an enemy — but not quite the enemy he supposed.

"Lady Eden is preparing to receive a guest," Claudia said, smiling just enough to make Shaw understand her meaning. She held out her hand. "Come, Donal."

He did so with reluctance. "Lady Eden wishes to see me," he told Shaw.

"I will see you tomorrow, then." Shaw smiled at the boy the same way he had in the forest. "You did well today."

Donal beamed. He dashed toward the house ahead of Claudia so that she had to hurry to catch up. She seized his hand just as he reached the door.

"You must learn to walk like a proper gentleman and not shame Lady Eden," Claudia said, striving to coax rather than scold. "Before you see her, you must wash off the stable dirt and change your clothing."

He looked down at his jacket and skeleton suit. "Very well, Lady Claudia."

How very much like a little adult he was. She brushed away another twinge of regret. "Mrs. Byrne will help you. Let us go to the nursery, and I will call her."

Temporarily domesticated, Donal permitted her to walk him to the nursery. She made a brief pretense of looking through his clothes, and then moved quickly to the door.

"I will come get you when Lady Eden is ready," she said. She closed and locked the door and waited for any sound within.

For inscrutable and doubtless inhuman reasons of his own, the boy did not cry out or pound on the door. His silence was not entirely reassuring. Claudia hurried down the stairs and to the servant's hall in search of Mrs. Byrne.

The housekeeper was in the storeroom, taking an inventory of kitchen supplies with Cook. Both women regarded Claudia's intrusion with the same wariness as had the men outside.

I shall see you discharged as well, if you do not learn your place, Claudia silently promised Byrne. "Mrs. Byrne, would you be so good as to go to the nursery? Donal is in need of a nap, and I do not wish him to disturb Lady Eden and her guest. Please keep him quiet upstairs for the next few hours."

Mrs. Byrne glanced at Cook. "Do you not wish me to finish preparing for Lord Rushborough's arrival? Lady Eden said —"

"No. I shall instruct the maids and Armstrong in what remains to be done. Please send them to the sitting room at once, and go directly to the nursery. Donal is waiting."

"As you wish, your ladyship." Mrs. Byrne gave a semblance of meekness, but it was not in her eyes or bearing. "Please excuse me." She stepped out of the storeroom.

Mrs. Beaton avoided Claudia's eyes and went back to work. *There* was one, at least, who presented no problem. Claudia gladly left the servants' domain and returned to her own. Now she must wait until the last possible minute and regretfully inform Eden that she had not been able to find Donal.

If all went according to Claudia's slowly forming plans, the marquess need never meet the monster's inhuman son.

Chapter 12

Eden barely made it down to the drawing room before Lord Rushborough's curricle pulled into the drive.

She smoothed her gown, pressing it to her figure as she gazed out the window. She had lost weight these past few weeks, and no wonder. Francis had known her in days of ease and plenty. What would he think of her now, with a trace of dreaded brown in her face and arms, and hair that wouldn't seem to stay in place? Their last meeting had not been auspicious, and she'd fled from him. She had apologies to make for her behavior at the party.

Did she want him to think well of her? Or did she want him to go away and leave her to . . .

Hartley rose in her mind as if he stood before her, grave and questioning. *Will it be him or me? Choose, Eden. Choose.*

She had not chosen. She had avoided Hartley as much as possible while her thoughts ran in circles. Every circle returned to the same beginning: Hartley Shaw.

What she'd said about Donal was not merely an excuse to postpone turning her life upside down yet again. Today's revelation to the marquess would help her make the deci-

sion that would alter her and Donal's life forever. It was a
great risk, and one she had but recently resolved to take.
But she had discovered that even she had honor that could
not be compromised. She could not live a lie with the man
she married.

The marquess descended from the curricle, attended by
his groom. Eden buried her fingers in her skirts.

"Eden! You will crush your gown." Claudia came to her
side and followed her gaze. "Do not worry, my dear; you
are lovely, as always."

"Am I?" Eden murmured. "Where is Donal?"

Her aunt hesitated. "I could not find him. But I have
asked Mrs. Byrne to send servants to search for him."

"It is my fault. I have neglected him too often these past
few days."

Claudia patted her arm. "Set such worries aside, Niece,
and compose yourself. The marquess is come."

Claudia took her seat and her needlework. Eden did the
same, though she dropped the pretense of pleased surprise
when the marquess entered the drawing room. Had this not
been planned days in advance? Did they both not know
why he was here?

She rose and curtsied. Francis bowed over her hand.
The three of them engaged in idle, meaningless conversation for the appropriate amount of time, and all the while
Eden listened for Donal's return. He would hardly make a
good impression if he appeared the untutored farmer's son,
but there was no helping that. Eden had made her decision.

After an interminable period, Claudia made some excuse to leave the room. Eden scarcely heard what she said.
The marquess had been staring at her for an hour, and she
probed and probed at her feelings as if they were a sore
tooth.

Yes, she was flattered. Yes, she still found him charming and handsome. But beyond that . . .

"I have awaited this day, Eden," Francis said, moving to
a chair much closer to her. "I had not realized how much I

missed your company all these months — not until this last parting."

"I am surprised that you wish for my company, considering my odious behavior toward you during the tenants' feast," she said gravely. "I must apologize —"

"No. It is I who owe you an apology for my boorishness."

Eden lowered her gaze. "We were both . . . a little distracted, perhaps." She looked up with a smile. "How have you been, truly? With the lack of diversions here in the country, you must be dying of boredom."

"Boredom is a small price to pay for seeing you again." He reached across the space between them and took her hand. "Ah, Eden. You know why I have come to the Lakes. It is not for the scenery, I assure you."

"I know." Eden made no attempt to embellish her speech with the usual wit and flattery. She hadn't the heart for it. "I wish our reunion could have been under more fortuitous circumstances."

He shook his head. "That does not matter. Eden, when you left me —"

"My husband was ill. He needed my care."

"Of course." He kissed her fingers. "You have such a generous heart."

How little you know me, Eden thought. She gently withdrew her hand from his. "Would you care for some tea?" She moved to serve from the tray, leaning away from him.

Francis straightened and accepted the tea, sipping it while regarding her over the rim of the cup. Silence hung heavy between them.

"I know your life has greatly changed," he said. "But I am in earnest, Eden. I would not have come here otherwise." He set down his cup. "It is not usually my way to act so hastily, but I find I have no choice. I wish to make you my wife."

It was said. Eden had expected it, but it still came as a mild shock. Her heart did not leap with joy nor her body warm with anticipation and relief.

Once again she saw Hartley, felt his kiss, heard his whispers in the darkness.

She rose abruptly. "Lord Rushborough — Francis — there is someone I wish you to meet before we discuss this further."

He got to his feet. "Indeed. By all means, if it will set your mind at rest, dear Eden."

She went to the door and glanced down the hall. Where was Donal? She felt a peculiar frisson of foreboding. A door slammed upstairs. Little feet came running down two flights, and Donal skidded to a stop just outside the door.

"Aunt Claudia forgot about me," he announced. "Mrs. Byrne let me out."

Let him out? Claudia forgot about him? Eden frowned. That made no sense at all, given her last conversation with her aunt. At least he had been washed up and dressed in his best clothing, appropriate to meeting callers.

"It doesn't matter," she said, combing his hair with her fingers. "You are here now, and I would like to introduce you to my friend, Lord Rushborough."

Donal tilted his head. "The man with the tight pantaloons and the tired horses?"

Eden stifled a laugh of chagrin. "Did you see him, Donal?"

His only answer was an evasive look. Eden sighed, took his hand, and led him into the drawing room.

Francis was waiting, his arm upon the mantelpiece. His first glance at Donal sharpened into a stare.

"Lord Rushborough," Eden said slowly, "I would like you to meet Donal . . . my son. Donal, this is the Marquess of Rushborough. Can you make your bow to the marquess?"

A little shiver ran through Donal, but he remained still. The marquess was obviously stunned by the announcement, but he had the good grace to conceal it. The seconds before he spoke were less dreadful than Eden had expected. Her ambiguous feelings made it all much easier to bear.

"Your son," Francis repeated. "Master Donal Winstowe?" His sentence held an upward lilt, half question.

God bless him, he was tacitly agreeing to accept any tale she chose to tell. She placed her hand on Donal's shoulder and drew him to her side.

"You must have many questions, Lord Rushborough. But I wanted you to meet Donal first. He is five years old, and only recently come from Ireland. He still has much to learn." She couldn't bring herself to apologize for him beyond the barest necessity.

Francis looked at her and then back at Donal. He took several steps forward. Donal shuffled back until his head bumped into Eden's middle.

"He is also rather shy with those he does not yet know," Eden added.

"Then perhaps we ought to let Master Donal return to his governess," Francis said. He smiled at Donal. "You should like that better than remaining here, shouldn't you?"

Explaining Donal's lack of a governess was not on Eden's immediate agenda. It was remarkable that Francis sensed and sympathized with the boy's unease . . . or recognized that they could not discuss Donal in his presence. She realized, with deeply mixed emotions, that Francis had already risen to the occasion very well indeed.

"You may go, Donal," she said, "but please find Mrs. Byrne and remain with her for the remainder of the afternoon. Will you do that for me?"

Donal nodded, cast a glance at the marquess, and bolted out the door.

"I am sorry —" Eden began, and stopped. No easing the way for herself with a show of embarrassment or false shame. She straightened and met Francis's gaze. "You may well ask why you have never met my son before, and why he is so wild. The explanation is simple. Until a few weeks ago, I did not know of his existence. And he is not Winstowe's child."

Once it was said, a peace settled over Eden. She resumed her seat and folded her hands in her lap, waiting for Francis's response.

In spite of his kindness, he did not spout comforting platitudes. He regarded her as if he were being forced to alter his perception of her, and not necessarily for the better.

"Of course you do not know what to say," Eden said to spare him the struggle. "You have known me in Society, and you know my reputation for having taken lovers. But of course that was after I was married, and such behavior became de rigueur." She sighed, when once she would have laughed. "Let me tell you a story. When I was very young, before I met Winstowe, I spent all my time between Seasons with my father at his various estates. It was during my eighteenth year that the earl summoned me to Hartsmere. That was the year that my cousin Cornelius Fleming stayed with us."

In terse, unadorned words she told Lord Rushborough how she had come to elope with her "cousin" and then learned something about him that made it impossible for her to wed him. Cornelius Fleming had fled, and she had gone home for her confinement, only to be told that her son had died at birth. She did not explain how she had learned of his existence, only that she had sought him out and brought him to live with her as soon as she became aware of it.

"So you see," she said. "I made a foolish mistake as a girl, but I did not realize the full consequences until I found Donal. Winstowe was aware that I had . . . committed an indiscretion. He nevertheless agreed to marry me." She swallowed. "Donal is my only child. I love him. I intend to give him the home he has been denied."

Francis stood and paced a tight circle about the room. "I confess that I never expected . . . never conceived of you as a mother," he said. The words carried a trace of strained humor, but Eden was not deceived. "It must have come as quite a shock to you, so soon after Spencer's passing."

Eden was relieved at Francis's bluntness. It spared her

so much. "Yes. A wonderful shock. I cannot regret him, Francis. I wished you to know this before . . . before we continued. There is another thing you must understand. I have made it known that Donal is the son of my late cousin, and that he had been living with my uncle in Ireland until Mr. Fleming became too ill to care for him. I intend to maintain that fiction, whatever I must do to keep it. I realize that you may not wish to be party to this . . . but I will be most grateful if you would keep this matter to yourself, whatever our future dealings." She let no emotion touch her face or voice. "Of course you will need time to consider what I have told you. And perhaps distance as well."

Now she gave him an easy escape back to London. Her heart beat fast, but she still could not decide what she wanted him to do, what would be best for Donal.

After a while, Francis went to the mantelpiece again and leaned on it heavily. "Forgive the question, but did Spencer — did your marriage suffer because —"

"It cannot have helped." She gave a small, crooked smile. "I cannot blame him. And though it is the way of the *ton,* I know I failed him as a wife in many ways." She closed her eyes. "If only . . ."

"This Cornelius Fleming. Did you ever see him again?"

The harshness of his voice revealed his true feelings. She faced them squarely. "No. And I doubt I ever shall. He is gone."

"The blackguard." Francis fisted his hand on the mantelpiece. "I will not ask you what you learned of him that made you break the elopement, but I cannot . . . I will not hold you to blame, Eden."

How could she have anticipated such acceptance? "You are generous, my lord," she said warmly.

He turned to face her. "Who told you that your son had died?"

Even now she could not bring herself to speak it aloud, but Francis would guess. "It is so long ago. The details no longer seem important — only the fact of Donal's presence in my life."

Francis resumed his seat, leaning forward. "You cannot have found this easy, Lady Eden. Your honesty is . . . laudable."

My very selective honesty, Eden thought. "There can be nothing but truth between us," she said. "That is why I confided in you. You have been a good friend, and I am grateful."

"Have been?" He gazed at her, unsmiling. "Is that your wish, Eden?"

How could she answer, when she didn't know her own mind or heart? "It is my wish, above all, to provide for my son and give him a loving home and the future he would have had if . . . if he had been Spencer's. Can you understand?"

"Yes." He rose. "It seems that there are depths within you I did not suspect. Perhaps even within myself."

And is that an answer, Francis? Have you, indeed, accepted so easily?

Eden got to her feet. "You are welcome to stay to dinner, but naturally I do not expect it."

He glanced toward the window. "You have granted me your confidence, Eden, and I will not treat it lightly. If you will forgive me, I shall spend a quiet evening at Caldwick."

"Of course."

With an air of distraction, he bowed and started for the door. At the threshold he paused.

"Whatever may happen, Eden," he said, "you will always have my friendship."

"Thank you. Thank you, Francis."

"Good night."

Armstrong gave him his hat, gloves, and cane, and Lord Rushborough left quickly. Eden went into the sitting room and stared out the window as he walked, head down, toward his waiting carriage.

The emotions she ought to feel were completely absent.

But that had been the case for some time now, and she was almost used to the condition. Numbness seemed the safest course.

But that luxury was to be denied her. Out of nowhere, Donal burst into view. He ran up to stand before Lord Rushborough and spoke words Eden could not hear.

The marquess laughed. She could see his shoulders move. And then Donal turned around to face the carriage horses. One of them began to shake its head from side to side. The other half reared in its harness. Francis's groom rushed to quiet them, but they danced away.

Donal pointed at the horses and spoke again. Francis turned his head just enough so that Eden could see his expression. It was far more appalled than it had been when Eden had made her confession.

The groom made several more attempts to catch the horses, and then Donal calmly walked up to them and caught the near horse's bridle. At once the animals were quiet. Donal smiled at the marquess.

Francis glanced back at the house. Eden ducked behind the curtains, but not too soon to observe that the marquess was upset. The groom took his place at the rear of the curricle, and Francis jumped into the driver's seat, urging the horses into an almost violent start. The curricle flew down the lane as if the devil himself pursued it.

Eden dashed out of the sitting room and into the hall. By the time she reached the porch, Donal had disappeared. Her first thought was that he had gone to Hartley.

Halfway to the stable she caught up with him. He heard her coming and turned, flinching as if he expected a blow.

Eden's heart dropped into her stomach. She sank to her knees on the path and opened her arms.

Donal rushed into them. She held him until her own heartbeat had slowed. Only then did she set him back so that she could see his face.

"Do you want to tell me what happened between you and the marquess?" she asked. "I promise that I will not be angry, but I would prefer that you tell me the truth."

Donal searched her face. It was a terrible thing to see such conflict in a child so young. Eden wanted to weep.

"I . . . I told the marquess that I could hear his horses talking," Donal said in a small voice. "He didn't believe me."

Oh, Lord. She smiled encouragement. "What did you think the horses were saying, Donal?"

"They told me that he makes them go too fast on the roads, because it's too bumpy and hard here, not like where they come from." A flicker of mischievous spirit danced in his eyes. "I had to show him that I could talk to the horses, so I asked them to dance for me."

Eden remembered the rearing and head-tossing. "You . . . wouldn't let the groom catch them."

He shook his head. "The first horse wanted to run away. Then the second horse told the first one that he shouldn't think bad things about their master, but the first horse said that the man wasn't so much better than they were. The marquess chases fillies all the time, and sometimes he takes off his boots and stockings and picks between his toes, like he has thrush. Then I told the marquess what they said."

Eden was speechless. For a moment she didn't even question that the horses had, in fact, said what Donal claimed.

That was madness. But she had witnessed it all with her own eyes. Evidently Francis had believed it. How else to explain his look of horror and his hasty escape?

"What did the marquess say to you then, Donal?"

"Nothing. He was afraid. He just ran away."

Eden drew him close again. "Why did you do all this? Is it because you don't like the marquess?"

His body stiffened. "He doesn't like Hartley. Hartley said . . ."

"What did Hartley say?"

But Donal shut his mouth and would not answer. She didn't compel him. Altogether, the implications of what he had said were more than enough to worry her. She had been through this before. Either he was a master, at five years old, of entirely credible lies, or he was capable of something no child should be.

No *human* child.

"It will soon be time for dinner," she said with as much authority as she could muster. "Go to your room, and please remain there until Mrs. Byrne brings up your meal. Will you do as I ask this time?"

With a look of relief, Donal nodded.

She cupped his cheek in her hand. "We will talk more of this later, but I think both of us have had enough excitement for one day. Off with you."

He ran a few steps, paused, and looked back over his shoulder. A pair of turtledoves circled down out of the sky. One made a perfect landing on Donal's thatch of brown hair and balanced with a flap of its pale wings. Its mate settled at Eden's feet and bobbed a bow.

Eden looked from the bird to Donal. "Did you . . ." The question lodged in her throat. Donal gently removed his dove from its perch and cradled it between his hands. He held its darting head close to his.

"I promise," he said, and cast the bird skyward. Eden's dove followed, its wings nearly brushing her face.

Donal smiled at Eden and continued for the house as if nothing had happened.

With the feeling of walking on quicksand, literally and metaphorically, Eden made her way back into the house and to her room. She sat down at her dressing table and stared into the mirror.

She wasn't sure she recognized the face she saw. The younger Eden had witnessed the incredible and fled from it, refusing to accept its reality. That girl no longer existed. And yet only a few months ago, at the stables with Hartley, she had dismissed Donal's supernatural claims as childish fancies.

Could the woman she'd become face the possibility that the incredible might be a permanent part of her life . . . and of Donal's?

And what of the marquess and those like him? She had seen Francis's reaction to her son. If Donal could speak to horses and call birds from the sky, would his choice be to hide such gifts, or hide himself?

Can you ask your son to be what he is not? Are you not already doing so?

Unable to compass the enormity of such prospects, Eden's mind sought less oppressive worries. It struck her as odd that Claudia had not come to demand the reason for Francis's early departure. Donal's puzzling comment came back to her: "*Aunt Claudia forgot about me. Mrs. Byrne let me out.*"

Claudia had made clear that she thought Donal should not be introduced to the marquess until some indefinite time in the future, presumably when he had committed himself to marrying Eden. Had Claudia deliberately tried to prevent the meeting?

Is it possible that we have grown so far apart, dear Aunt? If Mrs. Byrne had let Donal out of the nursery, then she could provide answers.

Mrs. Byrne wasn't in her sitting room, but Hester directed Eden to the stables. Eden knew that the housekeeper and Hartley were friendly, but an inexplicable conviction came over her that far more was going on at Hartsmere than she comprehended.

Mrs. Byrne sat on a three-legged stool in the tack room, and Hartley leaned against a stall with his arms folded across his chest. He was looking toward the door when Eden entered.

The housekeeper stood and acknowledged Eden with an air of wary expectation, as if she anticipated the questions to come.

"Mrs. Byrne, I wish to speak to you." Eden looked toward Hartley, meaning only to steal a quick glance. But he trapped her with his eyes, and they were full of the same promises and questions they had held at the party.

Her mouth went dry. "Mrs. Byrne —"

The housekeeper followed her outside the stable. The

very openness of the yard made it as discreet a place as any for Eden's questions.

"Is it true," she asked, "that Donal was locked in the nursery?"

"Aye, your ladyship." Mrs. Byrne pressed her lips together. "'Twas Lady Claudia who asked me to watch over him there."

"And was this shortly before Lord Rushborough's arrival?"

"Aye. But the lad insisted that he was to see you, and . . . pray forgive me, your ladyship, but I thought I should let him go to you."

Eden clenched her fingers. "You did quite as you ought, Mrs. Byrne."

The older woman nodded once. Eden suspected that she harbored the same suspicions.

"Donal should be in his room, Mrs. Byrne. I have told him that you will take his dinner up and perhaps read to him afterward, if it will not keep you too long from your other duties."

"Of course, Lady Eden. 'Tis no trouble at all." The housekeeper set off without delay, leaving Eden alone in the stable yard.

Alone but for the man inside the stable doors. And she knew he was the one she truly wanted to see, to be with, to steal what solace she dared from the one man who saw her as she truly was. Whom she now believed loved her son almost as much as she did.

He stood just within the doorway, his face half hidden in shadow. He said nothing but took her hand and drew her into the room. It smelled of straw, clean leather, and horses. And Hartley.

"I have waited," he said.

"I know." She slipped free and took the stool Mrs. Byrne had left. Its uncertain balance seemed safer than the support of her own legs. "I have come . . . about Donal."

If he was disappointed, he didn't show it. "You met with your marquess today."

She suspected his statement was not a simple change of subject. "Yes. And I asked him to meet Donal."

Hartley cocked his head. In the next building, a horse whinnied. "And did your marquess find your cousin's son to his liking?"

"I told him the truth."

His surprise was almost gratifying. "You told him that Donal is your son?"

She met his gaze. "He was far more understanding than I had a right to expect."

"But?"

"Remember when you first came — you and Donal played a game about hearing the horses speak. I asked you not to encourage Donal in such fancies." She gave a brief laugh. "I did not really expect you to obey my instructions, but it has all become . . . I am beginning to believe . . ." The words trickled to a stop. How could she admit that she had allowed herself to consider that Donal might not be an ordinary child?

"That he is different," Hartley said, completing her sentence. "That he has special gifts."

She looked at him sharply, searching for the slightest hint of mockery or disbelief. He had never appeared more sincere than he did now. What had seemed ridiculous took on the weight of incontrovertible truth.

"You believe it as well?" she whispered.

"Yes."

"How can you be so sure . . . that it is real?"

"I, too, have seen the evidence." He stood over her, strong and immovable as an ancient oak. "You know it is true, Eden."

She shook her head, more in confusion than denial. "He . . . speaks to horses."

"To all beasts of wood, field, and pasture." Hartley smiled with a fondness that stopped Eden's heart. "He listens to them, and they speak."

The absurdity of the conversation gave this moment the air of a dream. "If you knew, why didn't you tell me?"

"But I did, and so did Donal. You did not wish to hear."

Nor did she wish to hear it now. The implications were staggering. If Francis had fled because Donal had actually done what he claimed, then the marquess also believed. And if he knew, so might others.

Others who would wonder, and question, and fear. Just as she had feared when she saw a man sprout antlers and work magic at an inn on the Scottish border.

"Has he . . . displayed these abilities to other people?" she asked.

"Not to any who can do him harm. Yet."

The air in the room turned icy. "Harm him?"

He leaned opposite her on a harness stand and captured her gaze. "Think how the boy's rare gifts at the track could alter the outcome of a race. Draw birds from the skies right to the waiting guns. Summon sheep from another man's pasture. Send a dog to attack an enemy. Even your city teems with animals who can listen and obey."

Indeed. Cats, stray dogs, mice. Rats. Terrible pictures formed in Eden's mind. She had thought of suspicion and misunderstanding from other children and adults, but not how Donal might be a tool to feed the desire for profit or power.

She did not know such people. But what if Spencer had lived and learned of this? He had loved the racetrack, and he was always in desperate need of money. Could Donal, as Hartley suggested, make some horses win and others lose?

Surely not. Not my son.

Did Donal even understand what he could do, and how he might use such abilities? Or was he only beginning to experiment, as children had done since the dawn of time?

Had her son deliberately set out to drive the marquess away?

"Do not make the mistake of thinking that Donal's gifts can remain secret," Hartley said. "Not even if you hide him at Hartsmere until he is old enough to understand why he must keep them to himself. And he must, Eden." He reached for her hand, hesitated, let his own fall. "He must learn to control what he can do, so that no one may ever use him. The world is a cruel place, Eden. It holds no mercy for those who are different."

Eden stared at him. "How do you know all this?"

"I have seen it before."

Seen what? A child who could speak to animals? Or similar, eldritch powers that did not belong among mortal men — that might only be granted to the children of those not . . . human?

"Where?" she whispered.

"You have trusted me with Donal, Eden. Trust me now. I have been watching, doing what I can to guide him."

"Your visits to the woods," she said. "Was that what you were doing — guiding him?"

"In every way I can." He leaned forward again, and she was reminded of Francis only an hour before, who had taken just such a pose as he proposed marriage. "I swear to you, Eden. I will let no harm come to him. He will not suffer because of who or what he is."

Her throat tightened. She nearly forgot that Hartley could make no such promises about Donal. If anyone was to protect her son, it would be a man like the marquess, who had wealth and power enough to shelter him from the world's harshness.

But the marquess had seen Donal's gift at work. If he never returned, the choice of marrying Francis for Donal's sake would be taken from her.

She rose and walked to the door. "I will speak to Donal, and explain to him that he must not talk to animals around other people, or make them do things that will attract attention. He is old enough to understand." She glanced defiantly at Hartley. "People will believe that he is a child, with a child's imagination."

"And when he is older? Will you deny him what is within himself — his rightful heritage?"

Her muscles locked in place. "What heritage?"

"You tell me, Eden. Who was his father?"

Chapter 13

To her credit, Eden did not falter. She met Hartley's gaze with that surprising fortitude he had come to admire and respect, and her eyes were clear. It was for Donal that she feared, not herself.

He fought the urge to pull her into his arms. The time was not right.

But soon. Very soon.

"I have entrusted only one other with what I am about to tell you now," she said. "But I can trust you, can I not?"

"Always, where Donal is concerned."

"Very well." She squared her shoulders. "Donal's father was my cousin, who came to live with us when I was still a girl. We planned to be married. We were not." Her eyes dared him to judge her. "I paid for my mistake, but it gave me Donal. I wish the world to accept him as my uncle's grandson. I wish him to have all the advantages of a legitimate birth."

He listened for regret in her voice, the wistful sorrow of love lost, but she spoke as if relating a household inventory. Even now, knowing what Donal was, she refused to admit that the boy's father might not be human.

"And the marquess can provide that," he said harshly. "The very same man who fled when he witnessed Donal's gifts?"

She took a step back. "How did you know? I did not speak of what happened, only that —" Her eyes narrowed. "You wished the marquess gone, did you not? You poisoned Donal against him."

"I did not need to. Donal is wise enough to recognize an enemy."

"Enemy?" She gave a breathless, strained laugh. "No, not Donal's — yours. Because he can provide for my son what you, a servant, cannot."

"Can he, Eden?" Hartley closed the space between them and grasped her arms gently but implacably. "Can he be a father to a boy who is not of his get or his nature?" He felt her pulse beating high and fast beneath her skin, the rising scent of mingled fear and arousal. His own body leaped in response. "Can he awaken you with sweet summer kisses and bring you flowers in midwinter? Can he make you feel as I do?" He gathered her nearer, increment by increment, timed to the precise moment that her resistance ended. "I make you feel, Eden, as no one has ever done."

"You . . . make me . . ." She closed her eyes and shuddered. "You make me want you. That is all."

"You do not want the marquess," he said, stroking the tension from her back with long, sensual sweeps. "How can you consider making him your mate when you do not know what you will be giving up?"

"You speak . . . as if we were animals."

"Ask your son if that is such a terrible thing." He drew her to the doorway and turned her to face the forest. "The world beyond your walls of stone and metal is his. He can be a part of it as few can hope to be." He pulled her against his chest and nuzzled the back of her neck. "Do you know what it is like to be a part of nature, Eden — to live as one with the ebb and flow of the seasons, to understand the soaring thoughts of the birds and fly with them, to feel the tiny spark of the seed as it waits in the earth for the coming of the sun?"

"No. I do not." She didn't struggle to free herself, but she wasn't yet at ease in his arms. Or with anything he said. "I have always . . . always hated coming to the country."

"And do you still?"

She turned slowly. Her eyes were so soft, so unguarded, that he lost all desire to do anything but drown himself in them.

"No," she murmured. "I do not hate it anymore."

Ah, Eden. I stopped hating you the moment I saw you again. He bent his head. Her breathing stilled. The kiss he gave her was almost spiritual, like a benediction. The next, when it came, would not be.

"Let me show you," he said, "how to begin to love it." He took her hand and led her through the door, across the stable yard, and beyond to the gate in the stone fence that marked the boundary of the home pasture. He started up the fellside, but Eden's grasp was an anchor that pulled him back.

She stood staring up at the forest. He remembered that look from the old days when, as Cornelius Fleming, he had tried without success to interest her in his world. Then, her thoughts had been focused entirely on returning to London after their wedding and teaching him the ways of the *ton*.

Yet in spite of her rejection of it, Nature was kind to her; the slanting late afternoon sunlight penetrated the sheer fabric of her dress, outlining her graceful legs as if she were some half naked wood nymph of the south, and the breeze caressed her face, stirring tendrils of hair and tinting her cheeks with rose.

He could see her as one of his own people in the time before so many had left — running with abandon through the wood, laughing, free of the human rules that forbade her to follow her deepest desires. If only he had time to teach her. . . .

Why was it so important that she understand the things

he loved and had devoted his life to protecting? For Donal's sake, yes — so that when he took his son to Tir-na-nog, she would know it was for the best. And he held the slim hope that she would become the land's guardian for the remainder of her mortal life, watching over the birds and beasts and untouched wood as she did her tenants.

But there was more to it than that. He need not take so much trouble to seduce her; she was nearly his, vulnerable in her confusion, prepared to throw caution to the winds. The marquess had helped, not hindered, his plans. A few more kisses would send her tumbling into his bed.

Seduction of her body was no longer enough. He did not know when his intentions had changed; he wanted to seduce her mind and heart as well, make her his in every way, even though he knew the cruelty in it if he succeeded.

When Fane wanted, they wanted with everything in their beings and would stop at nothing to obtain it. He was no different, whatever name he gave himself. Fane power was that of enchantment and the primal rhythms of the world; mortal power was the ability to fascinate the Fane into recklessness and, yes, even savagery.

The savagery to make a woman love, get her with child, and then abandon her, even though he no longer hated her or sought revenge. He did not have the excuse of such motives.

His soul was Fane: self-contempt was foreign to his nature. He had told himself that leaving Eden with a new child to replace Donal was a mercy and a kindness.

But in his time with Eden, he had begun to feel with increasingly human emotions. He had begun to hate himself even as he smiled at Eden and prepared to complete his seduction.

"What do you fear, Eden?" he asked. "There are no longer any wolves or bears or dragons in England."

"I . . . I do not know." She attempted a smile. "It is very foolish of me."

He cradled her chin in his hand. "You are safe with me."

But not from *me.* "No harm will ever come to you in the wood, or on this land."

"You speak as if you owned Hartsmere, though it has been in my family for generations. Why am I not surprised?"

"Because you have begun to know me, Eden." He took her hand again. "Come."

As if to compensate for her former hesitation, Eden let go of his hand and marched up the fell ahead of him. He caught up in time to help her over the escarpment that separated pasture from wilder ground. Then they were at the edge of the wood.

"Must we?" she asked.

He reached out with his thoughts and called to the birds: pipit and redstart, blackbird and goldfinch, wagtail and warbler, commanding songs to soothe a mortal's fears. From near and far, meadow and forest, mere and fell, the wild music rose in a chorus as magical as it was chaotic.

Eden looked up into the trees. Bursts of bright color flashed among the leaves as birds hopped from branch to branch.

"So many!" she exclaimed. "Where did they come from?"

"This is their home. They are welcoming you to it."

"How generous of them," she said with a laugh. "Do you hear them speak as Donal does?"

The birds fell silent. Her question hung between them, unanswered. Eden stared at him, the beginning of comprehension in her eyes.

"Is that it?" she whispered. "You spoke to the birds. You understand Donal because you . . . can do what he does." She shook her head. "Of course. The horses — the way you handled Atlas and Copper. You and my son are alike!"

If he denied it, she might never trust him again, but if he told her too much, she would guess the truth before he was ready.

"I am like him," he admitted. "We share some of the same gifts."

She released a long breath and gazed at the ground beneath her feet. "It explains so much. Why Donal liked you instantly, and why you have . . . cared for him." She looked up. "That is why you wish to protect him."

"And why I know what he will face in the world of men."

"There is no other world."

"Look around you, Eden. This is not man's realm."

"And you would have him live in the woods like a red Indian?"

"I wish him be happy, as you do."

"By denying him his birthright?"

"His birthright as a bastard and misfit?"

Cold fury blazed in her face. "Never speak so of my son."

"Eden." He enfolded her fist in his hands. "If you will not see the wonders of Donal's world, you cannot help him. Let me show you."

She searched his eyes. The muscles in her face and body relaxed. A bird sang tentatively, followed by another, and a third.

"Very well," she said, offering her hand. "Show me."

He led her into the forest, and all the discomfort he felt in man's world dropped away like a stag's antlers in spring. He paused, as always, to touch each of the Old Ones, the trees that had stood undisturbed for so many mortal years.

He brought Eden to one of the greatest, a massive wych elm who stood near enough the edge of the wood to look down over the lesser trees upon the dale below.

"This is one of the queens of the forest," he said, stroking the bark with affection. "She has seen many things men cannot dream of."

"Do you speak to trees as well?"

Though she made a jest of the question, Hartley saw the wariness in her eyes. He took her hand and laid it, palm down, upon the lady's trunk.

"She speaks to you, Eden. The life of the earth is in her veins, just as it is in yours if you will but listen for it."

She closed her eyes, and the childlike tilt of her head, her willingness to try in spite of her fear and disbelief, sent a bolt through him that was more than esteem or desire or obsession or any of the things he had felt in her presence. Her very spirit seemed to pour into the Lady Elm and flow into his body, purified and vitally precious, like sap rising in spring. So it would be, a thousand times more potent, when he joined with her.

Eden's face lit with amazement. "I think . . . I think I hear her," she said. She ran her hands over the trunk, reaching, until her fingers nearly touched his. She pressed her cheek to the bark with a sigh.

That was when she felt what he had. Her eyes snapped open, and she bolted away from the lady as if she had been stung. She rubbed her hands on her skirt, over and over again, until she noticed him watching. She tossed her head and smiled defiantly.

"Have you any other talking trees to show me," she asked, "or perhaps a shrub that quotes Byron?"

"Perhaps," he said. "Come and find out." He took her hand to lead her away, and the bond the tree had forged between them sparked anew. But Eden did not try to break free. She gazed at him, her lips slightly parted, while a dove alighted in the branches over her head and cooed its approval.

He could have taken her there, under the nurturing arms of the lady. But there was a better place, where his magic was strongest and that of men — of Eden — held little sway.

He led her deeper into the wood. In a small clearing lay a badger's sett, a mound of earth around a tunnel entrance. The sleepy sow climbed out to greet him, followed by her four bickering cubs. Eden knelt behind a yellow-flowered gorse and watched with obvious delight as the clumsy youngsters tumbled fearlessly over each other and their parent.

A few yards away, in a thicket of hawthorn, a vixen and her cubs played with the same careless joy. The vixen paused in her game and sat on her haunches, barking once at Eden as if to convey a secret message. Then she and her offspring vanished into the undergrowth with a final salute of their white tipped brushes.

"I do not think I shall ask you what she said," Eden remarked.

"She greeted you as a fellow female and warned you to keep a wary eye on your male, for they are not to be trusted."

"She is a most percipient creature indeed." But the look she cast him was anything but guarded. Already the things he had revealed to her had opened her heart and loosened the bonds of her world's expectations.

"Even the hedgehog finds his mate when the time is right," he said as the snuffling, bristly little male poked his head from his nest of leaves in the undergrowth. "It is fortunate that he seeks a hedgehog wife, for only another like him would find him handsome."

Eden laughed, and Hartley took unexpected pleasure in her amusement. "I think he is adorable," she said. "I would love to take him home to Donal."

"You would destroy him."

Her eyes widened at his harsh tone. *Fool. Do not frighten her away now.*

"Eden," he said gently, "I show you all this so that you will know why it must be protected and saved from men who would enter and kill, or cut down the trees that shelter so much life. So few of these places remain. They are as rare as Donal, and he is a part of this forest, as much as he is a part of you."

She wrapped her arms around herself and shivered. "Why does this forest mean so much to you?" she asked. "Did you lie to me when you said that you were not from this parish?"

"I have known of this wood for many years."

"And you wish to make sure that I protect it . . . from—"

"Men such as your father."

Her head lifted. "Did you know Lord Bradwell?"

"I have heard of him." He was uncomfortably aware that a look of suspicion had come into her eyes. She moved a step away.

"Were you in the dale five or six years ago?"

She wouldn't have asked that question if she had not begun to make certain connections in her mind and heart: connections between Cornelius, a certain incident at a border inn, and Hartley Shaw. She had not acknowledged them . . . yet. But he must tread carefully.

"Yes," he said. "I passed this way, and that was how I came to find this forest and to recognize its rarity. It is a treasure, Eden. Your treasure, if you will accept it."

"It is not yours to give, is it?" she whispered.

"But you have the means to protect it. Will you, Eden? No matter what happens between us?"

She turned her back to him. "I shall never allow any creature at Hartsmere to be harmed in any way. Not even so much as a mouse."

"Do you promise that, Eden?"

"Do you think, because you can speak to birds and animals, that no one else is capable of kindness toward them?"

"I think that men are often blind."

"Are you not curing my blindness?"

Your blindness will end only when I reveal myself. "The gift of seeing clearly brings a price."

"There is always a price, isn't there?" She looked back at him. "If you were here five years ago . . . is that how you deduced that I am Donal's mother? You knew of my—" She shook her head. "I should be grateful that you are far more astute than most who live here."

He moved to her side and took her hand. "I told you that your secret is safe with me. Believe it, Eden."

She sighed and nodded. Once more he led her closer to

the heart of his realm. He found the nuthatch's nest in a tree hollow, occupied by four gape-mouthed fledglings.

"How lovely they are," Eden said softly.

"The nuthatch has one mate in his life," he said. "He will never leave her for another. Can men say as much?"

She glanced away. "It is not always possible. Birds do not have the obligations of people."

"And their lives are so short. Every moment is precious. Yet they live each one without regret."

"Is that how you think we should live? Without regret?"

"Yes. For as long a time as we have."

Something unspoken passed between them, just as it had done at the Lady Elm. Hartley held out his hand, offering and asking for much more than a touch.

The entire forest fell silent. It waited, as he did, for her decision. Even the sun seemed to pause in its journey, poised on the peak of the highest western fell and casting the world in a red gold glow.

Slowly, never taking her gaze from his, she gave him her hand. The desire he had felt constantly in her presence broke free of its restraints. He could not stop it from spilling over.

Her eyes widened. "Oh," she murmured.

He pulled her close and kissed her. His need was too potent to be satisfied by a single kiss, but it was all he dared take.

It was not enough for Eden. As he withdrew, she wrapped her arms around his shoulders and kissed him in return.

The Fane race were expert in the ways of pleasure, if not of love, and they practiced it often in their own land. Hartley had been different, spending years alone in his wood, returning less and less to Tir-na-nog. But the sensual talents bestowed by his Fane birth were present in abundance.

As they were in Eden, human though she was. All her reluctance was gone. Her kiss was fire in the cool of the evening; she seduced him with lips as sweet as the mead of

Tir-na-nog. Soon he would drive all recollection of other lovers from Eden's heart and body. He would love her so well that she would carry the memory of this night forever.

With a great effort he set her back, though it was like severing a part of himself. "I know a place," he said, "where we will not be disturbed."

"Donal —"

"Is in good hands. Forget that other world, Eden, and give yourself to mine."

To me.

Eden trembled at the open desire in his eye. She didn't know when she had made the final decision; in the dimmest reaches of her mind, she knew she must have made it long ago.

Oh, she had had doubts, the most troubling within the past several hours. Some of the things Hartley had said reminded her in some inexplicable way of Cornelius. His attachment to the forest, his contempt for civilization, even his ability to captivate her. He did not look like Cornelius, but there was something . . . something that seemed to connect them. And he had the same abilities as her son. Abilities he had inherited from . . .

She gave herself a mental shake. As if the movement had awakened her brain, she caught a glimpse of an answer.

What if Hartley were like Donal in every way? What if he, too, had a parent who was not quite human? It would explain so well his devotion to her son. His complete understanding of Donal's situation. And his own extraordinary talents.

She could not bring herself to be horrified by the possibility. Her love for Donal had made her tolerant of what she would have rejected five years ago. This man had nothing in common with the creature she had nearly married. He, too, might be a victim.

Eden thought she had never seen Hartley clearly before this moment. The insolent servant was gone; in his place was a man stronger than any she had known, a wise initi-

ate to the secrets of life that had eluded her for five long
years. Many had offered so much more than this man
could hope to give, or would promise, even to win her
love.

He made no promises at all, and she did not care.

The forest cast a spell over her, urging her to become
like the animals Hartley and Donal loved: heedless, driven
by ancient instincts, sparing no thought for a future that
might never come. The tenuous barriers she had built to
contain her desire had turned to gossamer and air.

"Yes," she said, though she was not sure whether she
spoke aloud, or only in her heart. "I want you, Hartley
Shaw."

He kissed her hand lingeringly and then turned to lead
her away. She followed, her feet stumbling in haste, to
what must be the very center of the wood.

To paradise.

In a tiny clearing surrounded by the oldest trees lay a
carpet of wildflowers of every hue, many unknown in the
north: orchid, iris, bellflower, campion, foxglove, betony,
pimpernel, primrose, violet, and cranesbill. They were as
richly bright as if the sun shone directly upon them, though
night had begun to fall; they seemed to glow with their
own light. Their mingled perfumes were heady enough to
intoxicate.

Each tree surrounding the glade was the most perfect of
its kind, whether elm or oak or birch. Leaves of vivid green
lent cool peace to the hidden world they shaded, and the
branches seemed to bend and rustle in welcome.

At the foot of the most magnificent oak Eden had ever
seen was a nest of soft leaves and blossoms, laid out as if
it had been prepared for the marriage bed of a new bride.
A tiny beck traced a path of liquid silver alongside. Birdsong drifted overhead.

"I have never brought another to this place," Hartley
said. "I never will again."

She could well understand his reasons for keeping it a
secret, and she felt honored that he had chosen her to see

it. This was his gift to her: a bridal gift for one who could never be his wife. A hard lump formed in her throat, and she looked up into his face.

In the reflected glory of the wildflowers, his features lost their harsh angles and became unearthly, beautiful as few men were beautiful. His groom's apparel was as incongruous on him as a plow harness on a fine thoroughbred. He met her gaze, and though he did not smile, she thought that she might forget to draw another breath as long as she lived.

That was when she understood. It was not merely the magic of this paradise that made her see him thus. It was not simple desire that made her so ready to risk what she'd once held dear to lie in this man's arms.

It was love.

She swayed as the revelation swept over her. She burned when he caught her in his arms and held her close. Above all, she laughed inside at the irony of loving one for whom so much must be sacrificed to keep that love alive.

A love she did not even know if he shared.

"Eden?" he asked. "Are you well?"

How gentle was his voice. She shook her head and smiled and touched his cheek.

"Oh, yes," she said. "I am well." She gave a little gasp as he lifted her into his arms and carried her to the bower of leaves and blossoms. He laid her down upon the petals. The way he looked at her, with such a potent combination of lust and tenderness, left her limbs heavy and her mouth dry with anticipation.

In a few moments, she would know what it was to be loved by a man any one of her class would consider far beneath her — perhaps one not entirely human. He would be bold and strong and possess her without subtlety, and that was what she wanted: to feel him moving inside her as if he could pierce the last barriers that lay between them.

This was her choice. Letting go was more than surrender to this man she wanted so desperately; it was a release of her past, of the empty excitement she'd sought in London to quiet her aching, barren heart.

Her heart was barren no longer, but it ached — oh, how it ached, with a pain even a lifetime might not erase.

Once she had experienced the perfect joining of lust and love — innocent lust awakened by a man she had tried to forget. This very day she had faced the possibility of marriage with a respectable man who loved her.

But the marquess was not here. He could not exist in the same breath, in the same world as Hartley Shaw. If he courted her for another century, he could not awaken this need. Or this love.

All she would think of now was the need.

Hartley seemed to know when words were unnecessary and unwelcome. The haze of her bemusement gave way to something hotter and more urgent as he stood over her and swept her body with his scorching gaze.

She lifted her arms to draw him down, but he was already beside her. "Eden," he said, making her feel the paradise of her name. He pulled the pins from her hair and spread it out in a fan about her head. She reveled in the wanton freedom of it.

Then he kissed her. Not as before, lightly, but with force enough to match her inner fire. All gentleness was gone, replaced by hungers as primitive as they were overpowering. His mouth told her how much he desired her, but not in words.

She parted her lips. His tongue stroked over hers. Her body pulsed with a shock of pleasure, as if he had already stripped her naked and possessed her completely.

She might as well have been naked. His hands began to play over her, molding her gown to her body, seeking flesh beneath stays and chemise. Her bodice was fashionably low cut, and he wasted no time in sampling what lay bared to his caresses. He kissed the pulse points of her neck and under her jaw, allowing his tongue to linger at the hollow of her throat.

Each caress was expert, finding nerves in her body that

she had forgotten existed. No, this was no servant's skill. She set that thought aside, for he was working his way down the swell of her breasts with exquisite deliberation.

She wore only the least confining of stays, but the idea of taking the time to remove it was agony. Her nipples were already hard, aching for the touch of his mouth. She entertained the barbarous image of Hartley using his strong hands to tear gown and stays and chemise away like so much tissue, and felt no horror at her own licentious imaginings.

But he did not rend or tear. He gazed at her as if will alone could dispose of her clothing. Her stays suddenly loosened. A deep breath would send her breasts spilling free and into his eager hands.

He wasted no time waiting for her assistance. He bent over her and used his tongue to tease her nipples over the top of the stays. The sensation was erotic beyond anything in Eden's meager experience. She gasped and arched up, urging him to take more of her into his mouth.

He obliged. His hands cradled her breast and his lips closed on her nipple while his tongue swirled around it as if it were a favorite sweetmeat.

Eden pushed her fingers into the bed of leaves, clutching handfuls in an agony of pleasure. Hartley left no part of her breasts unexplored, but always he came back to her throbbing nipples, licking, kissing, suckling.

"Hartley," she whispered, "if you do not . . . stop . . ."

He lifted his head and met her heavy lidded gaze. "Do you wish me to stop, Eden?" He kissed the underside of her breast. "Do you?"

She closed her eyes, overwhelmed by her inundated senses. "No. No. Please do not stop. Hurry."

"After waiting so long?" He lifted one of her hands and kissed her fingers. "Did none of your other lovers pleasure you this way, Eden?"

Only one. She opened her eyes and forced herself to focus on his face and the words she must speak. "No." She shivered as he sucked on her little finger. "I . . . have had only three. Donal's father, my late husband . . . and you."

He went very still and stared down at her, expressionless. "But your reputation —"

"You have heard of that as well? My reputation was earned with innuendo, gossip, and mistaken assumptions that I chose to encourage. Even my aunt believed the rumors of my wanton voraciousness."

"Why?"

"I found it amusing to deceive the *ton*."

"Why no other lovers?"

"Because . . . because . . ." Her tongue was thick and inarticulate when her body spoke so loudly, begging for release. "Spencer . . . lay with me only once. He ignored me after. And then —"

"And then?" He slowly turned her hand to lick the center of her palm.

"I waited."

"For what, Eden?" He drew his tongue the length of her arm and kissed the inside of her elbow. "For whom?"

"For . . . for —" *No. If you tell him, it will become more than you can afford. It will become real . . .*

"Was it for me, Eden? Did you wait for me?"

Yes. But I did not know. She shook her head, and the perfume of the blossoms wreathed her face. "I did not know you."

"You know me now." He kissed each of her breasts in turn, lightly, and put his hand on her knee through the muslin of her gown. His touch threatened to scorch the cloth from her body.

"I . . . know you. Please, Hartley —"

"How many years without a man's touch?" He slid his hand up her leg, drawing her skirts with it. "Is that why you came to my bed, Eden?"

"No. I could have had —"

"Any man you please. The marquess." Her skirts were around her thighs, barely covering her drawers. "But

Rushborough is like Spencer — only half alive." He parted her thighs and knelt between them.

"Show me," she whispered. "Show me, Hartley, what I have been missing."

He showed her. She felt the cool air between her thighs, and then a jolt of sheer pleasure as he touched her intimately, stroking his fingers over her wetness. He unerringly found the one part of her that held the center of all sensation, and teased it with his fingertips.

A moan escaped her. Then even that required too much effort, for his finger slipped inside her while his thumb continued its caresses.

Tension began to build in her, pulsing outward from the place he touched. His finger moved in and out, testing, preparing her for what was to come.

And she was ready. She pushed up against him, begging him silently to give her all of himself. But he was not finished. His hand withdrew, and she felt his hot breath before his mouth and tongue replaced his fingers.

This had not happened before, even with Cornelius. She couldn't manage so much as a gasp. With long strokes and tiny flicks of his tongue, Hartley tasted every part of her. It was impossible to tell where she ended and he began. All the world was hot and wet and filled with rapture.

The forewarning of ecstasy she'd experienced before, when he touched her breasts, returned tenfold. She wanted it to come, desperately, and yet she wanted this feeling to last forever. For she knew, at the core of her being, that there wouldn't be another after Hartley Shaw.

Blindly she reached down for him and laced her fingers in his hair. He looked up, licking the moisture from his lips.

"Now," she said, holding his gaze with all the discipline she had left. "Now, Hartley."

"Is that a command, your ladyship?" he asked softly.

She hated him, then, as much as she loved him. "Do you want me, Hartley Shaw?"

His answer was everything she could have wished.

With a haste that betrayed his ardor, he stripped off his shirt and unbuttoned his trousers. She was granted her first full look at his maleness and knew there must be very few like him. Certainly Spencer had not even come close.

But her body would take that magnificent instrument, every inch of it, with gladness. She gazed at his sleek, strong muscles, the power of arms that she had seen before and the thighs that she had not. His stomach was flat and ridged, without an ounce of fat. The coarseness of a laborer was nowhere to be seen, nor a single scar or imperfection of flesh, form, or bearing.

She reached for him, and he came down over her. He kissed her, and below she felt his hard length stroke her inner thigh in search of admittance.

"I have waited for this, Eden," he said. "Look into my eyes. I want to see yours when I take you."

His brazenness only excited her more. She clutched his shoulders and lifted her hips. His first thrust was true, deep, and potent, but she felt only a slight discomfort that was gone in an instant. Then came the withdrawal, and a second thrust, and the steady rhythm that began the ascent to paradise. She wrapped her legs around his waist to draw him deeper still.

And he looked into her eyes. If he blinked, she did not see it. The deep green of the forest, of growing things, swallowed up the black of his pupils. Pleasure, satisfaction — she could only guess what lay behind them.

She knew what her own eyes might all too easily reveal. She drew her emotions inward, hoping he wouldn't see.

He cupped her buttocks and watched her face as he drove his full length into her. She let her head fall back, panting in time to each thrust. She was nearly there, nearly at the top of the mountain. He need only guide her the last few steps.

One. Two. Three. For the second time in her life, she felt what it was to burst free of her body and soar skyward without wings, higher than any bird that came to Hartley's call.

She was not alone at the summit. Hartley shuddered, his hips moving faster and faster, and then his weight settled on her, damp and heavy. He remained there for a span of minutes, breathing deeply, while she put her arms about him and nuzzled his damp skin. His muscles clenched, and with a groan he lifted himself on his arms and rolled off.

So suddenly it was over. Eden lay very still while the pulsing of her body quieted and the rapture faded. Gradually she remembered that her breasts were bare and her skirts around her waist. She tugged her clothing into some semblance of modesty and turned her head toward Hartley.

He lay on his back with his arm flung over his eyes. He looked cold, bereft, when all either of them should feel was joy and completion.

"Hartley?"

He said nothing for a long, long time. Her happiness shriveled, sinking into the pit of her stomach like sour wine. Why would he not even look at her? Was he ashamed? Had she proven so great a disappointment to him?

Or was he disgusted that he'd had his way so easily with his employer, and now had no further use for her?

That thought was too painful to bear. Eden sat up, trying without success to fasten her stays and gown. Suddenly Hartley was beside her again, and her clothing fell into place at his lightest touch. He was, she thought bitterly, very adept with women's garments.

"Thank you," she said. She tried to stand, but Hartley caught her arm and helped her up, like any true gentleman who had his way with a woman.

"I will take you back to the house," he said. That was all. His voice was flat and uninflected. He would not meet her eyes.

Why, Hartley? What have I done? But such questions would rob what little composure she had left, and she refused to so humble herself. All her knowledge of men — men of the *ton,* every one — could not help her now.

She still had her rank and her dignity. Squaring her

shoulders, she marched in the direction she thought they had come. Hartley caught up and moved a little ahead of her, taking great care not to touch her again.

What had she been thinking about her aching heart? Now she knew that it could break into many pieces and still keep her body alive. Yet cursing herself for a fool was futile. If it happened all over again, she knew she would do the same.

Even if Hartley Shaw never knew that she loved him.

Chapter 14

The plan upon which he had built his hopes was a failure.

Hartley ached with the need to touch Eden, to reassure her with soft words, erase the stiffness of her expression and carriage with caresses she could not resist.

He did not touch her. He could not even speak. The loathing he felt for himself in that moment muted him as surely as any spell.

He had seduced Eden for a purpose: to give her a child of her own and sever the ties that bound him to her and to her world. Once he was free, his Fane heart would return to its normal condition and cast off the guilt that tormented him at the thought of taking Donal from his mother.

But his heart had not changed. Or it had, but not in the way he had wished. He felt as if Eden had taken a more binding possession of his soul even as he found release deep within her body. And he knew that she was not with child.

It seemed impossible that he had failed in so simple a task. Had he lost the ease of his old powers? Yet the foliage grew lush at his command, and the animals were fertile.

Where was his mistake? Had her very body rejected his seed, as she had rejected him six years ago?

That knowledge was bitter indeed. Doubly so because he felt her pain and refused to ease it with the words mortals required at times such as this.

Words he could not speak. His only relief lay in the fact that she had declared herself incapable of love for a man. That was one loss he'd not inflict upon her.

They walked in painful silence back to the house.

Eden left him at the door and didn't look back. His immediate thought was to find Donal, but he knew that would be Eden's desire as well. He turned, instead, for the stables and set about grooming the horses, seeking some measure of peace in the repetitive motion and the easy company of the animals. He worked until the horses gleamed like satin, yet he found no serenity.

The night was well advanced when the fox slipped in the stable door and curled about Hartley's feet. The horses snorted and sidled, but only for a few moments. Tod was no threat to them.

Indeed, Tod was far more distressed than the horses. He quickly changed from fox to man and bounded up to the top of the stall partition. He grimaced and rolled his eyes, pulling at his hair as if he would tear it out by the roots.

"No more," he said. "No more, my lord. Can't stay by the mortal and keep her away, not now."

Hartley dropped his brush. He had almost forgotten that he had set Tod to create minor mischief in the dale to keep Eden occupied and away from Donal while he taught his son how to use his Fane gifts. He suspected now that Eden would not have objected. He had caused her much vexation.

Tod looked pleadingly at Hartley through his long red lashes. "Release Tod from his duty, Mighty One, Tod begs."

"What is wrong, Tod?"

"She weeps." He bared his teeth and covered his eyes. "Weeps and weeps in her cold chamber, so soft no mortal ear could hear. But Tod hears. Mortal weeping makes Fane mad. Can't go back!"

Hartley leaned against Atlas's flank and closed his eyes. Eden's tears might disturb Tod, but it was Hartley they were likely to drive mad. She wept because of him.

Why? She had admitted her desire, and that desire had been fulfilled. Was not honesty what she wanted? But the thought of her pain plunged into Hartley's gut like a deadly knife of Cold Iron. His Fane senses betrayed him, seeking the mother of his son and carrying back to his ears the low, broken sounds of her sorrow.

He could not bear it.

"I release you from your task," he told Tod in a whisper.

Tod leaped from the stable wall and hopped from the back of one horse to another, feet never touching the ground until he had reached the door. Atlas snorted and slued his head about to gaze at Hartley.

Every other equine head followed suit. Large brown eyes watched him, waiting for his decision.

There was none to make. Hartley cloaked himself in a glamor of invisibility and strode from the stables to the house. He entered the servants' door and took the most direct route to Eden's room.

The door was closed. All was silent within. He had never been inside Eden's chambers. They were not for the likes of Hartley Shaw, not even when she took him for her lover. No one would see him enter now. Her honor was safe.

He was the one in danger.

The door opened at a pass of his hand. His Fane eyes pierced the darkness, found her huddled upon the bed like a child being punished for some wrong she did not understand.

"Eden," he said.

Only the tiniest movement betrayed that she had heard him.

"Eden, look at me."

She obeyed, but surely not to please him. Her face was

puffy and streaked, her eyes red and filled with defiance. "Go away."

He remained where he was. She felt across the counterpane until her fingers connected with a pillow. He could see her debating whether or not to use it as a weapon, and the crack in his heart extended. What weapons did they truly have against each other?

"Leave, at once," she whispered hoarsely. "Unless it is your intention to . . . ruin my life completely?"

"I will not, and it is not. No one has seen me." He advanced farther into the room. Eden recoiled — not afraid of him, but of herself, and the desire they shared. In the confines of her chambers, it was almost smothering.

Hartley understood such fear. His heart raced like that of a stag pressed to extremity by ravenous hounds. He was beyond what mortals called common sense. But he knew what must be done. They both were torn, he and Eden — torn between necessity and desire, repulsion and obsession. Neither of them would be free until each had his or her fill of the other: Eden free of shame and temptation, Hartley free of guilt and mortal obligation. He had the power to give Eden pleasure beyond mortal imagining . . . and there was still a child to be made.

It was time to strike a new bargain.

"Eden," he said, "I have come to make a proposal."

She laughed under her breath. "Could it be that you intend blackmail, now that you have had your way with me?" She sat up, ineffectually smoothing her crumpled gown. "Perhaps you believe that I have some hidden wealth to pay you off. After all, you know I would do anything to protect my son."

Her suggestion astounded him. When had he ever done aught to make her attribute such motives to him?

"Oh," she said with feigned contrition. "Do I offend your honor, Hartley? I do apologize."

He laughed at himself, at her folly and his. His intended treachery was of a much more permanent nature.

He went to her bed and knelt beside it, humbling himself. "You are wrong, Eden." He released a long breath. "It is not my way to beg pardon, but I ask yours now if I did anything to put such thoughts in your mind. If I have behaved wrongly, I . . . am sorry."

She drew the crumpled bedcover up to her shoulders, her face expressionless. "Behaved wrongly? By stealing my virtue, which was gone long ago? I can hardly claim to be an innocent victim, can I?"

Her mockery cut, but not at him. She turned her bewilderment into rage against herself, like a beast tearing at its own limbs to escape man's trap.

Such confusion, such bitterness, such passion accompanied one human emotion above all others. But she had said she could not love again. He had no cause to doubt her. They had lain together, pleasured each other . . . that was all.

Or was it? Did he misjudge her now, as he had six years past? Was it possible . . . that she loved him?

Loved him as she had claimed to love him before, when she'd believed she had nothing to lose and the world at her feet?

Old bitterness gave his words a harshness he had not intended. "I do not apologize for taking you," he said, "but I was . . . cold to you. I caused you pain you did not deserve."

Eden inched back on the bed until she was encased in a fortress of pillows heaped against the headboard. "How kind of you to say so. May I assume by this affectionate declaration that you do not intend . . . do not intend to —" Her words were lost in a low sob. "You will not . . . take advantage of . . ."

He reached across the bed for the only part of her he could touch. Her bare foot was icy cold. He thought of warmth, and felt her flesh come back to life under his hand.

"You know me so little," he said thickly. "Have I been so heartless, Eden? Have I ever treated you so ill?"

She was fighting tears with all her strength, determined

not to let him see her vulnerability. He stroked her foot from toe to ankle, soothing with no intent of seduction.

"We wanted each other," he said, "and we gave each other pleasure, did we not? But I . . . it has been very long since I have been affected by a woman as I have been by you."

He said it for her sake, and then he realized that it was true. Even more true than it had been when she was an innocent, and he so certain of his Fane superiority.

The frozen rigidity of her face gave way at last. A tear slid down her cheek. He caught the crystalline drop on a fingertip.

"Don't," she protested, averting her head. "When you are gentle like this, I —"

"Believe me? Believe that I wish no harm to you, Eden." He caught her chin and turned her to face him again. He closed his eyes and forced out another truth. "I . . . care for you."

She trembled. "Do not attempt to be kind —"

"I have not often been called kind. What kindness I possess you have awakened. But I do not make promises that I cannot keep."

She looked at him, clear-eyed and suddenly done with weeping. "You never did make promises, did you? Nor did I. As I can make none now."

"No."

She remained burrowed among her pillows like a hedgehog halfway coaxed from its nest. "All of this . . . seems somehow beyond our control."

"Then why struggle, Eden?" He took her small, cold hands and kissed her fingertips. "You behave as if you have earned punishment, when it is pleasure you deserve. That I can promise you. I did please you?"

Her breathing quickened. "Yes."

"And you, Eden . . . you pleased me very much. Why can we not continue to please each other?"

She withdrew her hand from his. "But for how long? A week? A month?"

Her voice was completely calm, her words measured and rational and unweighted by emotion. Surely he had been right to believe her that night in the park, when she had told him that love was impossible. She did not love him. Already she accepted that there could be no future for them, though her reasons came of ignorance. She didn't question why he did not offer marriage. She would have been appalled if he had.

Appalled no matter what guise he wore.

But a proposal was the last thing she need fear from him. "You speak of time as if it were solid and unchanging," he said. "A day can seem a week, and a month a year."

"Why?" she asked. "What do those days and weeks bring to you? This was not simply a challenge for you, a conquest, to prove yourself my equal. It was not for power or money or ambition." She counted all the motives she must have ascribed to him in the past few hours, rejecting each one in turn, and yet her eyes continued to search his. "What do you want, Hartley Shaw?"

He leaned close, brushing her lips with his. "What you want, Eden. No promises, no demands. Only this."

There, in her widow's bed, he kissed her, and began to make her believe that a minute could last an hour. He kissed her again, and tried to make himself believe that he might, against all evidence to the contrary, sate himself with her body as she did with his, get her with child, and leave her content — yes, even content to surrender her son. He salved his guilt by thinking only of what he would give her, not what he would take away. He shrugged off his absurd and all-too-human urge to seize her and make her confess that she loved him. And he called what he felt for her obsession, lust, admiration, affection.

Even Fane could lie . . . to themselves most of all.

Summer began with a riot of growth and color that the villagers and dalesmen hadn't seen for many years.

Young women continued to apply for positions at
Hartsmere; young men returned to the dale, including the
errant Mr. Singleton. Sturdy Berwick lambs gamboled on
green hillsides, vegetable gardens thrived free of vermin,
and the weather was a perfect balance of rain for the crops
and sunshine for the soul.

For Eden, it was an idyll such as she had not imagined
could exist in her life. She had taken Hartley as her lover,
casting off all doubts and regrets. Her heart blossomed like
the land; new energy coursed through her body, and she
could walk miles without fatigue, alert to every joy the
countryside had to offer. It was as if she had been blind,
deaf, and incapable of all understanding before this miraculous season.

Incapable of loving as she loved Hartley Shaw.

She had made peace with her emotions. Not once did
she demand that Hartley reveal what he felt for her, beyond
what he had done that day in her bedchamber. She did not
want to know.

If he loved her, then giving him up when the time came
would be that much more difficult.

For he never attempted to suggest that they ought to
marry. She loved him all the more for his perception, that
his pride did not extend to an ambition to wed so far above
his station, and thus endanger her hopes for Donal.

It shamed her now to think that once she'd considered
him capable of such scheming. She had come to realize
that his coldness after their first time had been his way of
dealing with the unexpected: the powerful magic they
made together in the act of love. If he had ever possessed
ulterior motives in pursuing her, they had not survived that
night.

But so much else had. So much more had altered forever.

They sought the magic together, night after night, stealing what moments they could. Sometimes, when it seemed
safe, he came to her bed; at others, he took her back to his

forest bower or introduced her to some new sanctuary where they could not be discovered.

During the day, no one seemed to suspect. Hartley became a model servant, showing her more deference than he ever had when she'd regarded him as such. Donal continued to worship him, and though Eden knew that her son, like she, would suffer Hartley's inevitable loss, the things he could teach outweighed all other considerations. Hartley understood him. Hartley loved him. No declaration was required.

And whenever she wondered at his true origins, she laughed off her misgivings.

Aunt Claudia continued to speak of marriage and the marquess. Lord Rushborough had returned to London for the Season, but Claudia dropped hints that he planned to return in early autumn. His letters, addressed to Eden, continued to arrive — brief and irregular, but proof that he had not been discouraged by Eden's confession or Donal's display.

Eden was glad that she had not lost his friendship. His acceptance was tacit agreement that he would support the story she chose to tell about Donal's background, and that he would not betray her confidence. He was even vital to Donal's future, for he could be an influential sponsor. But any thought she had held of nurturing his affection, or his proposal, had died when she gave herself to Hartley Shaw. She could neither delude the marquess nor discard her lover.

Autumn seemed very far away. It might never come at all. The days moved with glacial slowness, just as Hartley had promised. Each hour gave up every joy it could hold.

The natural world she'd once disdained revealed its secrets one by one. She and Donal would meet Hartley near the wood, and the three of them dined by the beck among trees that shielded them from Hartsmere's view. The birds and animals came to Donal, and soon they came to her as well, unafraid.

The only remaining mysteries lay in Hartley's eyes.

Eden refused to pursue them. What the two of them had shared was like some treasure in a fairy tale, apt to vanish if examined for flaws. When he showed her a hidden wild-flower, or loved her under the stars, that precious magic created a timeless world of its own.

And if sometimes she caught him gazing at her with an unspoken pain, his brows creased in a frown, she pretended not to see.

The familiar rhythms of dale life continued with no regard for her petty concerns. Care of the flourishing flocks and fields kept the people of Hartsmere busy, and they revealed their contentment with much laughter and song. Such good fortune had come to the dale that Eden had little to do in supervising the needs of her people. Instead, she found many excuses to hold celebrations at Hartsmere, and farmers who had once regarded her with suspicion now openly displayed a fondness that compounded her happiness. Eden and Hartley were considered good luck, and almost every farmer found an excuse to summon them both for any project dependent upon good fortune.

As if blessed by the same fertility, daleswomen began to show certain signs beneath their aprons; Mr. Appleyard was pleased to note, with some diffidence, that most of the expectant mothers were married. A little persuasion brought to bear by the lady of the manor would surely un-cover rightful husbands for the rest. Eden was happy to do her part and encouraged reluctant suitors by promising a generous contribution to a dowry or a wedding gift.

The farmers and their families who attended the simple weddings would never have guessed at Eden's inner turmoil. She had told herself many times that one disastrous near marriage, and another ending in bitterness, had extinguished any romantic notions she had about such unions. But she watched the brides and grooms at the altar, and she envied them, nevertheless.

Claudia certainly did not let her forget the prospect of a most admirable future union. She showed no sign of being aware of Eden's liaison with Hartley. Her dislike of Hartley was pointed, but she had no grounds to complain of his public behavior.

Instead, she threw all her efforts into promoting the marquess and joining Eden on visits to nearby landowners, squires, and gentry. Eden had proceeded well into her half mourning, and lacked an excuse to remain a recluse among those of her own rank. Still, she was reluctant to return to the world she had known, so distant and unreal.

Society could be spared the knowledge that she was living the happiest time of her life without the company of a single one of its members.

The dale's fine weather and ideal conditions were so extraordinary that the time of sheep-shearing came early, and Mr. Appleyard suggested a competition among the clippers, both native and hired, to celebrate the harvest of thick wool that the rich pasturage had produced.

Eden was glad to oblige. She met with several of the dale's prominent farmers to discuss the details, and the competition was set to be held at Mr. Topping's great stone byre on St. John's Eve. Two days before the event, Aunt Claudia was unexpectedly called to London to visit an ailing friend. She did not bother to pretend that she would regret missing the sheep-shearing contest.

Eden was relieved. Claudia never attended such events in any case, and she remained critical of her niece's active participation in the affairs of the dalesmen, as if the farmers' dirt might somehow rub off on her.

On the day of the shearing, Donal woke Eden before dawn with excited, almost indecipherable chatter about the coming contest. His sleepy nursemaid — Jane Singleton, Mrs. Singleton's eldest — apologized, but Eden only laughed.

"Never fear," she said, scooping Donal up and setting him beside her on the bed. "I am used to rising early. It is you, Jane, who look most in need of sleep!"

Jane smiled sheepishly. "No, my lady. With Papa home, and the new baby born, and Mama so happy . . ." Her eyes lit. "Samuel Topping is to be in the contest, my lady. May I go?"

"Is Samuel your sweetheart, Jane?"

The girl blushed. "Aye."

"Well, then, I shall not deny you the pleasure of watching him win. Donal will come with me today."

"Oh, yes!" Donal said. "But Samuel will not win."

"It is hardly polite to say so, Donal," Eden chided gently. "Have your breakfast, Jane, and I will bring Donal down myself."

"Thank you, my lady!" Jane curtsied and made a swift exit, doubtless to primp for Samuel Topping.

"Mother," Donal said, tugging at her dressing gown, "We are not supposed to lie, are we?"

Eden whispered a prayer for her own many falsehoods. "We must strive always to tell the truth."

"Well, then, I was telling the truth when I said Samuel will not win. Hartley shall."

As always, when anyone spoke his name, Eden experienced a peculiar fluttering in her stomach that spread throughout her body, leaving her both languid and invigorated. And very much aroused.

She was not surprised that Hartley planned to enter the contest. How could she blame Donal for assuming that he would win? If anyone knew what a sheep was thinking, Donal did. And so would Hartley. The beasts would very likely find a way to shed their wool and lay it at his feet.

"You may be right," she said, lifting Donal to the floor as she got up to dress, "but it is more gentlemanly to pretend that you are not quite so sure." She gave him the sternest glance of which she was capable. "You must not tell the sheep what to do, Donal. It would not be fair."

He grinned. It was so wonderful to see him grin, which he did more and more often now that Ireland was but a memory. Now that he had a real mother . . .

And almost a father.

"I promise," Donal said.

The mischief in his eyes gave another message, but she

chose to take him at his word. She rang for her own maid, Nancy, who had proved adequate, if not yet polished in her duties. "Let us fetch one of your toys, and you may play here while I dress. After that we shall go down to breakfast together, and then . . ." She tickled him lightly under the chin until he giggled. "Then off to the contest!"

Donal hardly fidgeted at all while Nancy saw to Eden's bath, fastened her dress, and fixed her hair, and he was most cooperative when Eden helped him put on his clothes. After breakfast, he consented to walk out with her like a little man rather than rushing ahead to greet Hartley.

Hartley waited for them by the dog cart, which she still used for visits to the village, even though Claudia had insisted upon the purchase of a modest but more fashionable equipage. The landau was one of several luxuries that they could afford because of the dale's new prosperity, which permitted the payment of delinquent rents, added new tenants to fill the vacancies, and lessened need among the farmers.

But the dog cart would always hold a special place in Eden's heart. Dalziel had responsibility for the landau, but Hartley continued to drive the cart because it enabled them to be together.

As Hartley looked up from Copper's harness, she had to stop just to catch her breath. It was part of the magic that she still felt so, still anticipated his smallest touch after so many weeks.

He smiled. She forgot how to walk.

Donal tugged on her hand. "Mother, we shall be late!"

Eden took herself in hand and walked at a steady pace until she reached the cart. Donal held up his arms, and Hartley swung him about to deposit him in the rear seat. His gaze met Eden's with a conspiratorial glimmer.

"Is your ladyship ready?"

"Always." She offered her hand. He took it, squeezing lightly, and helped her up.

He held the ribbons only as a pretense while Copper pulled them down the lane at a brisk, cheerful pace. Wildflowers lining the way — eyebright, buttercup, and globe-flower — swayed and nodded in the warm summer breeze, and the smell of ripening hay was everywhere. Soon it would be cut and heaped in great mounds in the fields to be dried. A bee set aside its diligent quest for nectar and buzzed lazily about Donal's head as if confiding its secrets.

Near the village, children searched among the goose-berry bushes for early ripened fruit, eating as much as they gathered. They stopped to wave at the cart as it passed. Farmers and laborers, with families or without, made their ways singly and in groups to Mr. Topping's byre, eager for the match.

Hartley exchanged more than one secret glance with Eden, and every so often he would point out a rare flower to her and Donal, or make a teasing remark that sent the boy into sudden laughter. That was something that had changed in him; he had learned to laugh, even jest, with genuine pleasure.

"Tell me another story about the Faerie Folk," Donal said.

Eden realized that he was speaking to Hartley. Unease blossomed in her chest.

"What stories are these?" she asked.

"Hartley tells me about the Faeries, who used to live all over England," Donal offered helpfully. "Only they don't call themselves Faeries."

"Indeed?" She glanced at Hartley. "It sounds . . . most entertaining."

Was it her imagination, or did he seem to share her discomfiture?

He shrugged. "They are merely stories I have gathered in my travels," he said, gazing at the road ahead. "This country is rife with them."

"Like the one Kirkby told us — about the Faerie king who dived in the forest and cursed the dale?"

"No." His jaw flexed under tanned skin. "Not like that."

"Tir-na-nog is the place the Faeries go when they leave

here," Donal piped in. "It's never cold there, and the trees are always green."

"Are all the Faeries there now, Donal?" she asked with a tense smile. "You have never seen one, have you?"

"No," he answered seriously. "Even when there were lots of them, they were hard to see. Some of them were very small. Some of them were as big as we are, so they could pretend to be real people. They were the ones who left first."

Pretend to be like real people. Eden's mind lost its way in a memory, in an image of Cornelius and the antlered man-beast he had become. Once more she thought of her notion that Hartley was somehow related. Who better to tell these tales than one of the Fair Folk himself?

"Why?" she whispered. "Why did they leave?"

"Because of the cold iron and all the mortals who cut down the woods." Donal sighed, the sound as precociously adult as his words. "And because people didn't want them anymore."

She looked at Hartley. "Did you ever hear of one of these Faeries who . . . looked like a man, but had antlers growing from his forehead?"

"I see such creatures every day. Don't you?" He laughed. "You refer to the old legends of horned gods. Those tales are also common here, and all throughout Britain. The priests took the old gods and shaped them into your devil. But they were never evil, only different."

Different. "Are any of them . . . still here?"

"Oh, yes," Donal said. "Sometimes boys and girls had a Faerie mother and a mortal father. Most of them went away, but some stayed."

Though the sun was warm, Eden gathered her shawl more snugly about her shoulders. "What of . . . mortal mothers and Faerie fathers?"

"Yes. *They* could do magic, too. They must be sad to stay here and hide instead of going to Tir-na-nog."

God help me. "Hide . . . their magic?"

He nodded somberly, then brightened. "But sometimes you can go there if you know the way."

"And do you know the way?" she asked, staring at Hartley.

He glanced at her with a wry smile. "Every night the Faeries come to me and whisper their secrets. But I have no desire to leave you, lovely Lady Eden." He slapped the ribbons lightly on Copper's back and turned down the rutted path to the Toppings' farm. And Eden, knowing the topic was closed, worked to fix a smile on her face and play lady bountiful to the people who expected her to reign graciously over the competition and the feast afterward.

In such a pragmatic undertaking as a sheep-shearing, Faeries had no place. The farmers placed her and Donal on chairs beneath a crude arch woven with flowers just at the entrance to the byre, beside the other officiator, Mr. Appleyard. The curate greeted them with a bow and a smile, while Hartley slipped away to join the contestants. Eden recited the little speech she had prepared, and then Mr. Appleyard read a blessing over the sheep and the parishioners.

That was the last peace and quiet for some time. Soon the byre was filled with the bleating of sheep, the snipping of shears, and the laughter and shouts of the dalesmen, urging on their favorites. The air grew thick with the scent of sweat and wool. Shorn sheep were let loose into a pen, where bewildered lambs cried for their denuded mothers.

Great tankards of beer, brought in from the alehouse in the neighboring dale, were consumed by thirsty contestants and observers alike. Eden had arranged for quantities of food to be delivered in time for the feast. As always, it gave her great satisfaction to see the people taking such pleasure in her small gifts.

But her greatest joy lay in watching Hartley. Her chill feelings of foreboding could not survive the melee in the byre, or Hartley's warm glances. As Donal had predicted,

he soon outmatched even the most experienced clippers as
if he had been born to it. Hardly a sheep offered so much
as a token struggle.

Yet, when the hours-long contest neared its end, Hartley leaned back and slowed to a crawl, yawning as he
worked. Others caught up with him and finally surpassed
him. In the end, it was a young man — Jane's young
man — who took the coveted first prize of six shillings
and a new pair of shears. Jane shrieked and ran to embrace
him, which no one minded at all given the general merriment and chaos.

After that, everyone settled in for the feast. They
spread blankets on the meadow and laid out the food with
much animated conversation. While Donal went to see the
shorn sheep, Eden took her place at the top of the head
table, as hostess, seated with the winner and a few other
leading dalesmen. Hartley sat two seats away. They did
not look at each other too often. Gossip need not be encouraged.

The talk was casual and idle, mainly of sheep and the
haying. Eden excused herself after an interval and threaded
her way among the blankets to visit the people she had
come to know. The reunited Singletons sat close together
with their children about them. Mr. Singleton bolted up
and offered Eden a jerky bow.

Mrs. Singleton joined him, her babe in her arms. "Your
ladyship," she said, "we cannot thank you enough for all
you have done. Now that John is bailiff again . . ."

It was not the first time Eden had met the wandering
husband and father, though she had left his reemployment
to Mr. Rumbold. Singleton flushed, with good reason.

Yet Eden glanced at Mrs. Singleton's face, saw the joy
in it, and knew his return was far better than his absence.
Throughout the world, women needed their men to prosper
and be happy.

Yes, even she.

"You are content with your work?" she asked Mr. Singleton.

"Aye, my lady. As my wife says . . . we're grateful. I don't know how we can make up for it."

"I ask only that you take good care of your family, and come to me or Mr. Rumbold if there is trouble of any kind." She smiled at Mrs. Singleton. "Your children are well? Adam appears to thrive."

Hearing the beginning of woman's chatter, John retreated, and the children tumbled after him. Eden relaxed.

"That he is, your ladyship," Mrs. Singleton said, beaming at the little boy. "It meant the world to us that you were there for Adam's christening."

Eden could never become used to such open gratitude from the proud, self-sufficient dalesmen. "I am glad that you have found happiness, Mrs. Singleton."

"As you have." The woman's words were so soft that Eden barely heard them.

"I beg your pardon?"

Mrs. Singleton smiled, an expression any other woman would recognize. "Hartley Shaw is a fine man. It was a kind thing he did for Samuel, letting him win. No one in the dale believes he was born to a farmer's life. That is why people are glad."

She spoke with great forwardness, but Eden heard sincere support and friendship. Mrs. Singleton as much as said that the dalesmen of Hartsmere approved of the "secret" affair, when they might have despised her for taking a lover who compromised her class and thus her standing as their lady.

They sensed, as she did, that Hartley was no ordinary countryman.

"Thank you," Eden said, deciding to be equally frank. "What you say gladdens my heart. But others beyond the dale may not feel as you do."

"No one beyond the dale will ever find out." Mrs. Singleton smiled again knowingly. "We gossip, right enough, but we also keep our secrets." She performed an incongruously formal curtsy. "Be happy, my lady. That is all we ask."

It was all anyone could ask. Whatever fairy tales might be told in the dale, whatever the nature of the man she loved, Eden intended to make her happiness last as long as possible.

Chapter 15

In the elder days, the night of Lammas had marked the beginning of one of the year's great celebrations, the time of the harvest. The festival honored Lugh, last leader of the Tuatha de Danaan, adopted as a god by many of the peoples of these islands. They had called the festival Lughnasadh.

Old days, almost forgotten. But Hartley remembered the one they had called Lugh, a great Fane lord who had fled when men of the cross came to Albion and Eire. He, like Hartley, had never sought mortal worship; with it came responsibilities that no Fane savored. Most were glad to abandon it and return to the homeland.

But traditions lingered. All day, working in the gardens and stable, Hartley had smelled the Lammas bread Mrs. Byrne baked in the kitchen. He had also seen her making a corn doll, constructed of braided straw, in the privacy of her sitting room. In times not so long past, she might have been burned as a witch for such practices.

As *he* might have been, had others seen his true nature. But centuries ago he had ceased revealing himself to mortals, except on rare occasions.

Now he waited for the one mortal who wielded power over him as none ever had. Here, at the edge of the wood, where crickets sang and darkness came early, his thoughts were filled with Eden and the long, sweet night that lay ahead.

For the past month there had been many such nights, each one only increasing his hunger for Eden. Claudia had been absent from Hartsmere longer than anticipated, and with her absence came a freedom that made Eden ever more daring. She had become a wanton in truth. She hardly bothered to hide her feelings from the servants; twice he had slept in her bedchamber until dawn.

At last he, incongruously enough, had been the one to caution her. His warning came none too soon. Claudia had returned yesterday, and the way she smiled at Hartley in the garden made him understand why mortals referred to cold-running blood. Though Eden insisted that her aunt was unaware of her physical relationship with him, he could not dismiss the elder woman as that much a fool.

He had lived too long among the beasts not to sense danger. But she was still mortal, and limited in her powers. He set Tod to watching Claudia and put her from his mind. Tonight she kept Eden late at the house, but nothing short of disaster would prevent Eden from coming to him.

Their trysts were for a greater purpose than physical pleasure. Hartley had still not gotten Eden with child. It was the one darkness in the world of light they created together, and his failure continued to trouble him. It was almost as if his own fertility was the price for the dale's.

Tonight, in the spirit of the ancient rites, he had prepared the wood to welcome Eden as if she were a goddess and he was about to take her in ritual marriage. The birds would sing late this eve; their song would join that of the beck and the wind in a symphony sweeter than any mortal man could devise. The path to his bower was lined with summer wildflowers, chosen for their beauty and scent. And he had gathered berries and fruit as ripe and delicious as any found in Tir-na-nog.

If he could go to that happy land and bring back a thousand treasures for her, he would do so. But once he passed through that gate, he would not return.

A rush of wind warned him that Tod was near. He materialized close to Hartley's perch in the fork of a birch and sat cross-legged on a young branch that would have snapped under a mortal's weight.

"She comes," he said with a grin. "The lady comes, like Titania to Oberon."

"Tonight I am as powerful as Oberon," Hartley said. He leaped down from the tree. "And you are as swift as Puck himself."

Tod laughed. "Swifter by far. The sour-faced mortal had to be convinced to seek her bed."

Hartley did not ask how Tod had convinced Claudia to retire. Eden had come, and all else was unimportant. "Go back and watch," he commanded.

Eden floated into Hartley's view dressed as the sylvan nymph he had imagined her, clad in an insubstantial, nearly transparent gown that hinted at her body without completely revealing it. The silky fabric slipped between her thighs, caressing her with every step. She wore no undergarments. Claudia could not have seen that gown without understanding Eden's reason for donning it.

With hungry impatience, Hartley strode to meet her. He lifted her high in his arms and kissed her urgently. She opened her mouth to accept him with a soft groan. Her nipples were firm nubs against his chest, begging to be suckled. The scent of her body grew rich with arousal.

He had wanted her to see what he had prepared, but all his intentions fell by the wayside. Her mortal steps were too slow for him now. He swept her up and carried her through the woods, over hidden paths that revealed themselves only to him. Her breath came swift and shallow with the same desire that raged in his blood. When they reached the bower, he forced himself to set her down gently and allow her to keep the gown in one piece.

But her hands were already at work on his shirt before

her feet touched the ground. He tugged it off over his head. Her cool hands rested on his chest, and then her hot mouth kissed and caressed where her hands had been.

He bent back and allowed himself a moment of surrender. Eden had learned the arts of love with remarkable speed, enough to more than match her reputation among her own kind. And all of her skill and enthusiasm was for him.

She nipped the skin of his shoulder, and he grinned fiercely at the challenge. There were still some things at which she could not best him. Tonight he was not the gentle lover, one who might find a place in the Fane queen's elegant court. Tonight he was like the stag whose form he could assume, intent upon only one conclusion.

With consummate care he pinned her arms to her sides and nipped her ear in return. Then he soothed the mock bite with his tongue. When she was pliable in his arms, he rained kisses from her neck to the barely contained swell of her breasts.

After months of loving, she still gasped when he caressed her. Her nipples were firm and dark beneath the diaphanous bodice. They grew darker as he covered her breast with his mouth and wet the fabric until it was almost invisible. He lifted her higher against him and suckled. Her hair came loose and draped like a veil over his head. She wrapped her legs around his waist, and he knew he could wait no longer.

He freed himself from his trousers and pushed her skirts about her hips. With a thought he transformed the bark of the nearest oak from rough to smooth, a soft resting place for Eden's skin. He carried her to it and held her there, hands cupping her round bottom, while he made ready to enter.

Eden gave a faint cry of shocked pleasure as he thrust deep and true. Hartley had never taken her like this, but tonight his need was almost reckless, wild, and if she had any notion to resist, she would have been helpless against him.

But she had no wish to resist. She reveled in his fierce possession, in the excitement of being held so effortlessly while he took her.

He thrust again, pinning her to the tree that was smooth as a cushion. She locked her legs about his waist and dropped her head back, lost in erotic sensation. The whole world seemed to spin around her. Deeper he moved inside her, impossibly deep, and her body drew him in and closed around him as if he could drive straight to her heart.

But he had done that long ago.

He pressed close, burying his face in the hollow of her neck. "Eden," he whispered. "My love."

She closed her eyes. The pain of his first declaration was so much worse than she had expected. Men said such things easily when they took their pleasure, and she did not believe that Hartley was an exception. But his movements came more rapidly, and her ecstasy built until it spilled over and carried her into oblivion.

She needed Hartley's support when her feet came to rest again on the earth. She looked up into his eyes, clear now of the lust that had driven him. He cupped her face in one hand and brushed back her hair. His eyes seemed to repeat what he had told her in his elation.

My love.

She smiled sadly to herself and touched his lips. "Tonight was worth waiting for," she said.

"I did not hurt you?"

"No." She laid her hand over his. "I am not so fragile as that."

"When I'm with you, I forget myself." He kissed her forehead. "You must tell me if I am too rough."

"Not rough, merely . . . enthusiastic." She looked up into the boughs of the trees. "Is it not late for skylarks to be singing?"

"They sing for you," he said. His face grew serious. "Eden . . ." He stopped, but the look in his eyes made Eden's legs unsteady all over again.

Surely he was about to tell her something important. Something that would not come easily to a man like him.

What if he had meant the words murmured in the heat of passion? If he were to repeat them now, deliberately admit that he loved her . . .

Had she the courage to hear him say it?

He raised his other hand to frame her face. "Eden, there is something I must —"

The sentence was never completed. A strange, high whistling cut it off, followed by a whoosh of air and a low thump very near Eden's face.

Hartley's expression alarmed her before she understood the source of the sounds. She turned her head to follow his gaze, and found a lock of her hair pinned to the tree by the still-quivering shaft of an arrow. Instinctively she held very still, hardly daring to breathe.

Hartley seized the shaft and jerked it from the trunk. The arrow was capped by a wickedly sharp head forged of metal; he tested it carefully on the tip of one finger. With a hiss of pain, he dropped it to the ground and stepped back, searching the surrounding forest with raised head and body as taut as a bowstring.

Eden stared down at the fallen arrow. Quite apart from the fact that it had nearly killed her, she was at a loss to imagine how such an antique should have come to Hartsmere's wood in midsummer. It was not yet the hunting season, and no one pursued game with arrows in these modern times. Such methods had been abandoned centuries ago.

She might have thought it the work of a child playing pranks, but this was no child's toy. Such a close shot could not have been an accident.

And if not an accident, it was deliberate — a deliberate attempt to wound or kill.

Hartley crowded Eden against the tree, making a shield of his body. The forest had grown utterly silent, warning of the intruder by the very absence of sound.

He smelled the scent of man. Man — *a* man — who had entered his realm for a purpose he could not mistake.

"Hartley —"

He held up his hand to quiet her. "We are not alone," he whispered harshly.

Eden's shiver passed into his own body. "What is it? Who —"

"I don't know. But someone is here in the wood . . ." *Someone who knows what I am. Someone who knows enough to use Cold Iron in its purest form.* ". . . and he meant that shot to kill."

"But who could possibly . . ." She wet the lips he had kissed only moments ago. "People do not go about murdering other people with arrows. We have no poachers at Hartsmere — not that I've ever heard. Who could wish to kill either of us?"

Considering how close she had been to death, her voice was remarkably steady and her questions perfectly sensible. He felt behind him, reaching for any part of her he could touch, as if to reassure himself that she was unharmed. Her fingers found his hand and clutched it tightly.

Had his head been a fraction of an inch to the right, that arrow would have pierced his neck. And the poison of Iron would have killed him more surely than the wound itself. But had it struck Eden, she, too, would have died just as surely.

He wanted to bellow and paw the earth and charge off to hunt down the unknown enemy who had endangered his woman because of him. He locked his knees to battle the impulse and gritted his teeth against the pain in his forehead.

The man had already fled; he was sure of it. If the hunter knew Hartley's nature, he would not linger once he had failed in his mission. Hartley was too distracted to summon help from the forest creatures, at least until Eden was safe.

But as long as the enemy remained within the dale, Hartley could find him. And discover his purpose.

"You must go back to the house at once," he said, turning to her. "I will accompany you as far as the garden wall."

She frowned at him, all the softness of their loving gone from her eyes. "And then? Do you intend to seek this person? Why are you so sure that he meant to —"

"I know."

"Even if what you say is true, and someone wishes to kill us"— she shook her head in disbelief —"surely this is a matter for the constable. I shall —"

"No." He took her arms and forced her to look at him. "Do as I say, Eden. Go back to the house and remain there. Speak of this to no one. Do not let Donal leave the house for any reason. When it is safe, I will tell you."

"Donal?" Her body grew rigid. "Is he in danger?"

"That is what I intend to learn."

"By placing yourself in danger as well? This person must be a madman." She twisted her arms so that she could grip his. "Please, Hartley. Do not risk your life."

He swallowed the sudden thickness in his throat. "I promise you that I will come to no harm."

"You know more of this than you are telling me. Hartley, is it something from your past? Have you enemies?"

His laugh remained safely within his chest. "I cannot speak of it now." Without further warning, he picked her up and began to run toward the edge of the wood.

"I can walk," Eden protested.

"Not fast enough." He increased his pace, flying over obstacles and through impenetrable thickets. If Eden was afraid of this precipitous flight or wondered at his ability to move so swiftly in the dark, she did not reveal it. She merely clung to his neck and let him keep his breath for the run.

At the edge of the wood, where moonlight made a silver ocean of the sloping pasture, the hunter tried again. This time the arrow went wide and buried itself in the tall summer grass. Eden gasped. Hartley never paused, but leaped the rock wall and hurtled down the fell to the park and then to the border of the garden.

He set Eden down. "Go inside," he commanded. "Do not speak of this until I return.".

"No. I shall send for the constable —"

"What if this poacher is a madman, bent on killing any within his reach?"

The lie was convincing, for it was what Eden was most inclined to believe. She touched his face with anxious fingers.

"If you do not return quickly, safe and sound, I shall be forced at last to discharge you."

He smiled, his heart too full to admit fear. "You cannot expect me to begin obeying your commands at this late date." He drew her into the shadows of the wall and kissed her deeply and passionately. "Give Donal my love."

Her body stiffened and then relaxed. "I shall." She stepped back, her expression almost invisible even to his keen sight. "Take care, my . . . dear friend."

She slipped through the gate before he could answer. He had no time to ponder her final words. Wheeling about, he ran across the park and pasture and onto the fell, searching for a scent and a sign of passage.

Come to me, my brethren, he called to the beasts pursing their nocturnal business. *Find the one who dared to enter our sanctuary with the weapons of man's violence. Find him, and hold him.*

From all about came the rustlings of many tiny feet, the brush of fur on grass, the puffing of breath low to the ground. Stoats, foxes, weasels, badgers, hares — all that could run — set out in pursuit. Hartley did the same. Rage and hatred, born of Eden's danger, fueled him as nothing else could. He let go all restraint and became the stag, covering many human paces in a single leap.

The man was clever. He knew the wood and the field and how to hide his track. But he was still mortal, and in his foolishness he had run higher up the fell, away from his own kind. Hartley traced him to a narrow cleft between two great boulders, barely wide enough to permit him passage.

None of the other beasts had caught up with him. He could smell the enemy beyond the cleft. Shedding his stag's form, he prepared to enter.

"No!"

Tod appeared before his face, the hob's expression twisted in terror. "Cold Iron, Cold Iron!"

Almost too late, Hartley smelled the bitter tang. Far more Cold Iron than existed in a single arrowhead or a dozen.

A trap. He leaped back, and Tod began to spiral out of the air. Hartley caught the hob as he fell.

An arrow's broken shaft was buried in Tod's shoulder.

Hartley howled. He ran far from the cleft and his quarry, cradling his servant in arms grown numb. The beasts he had called ran beside him. He found a hollow in the center of a thicket and set Tod down, closing the shrubbery about them like a fortress.

"Go," he said to the beasts. "Follow the man when he leaves the cleft, but do not let yourselves be seen. Tell me where he runs. I shall find him."

The beasts left again. He knelt over Tod. The small Fane's body was slack as the poison worked its way into his blood. The longer the arrowhead remained in his body, the less his chance of survival. It might already be too late.

Hartley summoned all his power. He set his hand on the broken shaft and imagined the poison at the farthest points of Tod's body, imagined himself drawing it out and up the shaft and into his own hand.

It came, and with it pain almost beyond bearing. Hartley did not stop. The shaft burned his hand, and fire moved up his arm. Still the poison flowed. After an eternity of torment, Hartley's agonized nerves felt the change in Tod's being. The shaft jerked in his grip as the wound began to close, forcing the arrowhead up and out.

He flung the arrow away with all his remaining strength

and collapsed, lungs afire. He was so weak that should the hunter come upon him now, he would be helpless to fight back.

But no one came. Some beasts had remained to guard him, and the normal forest sounds had resumed, signaling peace.

And the likely escape of the enemy.

Hartley lay still until his body demanded a deeper rest. The pain faded into an oblivion that passed for sleep.

"My lord?"

The whispered voice wakened him. Tod crouched over him, hand hovering above his face. Tears filled the hob's eyes.

Tears. Like a mortal.

That shock alone roused Hartley. His body still hurt, but the pain might linger for days as he cast off the effects of the Cold Iron he'd absorbed.

"My lord?" Tod repeated. "You saved Tod."

Hartley winced. "I merely repaid you for saving me. You warned me of the trap."

Tod shivered. "A cage, with great teeth of Iron. The man was waiting."

A cage. A trap. Hartley fought to his knees. "We must find a way to destroy it."

"It is gone. The man took it, so the beasts say."

Hartley listened, and he heard what Tod had already learned. The man had indeed gone and taken his trap with him.

Renewed sickness washed over him. "I must . . . speak to Eden," he said. "Rest."

Tod's hand brushed his arm with a feather touch. "Do not go to the man place, my lord."

"I must." Using the support of the shrubbery about him, he pulled himself to his feet and staggered from the hollow. Tod moaned behind him.

With but half his usual energy, Hartley crept toward the house. His muscles were flimsy flower stems, and his heartbeat the tap of a dead leaf against a branch. Now he knew how mortals felt in their frail, short-lived bodies.

But he knew more than the feel of a mortal body. As he walked, reeling from tree to tree, he relived the moment when the arrow had nearly buried itself in Eden's head. The thud of the point hitting the tree had seemed like the wail of the world's ending.

Eden had nearly died.

Eden. Dead. Because of him.

He stopped and flung back his head and gave a cry that set the leaves to showering about him and the ground to trembling under his feet.

If Eden had died, his world *would* have ended. It mattered not if he lived a thousand thousand years, here or in Tir-na-nog.

Without Eden, endless life would become endless torment.

He moved again, blindly. But with each step, his vision grew more clear, and he saw the path before him.

He must tell her.

The rightness of it filled him, even as he trembled with the realization of what it meant.

Eden must be told the complete truth of who he was. Only then could he know if the things he contemplated were possible.

If he could forgo his homecoming, and Donal's.

If he could give up everything for Eden.

If she could . . . love him.

Fear choked him as it had not when he had been so near his own death. When Eden learned the truth, she might hate him. Hate him for the past, for his deception, for his very inhuman nature.

He might lose her forever.

The thought was too monstrous to hold. He continued down the fell and cloaked himself in shadow as he reached the garden gate.

She would know, tonight, or he would give himself to the hunter's Iron.

•   •   •

The fool. The wretched, bird-witted fool.

Claudia looked at the clock once more. It was well past midnight, and still he had not come with proof of her enemy's death.

She turned from the window and paced the length of the drawing room and back again. All the time Eden had believed her to be visiting friends in London she had been seeking — painstakingly and with much frustration — for a certain man. She did not know his name, or even his everyday occupation. Her search began in blindness. But she knew she must find him: a hunter skilled and intelligent enough to kill the monster of Hartsmere.

Such men were uncommon in England, where game laws and land ownership were so restricted. A mere poacher would not do. And the man she hired must also follow her instructions to the letter . . . and believe the wild tales she told without question.

Miraculously, she had found the perfect candidate. In the intervals between her searches, she had attended a few parties held by friends. At one such event she had spoken to a clergyman with whom she was somewhat acquainted, and they had fallen into a curious conversation.

The clergyman had told her of a very strange man, a near savage from the former colonies of America, who had come to him asking about "demons" and "wendigos." He had insisted upon the existence of such supernatural creatures and said that he had forged paths across the trackless wastes of forest and plain in pursuit of them. He had not been shy of boasting about his God-given calling to destroy them wherever they nested. He had come to England because he had heard that these "wendigos" still survived in the island's hidden corners.

When the clergyman mentioned that the American was skilled with a bow such as the red Indians used, Claudia knew that she had found the man she sought.

Obtaining an introduction to him had been easy. Convincing him to help her, for a very generous fee — and by

emphasizing the evil nature of the beast he must hunt—
hadn't been much more difficult. The creature she de-
scribed was much like the demons he pursued in his own
land. In the end he had agreed, eager for the challenge and
the chance to save a maiden in distress.

So he had come to Hartsmere in secret. And she had
given him his instructions and all the warnings she could
think of. The arrows he would use were swift, silent, and
armed with deadly tips of iron. All he need do was find
Hartley Shaw, slay him, and return to collect the second
half of his reward.

But he had not come. Claudia had kept Eden with her as
long as possible tonight, well aware of her niece's intended
meeting with her lover. She would not risk Eden's life. But
there had been no way to keep her in the house save telling
her the truth, and that was out of the question.

When Eden had returned only an hour later, disheveled
and distraught, Claudia guessed what had happened even
before her niece spoke of the unseen intruder.

The ill-bred fool. Oh, yes, he had found Hartley Shaw.
But his shot had missed, nearly hitting Eden in the process.

Eden told her that Hartley was searching for the intruder, and that was Claudia's one remaining hope.

She strode back to the double doors and twitched at the
curtains. The wretched Colonial had no doubt failed in his
task and chosen the better part of valor rather than continue. Either that . . . or the creature had turned the tables
on him. He could be dead.

God forbid.

Out in the garden, beyond the wall, something moved.
Claudia let the curtain fall and opened the doors. A man
walked into the light cast from the windows.

Not the American, but Hartley Shaw. The taste of bitter
defeat filled Claudia's mouth. He was not even wounded,
though he looked as though he had been running.

The hunted after the hunter.

He strode toward the doors and saw her. Instinctively,

she smoothed her expression and replaced it with one of worry and concern.

Think, Claudia.

Her first plan had failed. There would be other ways, other opportunities, but in the meantime she must take advantage of any small opening given her. Perhaps . . . just perhaps she could buy more time and separate Eden and Shaw for a little while longer.

"Shaw," she said, stepping into the garden. "Lady Eden told me of the intruder. Did you find him?"

He stopped in his tracks, suspicious of her sudden willingness to address him after weeks of shunning and contempt. She saw his frown and his hesitation. But Eden's name had some power over him; he moved closer and shook his head.

"I did not find him. He has fled." He looked past her, into the drawing room. "Eden —"

"Is resting. She has had a most unpleasant experience, but thank God she was not injured." Claudia forced herself to carry out the deception. "And you?"

His eyes narrowed. "I am unhurt."

"I am grateful that you saved my niece's life."

He did not respond immediately. She could see his alien mind pondering her change of attitude and considering what to make of it.

"The arrow flew before either of us were aware of a trespasser," he said. "I brought Eden back immediately. She is in no further danger."

Either of us. He could not make clearer that they had been together, alone in the wood. But that was no secret.

"I see," she said, allowing some of her disapproval to seep through. He would not believe her apparent change of heart if she seemed too accepting.

"Whatever you think of me," Shaw said, "you may believe that I would protect Eden with my life."

She clenched her teeth behind half-smiling lips. "I do believe it. And that is why . . . especially after tonight . . . I wish to declare a truce."

His brow arched high. "A truce?"

"Let us be frank with one another. I have told you that I would not permit my niece's involvement with a servant. My feelings have not changed. But Eden is not a child. My influence over her is limited. It is folly for you and me to be enemies, when we might deal reasonably together."

"As you tried to *deal* with me before, Lady Claudia?"

She retreated through the doors. "Come inside. There is a dangerous madman abroad."

He followed her as reluctantly as if he walked into a cage. What had become of the trap the hunter had set? Did it still lie in wait where the monster might come upon it?

"I promise that I will not bite," she said with a twist of her lips. "I think it best if we continue our discussion in the sitting room, where we will not be disturbed."

"Am *I* to be permitted such a privilege, my lady?"

She chose to ignore his sally. "If you will wait here but a few minutes, I will make certain that the household is asleep. Eden has already retired."

"I wish to see her."

Claudia bit hard on the inside of her lip. "Very well, if you keep quiet and do not wake her. I'll meet you in the sitting room at half past the hour."

He nodded dismissively and strode for the hallway. The moment he was out of sight, Claudia put on a pair of gloves and went directly to Eden's secretaire in the sitting room.

The letter she sought was still there. Though Rushborough's invitation had come a week ago, Eden had struggled over her response, seeking just the right balance of gratitude and distance. She had declared her initial efforts much too warm, and a number of rejected missives lay stacked in a drawer. Claudia found the one she wanted and carefully smoothed it out on the desk, where the invitation still awaited an answer.

Very little remained to complete the letter. Carefully Claudia arranged the invitation and the response so that they appeared to have been laid aside, forgotten in a moment's distraction.

It might not have the desired effect. She did not pretend to understand a monster's motives and concerns. But there was a chance, and that was enough.

She left the room and waited in a place where she could hear Shaw return. Soon he came down the stairs, mouth set, and went into the sitting room.

Silence. The hall clock ticked. She crept close to the door and listened.

Footsteps. Then the rustle of papers. An indrawn breath. More rustling, and then footfalls approaching the door.

She hid until he had gone down the hall, into the drawing room, and out the garden doors.

Success.

The garden doors were wide open to the night air. Claudia closed them firmly.

The papers in the morning room had been shuffled and replaced in almost the same position she had left them. She picked up the invitation, read it through once more, and then perused the reply she had chosen for Hartley's edification.

My Dear Lord Rushborough:

It is with pleasure that I accept your kind invitation to join your house party at Caldwick on the eighteenth of October. I offer my congratulations on your recent purchase of a hall that has a fine reputation throughout the Lake District. I shall look forward to meeting old friends and making the acquaintance of those I have missed.

I had meant this letter to be a formal acceptance, but now I find that I must add a message of a more personal nature.

I have been a very poor friend indeed, and I have much to atone for. Your invitation is proof enough that you have forgiven my lapses of hospitality and manners. Your very generous offer to spend time

with my son, in spite of his lack of social graces,
goes beyond the duties of friendship.

I regret that I have neglected to show my grati-
tude properly these past months. In my distress over
recent events, I have behaved intemperately. I hope
and trust that my visit to Caldwick will go a little
way toward making up for any wounds my poor
judgment may have incurred.

>   *Yours in friendship,*
>   *Eden Winstowe*

Claudia set down the letter and laughed.

Chapter 16

For the first few days after he read the letter, Hartley could not bring himself to return to Hartsmere.

He knew he was unreasonable. He even told himself that it was for the best. But he had come so close to a declaration that would bind him to Eden and her world forever — and it would have been a terrible mistake.

Deep in his woods, he raged and brooded. He beat his antlers against inoffensive trees and tore the ground with platter-sized hooves. The animals fled his company, and he could not blame them. Even Tod avoided him.

Eden. Eden. Eden. She filled his every waking thought and even his dreams. He might stay away for days, but no longer. He was a slave — he, a lord of the Fane — grateful for any scraps she might throw his way.

Scraps left from the lordly table of the Marquess of Rushborough.

After he had exhausted his wretched emotions, he went to Hartsmere's kitchen, where Mrs. Byrne often spent her evenings chatting with Cook. When the Irishwoman saw his face, she glanced at Mrs. Beaton and quickly left the table.

"Come to my sitting room," she said.

He slumped in the chair she offered and refused the tea. "How is Eden?" he asked.

"Worried. Waiting for you."

Mrs. Byrne's forthright directness was what made her one of the few mortals he could endure as a confidante. He had been aware for some time that she knew of his relationship with Eden and had not disapproved.

Hartley suppressed a scowl. "She has not come looking for me."

"There was word of an intruder," the older woman said dryly. "Would it not be unwise for her to venture into the woods at such a time?"

He stared at his boots. "I looked for the villain. He is nowhere to be found, nor did anyone else in the dale see or hear of him. He has not come back." His first wild thought — that it might even be Eden's aunt who had set the hunter on him — he dismissed as ridiculous. She was a town-bred lady, with no knowledge of hunting or weapons, and certainly none of the Fane.

"Then he is gone," Mrs. Byrne said, interrupting his thoughts, "and good riddance." She sighed and took a sip of tea. "I heard the whole tale from Lady Eden the morning after it happened." Her knowing gaze hinted that she had surmised much more than she had heard. "But something else besides the attack happened that night. It has kept you away from the woman you love so soon after she almost died."

He nearly bolted from his chair. *The woman you love.* How dare she speak so, as if she knew his mind?

He subsided back into the chair, stunned by the intensity of his feelings. Was it love, that he had been prepared to give up Tir-na-nog and stay with Eden until death? That he would sacrifice everything, even Donal's chance at perfect happiness among his own kind, to remain with a mortal woman?

He could not absorb the idea of it, let alone the emotion. And at the moment his jealousy and anger were sufficient.

"Something else happened," he agreed heavily. "I learned that Eden has dallied with me while she prepares to go to another man." The last words came out as a growl, and Mrs. Byrne raised her brow.

"Is that it, now? The other man being the marquess, I presume?"

"Who else?" What was the point of this conversation? He only humiliated himself before a mortal to no purpose.

"Ah, jealousy." Mrs. Byrne set down her cup. "It makes men do very foolish things, such as reaching false conclusions about those they care for. The greater the love, the worse the fool!"

Hartley bristled. He considered striking Mrs. Byrne mute or calling a mouse to chase her.

"Even a fool can read," he snapped. "I saw the loving missive Eden wrote in accepting Rushborough's invitation to his house in October," he snapped. "She made it very plain that she regards him as —" He could not complete the sentence. "She made me no promises, as I made her none. It is natural that she should —"

"Of course," Mrs. Byrne interrupted. "An incriminating letter, which undoes everything you and the lady have shared this summer, and which you happened to run across at a very convenient moment."

Something in her tone made him study her with greater attention. "It was in the sitting room."

"And who was the last person you spoke to before you found it, pray tell?"

"Lady Claudia," he said slowly. "She met me when I came to see Eden, after I searched for the trespasser. She was uncommonly civil, even —" He slammed his fist on the arm of the chair, and Mrs. Byrne winced.

"Lady Claudia is a very clever woman," she remarked. "She knows what has gone on between you and Lady Eden. She has grand ambitions for the girl, and you are an obstacle. But she also realizes that open interference will only drive Eden into your arms. So she must find other ways of separating you."

"But Eden did write that letter. I —" How could he admit that he had smelled Eden's unique scent all over the paper, when his senses were beyond those of men? No one but she could have written it. She had simply not intended him to see it.

Claudia had made sure he *did*.

Mrs. Byrne leaned back, her lean, wrinkled face sharp with rebuke. "You're double the fool for turning your back on your sweetheart without letting her speak for herself."

"I have underestimated Eden's aunt as an enemy," he admitted.

"And you have done Eden a great injustice. She and she alone knows the truth of her heart." Mrs. Byrne refreshed her dish of tea. "What is it that you wish, Hartley Shaw? To enjoy yourself with the lady of the manor until you tire of her? Or do you love her enough to want more for both of you?"

The housekeeper knew him only as a servant, an unsuitable match for a lady such as Eden. What was she suggesting? That he ask her to marry him?

"I have much to think about," he said, rising. "Thank you for your hospitality . . . and your wisdom."

"Do not think too long, lad." She picked up her knitting. "You will find Lady Eden in the garden."

He smiled wryly at her endearment, knowing himself to be many hundreds of years older than she. Yet he had, on more than one occasion, behaved like a youth of less than twenty summers.

Had he learned enough?

Eden walked in the garden, her head bent in thought. Hartley stopped before she saw him, struck to the heart by her beauty and her loneliness.

She *was* lonely. For so many centuries he had not really understood what loneliness was, content to be alone and free of all ties. That had changed. He had hoped to return to Tir-na-nog out of loneliness, but now he knew that he had hardly begun to recognize the meaning of the word.

Loneliness was being without Eden — for a day, an

hour, a minute. Loneliness was discovering that one needed companionship after all. That one might even need love.

"Eden," he said softly.

She looked up, and her countenance unfolded like a newly bloomed rose.

"Hartley! Where have you been?" She ran halfway to him, paused, and reassembled her dignity. "I had feared . . . had thought . . . the intruder —"

"Is gone and has not returned." He held out his hands, and she took them. They gazed at each other at arm's length. Hartley would gladly have found some sheltered place and loved her there and then, but that must wait. "I should have sent word, but you know that I would not allow any harm to come to you or Donal or any of the folk here."

"I know." She squeezed his hands. "But I worried for you. I would have come looking, if not for my son."

Shame bowed his head like antlers in autumn. "I could come no sooner."

"Thank God you are well." She glanced toward the garden doors — old habit, now that Claudia was in residence again — and led him to a bench behind a rhododendron. "I still do not understand what happened or why."

If he told her everything, here and now, she would be able to understand why a hunter with iron-headed arrows might pursue him. But this was too public a place. "Can you come to the wood tonight, after the others are asleep?"

He could tell by her breathing that her thoughts followed the same paths as his, but she shook her head. "I cannot. I promised my aunt that I would look at fashion plates she brought from London and select several new gowns."

Claudia. "I had thought such matters as fashion and vanity were no longer important to you."

She blinked, startled by his tone. "They are not. But I have obligations to my neighbors, and I must be respectably dressed in their company."

"Your neighbors?" He tightened his grip on her hands. "Like the ones you had in London?"

"The local gentry, landowners —people with responsibilities similar to my own." She smiled uncertainly. "Surely you can understand the necessity of my associating with those from whom I can learn so much. Now that my mourning is nearly over, I can do more to help the people of Hartsmere."

"How much more can you do? The folk here are prosperous enough." He tried to modify the harshness of his voice, but it refused to obey his will. "Are you sure it is not because you miss your old life of carefree pleasures?"

A frown creased her brow. "Why do you speak so, Hartley? I have spent the past few days worrying about you, we have been apart, and these . . . accusations . . . are all you can offer?"

"Ah. That is it, isn't it? I can offer so little, and the marquess so much."

"I do not understand you, Hartley. We have been through this before —"

"Without having reached a satisfactory conclusion. Is that not true?"

An odd, fleeting expression crossed her face. "I had not thought that you wished to reach a conclusion. Has that changed?"

Yes, he bellowed inwardly. *Yes.* But the words — human words — caught in his throat. The letter had burned itself into his memory. What emerged from his mouth bore no resemblance to what he'd intended to say.

"Did you accept an invitation to stay with the marquess?"

Her lips parted and then pressed together. "How did you know of that? The invitation only arrived the day of . . . the day the trespasser attacked us."

"I saw the letter you wrote to him. 'I hope and trust that my visit to Caldwick will go a little way toward making up for any wounds my poor judgment may have incurred,'" he quoted savagely. "How will you make it up, Eden?"

She pulled her hands free of his. "What right have you to go through my private correspondence? Lord Rushborough has been my friend for many years, and I shall not cut him as if he were an importunate mushroom."

"Do not see him. Stay away from him, Eden."

"Hartley, you are behaving as if —"

"I *forbid* you to see him."

She laughed. Perhaps it was only surprise, but his emotions had snapped their leash and there was no recalling them. He heard it as mockery. He surged to his feet.

"I forbid it, Eden. I can enforce my commands."

"Oh? I have seen you behave intemperently, Hartley, but never with violence. You have no reason for jealousy —"

He recognized her overture for peace and swept it aside. "You do not love him, Eden." He loomed over her. "You love *me.*"

Once more her lips parted, as if she invited him to kiss her. Her face flushed, and her eyes grew soft and vulnerable. Only the barest veneer of sanity kept him from laying her down on the bench and branding her as his.

"Is that what this is about?" she whispered, searching his eyes. "You never demanded such declarations from me. And you have never given them."

"And if I did, it would change everything, would it? You would give up your Society — the marquess, all of them — and stay here with me?"

Even in his blind ferocity he saw that he had pushed her to the brink of her composure. "Do you think that you can buy my love?" she asked, her voice shaking. "That you can command it? Oh, Hartley. Can you give me what *you* demand? Can you speak the words?" She smiled unsteadily. "Can you?"

Behind the throbbing in his temples, beyond the demon in his mind, he knew perfectly well what she asked. What she *demanded*. She, a mortal, demanded it of *him*.

"Will that be enough for you, Eden?" he asked hoarsely. "Will that ever be enough for the great Lady Eden Winstowe, who sleeps with a servant but pursues a marquess? The lady who bore a fatherless child and would deceive the world rather than sacrifice even a portion of her social position?"

Eden stopped breathing. Her face went pale and still. Slowly she drew herself up, never averting her gaze.

"I can see that our passions have had the better of us both. Perhaps we must reach a new understanding of what we want from each other."

"Have I not made clear what I want from you, Eden? Let me remind you."

He kissed her, and all the anger and frustration and confusion in his own heart was transformed into punishment for the woman responsible.

But he could not sustain it. He could not hurt her. His lips gentled, and he drew her into his arms and tried, in earnest, to show her what he could not express and had come so close to destroying.

From the corner of his eye he caught a whisper of motion at the double doors. The curtain twitched back into place, but not before he saw the eavesdropper's face.

Claudia. Was she gnashing her teeth at the failure of her scheme to separate them?

Eden laid her cool hand on his cheek. "Let us not quarrel. Let us not ruin what we have."

The look in her eyes could bring a strong man to his knees. Or a Fane. "Will you see Rushborough?" he asked stubbornly.

She sighed and stepped back. "We come from two different worlds, you and I. I will not sever all ties to mine, not even for your sake. I have Donal to think of now. That does not mean . . ." She shook her head and looked away. "Perhaps you cannot understand."

Perhaps you are right. Yet when he spoke, it was if a stranger composed the words. A humble, desperate stranger unwilling to lose the two most precious relationships in his life.

"I am not eloquent like your marquess. You say that we

come from different worlds, and you are right. But something has happened to my world, Eden. Once it was complete unto itself, needing nothing, no one. I was absolute ruler. If another attempted to enter, I drove him away. Then you came, and it shook to its very foundation."

She looked up. He smothered his rebellious pride and continued. "I fought back as any conquered monarch fights, with every brazen tactic I could employ. But I discovered that my world could no longer thrive without you. It shriveled and died where your touch did not nourish it."

She said nothing. A nightingale called from the direction of the forest. Hartley's pulse pounded in his ears. He began to turn away.

"Hartley." She raised her hand, and it hung suspended between them, like the words that remained unspoken. "How can say you are not eloquent? It is I who have only the simplest phrase to give in return." She laid her palm over his drumming heartbeat. "I love you, Hartley Shaw."

He had not truly comprehended, until this moment, how much he had wanted to hear that phrase. His heart swelled until it filled his chest, crowding out every other organ, making air and water and nourishment and all the necessities of life unimportant.

No time was better to reveal himself for what he was.

But he was afraid. He, who had seldom known fear in his long, long life, feared transforming that adoring look to one of terror and loathing.

Tell her he must, and soon. But not yet. Not yet.

He leaned forward, took her face between his hands, and let his lips speak for him.

Chapter 17

"*There,*" *Aunt Claudia said with satisfaction.* "*The gown* is absolute perfection. No one at Lord Rushborough's house party will believe that you have passed your twenty-fourth year."

Eden accepted the compliment with a bowed head and ran her hands over the expensive violet satin of the evening gown. Of those dresses and trappings that Claudia had insisted she purchase, this was the finest and had given her the greatest qualms in ordering. Its rich color was vastly unlike the blacks and dull hues of mourning. She felt almost naked in it.

But this gown, like the others, was a necessary investment if she was to be a proper lady of Hartsmere and mingle with her fellow landowners. Left unvoiced was her aunt's assumption that such a rusticated situation was temporary, and soon the wardrobe would be put to much better use in London . . . when she was Marchioness of Rushborough.

So Claudia hoped.

"It is still a wonder to me that Lord Rushborough purchased the estate near Patterdale," Claudia remarked. She began to undo the tapes along the back of Eden's bodice. "He has no love for the country, and I can conceive of only one reason that he would do so."

Eden bit the inside of her lip. She knew that her aunt had a large part in the invitation to Lord Rushborough's grand house party, but she had not yet found the heart to tell Claudia that her principal reasons for visiting Caldwick did not include encouragement of the marquess's suit. To the contrary. It was time to lay Rushborough's marital hopes to rest.

She had another purpose in maintaining some connection with the marquess, however platonic. Rushborough's continuing friendship meant connections for Donal, and those she must continue to establish, no matter how small her interest in resuming her old way of life.

Francis had made a considerable effort to accept her son. He had invited Donal to a children's gathering to be held one day during the party, and offered to take him riding. Eden was determined to keep the marquess's goodwill — if she could let him down gently enough.

"How fortunate that there was one decent mantua maker in Ambleside, at least," Claudia said, obviously hoping to engage Eden's enthusiasm. "I would have preferred that you had gone to London for the fittings, of course —"

"But I could not leave for such an extended time, Aunt, with so much to be done at Hartsmere," Eden finished firmly.

God knew that she had been constantly busy since her declaration to Hartley. The harvest had come and gone, and October was nearing its end. The people continued to grow fat and merry and prosperous, as if they had never known want. All the neighboring dales wondered at the enormous crops of hay, the prize-winning ewes and tups, the vegetables lush and sweet as if from the soil of some soft southern shire.

Every day she found some new aspect of her duties as lady of Hartsmere — and as mother to Donal — to learn or perfect. Since the invitation's arrival, she had worked to prepare her son for his first significant social appearance. Presentation to Rushborough's *ton*nish friends — once her friends as well — would be an important first step for his future.

Every day was filled with satisfying work and friendship.

But every night . . .

Every night was Hartley's.

Her joy had not fled with summer's warmth. Leaves fell, flowers withered, and animals and men began to prepare for winter, portending the season of cold to come. But the looming year's end no longer seemed the death of love and contentment. It was only the epilogue of the life she was leaving behind. The long, cooler nights gave her and Hartley more hours to spend talking, caressing, loving. He was by turns tender and wild and always concerned with her happiness.

Hartley's speech after their quarrel over Rushborough had banished almost every doubt from her heart and mind. They had not argued since. Nor had he brought up her forthcoming visit to Caldwick.

He had also failed to return her avowal of love. Yet whenever they lay together, or walked in the wood, or shared laughter with Donal, she saw something in his eyes that told her she had nothing to fear in his silence.

The party at Caldwick was a test of sorts, and she intended to pass it. She would prove to herself that she had no regrets in abandoning the former Lady Eden Winstowe. That she could play society's games for Donal's sake but keep her heart untouched and free. For Hartley.

The thought of Hartley made the room uncommonly hot for a mid-October day. Thank God Claudia had not spoken of him, though Eden had come to realize that she had been naive to think her aunt unaware. It wasn't anything Claudia said but the way she so completely avoided any mention of him.

"It's done," her aunt said. "There are no more adjustments to be made. Your wardrobe is complete, and I have no doubt but that it will dazzle our marquess."

Your marquess. "How shall I compare to you, dear Aunt? Everyone will believe that we are sisters."

Claudia couldn't hide a smile of satisfaction. At last, poring over patterns and ordering gowns, she had been in her element. "Tut tut, Niece. You know that is a patent falsehood. I shall look well enough for my age, nothing more." She examined herself in the cheval mirror. "I am happy to bask in your reflected glory."

Eden did not relish the prospect of shattering Claudia's illusions. "Oh, Aunt —"

"No false modesty, my dear. Even with half your former looks, you would outshine all the rest."

"We shall see. Now it is time for me to help you with *your* gowns."

Claudia's eyes lit up like those of a girl on her coming out. "This is exactly what we both required at this dreary time of year — new clothes and a Society gathering to attend!"

Eden smiled and resolved not to ruin Claudia's enjoyment.

The first day of the house party arrived with a bustle of packing trunks and last-minute adjustments of coiffure and hemlines. Eden made sure that everything regarding the estate was in good order for her days-long absence. Mrs. Byrne promised a smooth-running house and prompt delivery of Donal to Caldwick on Saturday afternoon.

But all the time the landau traversed the rutted roads out of the dale and over the rolling fells to Caldwick, Eden was composing in her mind how best to refuse the expected renewal of Rushborough's proposal.

She and Claudia were not the first to arrive at Caldwick. Eden caught sight of another carriage being driven to the stables, and a distant pair of walkers across the fine park. She swallowed and tugged at her gloves.

"You look lovely, my dear," Claudia said. "At last you

are returning to your rightful place. I know you will find it all much easier than you currently suppose."

"Is it so obvious?"

"Only to those who know you well." Claudia patted her hand. "I shall watch over you, as I have always done."

And how disappointed you will be in me, Eden thought. She avoided Claudia's piercing gaze and took the footman's hand to descend from the carriage.

As if he had been watching for their arrival, Francis met them at the door. His display of unfashionable eagerness was humbling indeed, and while his greeting was impartially warm to them both, his intimate glance was for Eden alone.

Flustered, she was grateful to follow a servant to the room set aside for her, next to Claudia's. She saw at once that someone had been at great pains to make it suitable for one of her taste and experience. The walls were hung with silk, the floor covered with Axminster carpets. Gilded Grecian-style furnishings lent the room a refined elegance.

Francis's housekeeper arrived in person to offer her services and every comfort his lordship's guests might require. Nancy had her own small room adjoining Eden's, and she had plenty to say about the magnificence of the chambers.

It was a grand house indeed, twice the size of Hartsmere. A few hours before dinner — held on London time, not country hours — Francis took her and Claudia on a tour of the house. The way he spoke of it gave Eden the uncomfortable certainty that he soon expected her to become its mistress.

Nevertheless, she found herself relaxing in his company. It was almost like old times, when careless, light conversation was the order of the day, and flirting came as naturally as breathing. As the other guests began to arrive, her nervousness vanished amid the surprisingly warm greetings she received, from friends and strangers alike. The men were uniformly gallant, the women solicitous.

All of them were her kind: of the *ton,* the sons and

daughters of peers and gentlemen. They knew the games as well as she. The glossy veneer of Society lulled her into an illusion of contentment. Suddenly her collection of gowns seemed very modest indeed. She missed the jewelry she had sold to bolster the estate. She found herself at the mirror in her room, looking for new wrinkles or sun spots.

Every hour she rediscovered some forgotten amusement or turn of conversation. Everything she saw was stylish and beautiful and expensive. Dinner was a lavish, sparkling affair that might have been held in one of London's finest dining rooms. Duchesses and marchionesses, viscounts and earls sat side by side with distinguished knights and wealthy gentlemen. No expense had been spared. Eden felt simple pleasure in just holding the crystal goblets and sipping the costly French champagne, luxuries to which she had once been accustomed and seldom questioned.

That evening, Francis escorted her to her room to say good night. Everyone else must have seen, but he was scrupulously proper and not in the least forward. She tried, and failed, to broach the topic that was sure to give him pain.

In the morning, Eden slept late and was still one of the earliest down to breakfast. The next day went by with the speed and fantastic, unreal atmosphere of a carnival, and once more she was unable to meet the marquess alone.

On the second morning, the men went out to observe a fox hunt with the local fell pack, kept by the neighboring squire.

Among those women who had elected not to join them, Eden sat in the shade of a grand old beech, struggling with the disquiet that had settled over her since she had learned of the hunt. She ought not to have been surprised; this was shooting and hunting season, and it was no wonder that Francis's sporting friends should wish to partake of his generosity in sharing his coverts. There was already eager talk of a shoot tomorrow, since Lord Rushborough had hardly touched his birds.

This was an aspect of Society she had tried to forget. Who had been a greater sportsman than her father? How many autumns and winters had she been forced to endure the countryside she loathed, and produce great mountains of embroidered handkerchiefs and pillowcases, because he had insisted upon having her with him when the Season was finished?

But she had stayed away from the hunting fields. She had carefully not looked at the bagged birds Lord Bradwell's servants brought into the kitchen. And now . . .

Now she knew something of the creatures who lived in those woods and fields. The creatures facing death at the hands of her own kind. They were no longer merely dumb beasts to her — not fox nor pheasant, badger nor rabbit, mouse nor stag.

Hartley would be ashamed of her for permitting such cruel sport. She saw his face, and behind it the noble head of a stag, antlers branching high and wide against a blue sky.

Unreasoning terror halted all other thoughts and left her mind spinning. *Hartley. The stag.*

It could not be. They had lain together, laughed, loved. She had accepted that Hartley was not an ordinary man, but she would have known if he and the creature who called himself Cornelius were one and the same. She would have felt it in her very soul.

But he knew so many things about her that he should not. He behaved like a peer of the realm, not a laborer. He acted as if he were Donal's father.

Her stomach in knots, she rose unsteadily and strode away from the house, seeking answers no one at Caldwick could provide.

"Ah, my dear." She stopped abruptly at the sound of Francis's voice. He stood before her, looking bemused. "You seem troubled. Is something not to your liking at Caldwick? Please tell me at once, that I may correct the omission."

"No. No, my lord." She forced a smile. "Your hospitality lacks nothing. Please forgive my freakish tempers. I have become quite unused to such luxury."

"How formal we are." He tucked her arm through his. "Here it is, a beautiful morning, and at last we have a moment to ourselves."

The opportunity could not have come at a worse time, but she had to take it. "You did not join the hunt?"

"Not today." His eyes were very warm. "I had promised myself to take you on a drive about the estate upon the earliest possible occasion. I can think of none better than now. If you agree . . ."

Eden's stomach completed its plummet to her toes. "Of course."

"Excellent." He turned her about and led her to the carriage house, which in itself was fine enough to accommodate a baronet. The waiting horses were the best matched pair she'd ever seen, and the phaeton gleamed with newness. They might as well have been nags pulling a ragpicker's cart in Seven Dials.

Eden sat beside Lord Rushborough, watching his deft hands on the ribbons. But other hands superimposed themselves upon his spotless gloves: rougher, larger hands, equally skillful, and gentle with instinctive understanding of the beasts he drove.

God help me.

Francis drove the carriage down the lane through the park, over rolling ground that gradually started uphill along a sloping fell. The coppices and woodlands were painted with color, and the smell of woodsmoke drifted on the breeze.

"It is beautiful," Eden said, speaking the first words that came into her dazed mind.

"Thank you." He was silent for a moment, clucking to the horses. "I have seen the miracles you have wrought at Hartsmere. I can only imagine what you might accomplish with . . . greater resources."

"You compliment me too highly."

He reined the horses in. "When will you call me Francis again, Eden? Must I beg you?"

"Please, do not. Francis."

He nodded with an air of victory and urged the horses onward, up a gently winding road that climbed the fell. He kept up a largely one-sided conversation, but Eden knew that he was biding his time for far more serious discourse.

When he stopped the carriage again, it was at a glade beside a lovely little beck, a level portion on the fellside secluded from the outside world by a thicket of alders. Eden braced herself.

"I have had much time to think, Eden," Rushborough said, "and I have come to realize that my feelings for you have not changed." He met her stricken gaze. "I think I may reasonably hope that yours have undergone a corresponding alteration since last we were together. I am no callow youth, Eden. I can provide your son with the advantages you wish for him. The boy may not bear my name, but he will have everything else befitting a gentleman."

He swept his hand wide to encompass all that lay below them. "I bought this estate for your sake. Hartsmere is not a proper setting for you, my dear. I would give you free rein to make any changes you wish. Indulge yourself, with no thought of expense." He finally smiled at her, certain that what he offered was impossible to refuse.

He knew as well as she that a woman in her situation must be an utter fool, or mad, to turn him down. For Rushborough to promise to give up his carefree bachelor's life for her sake, and Donal's — her illegitimate son — she could scarce credit the change in him. It was almost as great as the one in herself.

"What you offer . . . is beyond generous."

He seized her hands. "You know what you can do to make my life complete. Ah, Eden . . . once we are wed, nothing can prevent us from becoming the most sought-after couple in London. Those who cut you before will come begging to your door. You may have all the servants you wish. You need never lift your hand to any labor. You can devote your life to pleasure once again, as you deserve." He kissed her hands, one after the other. "Say yes, Eden."

Her throat closed, barring the painstakingly phrased speech she had prepared for this moment. Rushborough gazed at her unflinchingly. Confidently. Believing he had left nothing unsaid.

The same words that Hartley had left unsaid.

Hartley . . .

The horses shied violently, nearly upsetting the carriage. From the midst of the undergrowth a fox came running, low to the ground and frantic with fear. It dashed between the phaeton's wheels, through the trees, and onto the open fell.

From the distance, growing nearer by the second, came the fierce belling of the pack.

"The hunt!" Rushborough cried. He steadied the horses and guided them out of the glade. "Look!" He pointed up the fell, where the first of the hounds was just cresting the rise. "They are much closer than I had suspected." He watched with keen interest as the fox zigzagged an uneven course toward the level ground of the park. Spotted hounds, in full cry, barreled down the hill in pursuit. Eden felt a stab of fear that was not for herself or for anything human.

"The fell packs are unlike those of the south, in that men follow afoot rather than on horseback," Rushborough said, an edge of excitement in his voice. "This country is too dangerous for galloping horses. And the local folk pride themselves on their sturdiness and stamina. There is sure to be an excellent kill today."

He nodded up the fell, where the dogs had been. A handful of men appeared at the crest, bristling with guns and holding still more panting, straining dogs. One of the hunters pointed downfell and gave a cry.

Sick with dread, Eden held her seat. She had the absurd

desire to run after the fox and place herself between it and the bawling hounds.

"I do not care for this, Francis," she said. "It is cruel, and if I had my way, I would banish such hunts entirely."

He stared at her in surprise. "Cruel? Why, we do the farmers and shepherds a great service by killing their vermin. They'd destroy the foxes themselves if we did not. For what purpose were such creatures born, if not to amuse us?"

Eden clutched the side of the carriage. The dogs, growing more distant, were closing in on the hapless fox. Soon it would go to earth and wait to be dug out and torn apart by the terriers.

She could do nothing to save it.

"You do look pale, my dear," Francis said, smiling indulgently. "It is your womanly nature that is offended. I shall take you home at —"

He stopped short with a gasp. She followed his line of sight to the place where the fox had last been.

The fox and the hounds were no longer alone. A human figure was with them — but one far too small to be one of the pursuing hunters. He stood between the snarling, snapping dogs and the fox crouched at his heels.

Some primal instinct told Eden who that figure was. She tried to scream, but her breath came out in a long, high wheeze. "Donal," she whispered. "It's Donal."

"Your son? Impossible. Was he not to come tomorrow? Hartsmere is miles away —"

"It is my son, I tell you!"

Rushborough frowned. "You are unwell, my dear. Let me take you back —"

She snatched the ribbons from his loose grip, slapped them down on the horses's backs, and drove a reckless path down the fellside. The marquess sputtered a protest, which she ignored. She had no thought for him now. The carriage bounced and jounced over rough ground and stones, but her grip on the lines was iron.

Donal's pale, set face looked up as she drove near. He

bent over the fox, protecting it with his body, while the hounds circled him with deep, menacing growls.

Surely they would not hurt a child. Surely not a boy like Donal.

But whatever Donal's natural skills with animals, they had deserted him now, or he had forgotten how to use them. He caught up the fox, made himself very small, and tried to face all the dogs at once.

Eden tried to jump out of the carriage, but Francis seized her by the arm. "Eden!"

"Let me go!" She turned on him savagely. "Find a gun! Get help!"

With a look of astonishment, Francis glanced from her to Donal and jumped from the carriage. He ran up the fellside toward the descending hunters.

Eden dropped the ribbons and let the plunging, wildeyed horses bolt away. She darted toward the nearest of the dogs, shouting and waving her arms. Several of the hounds spun to face her, bristling.

With another silent prayer, Eden walked directly into the seething pack. A tooth-filled maw snapped at her hand. Another dog caught the hem of her pelisse and began to tug.

Then, all at once, one of the dogs yelped and the others cowered back from her and Donal. A shadow fell over Eden. She turned, and nearly fell in her amazement.

An enormous stag, its head crowned with a vast rack of antlers, stood over the dogs. It bellowed, shaking its head in threat.

So many dogs might have brought the beast down, if they had been so inclined. They were not; this was no helpless fox. Several broke away, tails tucked, and even the bravest fled when the stag took several bounding steps forward and nearly impaled the importunate beast on one long, daggerlike tine.

Safe. They were safe — at least from the hounds. Eden ran and caught Donal in her arms, fox and all, putting herself between him and the stag. Vaguely she was aware of the hunters approaching, raising guns, taking aim.

She stared up at the stag's bright eyes. It dropped to its knees, lowering its great head nearly to the ground.

Donal wriggled free of her hold and dashed toward the stag. He leaped onto the stag's back with the skill of an experienced rider, and the animal surged to its feet. It wheeled on its haunches and plunged into a full gallop toward the nearest trees.

Chapter 18

New terror clawed at Eden's chest. She ran after the stag, knowing it to be hopeless, ignoring the shouts of the men. She ran as she had run but once in her life.

Branches whipped across her face as she entered the glade. Donal knelt beside the beck, calm and unafraid. The fox and stag were nowhere in sight.

She fell to her knees beside him and hugged him with all her strength.

"Donal, are you all right? Were you hurt?"

He squirmed until she loosened her hold. His large green eyes widened at the look on her face, and he patted her arm.

"I'm all right, Mother. The dogs didn't hurt me." He sighed. "They wouldn't listen when I talked to them. They were too angry. But it isn't really their fault."

Eden almost laughed in exasperation. Trust Donal to worry more about the animals than himself! She sobered instantly at the thought of the stag.

The beast that had not behaved like a beast, that had saved her son. The very creature who had figured so powerfully in her imaginings.

"He's gone," Donal said, "but he's not far away."

Eden snatched him up again and refused to let go. "We must leave at once."

"But he said to stay here —"

She clamped down on her panic and looked wildly about the glade. There was a sudden swell of renewed howling and barking out on the fell. Eden didn't let Donal go long enough to learn the reason. She listened until the sounds grew faint and disappeared.

Donal smiled. "They won't come back for a long time. Tod is leading them away. The other fox is safe."

Tod? Who was Tod? Such questions must wait until Donal was safe. She grabbed his hand and started out of the glade, nearly colliding with three men: two hunters and Francis.

"Thank God you are all right," Rushborough said. He opened his arms as if to embrace them.

Donal hid behind Eden. Doubtless he was far more shaken than his calm words revealed, and she would certainly not subject him to the company of a man who had not thought to place himself between her son and vicious dogs. But as long as the marquess remained, the creature she feared would stay away.

"Please," she said, barely maintaining her civility, "let us take a few moments to recover, Lord Rushborough." She looked beyond him to the two hunters, farmers both by their appearance. "If you will bring the phaeton —"

"But you cannot drive in this state — and what of the stag? It carried the boy away . . ." A peculiar look crossed Rushborough's face, as if he was recalling how Donal had vaulted onto the stag's back, riding a wild animal like a horse.

"I am fine. Donal is unhurt."

"Nevertheless, I will drive you myself." He signaled to the hunters. "Remain here with Lady Eden."

He looked at Donal as if he would like nothing better than to give the boy a good thrashing, and then strode from the glade.

Eden released her breath. She closed her eyes and listened. All that broke the silence was the sweet burbling of the beck and the rustle of the trees. Until a wind came up, shaking loose a shower of leaves and drawing a moan from the branches.

The hunters exchanged uneasy glances. Thunder growled. Needling drops of rain began to fall, but they did not touch Eden or Donal. Within seconds the farmers were drenched. The downpour was followed by a searing flash of light, a loud crack, and a large tree limb plummeted to the ground at the farmers' feet.

As one, the hunters turned on their heels and fled.

"Mother?" Donal said, tugging her torn skirts.

The rain had stopped, and so had the wind and thunder. Another man stood where the farmers had been.

"Hartley," she whispered. She wasn't shocked. She felt quite numb, as if the part of her body that produced astonishment had become weary of supplying the emotion.

"Donal is safe," he said. "I am sorry I did not realize earlier that he had run away from Hartsmere. He found this place all on his own." He looked at Donal with unmistakable pride. "You were very brave, both of you."

She finally laughed, half afraid that the laughter would become helpless sobs if she did not control it. "I have never been brave."

"Yes you were, Mother." Donal gazed up at her gravely. "I came to bring you home. And then I saw the fox."

She caught her breath and cradled Donal's head against her hip. "And the stag," she said.

And the stag. Hartley met her eyes, unblinking. He recognized her question for what it was.

The air prickled with building tension, electric currents that wove back and forth between her and Hartley. She knew with utter certainty that something was about to happen. Something more terrible than anything that had occurred in the past fifteen minutes.

She could not move. She could only stare into those forest-green depths and wait.

"There is something I must tell you, Eden," Hartley said in a halting voice. "I should have told you long ago."

Incredibly, he was afraid. She sensed his fear, and it only increased her own.

"Please," she whispered. "Let us go —"

"The time has come," he said. He seemed to grow larger before her eyes, taller, more imposing. The lines of his face lengthened, smoothed, became oddly and terrifyingly familiar.

And then he vanished. In his place was the stag, still as a marble sculpture. She had only a handful of heartbeats to recognize what she had seen when the stag vanished and Hartley was back again.

Only it was not Hartley. Not this godlike creature dressed in flowing rags of green and brown, handsome beyond even Hartley's good looks.

Antlers, many-branched and hung with leaves and moss, sprang from his brow.

All the blood rushed from Eden's head. It was true. Good God, it was true. She swayed, and Donal's small, strong body supported her.

"Eden," the creature said. Its voice was deep and commanding and utterly beautiful. It was a voice she had heard before. A face she had seen before.

Once it had called itself Cornelius Fleming.

"Eden," Cornelius/Hartley said from very far away. He raised his long, elegant hand. "Do not be afraid. Nothing has changed. Nothing." He almost seemed to smile. "Donal — Donal is our —"

Roaring filled her ears, cutting off his last word he did not need to say.

Donal was his son.

H artley saw her face, and his hope shriveled like Fane-cursed crops.

It was not simple shock, or consternation, or any of the less devastating emotions she might have displayed. It was not even horror, or disgust, or open rejection. She simply stared at him as if her entire world had collapsed for the second time in her life.

That was most painful of all.

He had not wanted this to happen under any circumstances. Eden had undergone a great trial in witnessing Donal's danger and trying to save him. He cursed himself for not having watched the boy more carefully at Hartsmere. Instinct should have told him what Donal might do.

Instinct was useless to him now.

"Eden," he said, his voice cracking. "Look at me. I have not changed. I still . . . care for you above all others, you and Donal. I would die to protect you. To . . . stay with you."

She continued to stare, her hand clutching Donal's. "You are the one who bargained with my father. Who wanted me just for . . ." She swallowed convulsively. "What *are* you?"

"I am Hartley. Your lover. The father of our child." He took a step toward her. She flinched.

"You are not a man," she said. "You . . . are not human."

"No, I am not. But —"

"You lied," she said. "You lied six years ago, and you lied when you returned to Hartsmere."

"Yes," he admitted, sickness in his belly. "I thought I had good reason. But I came to see . . . that it was wrong, Eden. Because I had learned . . . I had learned to —"

Eden covered her ears with her hands. "Stop. Stop. I will hear no more." She turned about and seized Donal's shoulders. "Run, Donal! Run down the fell to the house." She gave him a little shove, and he looked at Hartley with a question in his eyes.

"Da?"

"No!" Eden propelled him to the edge of the glade. She cast one glance back at Hartley, and in that glance was everything Hartley had feared.

Then she began to run. She carried Donal along with her by sheer force of will. Donal did not resist. He knew that his mother needed him now.

When they were beyond his sight, Hartley sank to his knees. He willed the antlers gone, and his form to its now-familiar shape. As he cast off his Fane body, the weight of the mortal world seemed to settle upon his shoulders. The weight of grief, and sorrow, and self-hatred.

It was just as if the events of six years ago had repeated themselves. He had lost her. Surely he had lost her. And in that knowledge he raged: against himself and against Eden. Eden, who would not accept or forgive.

He tore at the earth with his fingers. Tree branches tossed violently over his head, though there was no breeze. Clouds gathered thick and heavy over Rushborough's new estate. Not a sound was heard from bird or beast.

When his rage was past, Hartley sat back and gazed up at the sky. Slowly it cleared, and a shaft of sunlight found its way onto his little patch of ground. He closed his eyes and let it bathe his face.

All the Fane that he had known, long gone, marched through his memory: those that had been contemptuous of man and fled when mortals became too numerous; those that had fallen under the mortal spell and been drawn to mate with them and help them, sometimes to the Fane's ultimate peril; those who had merely used men for their own amusement without a thought to the consequences. And those like himself, bound longest to earth by affection for its creatures.

But rare, rare was the Fane who gave his or her loyalty to one thing or one being.

Hartley looked up at the sun. Awed wonder filled his chest and spilled through his body.

He had become like the sun with its constancy and steadfast light. He could not simply run way, turn his back on Eden, and pretend she meant nothing. He could — must — persist when others of his kind would yield, swallow the pride that came as naturally to his people as magic.

This had been a test: a test of his courage and of Eden's. A test, too, of the depth of her feelings. But perhaps she had not failed. Perhaps she, being mortal, needed more time to absorb what he had revealed. To know her own heart.

Yes. Hope was not yet gone. Time she would have. He would send Tod to leave her a message: for three days he would wait for Eden in the wood at Hartsmere. And if she had not come to him by then . . .

At this moment he felt very, painfully human.

By the time Eden reached the house, her legs would scarcely carry her another step. Donal, fresh as he had been at the top of the fell, showed no expression. He looked up the fell.

For *him*.

She must get inside. She must protect her son. She must think.

As if thinking would alter the circumstances one jot.

She led Donal into Caldwick's rose garden and sat down on a bench, resting her hot face in her hands. Donal sat beside her, legs dangling.

"Mother?" he said, patting her shoulder. "Don't worry. It will be all right."

Eden hugged him against her. God love the child; he had obviously accepted his father without fear. And just how long had he known? Had . . . *he* . . . told Donal from the beginning?

How had a young boy kept such a secret from his own mother?

She took firm hold of her emotions and smiled at her son. "Donal, you know that . . . Hartley is your father."

He nodded, eyes wide and solemn.

"When did he tell you?"

"He didn't tell me," Donal said. "I just knew. Like I knew who you were."

Memory blinded her. That first day she had found

Donal at Hartsmere, he had called her "Mother." But he had never seen her before.

He had simply known. And given her his heart. As he had done with . . . *him*.

You cannot keep this up forever. Pretending he does not have a name, that you did not lie with him night after night, and swear that you loved him.

Once she had believed she loved him in another guise. Now she knew that the love she'd felt as a girl had been a mere shadow of the reality. She had been flattered by masculine attention, attracted to wealth and looks, certain of her own ability to mold her cousin into what she wanted.

What she felt for Hartley — what she *had* felt — had grown deep and strong like the roots of a great tree. She had ceased wishing to change him or expecting him to be what he was not.

And all the while, he hadn't been what she'd believed.

She called up the vision of the being she had met in the glade. The magnificent, larger-than-life form, like a god . . . like Hartley but somehow more so. The clothes that seemed assembled of moss and bark and leaves. The rack of antlers that matched those he had worn as a stag.

He not only understood the beasts, he was one. And not.

For his eyes had been Hartley's. They had pleaded for her forgiveness, her acceptance, casting aside the pride that he wore so naturally in all his forms.

Hartley. Oh, Hartley. If only I had never known.

If only she had lived in ignorance, denying her doubts, deceived by the man she loved, who was not a man at all. If only they could have gone on as they had been, forever.

But that was not to be. *Two different worlds.* Worlds father apart than she had imagined, even in her wildest speculations.

The sole bridge between them sat beside her: Donal. A boy who was also more than human. Whom Hartley had saved twice from death. Whom he would risk everything to protect. As she would.

Donal's fey nature had no bearing on her love for him.

Why was it so different with Hartley? Because he had lied to her not once, but twice . . . and all but destroyed her life? Or was this a deeper, more primitive fear?

If he is not human, what is he?

But she knew. Mrs. Byrne had told her, and so had Mr. Kirkby. She had guessed part of the truth when she'd decided he might be, in some way, like Donal. Or Cornelius.

He could speak to animals. He could change his appearance. He could take the form of a stag and God knew what else. He sprouted antlers from his forehead, and perhaps had other powers she could scarcely imagine.

But he could also lie with a woman and father a child who looked and behaved human in nearly every way. He could love her with the greatest tenderness and defend her ferociously. He held his son like any father, pride and love burning in his eyes. He worked with his hands in the earth, and gentled the most frightened horse with a touch.

That was Hartley Shaw. *That* was the man she loved.

She straightened on the bench and looked up toward the glade, a splash of autumn color against the brown fell. Was he still there? Did he wait for her, hoping she would relent? Or had he accepted her rejection and fled, never to return?

No. Not to see him again? Not to watch him with Donal, teaching her son — *their* son — with infinite patience? Not to be held in his arms, feel him moving inside her? Not to know that wherever she went, he would be waiting for her at the stable or in the wood, his green eyes alight with passion as she drew near?

She clenched her fists and stood up. *Decide,* she demanded of herself. *Which is the greater fear: to face what you do not understand, or to live without love?*

Donal took her hand. His touch comforted her. Donal was the very essence of love: his own, hers . . . and Hartley's. To reject that love was to deny the happiest days of her life. To deny that Hartley — whatever, whoever he was — had the ability to love, to suffer, or to feel the bitter pain of loss.

Who was she to make such a judgment?

"I still . . . care for you above all others, you and Donal," he had said. *"I would die to protect you. To . . . stay with you."*

She believed him.

The tightness in her chest gave way. *God help me. I must go back. I must talk to him. I must let him speak and ask a thousand questions, and dare to fight for this love. . . .*

She squeezed Donal's hand. "Go inside to your room. You have had a very busy day. I will come and speak to you later, about all that has happened."

"Da?"

Such a simple question, with a world of meaning behind it.

"I must talk to him, Donal. Just . . . your father and I."

He nodded and kissed her hand. "Don't be afraid, Mother," he said. He turned and marched into the house.

Eden felt as if she had lost her only ally. She looked down at her soiled dress and knew there was no point in changing. Not for Hartley. The stains and tears would only match his odd clothing that much better.

All the tension inside her released on a laugh. She had the wild urge to unpin her hair and shake it about her shoulders, like a wood nymph of myth. Would that, too, not be appropriate to the occasion?

"Eden? Good lord, are you all right?"

Claudia swept into the garden, her expression sharp with alarm. "We have been searching everywhere for you," she said. "Lord Rushborough said you were not where he had left you. He told us about Donal and the hounds . . . My dear, what has happened?"

Eden had no time for her aunt now, for the inevitable recriminations and explanations. Her mind must be clear and focused on one goal. One man.

"I cannot speak of it now, Aunt," she said, already starting for the gate. "Donal is safe and in his room. I may be gone for a while —"

"Was it *him?*"

Claudia's tone was so heavy with dread that Eden's muscles locked into place. "What?"

"The man who is a beast. The one you know as Hartley Shaw."

Three things warned Claudia that she could wait no longer. One had been Lord Rushborough's account of the stag and Donal's incredible ride. The second had been overhearing Donal's excited speech to Nancy in the hall, about meeting his father on the fell.

The third was the look of grave distress on Eden's face.

"I . . . do not understand you, Aunt," Eden said. She appeared very close to collapse, driven to distraction by the shock she must have suffered. But she had enough presence of mind to lie.

"I am sorry that I did not tell you sooner," Claudia said. "I know what you saw on the fell. I know who it was that carried Donal on his back."

Claudia felt behind herself for the bench and sank down. "A stag . . . it was a stag —"

"A stag who became something very much like a man, but not a man. A creature who has deceived you from the first."

Eden's eyes told her that her guess was correct. He had revealed himself, either by accident or design.

Even his kind could make dire mistakes.

"Oh, my dear," Claudia said. She sat beside Eden, pitying her, yet knowing she must be ruthless. "I swore to your father than I would never reveal what I am about to tell you. My brother did a terrible thing when he promised you to that creature, and perhaps it is not too late to undo the damage he caused."

"Papa," Eden whispered. "What are you saying?"

Claudia sighed. "It will not be easy for you to hear. You must be very strong, dearest Niece." She glanced up the fell. "The man you knew as Hartley Shaw has worn many faces. Six years ago, he was Cornelius Fleming. But I did not recognize what he was. It was only much later, when your father told me all, that I understood. And it has taken me years to discover the handful of facts and legends that have enabled me to uncover his nature and his purpose here."

Eden put on a brave face. "He told me he was . . . Cornelius. He admitted —"

"That he had lied to you, again and again?" She took Eden's cold hand between her own. "Did he also tell you that he is the last of what were once called the Fair Folk, Faeries, Fée, Fane — immortal, soulless creatures incapable of love or human virtue? That he left his forest only to obtain a son from a mortal woman, by any means necessary — and that he intends to take Donal from you?"

Eden's eyes stared at nothing, as if the pictures within her own mind blotted out reality. "Faeries?"

"They are not like the fairies in the childish stories you have heard. Not mischievous and tiny and easily frightened away. They were a powerful, sorcerous race that once inhabited the earth, but fled when men came. Only a few remained. The one who now calls himself Hartley had many names over many centuries. He has been called Kernunnos, and Cocidius, and Hern — pagan words from savage times, when men were little more than beasts themselves." She stroked Eden's lifeless hand. "Did you not wonder why your father, so avid a sportsman, never hunted at Hartsmere until just before Cornelius appeared? This Hern protected the forest at Hartsmere. He hated men, Eden — he still does. He is like the beasts he guards." She closed her eyes. "God help the man who enters that forest uninvited."

Eden tried to stand, but Claudia was afraid she would fall. She kept a hard grip on Eden's arm.

"You must listen, Eden. These Fair Folk have been known since time began for stealing human children. They have few weaknesses, but one is an attraction to mortal emotion. They long to experience what they do not possess, but they discard that which they desired when it is no longer new and fascinating."

"He . . . wants to take my son?"

"The Faerie race have very few offspring of their own, and so they seek mortal men and women as mates to produce half-breed children. For centuries this Hern avoided men and remained in his forest. But something happened that caused him to seek a mate so that he could sire a child. His motives I do not pretend to understand. But I do know how he found you, Eden."

"Papa."

"Yes. Your father was a weak man, Eden. One day, he made the foolish mistake of hunting near the wood at Hartsmere, even though the Flemings had not done so in memory. He had been told, like all the heirs of Hartsmere, that hunting in the dale was forbidden, and that the prosperity of the family and the dale depended upon keeping this pact."

"The legends," Eden said dully. "The ones the dalesmen spoke of."

"Indeed." Claudia shuddered with her own dark memories. "But your father scoffed at the stories. I had not heard them myself, since the secret was kept strictly among the lords and their heirs, but I had . . . other reasons for avoiding Hartsmere. I remained with you there after Cornelius arrived because I sensed that something was wrong and desired to protect you. In that I failed."

"But Papa —"

"He pursued a hare to the edge of the forest, and then saw a great stag. He could not resist the chance to hunt such a rare creature. But when he followed it into the wood, he was met by a man — a man who commanded the beasts and bore a set of antlers upon his head. This creature, Hern, told him that he must sacrifice his own daughter to bear Hern a son, or suffer the loss of everything he owned, and worse. And he revealed his inhuman powers so that your father could not doubt him capable of carrying out his threats.

"Your father loved you, Eden, but he was afraid. He found enough courage to bargain with the Forest Lord — to ask that he court you as human, posing as a distant cousin just returned from India. He demanded that you agree, willingly, to marry Hern in his human guise, and that the world should recognize the marriage as real and legal. But he knew that Hern did not intend to remain with you. He knew that Hern wanted a child and that he would take that child away soon after its birth. The only thing you would have left was your reputation, and a chance to marry again."

Eden covered her mouth with one hand. Claudia embraced her gently.

"Your attraction to Cornelius Fleming was understandable. He appeared to be a respectable young man, the likely heir to the Bradwell estates if your Uncle Fleming died without sons. You were young and impressionable, and there is no telling what sort of evil spell he cast upon you. The fault was not yours."

Eden shook her head with a sharp jerk. "I agreed to elope with him because I could not wait for a regular marriage. I was so in love." She laughed. "I heard him . . . the night at the inn near Gretna . . . bargaining with father. About me, but I didn't completely understand. Then I saw him as he truly is. As he was today. And I ran."

"Into the storm." Claudia stroked her hair. "You never spoke of what had happened. Your father and I thought it best to help you avoid the memories and all thought of the creature. He did come after you . . . but you were ill, and your father convinced him to come back only when the child was born."

"And he did come back, didn't he?" Eden whispered. "He came back for my boy."

"To take it from you, as he had bargained." Claudia pressed Eden's face against her shoulder. "But your father thwarted him. Bradwell could not surrender his own blood to such a monster. He told Cornelius that the child was dead. He swore me to secrecy and sent it away for its own protection, intending to tell you what he had done when you were well again."

"To Ireland. But how could Papa send him to poor folk, who could not care for him? Why not to my Uncle Fleming?"

"I do not know, Eden. Something did not proceed as planned, and he left England soon after, broken in purse and spirit."

Eden's eyes were haunted. "Oh, Papa."

"He was bitter about what he had done to you, Eden. He hated himself for it. The creature went away and did not return. We believed we were safe." She allowed herself a bitter smile. "But the beast did not leave. He has waited for your return to Hartsmere."

"And he learned that Donal was alive . . . when I did," Eden whispered. "He believed I had betrayed him, as Papa had."

"Can one betray a minion of the devil?" Claudia asked. "No, Eden. Do not attribute human motives to him. All he wanted then — as now — was the unnatural son he had fathered. If Donal had not come to Hartsmere, if his guardians in Ireland had not sent him back, he would have been safe. But now all that has changed."

"He was not safe in Ireland," Eden said. "He has never been safe, except —" She broke off and subtly shifted out of Claudia's arms. "I will do anything, anything at all, to protect him."

Yes, Claudia thought. *I know you will.* "And that is why I have revealed all this to you. So you will understand that this creature who calls himself Hartley Shaw has insinuated himself into your life, and Donal's, for the sole purpose of stealing your son away to his blighted realm."

"He could have taken Donal a thousand times. Why didn't he?"

"I assure you, that has been his aim from the first moment he courted you as Cornelius Fleming. Perhaps he preferred to win Donal's affection so the boy would go with him willingly. Or perhaps he hoped to get you with another half human child by seducing you once more — this time without a false promise of marriage."

Her crude words were effective. Eden's fingers curled into fists. "If what you say is true," she said, "then everything I have come to believe during these past months is a lie. Everything but Donal."

Claudia saw the lingering doubt in her eyes. A part of the girl was desperate to believe that love could exist between a mortal woman and a creature such as Hern.

. "Do you remember when we first came to Hartsmere, Eden, and witnessed the sad state of the dale? When your father defied the Forest Lord, he ended many years of prosperity. But Bradwell also lost his fortune, all the luck that had sustained the Flemings for centuries. Hern ruined your father, Eden. He punished many innocents who had never offended him. He can destroy you just as surely. Once he has what he came for, he will take your son and abandon you."

Eden stumbled to a trellis decked with an autumn rose and rested her forehead against it, heedless of the thorns. Perhaps she welcomed the pain.

"Should I believe you?" she whispered. "You say you tell me this for my sake, but your feelings . . . surely there is more to them than fear for me." She turned from the trellis, unaware of the trickle of blood on her brow. "There is something personal in your hatred, is there not?"

Claudia pressed her hand to her breast and let tears fill her eyes. "Have I failed you so badly that you question me thus? Is it not personal that this monster drove my foolish brother to near insanity and, for all we know, to his death in some foreign country? Is it not personal that he took your innocence and forced you into an odious marriage with Winstowe — you, whom I love above anyone on this earth?" She felt for her handkerchief. "I have seen what he can do, Eden. I cannot let him make my nephew into the monster he is. I will not let him finish what he began."

Eden sat beside her and touched Claudia's rigid fingers.

"I have hurt you," she said, her voice as calm as a windless dusk. "I am sorry. What shall we do?"

Claudia savored her bitter victory in the privacy of her own heart. "Trust me," she said. "I will help you to save Donal. And the first thing we must do is leave Hartsmere and return to London."

"How will that save Donal? *He* will simply follow —"

"No, Eden. These creatures are not the gods they once claimed to be. For a thousand years or more, Hern has been bound to the forest of Hartsmere. He cannot leave it for long, or he grows weak. The farther he goes from the forest, the more his powers — his life — drain from him. And like all his kind, he cannot touch iron without suffering great pain and risking death. He will not follow." She stood and took Eden's arm. "You will not be alone in London, my dear girl. Just an hour ago Lord Rushborough confided to me that he intends to remove to London for a few weeks before returning to his estates in Kent. He has invited us both to stay with his sister in Mayfair should we choose to visit before Christmas."

"But he must . . . *you* must understand that I have no intention of —"

"He adores you, Eden. That is why he has been so patient. But he also told me that if you choose not to accept his invitation this time, he will trouble you no longer."

From the look on Eden's face, she was quite troubled enough without the complications presented by the marquess. But it was her supreme vulnerability that would aid Lord Rushborough in winning the affection she had thus far denied him.

After all, who else could Eden go to now? What else, except her former life?

"Come," Claudia said. "We must leave for Hartsmere immediately if we wish to prepare for a morning departure."

Eden did not glance up the fell as Claudia led her into the house.

Chapter 19

The weather was unseasonably violent on the morning they left Hartsmere.

Snow fell in great gouts from the sky, as if nature itself conspired to keep them from escaping. It was seldom, the servants said, that snow fell in October, and never so steadily.

Eden and Donal, bundled in furs and blankets, sat in the inelegant post chaise Claudia had hired to convey them to London. The postilions stood beside the horses, stamping their feet to keep warm, while their animals blew clouds of mist that quickly dissolved in the lashing snow.

Claudia's form was just discernible through the window, consulting with Dalziel, who was to drive the old berline that would carry her, Jane, and their few hastily packed trunks. Any notion of using the landau had been discarded because of the harsh weather. Dalziel perched in the berline's driver's box, so wrapped up in scarves, hat, and greatcoat that only his eyes were visible.

Eden was as numb as the stinging cold that bombarded them from every side, blanketing the world in the white of death. The death of dreams.

She held Donal tight against her, as much for her own peace of mind as to warm him. His little body gave off more heat than the bricks under their feet. She looked outside the window and wondered how far they could go before the roads became impassable. Now that she had made her decision, all she could think of was to be gone from this place.

Hartley — Hern — had not shown himself again. Every moment since last night she had expected him to appear from behind a tree or rock, glaring at her with accusing, inhuman eyes.

But she could not maintain that image long. The eyes she remembered were warm and filled with pain as he begged for her understanding.

No. A deception. A lie. It must be. Because if it were not, she could not live with herself. And she must go on living — for Donal's sake.

Nothing was worth risking her son. Donal was real, and his love — her love for him — must be the only happiness in a future where sorrow was the one abiding condition she could expect. She no longer believed in some ephemeral happiness based on false hopes, not even the fragile chance that love between a man and woman could survive the wreckage of shattered beliefs and broken trust.

"Mother, why do we go to London?"

Eden had prepared herself for the questions she knew must come — those which, in the rush of preparation, had been blessedly spared her until now. She squeezed Donal's mittened fingers.

"You know that I lived in London for many years before I came here, Donal. I left there very quickly. There are still a few things . . . that I must do that I did not get a chance to finish."

"When is Hartley coming to London?"

Her heart seized in midbeat. Donal had not called Hartley "Da" since that disastrous meeting. It was as if he knew how that word upset his mother. Just as he seemed to know better than to speak of what had happened on the fell.

He did not know of the message she had found tucked beneath her bedchamber door at Hartsmere. She feared to speculate how it had arrived there, but Hartley's brief words had both tormented her and given her the hope that he would not realize they had left until it was too late. In three days, they would be over halfway to London.

"I . . . am not certain, Donal," she said. "He has duties at Hartsmere that he cannot abandon." She tried to smile. "Who else can care for the animals so well as he?"

Donal looked at her, and she could hardly meet his gaze. He knew she was lying. He knew, and forgave.

"Will Mrs. Byrne be there?"

Eden breathed again. "Someone must stay to look after the house — but we shall see."

"When do we come home?"

She owed him the truth at least once. "I do not know, Donal."

He absorbed this gravely and turned to the wooden soldiers she had given him for the journey. His very silence was worse than any accusation. But, mercifully, he did not ask for her reasons. She could not have answered. She tucked the blankets more snugly about him.

A tap came on the window.

"My lady?"

She glimpsed one of the postboy's faces through the frosted glass and opened the door. "Is it time?"

"Aye, your ladyship."

Claudia appeared, as bundled as the rest of them and equally unrecognizable. "I shall be right behind you every moment, my dear," she said. She took a steaming tankard from Armstrong, who was to ride at the back of the berline, and offered it to Eden. "Drink this. It will warm you and give you a little extra courage to face what lies ahead."

The mulled wine was hot enough to burn her tongue, but Eden welcomed the bite. She took a few sips and returned the tankard to Armstrong.

"Now we shall go," Claudia said. "Have faith. This will soon be over."

As the post chaise began to move and the berline followed in its wake, Eden tried to see through the endless white to the house and the garden. It might be the last glimpse she would ever have of Hartsmere.

Home, Donal had called it. She realized, now, how much she had begun to think of it as her home as well. Its people her people. Her friends. But as long as things remained as they were, she dared not come here again with her son.

In Mr. Rumbold she had an excellent steward to look after the estate. She would continue to send what funds she could spare to support the dale, and pray that the people continued to prosper.

Pray that Hartley surrendered and returned forever to the unearthly place from which he'd come.

A stab of soul-deep pain struck at her heart. If he left, all her problems would be solved. But if he remained, and the dale suffered because of her as it had when her father betrayed his promise, then she would return and beg him on her knees to have pity. She would give him anything he wanted, except Donal — even herself. She would find a way to appease the monster.

A monster who had helped the dalesmen time and again, taught Donal with patient affection, loved her so tenderly.

Who had bargained for her body, her child, and cursed her father for refusing to carry out that devil's pact.

Dry-eyed, Eden pulled Donal into her arms and watched Hartsmere disappear behind a sheet of snow. Love was dying in her once more, and she thought this time must be the last.

Let it be the last. Let it not struggle for existence when there was no hope.

The park was like a counterpane of bleached muslin, broken only by the darker upthrust of trees and shrubbery, and the rapidly disappearing drive upon which they traveled. The carriages passed through the gate and down the slope into the heart of the dale.

That was when a figure stepped out from among the trees, directly in the chaise's path.

Eden's heart slammed wildly within her ribs as she pushed Donal behind her.

It was not Hartley Shaw who stood before the coach. It was the Forest Lord, with his antlers and his aura of power, larger than life or anything human, his hands raised in a gesture of warning. The green and brown scraps of his ragged clothing floated gently about him, as if the harsh wind did not touch him. He spoke words she could not comprehend.

She did not need to. "Fly!" she cried to the postilions. *"Fly!"* But the men did not hear her, or could not obey.

"Mother?" Donal whispered. "Is it —"

She muffled his words beneath the blankets, as if she could hide him from eyesight so much keener than hers. The Forest Lord moved toward the side of the coach, every line of his body conveying predatory desire and fierce purpose. He reached for the door handle. Eden searched desperately for a weapon, anything to use against him. A wave of unexpected weakness swept over her.

A sharp, reverberating crack shattered the quiet. It sounded very much like a gunshot, but who would dare hunt here? Donal struggled in her arms. The weakness had grown so intense that she could scarcely hold him. Through dimmed vision she saw that Hartley was no longer trying to enter the chaise.

When next she opened her eyes, the window framed a different face. The door opened. Cold air rushed in, followed by Claudia's mittened hand.

"Eden! Are you well?"

"Aunt, what . . . I . . . ." Words became all twisted in her head, impossible to force past the malaise. "He . . . he came after Donal . . ."

"You need not fear. He is gone. Dalziel frightened him away with his pistol." Claudia's voice remained calm and unafraid. "You are both safe — for now. But we must change our plans, Eden. He knows Donal is with you. He will pursue you if he can. We must separate."

Hartley had gone away, but he would come back. "Change carriages," Eden murmured through lips thick as sausages. "Donal and me . . . in the berline . . ."

"That is not enough. You must send Donal with me. I know of a place to go where he will be safe."

Send Donal with Claudia? Let him go? Eden tried to shake her head, but even so small a motion made her faint.

"It is the only way," Claudia continued. Her voice had begun to echo, as if at the end of a very long tunnel. "We will change coaches. Donal will come with me, and you will proceed to London. The monster will not believe that you would let Donal out of your sight. If he follows, he will follow you."

It all made sense to her befogged brain, though her emotions cried out in violent protest. She could feel herself slipping close to unconsciousness. Soon she would be in no state to look after Donal in any capacity, let alone defend him. "Ill," she whispered. "I am . . . ill."

Claudia's soft, bare palm pressed her forehead. "You do not feel feverish. You are overtired, and your strength has been taxed too far. You should stop at Ambleside. You must rest there until you feel able to continue, while I take Donal ahead. That will be even more sure to throw the monster off."

Claudia's face had become a blur. "Where? Where . . . take Donal?"

"It is best that you not know, in case he finds you and uses his enchantments upon you. Nancy will go with you. I will send word to London as soon as we are settled."

She withdrew, and Eden felt herself being shifted about. Donal's warmth left her side. "I'll take her, your ladyship," Dalziel's distant voice said, and she was lifted into strong arms and carried from the post chaise and across the snow. The whole world was a mass of white streaked with black and red.

"Donal," she whimpered.

"There, lass," Dalziel said. "It'll be well, you'll see. You come with me, now."

Struggle was beyond her. Her body came to rest amid blankets meant to cushion the berline's hard seats, and more were tucked around her. A soft woman's voice murmured above her. She could not get warm.

Donal was gone.

Tears came, at last — quiet tears that seemed to fall from someone else's eyes. They dampened the blanket wrapped over her chest and shoulders, but she couldn't lift her hand to blot them away.

After a time the berline lurched forward again. Eden had very little sense of movement, anything beyond the suffocating universe of the berline's interior. She forgot where she was going and why. The more she labored to remember, the thicker grew the fog in her head.

In her dreams, Papa held out his blunt-fingered hand with a broad smile and called her name.

"Let go, my pet," he said, as he'd once called her so long ago. "It's not worth the candle."

At last she stopped struggling and surrendered to peace.

Like any wounded creature of the forest, Hartley sought the darkest and most sheltered place he could find in which to battle death.

This enemy was no stranger to him. He had seen countless humans — mortals — come and go, though he had been close to few of them. He had seen great trees topple and mighty stags driven to their end by young, vigorous rivals. He knew that death was a part of life on this earth.

But never had he faced it himself, not like this.

The iron ball had worked its way deep into his body from the wound in his side, tracing a path of searing agony, it had come to lodge very near his heart, leaching its poison into his blood.

Had he seen the shot coming, he might have made himself insubstantial, a wraith that the ball could not touch.

But he had been caught off guard when Claudia raised the pistol and fired. He had been completely vulnerable.

And Claudia had known exactly what to use to hurt him.

Iron. Cold Iron, the deadliest weapon man could wield against the Fane.

He crawled into the hollow of the fallen oak, where brown leaves pressed against him in a rustling cocoon. Each movement sent the poison coursing more swiftly through his body. Each breath brought screaming pain.

Claudia had shot him. Claudia *knew* what he was. Had Eden told her?

He ground his teeth to fight the greater anguish of that possibility. Had Eden warned her aunt what to expect? How had either of them known the way to disable one of his race?

He had no doubt that Claudia meant his death. But had Eden done the same?

No. He refused to accept it. She had rejected him a second time when she'd not returned to the forest, but she would not seek his death. She could not have known what Claudia intended.

But she must have told Claudia what he was. And made her aunt believe.

Hartley closed his eyes and concentrated on drawing air in and out of his burning lungs. That he was not already dead was a mark of his tolerance for exposure to Iron that would cripple another of his kind. He had handled bits, harness buckles, gates, nails, and other iron implements and tools used in everyday mortal life. He had become used to the constant discomfort.

But touching Iron with his hands and having it planted within his body were two different things. And this wound would even kill a human, for whom the metal was no worse than any other.

He did not dare use his magic to close the wound and stop the loss of blood, for the blood kept the metal from concentrating in his body. He knew what the next few days would bring: stillness, silence, enduring endless pain, and fighting every moment for his life. Fighting with all the tricks his Fane body could devise.

And most of that fight would be utterly beyond his control.

He heard the scrabbling of small animals about him, gathering to the silent call of his distress. They could not help him, either. But he took comfort in their nearness and their gentle, hesitant concern.

It was the only comfort he could find. The thoughts circled about in his head, becoming more bitter with every turn. Did Eden know he had been shot? Had she even thought to help him? Had she simply driven on, watching him bleed into the snow?

And Donal — had he seen his mother's aunt try to kill his father?

No answers came. But amid the haze of his pain, Hartley clutched at the plans forming in his mind: plans of tracking Eden wherever she might run, of finding her, standing before her and forcing her to confess her perfidy.

And of taking Donal from her, away from this tainted earth.

Healing sleep enfolded him: a sleep that would end with his body whole or dead. It was said that no Fane dreamed like mortals, but Hartley did. In his dreams, Eden lay in his arms and repeated the words she had said once, an eternity past: *"I love you."*

In his dreams, he believed her.

On the second morning at the inn in Ambleside, Eden forced herself to rise. She ignored Nancy's protests and asked the maid to help her dress. Each small motion required utmost concentration, but with her abigail's help she managed to wash and don her half boots and pelisse.

Nancy insisted that she drink at least a few sips of tea, and she did so, though nothing tasted pleasant on her tongue. She was still very ill. Walking had become as much a challenge as climbing the steepest fell.

But she had to get to London. That was where Claudia would send word. Claudia had Donal. She was keeping him safe from Hartley.

She *must* be keeping him safe.

Eden had dreamed during her first long period of sleep at the inn, the night after their departure from Hartsmere. She had dreamed, not of Donal or Claudia, but of her father as he had been in his youth: bluff and stout, good natured, more a country squire than a belted earl, casually affectionate with her when he did not forget she existed, and always a little surprised at her detestation of the countryside.

That was the way she tried to remember him, not as the man who had sold her to an inhuman creature, married her off to Spencer Winstowe, and then abandoned her. But she had no curiosity to expend on the cause of such dreams.

During her brief intervals of consciousness, Eden had tormented herself trying to remember what had happened before she and Claudia separated. So much of it was like a nightmare. First Hartley's appearance . . . then Claudia insisting that Donal could not be safe with his mother. Eden's sudden illness, that made her aunt's suggestion seem the height of good sense. Of necessity.

But Hartley had not followed her to the inn. Perhaps he had followed Donal instead.

The need for grim focus on simple actions kept Eden from driving herself mad with such thoughts. She called for Dalziel and accepted his help, along with Nancy's, to make her way downstairs to the inn yard. The anxious innkeeper followed, offering every sort of aid but the kind she needed most.

The berline stood waiting with the well-rested horses. Eden fixed her eyes on the coach and took one step after another, leaning heavily on Dalziel's arm.

A man stepped directly into her path. Dalziel and Nancy

stopped, clutching Eden to keep her from falling, and Dalziel opened his mouth to rebuke the human obstruction.

The man turned about. His clothing was of good cut but well worn and too large on his thin frame, his hair in need of cutting, and the valise he carried had seen much abuse.

Even so, Eden recognized him. And all the shocks of the past week crashed in upon her with renewed force. Only Dalziel's firm grip kept her on her feet.

"Papa," she whispered.

Had there been any way to do so, Eden would have continued on and ordered Dalziel to drive away. But her father stood there, staring, by turns flushed and pale. And her ravaged body had become paralyzed by a score of conflicting emotions.

Anger was first. Wild, unreasoning anger. Then came joy that he was alive and had returned. Next was grief, and then the lunatic desire to laugh and laugh and laugh.

But such violent emotion sapped too much of her precious strength. She shut it all away in a part of her mind where she could find it again later, and faced him.

His lips moved, forming a name he didn't speak. His throat worked. She realized with dull amazement that he was afraid. In all her life she could remember seeing him afraid only once before, and that was at the border inn when he'd bargained with Cornelius.

"Eden," he whispered. "Lass, to see you again . . ."

"Lord Bradwell?" Dalziel stammered.

A public inn was no place for a painful reunion. "It is all right, Dalziel," Eden said. "If you would help me to the coach, I shall sit down. Father —" She could not bring herself to call him Papa again. "I am glad to see that you are well. We will have some privacy in the coach."

As unsteady on his feet as she, Lord Bradwell turned and stumbled after her and Dalziel. Nancy fluttered about her, but once Eden was seated, she asked the abigail and coachman to wait inside the inn.

Her father sat opposite, clasping and unclasping his hands. "I cannot believe it," he said hoarsely. "I have been searching for you, Eden, all over London. They said you had gone to Hartsmere, so I came north. I was just about to leave the inn when —" He swallowed. "It is a miracle that you are here. I have so much to explain . . ."

Why did you take my son? Eden bit her tongue to keep from screaming the question. "Where have you been, Father?"

"On the continent. Nowhere, and everywhere. But you . . . they told me that Winstowe was dead."

"Yes. I have spent the past ten months at Hartsmere."

He looked at her as if seeing her clearly for the first time, taking in her half mourning and the signs of recent illness. "You go there now?"

"I am bound for London." She closed her eyes. Her sickness, which had briefly abated, was seizing upon the strain of this unexpected meeting. "Why did you not write? I did not know if you were alive or dead."

His voice cracked in a sound that might have been a laugh. "I might as well have been dead. Losing everything due to my own folly and cowardice, leaving you to make your own way . . ."

"I have been well," she said. "Hartsmere is prospering."

"Hartsmere," he whispered. "I had not thought that you would go back."

"Nor did I." She looked down at her remarkably steady hands. "Spencer died almost a year ago. It was necessary to retrench and restore my income. Hartsmere seemed the best option at the time."

Lord Bradwell bowed his head. "I believe I understand you. Spencer left nothing but debts."

"Yes."

"And when the allowance stopped coming — when I disappeared — what remained could not have lasted long. Spencer —" He pulled his hand over his face. "Eden, I did not realize his true nature when I encouraged you to wed him. All I could think of was to . . ." He shook his head. "I am . . . deeply sorry."

So he had known what Winstowe was. But he had not

remained to support her with a father's love, even his haphazard sort of affection.

And he had stolen her child.

"I have much to atone for," he murmured. "So much."

"Such as sending my son away to strangers?"

His head jerked up. "What?"

"My son, Donal — the one you sent to live in Ireland."
Her bitterness leaked out. "Spencer told me of his exis-
tence before he died. Donal has been living with me at
Hartsmere."

"But that is im —" He looked as ill as she felt. "The boy
is alive?"

If this was some cruel game on his part, he had changed
more than she could imagine. "Why do you ask, Father?
Did you not know? Did you not lie to me by telling me he
was dead?"

He tried to stand, bumped his head on the coach's ceiling, and fell back into his seat. "No," he croaked, holding
out his hand. "No, Eden. I . . . I was told that the child had
died at birth."

Eden became perfectly composed, her mind working
like a machine made of frigid steel. If he spoke the truth,
then only one other person could have told him that Donal
was dead. Only one other person could have arranged to
have a child spirited away and maintained the fiction that
the tiny casket they had buried contained her son.

Claudia.

But why? What earthly reason could she have for saying Donal had died? Why had she given him to common
Irish peasants? And how had Spencer learned of Donal's
existence, when Claudia had so hated Eden's husband?

Papa had told Claudia of his devil's bargain and Cornelius's true nature. She must have sent Donal away for the
very reasons she had attributed to her brother — to protect
Donal from his father — and had feared confiding even in
Lord Bradwell. Perhaps, having failed to assure Donal's
welfare in Ireland through poor judgment or simple carelessness, she had been afraid to reveal her part in his ab-

duction and was now attempting to make amends for her mistakes.

But that explanation left too many questions unanswered. It made Claudia into a liar who had pretended surprise even after Eden learned Donal was alive, who actively discouraged her niece from seeking her son. It turned Claudia into a woman Eden did not recognize and could not trust.

Donal was with Claudia at this very moment, but she had no reason to do him harm. She was still his great-aunt. But suddenly, urgently, Eden wanted Donal safe and sound in her arms. And her thoughts flew to the man whose arms would never hold his son again.

Or hold *her* again.

A piercing headache started behind Eden's eyes, harbinger of another bout of debilitating lethargy. Where had Claudia taken Donal?

"I did not know, Eden," her father repeated, tears thickening his voice. "You must believe me. Where is . . . Donal now?"

How could she begin to explain all that had happened since her father's disappearance? He did not realize how much she understood of what he had done in offering her to Cornelius, let alone that the Forest Lord had returned to haunt her. She wondered if he ever intended to tell her the full truth.

Yet the old resentments seemed petty and unimportant now. "He is with my aunt. We are to meet in London and stay with Lord Rushborough's sister, Lady Saville. I regret that I cannot offer you hospitality, but I must —" She fought off a wave of weakness. "I must be on my way."

"There is so much left to say, to explain. Eden —"

"We will meet again, Father." *After I have my son.* "Will you . . . please send for my maid?"

"You are not well! Let me take you inside —"

"No." She braced herself on the seat. "I must . . . go to my son."

"Is your aunt in London now?"

She cursed herself, and the unspoken words bounced like loose pistol balls inside her skull. "No. I was ill, and . . . we left Hartsmere in haste, because certain threats . . . had been made against Donal and me."

"Threats? What sort of threats? By whom?"

She shook her head, a mistake she paid for dearly.

"Claudia—" *Claudia insisted that he go with her.* "She was to take Donal . . . to a safe place." *Why did I let him out of my sight?* "She . . . did not tell me where."

Lord Bradwell's forehead creased with worry. "I knew that something was wrong, Eden, and I shall not desert you again in your time of need. I am not the man I was five years ago. Please allow me to find my grandson and bring him to you."

"H-how?"

"There was a place Claudia sometimes went when she needed a sanctuary, one she would consider quite safe. Perhaps she has taken him there. I will inquire upon the road."

"Tell me. Tell me where —" Eden's head had begun to spin. Lord Bradwell gripped her shoulders to hold her upright. It was the first time they had touched in five years.

"I beg you to trust me, Eden. Please. You are too unwell, and I know my sister as even you do not. If Hartsmere is not safe, you must go where you can be properly cared for. I once had friends in the neighborhood —"

Trust you? "No." It was becoming very difficult to think, just as it had been when she left Hartsmere. "My son. I must . . ."

He made some reply, but she could not seem to make sense of it. She dug her fingers into his coat. "Help me."

"I shall, Daughter." He squeezed her hand. "We will be a family again, I promise you."

That was the last she heard for a very long time. She drifted through a series of dreams — dreams of rumbling, constant motion, floating through space, muffled voices, and gentle touches. Faces passed in and out of her vision. Someone told her to drink, and she drank. She fought to wake up, aware of some urgent matter that required her attention, but the void dragged her down again like a deadly ocean current.

What finally set her free was the complete absence of movement. She felt a soft mattress under her back and blankets drawn up to her chin. She opened her eyes. The dim room in which she lay was not that of an inn, nor was it her own chamber at Hartsmere. She attempted to sit, but her head immediately warned her that such an action was most unwise.

"My lady? Are you awake?"

She turned her head to see a girl sitting at her bedside, a maid too young to be anything but a tweenie.

"Where am I?" Eden said. Her voice felt as if it had not been used in ages.

The maid sprang to her feet and curtsied. "You are at Lady Saville's house, my lady. You have been ill. I was told to watch you until you woke up."

Lady Flavia Saville's. That had been where she was bound . . . when they left Hartsmere. Memory returned all at once, in perfectly distinct, vivid images. The flight, her illness, the stop at the inn. The reunion with her father, and what she had learned from him. Her determination to find Donal. And then the darkness.

"How did I come to . . . be here?" she asked. "What day is it?" *Where is my son?*

"I will ask for Lady Saville," the maid said. She darted out of the room before Eden could blink.

Her body insisted that she close her eyes again, but she'd had enough of oblivion. Grimly, she rested her weight on her elbows and pushed up. She had managed to prop herself against the headboard when the door opened and someone entered.

"Oh, my dear! You are recovered at last!"

Eden had met Rushborough's sister many times and was grateful she need not stand on formality. Under the circumstances, it would have been ridiculous to try. She was by no means recovered, and remaining civil and courteous would require all her efforts.

"Lady Saville," she said, clenching her teeth at the pounding in her head. "I am sorry that I cannot rise to greet you."

"Tut, tut. As if I would expect it! You remain where you are, and I will have food and drink sent to you at once. If you believe you can eat now? You have gone days without a bite! As I told Rushborough —"

"I beg your pardon," Eden interrupted, "but I do not even know how I got here, or what day it is."

"My word, of course you do not! You were quite insensible to the world." Lady Saville availed herself of the chair and leaned forward with earnest solicitude, ample bosom straining the bodice of her satin gown. "We were so very worried about you, my dear. Your abigail and coachman conveyed you all the way from Westmorland, at your father's request . . . Lord Bradwell! I had heard rumors that he was dead. Oh, I am so sorry, my dear. I am quite beside myself. Apparently you were ill during the entire journey, and of course we did what we could for you, but the doctor was quite —"

"I am grateful for your kind attention to my welfare, Lady Saville, but —"

"Rushborough came to visit every day, but you did not know him. You did not know anyone. That quack of a doctor insisted that you appeared to have taken laudanum. Can you imagine such flummery?"

Laudanum. Eden nearly bit through her lower lip. "How long have I been here?"

"You came to us three days ago. Your father left you a letter. It is here somewhere in the room —" She popped up and bustled to the escritoire, opening drawers. "Ah, here it is! Shall I read it to you, Lady Eden?"

Given the nature of her conversation with Lord Bradwell, Eden dared not risk Lady Saville discovering such a letter's contents. Her father did not know that she claimed Donal as her uncle's grandson and not her own child.

"If you will permit me, I will read it myself," Eden said with an apologetic smile.

Unsuccessfully hiding her disappointment, Lady Saville passed her the letter. It was still sealed. Breathing a sigh of relief, Eden waited until her hostess had stepped away. Eden opened the letter. A thin strip of sunlight between the curtains provided the only illumination, just enough for her to discern the hastily scrawled words.

Dear Daughter,

I pray that this missive finds you in better health than when we parted. Since you were no longer able to give instruction to your servants, I have ordered Dalziel to drive you and your abigail directly to Lady Saville's, with a note to her of your condition and a request for your care.

I go now to find your aunt and the boy. I will bring Donal to London and send him to you at Lady Saville's as soon as we arrive, no later than the last day of this month.

Have no fear, Daughter. You will soon be reunited with your family.

Bradwell

Eden set down the letter and leaned back her head. Bless Lord Bradwell. He had been discreet, in case the letter fell into the wrong hands. He was wiser now than he had been. Than *she* had been.

And had she any choice, now, but to trust him? Tomorrow was the day he had promised to bring Donal. If ever she had needed faith in another person — and in Providence — it was now.

But oh, how difficult it was not to fling herself from bed and dash madly in any and all directions.

"It is good news, I hope?" Lady Saville asked.

Eden folded the letter. "No other messages have been sent for me?"

"No, my dear. Are you expecting one?"

"Yes. A messenger may arrive at any time."

"I shall instruct Hoskins to watch for it."

"Are Dalziel and Nancy well?"

"Your coachman is lodged with our servants. The abigail —" She pursed her lips. "She remained long enough to see to your comfort and then disappeared."

Nancy, gone. And the doctor believed Eden had taken — or been given — laudanum. If Eden's illness vanished with Nancy's absence, she would know the source of her malaise. But Nancy would not have done such a thing on her own. Or willingly.

It all came back to Claudia.

"You are quite pale, Lady Eden," Lady Saville remarked. "I shall send up some nice tea and leave you to your rest. I do hope you find yourself quite well very soon; tomorrow is Rushborough's birthday fête, and he would so enjoy it if you could attend."

Attend a *ton* party? Nothing interested Eden less. But she smiled and pressed Lady Saville's plump fingers. "I shall do my best. Thank you, Lady Saville, for taking such care of me."

"Tut, tut. Rest now. We shall talk later."

She swept out of the room, and Eden discarded the mask she had worn for her hostess's sake. She buried her hands in the sheets and twisted the muslin into tortured knots.

Hartley. If only I could trust you. If only you were here with me now.

But even a Faerie lord's magic was not enough to bring about such a miracle.

Chapter 20

The guest list for Lord Rushborough's birthday celebration was most select. Only the most influential, most respectable members of the *ton* who remained in London had been invited to Lady Saville's stately mansion on All Hallows' Eve. However inconvenient it might be that her brother had been born when London was thinnest of company, Flavia Saville intended to make the best of it.

Lady Saville had tried to convince Eden to be the evening's second guest of honor. The only thing that spared Eden that trial was the excuse of her illness. In spite of her rapid improvement, lingering weakness had confined her to taking brief turns about her bedchamber. She had been able to eat a little and receive a few visitors, including Lord Rushborough. His possessive inquiries about her health did nothing to ease the state of her mind.

Even amid the relative peace of Grosvenor Square, the noise and bustle and excitement of the city, which she had once adored, grated unbearably on her frayed nerves. The constant racket overwhelmed ears grown used to the quiet of the country; the droning hum of the guests as they arrived and mingled downstairs was like the relentless buzzing of flies. Even the smells within and without the house made her stomach churn with nausea.

And her thoughts circled incessantly among Claudia, Lord Bradwell, Donal, and Hartley. Her imagination tormented her with dreadful possibilities: Claudia seeking to drug her niece so that she, not Hartley, could steal Eden's son for her own incomprehensible reasons. Hartley attempting to follow, and succeeding — or suffering the dangerous effects of leaving Hartsmere. Her father failing in his promise to find Donal. Donal crying for his mother . . .

It was those helpless worries that drove Eden to rise from her bed and dress on the night of the birthday fête. She had been counting the hours since dawn, listening and hoping for word that Lord Bradwell had brought Donal safe to London. She intended to be ready when the message came.

Let it come soon.

With her borrowed maid's help, she donned a simple long-sleeved carriage dress of Madras muslin and sent the maid downstairs to inquire once more. After an hour of pacing her room, she thought that she might well go mad if she remained there another minute. But if Lady Saville saw her on her feet, her refusal to join the party in Lord Rushborough's honor would be most awkward, especially in light of the assumptions his sister and the *ton* were already beginning to make.

By now, everyone guessed that Lord Rushborough had proposed to the widowed Lady Eden Winstowe, so eager a suitor that he had not waited for the end of her year's mourning. After all, had not she and the marquess been in each others' pockets before Winstowe passed away?

There had been no formal announcement, of course, but none was needed. Society had its own very effective rumor mill, fully as efficient as that of any fishwife at Billingsgate market.

Eden's hasty departure from Caldwick and Hartsmere, followed by her illness, had conspired to prevent her from refuting those assumptions. But once she appeared before her acquaintances and friends, she would have to do so. She dreaded that ordeal and the hurt it must cause. It did not matter that Lady Saville's sponsorship assured Eden's welcome back into Society. Such recognition was no longer Eden's ambition, except where it affected her son.

Donal. She went to the door and turned the handle to open it. Just a crack. Just in case . . .

"Lady Eden? Is that you?"

Lady Saville stood before the door, her beringed hand raised to knock. Eden fell back, knowing that she had been found out.

"Oh, I am so delighted to see you up and about!" Lady Saville exclaimed. "Are you truly better? The color has returned to your cheeks! I had just come up to make sure that you . . . but what excellent timing, when our soirée has just started!"

Eden could not bring herself to feign an illness that had finally — and suspiciously — released its grip. She managed a smile.

"I am . . . somewhat better, Lady Saville," she said. "It was kind of you to look in on me, but I fear that I am not in a fit state to attend your party." She gestured at her dress. "I have scarcely been up —"

"Nonsense! Anyone with half an eye could see that you are recovered. Where is Adele? She is quite proficient in arranging hair. I understand that you did not arrive with a great many gowns. No matter, I shall contrive . . ." She lost herself in her own musings, oblivious to Eden's wishes.

Blatant discourtesy to a hostess had never been one of Eden's besetting sins, and it would take pointed rudeness to refuse Lady Saville now. She could not help her father or Donal by doing so. She resigned herself to waiting out the rest of the evening in company rather than alone with her fears and worries. Lord Bradwell's message would reach her just as easily in the drawing room as it would in her own chamber.

And at last she'd lay the rumors about her "engagement" to rest.

"I will be happy to join you, Lady Saville," she said.

"Rushborough will be delighted! Now, you must come with me, dear Lady Eden, while we look through my gowns to find the one most quickly altered. You are so thin, my dear! How fortunate that my abigail works wonders with her needle. She will do it in a trice. . . ." Lady Saville took her arm and pulled her into the hall. The sounds of the festivities downstairs grew louder. Eden gritted her teeth and let herself be swept along in her hostess's wake.

An hour later, she was sitting before Lady Saville's dressing table, having her hair arranged while the older woman's abigail made final adjustments to one of Lady Saville's better gowns. Lady Saville was beyond generous, but she was also generously endowed in her proportions. The alterations had been significant, even on a modest but elegant gown of white satin that would not have been particularly flattering on its owner. Eden rose and was poked and prodded a few more times by the haughty abigail, who stepped back at last and pronounced the work finished.

"How charming you look, my dear Lady Eden," exulted Lady Saville, clucking about Eden like a well-fed grouse. "You suit that gown so much better than I ever did. I am so glad that I chose it for you." She clapped her hands. "It shall be just like a second coming out. Rushborough will be charmed!"

Lady Saville was sincere, good-humored, and impressionable. Her naïveté was almost comforting. But Eden remembered the last time she had been fitted for such a gown: on the eve of Lord Rushborough's house party. And she well knew how that occasion had ended. What it had brought to an end.

Hartley.

Lady Saville clucked at her as she set out the jewelry she had insisted that Eden borrow, tasteful pearls to match the gown. Once the necklace and tiny earbobs were appropriately bestowed, she took Eden's arm and led her grandly down the stairs to the great drawing room.

Eden felt as if she walked through a waking dream. Her enervation seemed to have passed for good, but the sense of unreality lingered. If Lady Saville noticed her constant glances toward the door, she was too polite to question it.

Lord Rushborough was at the center of a group of well-wishers. He saw Eden at once and watched her with an intensity that made her neck prickle. She felt his possessiveness, his confidence that soon she would be his. But she was spared close conversation with him by the sudden attention of Lady Saville's guests.

For Lord Rushborough's sister, it must have been one of those social triumphs that all London hostesses savored. Lady Saville presented Eden as if she were the queen of some distant but friendly nation.

Her efforts were not in vain. It seemed that Eden had been missed, after all. Lord Rushborough's country house party had paved the way. Eden had every reason to believe that Donal would find equal acceptance once he learned to get about in Society.

Surely Donal would arrive at any moment.

Just as at the house party, Eden was able to slip behind a mask and make the necessary conversation, showing the right amount of gratitude for the condescension of her peers and professing interest in the latest gossip. Entirely absent, however, was the heady sense of pleasure she had so briefly enjoyed at Caldwick. What had happened since then made that quite impossible.

And as she went through the motions, she was continuously alert for the footman who would bring her word of Lord Bradwell's return.

"She is more reserved than I remember," she overheard one bejeweled matron murmur to another between sets, "but I quite like the change. She has a dignity about her. I am convinced that is why the marquess proposed. He certainly had no need to, when one considers her reputation — and of course Winstowe left her with nothing."

"My dear," said another, "it is common knowledge that her affairs have greatly improved since last November, else she would not return to London. Her reputation is no worse than most, and she has certainly suffered, forced to rusticate as she has been. But you are right about the change in her, though I am not sure it is so much for the better. She has become quite brown in the country."

Eden listened without interest. Once she would have laughed at such talk, amused to be the subject of conversation and convinced that it could not hurt her. And indeed, it could not, but for different reasons. She knew now how unimportant it was.

"Lady Eden, I cannot tell you how very glad I am to see you returned to London."

With half her attention, Eden recognized Mrs. Bathurst, who had once been a frequent companion in her larks and capers. Mrs. Bathurst was very pretty, very young, and very fast, and had earned her reputation with enthusiasm.

"London has been insufferably dull without you," Mrs. Bathurst continued, as if Eden had welcomed her with great joy. "We must reassemble our merry band and set the city on its ear as we did before. You must have been so dreadfully bored in the country — you, who loathe it so!" She laughed, a high-pitched giggle that grated on Eden's ears. "I have an excellent idea for a most amusing pastime. You must have heard how inordinately proud Mr. Porter is of his new curricle. I thought that perhaps . . ."

Eden never learned Mrs. Bathurst's plan. A man entered the room, preceded by a nervous footman, and the young matron halted in midsentence.

The new arrival paused in the doorway, handsome, regal, and dressed in green so dark as to be almost black.

Eden's mind went blank. She watched the man walk into the room, saw all heads turn and conversation stop.

He was magnificent. He wore his clothes as if he had been born in them, as if they had grown to fit him like flesh. Their cut and color were just unusual enough to attract attention without evoking fashionable censure. He carried himself like a prince, like a king . . . like one who was so sure of his inborn superiority that he had no need to put it on display. His face was almost too perfect, as if it had never known worry and could not suffer the effects of age.

"My word," Mrs. Bathurst murmured. "Who is he?"

Eden knew the answer, though she could not have spoken it aloud even if her voice was capable of speech.

The Forest Lord had come to London.

T*he pain was constant, and had grown more intense* with every mile Hartley put between himself and Hartsmere. It was not fatal . . . not yet, in any case.

And he almost forgot it when he saw Eden.

He had prepared himself for the moment he would face her again, look upon her with accusation and contempt, and prove to her by his very presence that he was not so easily defeated. She would tremble with the realization of what he was. Her eyes would betray her guilt, and she would humble herself and admit that she was wrong.

So it had gone in his imagination all during the journey to London. He had not been fully recovered when he left; he had considered the risk worth taking. But he had exhausted his rapidly waning powers in his travel, forced to resort to human methods of transportation.

It was a wonder that he had found Eden so quickly. Such fortune came not from magic but from something he did not dare name. He sensed that Donal was not with her; that was doubtless part of her and Lady Claudia's scheme to throw him off the scent, should he survive to follow. But Eden would most assuredly know where the boy was.

He looked about at the glittering company. The last time he had ventured so far from his realm had been many centuries ago, and everything had changed.

The one constant was Eden.

She recognized him. The face he wore was his Fane visage, bearing only a distant resemblance to the man he had become at Hartsmere. But she had seen this face in the glade, for all that he had been wearing vastly different garments.

She controlled her shock very well. No one would realize she knew him.

Her gown was finer than any he had seen her wear at Hartsmere. But it enhanced her beauty no more than a candle flame increases the heat of a raging fire. Her golden hair gleamed like Fane treasure. What emotion she revealed only added color to her cheeks and a sparkle to her eyes. Amid this glittering company, mortals who represented the highest ranks of men, she might have been one of the Fair Folk who had deigned to grace London with her presence for a few magical hours.

He could not take his eyes from her.

Whispers resolved into snatches of conversation, all covering the same subject: Who was this mysterious stranger? No one recognized him, though clearly he was good *ton*. Yes, there could be no doubt of that. Only look at his clothing, his bearing, his face. But who *was* he?

Hartley met Eden's frozen stare across the room and waited for her to act.

She gained a few moments' respite as a pretty, plump woman approached Hartley. She smiled with an air of bemused uncertainty, smoothing her gown as if she feared that her appearance was not quite up to snuff.

"Good evening," she said a little breathlessly. "I am Lady Saville." She cleared her throat. "I am terribly sorry, but I . . . do not believe we have met."

Hartley bowed. "It is I who must apologize, Lady Saville," he said. "I have been most forward in appearing at your doorstep without an invitation. I pray that you will forgive me when you hear my reasons."

Lady Saville puffed up her feathers. "Oh, you are most welcome to join us, Mr. . . . ?"

"Cornelius Fleming." He smiled and looked beyond her to Eden. "I am but recently returned from India, and I heard that my cousin was staying with you. I was most eager to see my family after so long an absence."

Lady Saville turned and followed his gaze. "Oh," she said. "Oh, my. Lady Eden is your cousin? But of course — Fleming! How wonderful! You are most welcome to join us, and if you will permit me —" She took his arm and led him directly to Eden. "My dear Lady Eden, here is your long-lost cousin from India! Is this not a delightful surprise?"

Like a sleepwalker, with the stares of every other man and woman upon her, Eden moved forward. The room hushed. With a visible effort, Eden met Hartley's gaze and offered her hand.

"It has been a long time, Cousin," she said with remarkable poise. "I trust that your journey was a prosperous one?"

Hartley lifted her hand to his lips. "With such beauty at its conclusion, the journey seems inconsequential."

Lady Saville pressed her hands together in glee. "How extraordinary this is. How pleased you must be, dear Lady Eden! And you, Mr. Fleming, pray take your ease and consider yourself most welcome in my home. Everyone will wish to meet you, and I am sure you have many a fascinating tale to tell of the exotic East!"

Eden attempted to retreat, but Hartley held fast to her hand. His skin burned where they touched, though two layers of kid glove separated them.

Eden flushed, and he knew that she felt what he did. She could not free herself without making a scene. After a silent struggle, she smiled and tucked her free hand through the crook of his elbow.

"Lady Saville," she said, "would you mind if I took a few moments to speak to my cousin privately? I confess that this has all been something of a surprise to me, and I am quite overwhelmed —"

"Of course, my dear. Of course." Lady Saville cast Hartley a solicitous glance. "I will see that refreshments are brought to you in the library."

Hartley bowed again, grateful that Lady Saville catered

so conveniently to his needs. He was keeping himself on his feet with only the most supreme effort.

And Eden would have no protection once they were alone. "Thank you, Lady Saville," Eden said. "If you will come this way, Cousin —"

Lord Rushborough stepped into their path. His gaze darted from Eden to Hartley.

"Ah, Rushborough," Lady Saville said, taking his arm. "We have a new guest. . . . May I present Mr. Cornelius Fleming, just come all the way from —"

"Fleming," Rushborough said, cutting her off. It was not a greeting. His eyes narrowed to slits, as if he recognized Hartley. But he would not be expecting a laborer in his home, least of all one dressed in expensive finery. Nevertheless, the way he looked at Eden suggested that he was disturbed beyond any passing jealousy.

Did he know the name Cornelius Fleming and what it meant to Eden?

Eden's expression did not change, but Hartley couldn't mistake the pleading in her voice. "Lord Rushborough, if you will excuse me for just a few moments . . ."

"Of course, Lady Eden," he said tightly. "But I insist upon being allowed your company for a little conversation when you are free."

She smiled, but her whole body stiffened. He was going to demand explanations, and she obviously feared that ordeal.

Hartley bristled. "I am honored to make your acquaintance, Lord Rushborough," he said. "I am very sorry to impose upon you, but I have been long away, and I am eager to be reunited with my dear cousin." He laid his hand over Eden's. "You understand, I am sure."

Rushborough merely stared, his jaw clenched. The scent of challenge overwhelmed the perfumes and pomades of the guests.

"Pray excuse us, Lord Rushborough, Lady Saville," Eden said, and tugged at Hartley's elbow. He allowed himself to be led away, but not before he heard Lady Saville's whispered hiss of reproval to her brother. "Really, Rushborough, how could you be so . . . so gauche? I cannot understand —"

Her voice was swallowed up in the chatter of the guests. Hartley and Eden entered a hallway, and then passed through a door into a shelf-lined room filled with dark, polished wood.

Eden shut the door behind them and leaned against it. She remained there, hands braced against the door, while Hartley found the support of the great oak desk and rested his weight upon it.

There was metal in the desk, to be sure, and the wood was long dead, but it gave him a moment's relief from the constant pain and weakness. He closed his eyes and focused on regaining his strength.

"So," he said softly, "you have returned to your old world. It suits you admirably."

She pushed away from the door, one hand extended. "Hartley," she whispered.

"Are you surprised to see me alive?" he asked coldly.

She blanched. "What?"

"Did you not tell your aunt who I was? Did you not know that she attempted to kill me with a pistol ball of iron?"

She shook her head wildly, loosening strands of hair from her elaborate coiffure. "No," she cried. "I did not! My aunt —"

"She knew what I was, and how to hurt me," he said. "How could she have known if you did not tell her?"

Eden's expression had gone beyond shock. "I told her nothing. I would never see you hurt." She reached out again. "Are you well? She did not harm you?"

Fear he had expected, but not this passionate sincerity. He shielded his heart. "Your aunt did not quite aim true. But Lady Claudia is a very clever woman. Most determined. It would have been convenient for you if she had succeeded, would it not?"

"No." She took a step toward him. "No . . . I do not know what to call you."

Reflected in her tear-bright eyes was the stranger's face he wore, neither Hartley's nor that of Cornelius. He let his shape change, and suddenly he was Hartley Shaw again, incongruously dressed in an aristocrat's clothing.

"Does this set you at ease? Or should I alter my dress as well?"

"Hartley." Her eyes pleaded with him, as they had done with Rushborough. "You meant to take my son from me."

"Not when I came to you at Caldwick. I had other plans then." The effort of speaking was beginning to tell on him. He spread his fingers on the wood as if he could draw its dormant energy into himself. "I waited for you, Eden. I even dared to hope." He laughed. "I offered you all I had to give. You had not even the courtesy to answer me."

Her posture straightened, like that of an errant soldier awaiting deserved punishment. "I was afraid to return. I was horrified at what you had revealed to me."

"That I am not human?"

"That you deceived me not once, but twice. That you intended to steal my son. And — " She bit her lip. "Yes. Because of what you are. And because my whole life, and Donal's, was shaped by your deception." She looked away. "Did you use your Faerie powers on me? Did you cast a glamor upon me, so that I would . . . do your bidding?"

His heart had begun to pound, battered by emotion and the workings of man on every side. "I never bespelled you; I only took on different forms. What I was did not change."

"And what is that?" She was calm now, unnaturally so. "A being who lives forever? Without a soul, or a heart, or the ability to love?"

His body shivered with warning. She understood much more than she had at their last meeting. She had talked to someone — someone who knew how to kill one of the Fane.

Claudia. Always Claudia.

An invisible fist slammed into his head. He sucked at

air that no longer existed. The blood seemed to drain from his body. Soon he would be too weak to stand or to speak at all. With a great effort, he concealed his pain. She would not pity him.

"Lady Claudia has taught you much, has she not?" he said, fighting for breath. "Did she tell you . . . why she wishes to destroy me?"

Eden backed away until she came to one of the bookcases. Her fingers felt blindly along the row of spines, as if she sought answers among the pages of mortal writings.

"She knew you," she said. "My father told her what you were six years ago, and of the bargain you made for my child. How you threatened Papa with death or worse if he did not obey. She thought you were gone forever, but then she discovered that you had returned, that you were Hartley Shaw. I did not even have to tell her. She *knew*.

"She told me . . . of your intention to put me at ease so that you could steal Donal from me. You must understand that I will not let that happen."

Each of her accusations struck at Hartley like iron-tipped arrows. How long had Claudia been aware of his true identity?

"Where is Donal?" he demanded.

"Did you think I would tell you?" she whispered.

"He is with Claudia, is he not? If you value his safety, you must tell me at once."

H*e waited for her answer, but all Eden could think* was that Claudia had betrayed her again.

She had tried to kill Hartley. She had stolen Donal at his birth, knowing that he was a Faerie's child. She had quite possibly drugged Eden so that she could take the boy without telling her niece where she was bound.

Claudia's behavior had ceased to be rational. She kept secrets and harbored intentions that were beyond comprehension. The sum of her actions began to form a terrifying pattern.

Eden had been afraid when Hartley walked through the door. Afraid that he would seek revenge for her flight from Hartsmere. Afraid that he would take her son.

That fear was nothing to what she felt now. *Does Claudia wish harm to my son? Why? Why?* Yet even as she confronted the terror that flooded her mind, her calm returned. Everything became very clear. Part of her had wished for Hartley, and he was here. She was no longer alone.

"I have been worse than a fool," she said. "Claudia took him, supposedly to protect him from you. I could not see that she was mad."

He took a step toward her and almost fell. She dove to catch him. Had he lied about Claudia's attack? Was he near death after all?

"You are hurt!" she cried. "Hartley!"

He shook her off. "We must find them. Where are they?"

"I do not know. I think she drugged me to make sure I could not protest."

He cursed in a fluid, lilting tongue. "Donal and I share a bond. I may . . . be able to find him, if I am not too —" He began to topple sideways. Eden caught him in her arms again and nearly fell beneath his weight.

A sharp rap came on the door, and it opened before either one of them could recover. Rushborough strode in, his face flushed and angry.

"I see that I have come just in time," he said, staring at Hartley like a belligerent ram. "Eden, I will not have this man in my house."

Eden felt Hartley's incredible effort to stand on his own feet. He pushed away from Eden and smiled. "Forgive me, Lord Rushborough, but I did not know we were . . . well enough acquainted to permit such rancor. Have we met before this evening?"

"We have not met, Fleming, but I know you. You are the man who seduced Lady Eden six years ago, got her with child, and abandoned her."

"Ah. She has told you, has she? Then perhaps she has

also mentioned . . . that it was her choice to leave me. I did not learn that she was enceinte until some time afterward."

"You cad. She left you because she learned —" He paused, briefly at a loss. He looked at Eden. She felt cold, remembering how much she had told Rushborough — and how little.

"Francis," she said. "It is so much more complex . . . The explanation . . . it must wait. There are more urgent considerations, and as you can see —"

"Surely you do not forgive this scoundrel! He has the unmitigated gall to return after all this time, to disrupt your life and mine —"

"I was wrong," Hartley said. His voice shook the room, echoing with inhuman force. Rushborough's mouth opened and closed.

"I did this lady a great wrong," Hartley continued hoarsely, as if he had expended the last of his strength. "I do not know if she . . . can ever forgive me." He met Eden's gaze. "She is blameless. I do not intend to remain to trouble her life."

"That is correct," Rushborough snarled. "I will see you out of this house and out of London by tomorrow eve. This lady is to be my wife, and nothing shall ever disturb her peace again as long as I live."

"I . . . will go," Hartley said. He bowed to Eden. "Lady Eden, I wish you every . . ." He gave a low gasp and collapsed against the desk. Eden rushed to his side.

"You can see that he is ill," she told Rushborough fiercely. "He cannot leave this house now. I do not believe that you have the authority to turn him out if Lady Saville invites him to remain."

Rushborough stared at her and turned abruptly on his heel. The door slammed behind him.

Eden laughed, because the only alternative was sheer panic. She doubted that Rushborough would now consider her a suitable marchioness. She was spared the need to explain that she would not marry where she could not love. That she would not marry, ever again.

"Come with me," she said, taking Hartley's weight upon her shoulder. "You must rest."

"Donal —"

"Someone is already looking for him, and we will go as soon as you are able." How easy it was to say "we" when their son might be in peril.

Lady Saville all but leaped upon them when they entered the hall. She prattled something about Rushborough and then noticed Hartley's pallor.

"Oh! Oh, dear! Are you not well, Mr. Fleming?"

"Would you be so kind as to allow my cousin to rest in a private chamber, Lady Saville?" Eden asked, continuing toward the stairs.

"To be sure! I will summon a footman at once, and have a room prepared. Shall I give your regrets to our guests?"

"Please do, Lady Saville." She half dragged Hartley, sensing with alarm that his condition was worsening with every step.

Somehow she managed to get him to the bottom of the stairs, and he pulled himself up by clinging to the bannister. Two footmen intercepted them on the landing and took Hartley's weight between them. A maid rushed out of an open door, flushed and breathless, and Lady Saville's housekeeper followed.

"My lady," the woman said, "We have prepared a chamber for Mr. Fleming. I shall send for the doctor —"

"That is not necessary," Eden said, following on the footmen's heels. "It is some recurring ailment from India, I believe. He only requires rest."

"Just as you say, my lady!" The housekeeper supervised the footmen as they carried Hartley into the room and laid him on the bed. Eden sat beside him.

"Would you bring clean water, and cloths, and a little food?" she asked the housekeeper.

"At once. Shall I leave Prudence with you?"

"No. I will care for my cousin."

She breathed again when the housekeeper, maid, and footmen had gone. Hartley's skin was like hot coals under her hand. He might be dying. Dying, while Donal was God knew where with a possible madwoman. What could she do now but trust her father?

"Hartley," she whispered, stroking his forehead. "Fight. Surely you are stronger than any mere mortal. Fight, for Donal's sake."

His eyelids fluttered and opened. "Eden."

"I am here."

"Donal —" He sighed and closed his eyes.

"You must regain your strength. What can I do to help?"

He tried to shake his head. "I am . . . weaker away from Hartsmere," he said haltingly. "My tie to the land is too strong. The journey was difficult. Iron is everywhere here, and the wound was deep. I have only so much . . . power."

"You risked your life coming after us. *Why* do you want Donal so badly? Why take him from me? My aunt . . . Claudia said —"

"She said too much. And you believed her." He laughed faintly. "The old tales. Men have always . . . shaped us to their image. Because they feared us, they gave us a hundred names and a nature they could despise. We were evil, and without souls."

"I do not believe that, Hartley." And she realized it was true; she did not believe it. "You must have a soul."

"I am no . . . philosopher, Eden, nor a theologian like your priests. I know only that . . . I am not without a heart."

She squeezed his hand, as if she could pour her meager strength into him. "I know that you love Donal." She did not let go, though she realized the things she must ask might bring only more pain. It was time to dispense with all the secrets, all the lies. "Why did you court me, Hartley? If you wanted a half-human child, there must have been an easier way. You could have found a woman who would not expect marriage or a lifetime of companionship. There are no doubt women who would . . . sell their own children."

He raised his head and let it fall back to the pillow.

"Stop," he whispered. "That time is gone. Is the present . . . not all the more precious to humans, who live such brief lives?"

"Is the past of no concern to your kind, who live forever?"

"The centuries can be very lonely."

"Was Donal to be your companion for eternity?"

His expression twisted, as if some inward pain overwhelmed him. "I came to . . . value your companionship, Eden. More . . . than I thought possible."

She swallowed the heavy ache in her throat. "And yet you used me, knowing you would take Donal from me."

"Yes. I used you, with no thought to your feelings." His hand moved restlessly under hers. "I believed . . . that all I wanted was a child. But that changed. It changed when you returned to Hartsmere."

"You hated me then, didn't you?"

"I believed that you had betrayed me . . . that you had joined your father in breaking our pact. I thought I wanted revenge. Fane can be merciless in vengeance. But you have also hated me, Eden. Do not your philosophers say that hatred is akin to love?"

"Your hatred, or mine?" She smiled sadly. "Do you claim to love me?"

No fear could match the one she felt for Donal or for Hartley's life. Yet she waited now with her hand folded around his, waited for the answer that might give birth to a miracle.

He shuddered and closed his eyes. She thought that he had fallen into unconsciousness and felt frantically for his pulse. But it was there, thready and weak.

He had given her his answer.

Someone knocked on the door, and a maid entered with a pitcher and bowl and cloths. A footman followed with a tray of biscuits, sliced ham, and tea. They set down the deliveries without a word and left. Eden rose, soaked a cloth in the cool water, and returned to the bedside. Hartley did not stir as she laid it across his forehead.

She had prayed, oh, how she had prayed that these feelings would not return. She did not want to keep loving Hartley. He had given her no reason to nurture what ought to be dead, and every reason to cast it aside. His weakness should give her an advantage in this ruinous battle they waged, if she wished to win at any price.

But victory was a sword that turned on its wielder. It cut deeply. She needed Hartley more than ever before, to save her son.

She fetched the tray and poured him a cup of tea. He took one sip and pushed it away. He rejected the biscuit and ham as well.

"You must eat, Hartley. If we are to find Donal, you must get well."

He opened his eyes and met her gaze. Pain had dulled the spring green to old moss. "There . . . may be a way, Eden. A way for you to help me."

"Tell me."

"Today is what men know . . . as All Hallows' Eve. The ancients called it Samhain. Once it was a sacred time for your people. They lit bonfires to welcome the spirits of those who had gone before. They believed — and it is true — that the veil between the realms of Fane and man . . . grows thin on this night."

"You waste your strength in talking —"

He lifted his hand to brush her lips with his fingers. "There was another name for Samhain: 'the time that is no time.' All boundaries are as nothing. Fane may give gifts to man . . . and woman may give her strength to Fane."

"I will give you all I have."

"Then lend me the magic of your body, Eden," he whispered.

Chapter 21

In his eyes she read his meaning. Her body came to instant readiness — treacherous body, that could still want him so much, at such a time. But her mind and heart knew that what he asked went far beyond a joining for the purpose of physical pleasure.

"I can make you strong again?"

"There is . . . a chance."

Maybe the only chance they had. She set aside all her questions and went to the door to lock it. Let Lady Saville and her guests think what they chose. This was life and death.

Did not life became most vivid in the face of death? Was that not why her body cried out for his when the world was crumbling about them?

Her gown was loose fitting enough that she was able to remove it by herself. The skirts puddled at her feet, and she kicked them aside.

Hartley had turned his head to watch her. She had learned to be a bold lover in his arms, but her boldness now was so much more than desire. She climbed onto the bed and knelt beside him.

"What should I do?"

"You do not know?" The corner of his mouth lifted in a crooked smile, and then he grew grave and intent. "I need your nakedness, Eden. Your complete surrender."

She pulled her chemise over her head and straddled his hips, highly aware of the sleek fabric of his pantaloons against the inside of her thighs.

"Free me," he whispered.

Her fingers slipped on the buttons of his trousers and found him hard and ready. The rest of him might be near death, but once more life found the way. She wrapped her hands around him and bent low to kiss his face.

He responded with lips and tongue. No weakness could disguise his desire or his need. His mouth moved so softly that it was as if butterflies danced upon her lips. His tongue slipped inside with the same tenderness. Their breaths mingled, a sweet alchemy of Fane and mortal.

She feathered her hands over Hartley's skin, caressed his jaw, traced the corner of his mouth and his parted lips. His fingers lifted to stroke her neck and shoulders, the touch as light as his kiss. If she had not come to know his body so intimately, she might have believed that he was a ghost, only half within this world.

He caressed her as if he were no longer convinced of his right to touch her. Yet already she sensed that he grew stronger. His manhood pulsed against her abdomen, seeking its true home. She understood that she must become something other than human this night, a creature of the elements, the pure force of life that beat in every mortal breast. Nothing must taint what she gave him. All fears, all despair must be forgotten for these few, fragile moments.

Take me, Hartley. I withhold nothing. Take my body and my strength and my love. Be whole again. Save yourself and Donal and you will save me. Let us light a bonfire of our own, and burn the veil between worlds to ashes.

But she did not speak. She proceeded, instead, to show him. She arched her back, curving her body into his, and seized his lower lip between her teeth.

His mouth fitted itself to hers in fierce demand. His palm cupped her breast, rolling her nipple to a hard peak. Arrows of desire that were almost pain shot into her womb and below.

She felt gloriously, wonderfully, tumultuously alive.

Hartley pulled her down and suckled her as if he drank some sweet and mystical nectar. She abandoned herself and moaned, lashing her hair across his face.

He slid his hand between her thighs. She wanted him so much that she nearly exploded before he'd done more than brush her with his fingertips. He drove her to the edge, but she could not make the leap alone. He must come with her, else the magic was void.

The magic was succeeding. Hartley felt his blood surge with renewed vigor as his fingers stroked inside her. He tasted her wetness on his own skin, and her body's elixir charged him with energy.

Death, such as the Fane knew it, stood by the bed like a jealous paramour. He had known She followed all the way from Hartsmere in hopes of claiming him. If not for Donal, he thought, he would gladly die here, in Eden's arms.

But Eden drove Death screaming back to Her dark and dismal abode. His golden mortal gazed down at him, the cascade of her hair sweeping over his waistcoat and loosened neckcloth. There was exultation in her eyes — the sweet madness that came of reaching for perfect union.

The same madness gripped Hartley. He sensed the inhuman tides within his body carrying a potency even Fane seldom knew. On this night, with this woman, he was a god in the old way, and Eden was his priestess. On such a night he knew he could give her a child of her own.

She tore the buttons from his waistcoat and shirt and spread her palms against his chest. He took her supple waist between his hands. Her thighs pressed tight to his hips, and she rocked up to position herself for his entry.

They remained so for minutes, or perhaps hours, their gazes locked. Hartley could see all the way to her generous and very human soul. That magnificent spirit had no room for hatred, even now. Even for him.

He slipped into a shadow world between mortal and Fane, his body neither one nor the other, an ethereal construct filled with very real memories. He remembered Tir-na-nog, and his ageless mother, and the Fane he had known who had abandoned the earth. He remembered Hartsmere: the common people with their unexpected complexity, the horses in the stable and the sheep on the fell, Mrs. Byrne and her uncommonly wise advice.

He remembered Donal in Eden's arms. Eden in his, as she was now.

He closed his eyes. Her hand traced across his cheek in a gesture almost like farewell, and then she came down upon him. She rode him like an Amazon astride her stallion, wild and wanton. Her hot body gripped his, tightened and released, driving him to ecstasies even Tir-na-nog could not match. And when she shuddered with release, flinging back her head on a silent cry, he was with her. His essence poured into her like molten flame. And into him poured everything she was: all the love she possessed in such abundance — love for her tenants, for Donal . . .

And for him.

In the small, private park beyond the window, a bird sang to herald the dawn. With the song came renewal and hope. Hartley sat up, pulling Eden against his chest, and buried his face in her hair.

It was over. Eden's breathing steadied and slowed, and her arms dropped to her sides. She had given of herself freely and asked for nothing in return but that he help her save their son.

But this had been their last moment of peace together. Eden's selfless love still reverberated through his body, sustaining him, restoring the powers he had lost. Yet in the very midst of his potency, he suffered from a wetness in his eyes and the weight of bitter despair.

For he understood, at last, that love was more important to Eden — to all her kind — than life itself. This — this blinding comprehension — was what Fane sought when they mated with men, or stole them away to the Faerie realm, or took mortal children. It was this dazzling flame that drew immortals to seek the one gift nature had denied them.

He wished with all his inhuman soul that understanding was enough. But it was not. He couldn't give Eden the one thing she valued most.

That last day at Caldwick, he had made a decision to remain with her on this earth. But love, such as men knew it, had been no part of that choice. The magic of mortal love was more powerful than any Fane enchantment. Neither Fane nor man could live in two worlds at once. To surrender to love was to reject all that was Fane and embrace all that was mortal, irrevocably, for himself and his son. There would be no turning back.

And so he recognized himself for what he was: a coward. Fane were masters of illusion; they believed themselves superior to every mud-crawling human ever born. They pretended amusement at the mortal passions they imitated, yet they feared those very passions. They had fled the earth rather than face the dominance of men or make any truce with humanity. No mortal could enter Tir-na-nog to taint its purity unless he carried the blood of the Fane.

Self-sacrifice was a quality unknown among Hartley's people, like humility. Like true love. He was no better than the rest.

Eden deserved so much more than the mockery of human emotion he could give her.

He gently lifted Eden from his hips. Their physical parting seemed to tear something inside him. She rolled away and slipped from the bed, her face closed to him as if the last minutes had never happened.

"Can you find Donal now?" she asked.

"Yes." Despising himself, he rose from the bed and buttoned his pantaloons. "And when I do, Eden, he must come with me to Tir-na-nog."

She did not react by so much of a twitch of her lips. "I am his mother."

"And you cannot protect him, even from your own kin. You cannot teach Donal to spend his life rejecting his true nature. He does not belong among men." He hardened his voice. "Accept the truth, Eden. Donal is more Fane than mortal."

"I will *not*. Unlike you, he can love."

He let the blow slide past him. "Then do not let this world destroy that gift. When he was in Eire, the mortals who kept him treated him with great cruelty. They beat him, Eden, and mocked him, and drove him away out of fear. Is that the life you wish for him?"

Her face grew white as bone. "He was . . ." She pressed her hands to her mouth. "Why did you not tell me?"

"And make you suffer as well?"

She looked so ill that he prepared to catch her if she fell. Tears streamed over her cheeks.

"He is five years old," she whispered.

"And in Tir-na-nog he will grow and live for many years. He will never want, I promise you. And I will not leave him." He swallowed. "You will not be alone. We have created a new child, Eden. One that will belong in your world. I have . . . made sure of that."

She touched her abdomen and stared at him, hollow-eyed. He knew he had killed any love she still had for him. Such was the mercy of the Fane. Yet it was her love that had finally unlocked his seed and made him fertile again.

She would not be alone.

"Eden," he said, the words cutting him like broken glass. "It is for the best —"

Whatever reply she might have made was lost in a whirring hum and a blast of air. A small figure tumbled into the center of the room and hung suspended several feet above the ground, darting this way and that.

"My lord! My lord, alive!" Tod flew in circles about Hartley's head and nearly crashed into Eden, who gazed at him in astonishment.

Hartley reached up and caught the little Fane by his ragged collar. "What are you doing here?" he demanded. "What possessed you leave the forest? You cannot venture from Hartsmere. You should be —"

"Not dead, my lord!" Tod squirmed in his grip like an otter. "Tod has a talisman against mortal magic!" He reached inside his russet shirt and pulled forth a silver charm on a chain. "This protects Tod, let him find you."

Hartley glanced at Eden. "You had better dress. We may have to leave very quickly."

With amazing self possession, she retrieved her gown and pulled it on. "One of your fellow Faeries, I presume?"

"Tod, the hob," he said, more proud of her than he had any right to be. He released Tod. "Where did you get such a charm? You cannot return to Tir-na-nog without me —"

"The Irishwoman gave it. She sent Tod!"

Mrs. Byrne had given the hob a talisman powerful enough to protect him in the mortal world? But Mrs. Byrne had shown no such talents. She was human. Hartley had not even taken his leave of her when he departed Hartsmere, let alone told her of Tod, or what he himself was.

But she knew. Somehow, she knew enough to command Tod and send him after Hartley. Mrs. Byrne would have many questions to answer when they returned to Hartsmere. If he ever had the chance to ask them.

"Tod has a message," the hob said, abruptly serious. "The Irishwoman sent Tod to tell my lord that the Angry One did not go away from Hartsmere. She returned, with my lord's son." He grimaced, baring his teeth. "The Angry One thinks my lord is dead. My lord must come at once."

Hartley froze. "Claudia went back to Hartsmere?"

He and Eden spoke at almost the same instant. They stared at each other with grim determination.

"She is not going to send for me," Eden said. "First she separated me from Donal, and then she tried to kill you." She squeezed her eyes shut. "Oh, God. She could not harm him."

"She will not. Tod, return with all speed to Hartsmere and do what you can to protect the boy. I will be right behind you."

The hob winked out of existence. Eden fumbled with the laces on her gown, and Hartley stepped up to help. Eden trembled so badly that he was obliged to use magic to complete the task.

He could wield it now because of Eden.

"We cannot . . . It is days to Hartsmere," she whispered. "Donal. Oh, Donal."

He turned her about and brushed her tears away with his thumbs. "You think like a mortal, Eden. There is an enchantment I could not use when I was weak, but now I am strong enough for both of us."

She opened her eyes and gazed at him with hope and devastating trust. "Take me to Donal."

He tilted her head and kissed her brow. "Hold tight to me," he said. In one motion, he swept her up in his arms and plunged toward the open window.

They never reached the ground.

Eden had no chance to scream. In the blink of an eye she found herself grasping empty air, and then her legs were wrapped around something warm and broad and strangely familiar.

She rode on the back of a stag, and the stag was flying.

She clutched at the thick mane mantling the beast's withers. The stag blew out a breath as if in encouragement and stretched out its body in an airborne gallop.

His body. She knew who carried her home.

The world passed by in a blur of color and formless shapes, one dissolving into another. She understood that they did not travel through space but somehow skipped over the miles like a stone upon a lake. The "time without a time" enfolded her in its enchantment, as it had done when she rode Hartley in Lady Saville's guest chamber. Fear was left behind amid the teeming London streets.

All that mattered was Donal, and reaching him in time. She had no sooner accustomed herself to the weightless sensation of Faerie flight than she felt the jarring impact of Hartley's hooves striking solid ground. The void resolved itself into a landscape she had grown to know well, and a great stone pile that brooded over a deep and silent lake. Snow mantled the land as it had when she had left.

Home.

All four of Hartley's feet touched the earth, and she tried to dismount from the great height of his back. He knelt to let her down. His sides worked like bellows, but he scrambled back up and swung his head toward Hartsmere.

Only the park lay between them and the house. "Donal?" she asked.

Hartley snorted and tossed his head. She did not question but set off across the park at a run. Snow flew from her feet, numbing them a little more with every step. When she paused to catch her breath, she discovered that Hartley was not with her.

He was no fool. She prayed that he used his magic to find Donal more quickly than she could, and make him safe. She picked up her skirts and ran to the porch as if she herself wore Faerie wings.

Claudia stepped out of the door, black clad as if in deepest mourning. Donal was not with her.

"Eden?" she said, unable to disguise her consternation. She searched the drive for a carriage and stared at Eden's wet-hemmed gown and sodden slippers. "What are you doing here? How is it —" She stopped, and her expression grew alien and remote. "Did my brother send for you?"

Eden knew then that her worst conjectures fell far short of the truth. Claudia's face was gaunt, with deep hollows under her eyes and cheekbones. She had clearly not been sleeping. But there was a frightening air about her, a look in her eyes that spoke of triumph.

If Eden's father was here, he had succeeded in finding Claudia. But something was very wrong.

"Where is Donal?" she demanded. "What have you done with him?"

Real pain was briefly visible in Claudia's face before she controlled it. "He is well. No harm has come to him." She sighed. "You should not have come here, Eden. You should have stayed in London with Rushborough."

"You drugged me. You lied. You took my son from me and brought him back to Hartsmere. I do not know what you intend, but it ends now. Take me to Donal at once."

Claudia's features relaxed. "You are so ignorant, Eden — ignorant and innocent. I had hoped to spare you what I have suffered. But since it is no longer possible —" She gestured toward the door. "Come inside before you take a chill."

Incredulous at her aunt's calm, Eden remained where she was. "All I want is Donal. I will take him away, and you need never see either one of us again."

"As simple as that? You have no desire, no curiosity to know why I lied to you, as you say, and drugged you, and sent you from Hartsmere without your son?"

The cold penetrating Eden's gown was as nothing to the chill brought by Claudia's words. "Aunt, you are ill. I can see that you have not slept. If you will only take me to Donal, we can talk about anything you wish."

"I am mad. Is that not what you mean?" She smiled sadly. "But I am not. I have been waiting for this a very long time." She gestured again toward the door. "You need have no fear of Hartsmere now, my dear. The monster is dead. I killed him. And if you wish to see your son again, you will hear what I must tell you."

Eden said a quick, silent prayer. She recognized that she would have to use deception to get Donal back, for there was no reasoning with Claudia. The only way she might gain the advantage was through understanding her aunt's motives, and making contact with Mrs. Byrne and others in the house. She would be cooperative for as long as necessary. And while she kept Claudia occupied, Hartley was free to act.

"Hartley is dead?" she whispered, feigning horror.

"You will come to understand why it was necessary," Claudia said, almost gently. "Come." She held out her hand.

Eden could not bring herself to take it. She stared at the open door, letting the whole gamut of her emotions reflect on her face. "I will hear what you have to say," she said. "And then you will let me see my son."

Claudia did not answer. She led the way into the formal drawing room.

"Where are all the servants?" Eden asked.

"They are otherwise engaged." Claudia sat and poured a cup of tea. She offered it to Eden, shrugging at her niece's refusal.

"There is so much to tell you," she said, gazing at Eden without a trace of shame or unease. "Let us speak of the past — both near and far away. Let us converse about love, and how it can destroy all our hopes."

"Love cannot destroy," Eden said. "Not a love that is real."

"Do you speak from experience?" Claudia sipped at her tea, but the cup rattled the saucer when she set it down. "You did not love Spencer. Or will you tell me now that you loved the monster?" She sighed. "I see that he succeeded in bewitching you after all. I am sorry for your pain, my dear niece."

The urge to shout a denial was overwhelming. *Find our son,* she wished Hartley. "You still have not told me why," she said. "I was right before, was I not, when I guessed that you had personal reasons for your actions? You hated Hartley enough to kill him, and it was not out of concern for me."

"It was, and is. But you have no conception of my reasons." She reached for the cup again and paused. Her hand trembled. "I shall explain, and perhaps it will make it easier for you to comply with my wishes. I would hope that you would do so willingly."

"Do what?"

Claudia felt as if she were drifting back to that terrible time, so many years ago, when the dreams of her young life had died with her husband. He must be dead, by now . . . foxes lived less than a decade, if that. For Lord Michael Raines, death would have been a blessing.

"Once upon a time," she said, "a man came to terrible grief when he trespassed upon the realm of the monster who fathered your son — before your father's mistake, before your own birth. But no one ever knew the truth of what became of my husband — until now."

"Your . . . husband?"

Eden's puzzlement only increased Claudia's pain. "We were both young and very much in love. We visited Hartsmere in the autumn, while Lord Bradwell was away shooting at one of his other estates. Hartsmere seemed peaceful and very private for a newlywed couple, and Raines was eager to try his hand at bagging a few grouse near the wood." She reached again for the cup and released her breath when she managed to pick it up without spilling the tea. "I knew nothing of the local legends or prohibitions against hunting on Hartsmere land, except the vaguest of stories that I naturally ignored. Raines had only his gun, not even so much as a dog, so it all seemed a lark. We took a picnic up the fell to the edge of the forest."

Eden's face was as pale as the morning mist. She guessed what was to come.

"Raines was an active man. Naturally his wanderings took him into the wood, so ancient and beguiling. When he had been gone some time, I followed him. And I arrived . . ." After all this time, it was still difficult to speak it aloud. "I arrived in time to see the monster cry the forest's wrath upon my love, and turn him into a fox — a creature to be hunted as he had hunted them. I never saw him again. Everyone believed the story I told . . . that he had fallen from a cliff. His body was not found."

Eden looked very much as if she wished to sink deep into her chair and disappear. She straightened instead, and reached out her hand.

"Aunt — Claudia — I am sorry. More sorry than I can express. I . . . grieve for your loss."

"Then you will understand why, when I learned Cornelius Fleming's true identity — when your father told me of his bargain — I could think only of revenge and protecting you from him so that you should not suffer as I had."

"Why . . . why did you not tell me what you knew, if you wished to stop the marriage?"

"How could I expect you, or any sane person, to believe me? And by the time I was able to act, you had eloped with him." She caught her breath. "After Raines's destruction, I learned all I could of the monster's nature. I consulted scholars and listened to the tales of country folk and madmen. When your father told me of your elopement and that he intended to follow and stop the evil marriage, I encouraged him. I gave him the iron filings I had prepared, and told him to put them in a drink for Cornelius Fleming."

Eden blanched. "I saw," she said. "I saw the cup on the floor —"

"Yes. He sensed the poison before he drank. Just as he avoided the traps laid by the American hunter I employed. But he did not survive the iron ball I had specially made for my pistol."

Eden bowed her head. Claudia wanted very badly to comfort the girl, but it would do no good. Not yet.

"When I realized that he had revealed himself to you at Caldwick, I knew that you would flee — and he would follow, to take back his offspring. I expected him to expose himself, sooner or later. And he did so. His death set us both free."

Eden stared at her. "And what . . . what has my son to do with this? What did you plan for him?"

"He is not human, Eden. He is the monster's child. Surely you see that he cannot remain with you in normal society." She closed her eyes. "I was prepared to do anything, commit any act, in my desire to protect you — lie, scheme, employ blackmail. . . . Yes, I forced Nancy to give you the laudanum daily, so that you could not interfere. I regretted the need for such acts. I had, at one time, even come to believe myself capable of harming your son. But I could not."

"You harmed him enough when you sent him to live with cruel strangers in Ireland," Eden accused bitterly. "You hid his very existence from me, not caring how much he suffered —"

"I did not know he had been mistreated, not until he arrived at Hartsmere. You see, Spencer was my tutor in blackmail. He discovered a letter I had written to the Irish family who were supposed to raise the boy and keep his origins secret. He was much amused to take revenge upon both of us by telling you as he expired. But the folk to whom I sent Donal were decent people, and I paid them well. My last inquiry revealed that they had died and left the boy to others, who resented the burden. By the time I had that information, Donal was at Hartsmere."

Eden worked her hands open and closed, open and closed. "And now you will send him away once more? As you did five years ago?"

"Yes, I sent him away. I misled your father into believing the child was dead and filled the coffin with the baby's swaddling cloths and a few strands of hair to deceive the monster. You have no doubt observed that his senses are very keen. Even so, I could not be sure that he wouldn't find the lad." She couldn't conceal her pity. "Donal, like his father, can bring only destruction upon you. I do this for —"

"No!" Eden shot up from her chair, her expression so violent that Claudia prepared for an assault. "He is *my son* —"

"And mine."

Claudia forgot the response she was about to make. She turned. Hartley Shaw stood in the doorway, very much alive, his eyes blazing with emerald fire. Something half visible flickered near his face and then disappeared.

"Eden," Hartley said softly. Claudia was sickened to see the tenderness in his eyes. "Are you well?"

She rushed toward him. "Where is Donal?"

"There is a stranger here, a man," he said. "He has the boy somewhere on the grounds. I go now to find them."

Claudia pushed aside her shock and stood. "How pleasant to see you again, Mr. Shaw. Not only alive, but still in control of my niece." She gestured about the room. "Won't you join us?"

Hartley's gaze shifted to Claudia. "I heard something of what you told Eden, Lady Claudia. I did not see you that day in the forest, long ago. I thought the trespasser was alone. I acted rashly and without mercy. I am sorry."

Claudia laughed. "Sorry. How touching. You have learned human emotions from Eden, have you? Pity and compassion, as well as mercy?"

"I have tried."

"But not love." She looked at Eden. "He has not told you he loves you, has he? But he has used every other means to keep you under his spell, just as I warned you."

Before Eden could respond, an intruder burst through the door. Breathing hard, Lord Bradwell looked about him, passing over Hartley without recognition. His gaze settled on Eden.

"I am sorry, Eden," he said. "I followed them here, but —"

"How did you get free, Cyrus?" Claudia demanded. "The American —"

"Mr. Blake detected the presence of one of his wendigos, and thought it expedient to take Donal from the house. Unfortunately, that made it impossible for him to continue guarding the rest of us. I was rather good at picking locks when I was a boy." He turned back to Eden. "I learned within days that Claudia had not gone where I expected but had returned to Hartsmere. When I arrived and tried to take custody of the boy, she . . ." He grimaced. "She has hired a henchman to do her bidding, an American. He has prevented me or the servants from leaving Hartsmere."

"Is Donal well?" Eden asked, ignoring Claudia.

"I saw him briefly when I first arrived, but yes — he has not been harmed. Claudia —"

"Will you speak of me as if I am not present, Cyrus?" Claudia said, mocking to hide her hurt. "Here we are, all together again. Where is the happy reunion?"

"Happy?" He moved by slow steps to Eden's side. "Not while you hold my grandson."

"Ah. I will enjoy hearing the tale of where you have been all these years, and how you came to assist Eden after abandoning her for so long. But that can wait for a more opportune moment."

"If one ever comes."

"It will, along with peace for all of us."

He shook his head. "Whatever your game, Claudia, you must return Donal to his mother."

"So that she may lose him to his father?"

"His father?"

Claudia smiled. "Yes, Cyrus. He is alive . . . for the moment." She gestured toward Hartley. "Do you not recognize your would-be son-in-law?"

He looked at Hartley, and slowly the knowledge spread across his face. "My God," he whispered.

"The situation is quite complex, as you can see," Claudia said. "But I assure you that I am in command of it. The monster can do nothing while my 'henchman' has the boy in his keeping. You have avoided responsibility for the pain you caused, Cyrus, but you are too late. You would be best advised not to interfere."

"But I will, as long as you intend my daughter and my grandson harm, even if I must —"

"*Your* daughter, Cyrus?" Claudia said. "No. I think it is time to end that fiction." She swept the group with her glance. "Tonight we are speaking the truth in our hearts. It is time for you to do the same, dear Brother."

All eyes turned to him. "Papa?" Eden whispered.

He covered his face with his hands. "Claudia —"

"Tell her."

Slowly, he dropped his hands. "Eden, my dear — I had

prayed it would never come to this. I have deceived you, hoping to protect you. In that, too, I have failed.

"You see . . . Claudia is not your aunt. She is your mother."

Chapter 22

Eden let the revelation sink into the calm, quiet center of her being, where it could neither hurt nor surprise her.

She supposed that she had always known in that same deep part of herself. She had simply never admitted it even to her innermost heart.

She met Aunt — Claudia's gaze. Claudia had behaved like a deranged stranger ever since Eden's arrival. Her obsession with Hartley was frightening in its power, and she posed a very real threat to Donal.

But now she looked at Eden and . . . waited. Did she expect her daughter to rush into her arms with a glad cry? Or did she find all this an entertaining pantomime that would somehow further her cause?

Half aware, Eden moved close to Hartley. He was the one person who had not changed beyond all recognition. He put his arm about her shoulder.

"I have been your father for four-and-twenty years," Lord Bradwell said, bowing his head. "I loved you like a daughter. But I am your uncle, Eden. My wife was your aunt." He faltered. "She loved you, too."

"Do not stop there, Bradwell," Claudia said. "Tell her the rest."

He closed his eyes. "Your . . . Claudia was married a year before your birth, Eden. It was a love match. But a tragedy occurred, and she lost her husband in a terrible accident on the fells."

Claudia laughed. "An accident, yes. That was what everyone believed. Do go on, Cyrus."

"Claudia was very ill for a time after that, and we learned that she was . . . with child." He flushed. "When the child . . . when you were born, Eden, she was still not in her right mind, and we feared for your safety. It was necessary that I and your aunt . . . care for you while my sister recovered from her grief."

"Recovered?" Claudia's eyes flashed with scorn. "Is that what you call sending me to an asylum for the mad?" She looked at Eden. "I was there for two years. Two endless years."

"We could not help you, Claudia," Lord Bradwell said. "Please, try to understand. You showed no memory of having given birth when you came back to us . . . and it was only much later that I suspected you did know. By then, she was our daughter, and you were content to be her aunt —"

"I was never content. You believed what you wished and neglected my child while you pursued your pleasures. I *was* a true mother to her when you all but abandoned her."

"I know. I know that now, Claudia. But I will make it up to her."

"As you have done so far? You would have served us all best if you had stayed away. Eden doesn't need you, and I certainly do not. Perhaps you should run now, or I may allow your daughter's suitor to take his revenge upon you before I take mine on him."

"I seek no revenge," Hartley said. He looked at Eden, gentle and sad and showing her everything she might have called love. "I hold no enmity against him. I . . . regret that

I ever threatened to do him harm, as I regret the pain I caused you. I ask your forgiveness."

"Yes," Eden said. "Yes."

"And I —" Lord Bradwell shook his head. "I am beginning to believe that I, too, was mistaken." His glance was for Eden alone, and with it he asked a question and accepted Eden's silent answer. "There are many things beyond mere human understanding, but I . . . hope to learn."

Eden's eyes filled with tears. There was a tiny oasis of sanity in this grim desert of pain and sorrow. She was deeply proud of Hartley and her father. Peace, and an end to the fear and hatred, was almost within their grasp.

"Poignant, indeed," Claudia said with a lift of her lip. "But have you forgotten, Eden, that this monster killed your true father?"

The knowledge cast a baleful shadow over her hopes. She forced herself to meet Hartley's eyes.

"I have not forgotten," she said, very low. "I forgive you, Hartley. You did not know. You were different then."

"But I do not forgive," Claudia said. "You may have bewitched my daughter, Monster, but you have not paid what you owe me."

"Is my grandson to be the price?" Lord Bradwell demanded. "Do you hate him, Claudia, as you hate his father?"

"No. But he will destroy my daughter's life as long as he remains by her side. He is his father's son."

"Yes, he is mine," Hartley said. He stepped away from Eden and stood toe to toe with Claudia. "You will give him to me."

Claudia did not move. "Are you prepared for violence, Monster? Believe me when I tell you that not even all your magic will persuade me."

"No!" Eden grabbed Hartley's arm. "No, Hartley. There must be another way."

"She must be stopped."

Claudia looked over Hartley's shoulder, catching

Eden's gaze. "It is he who must be stopped. Can you not see, my daughter? You must choose."

In place of the anger that should have come then, Eden felt pity. This woman had virtually raised her without benefit of a mother's name. She had taught Eden to thrive in Society and given her the strength to bear the past five years. The undying grief of a terrible tragedy had turned a decent woman into a pitiless stranger.

Eden could not stop loving her. In an odd way, that realization gave her the courage to go on and the determination to win. And it crystallized within her mind the decision she had been fighting since Hartley had revealed himself.

Donal would never be safe in a world containing those like Claudia Raines. Once he was with her again, she must choose — but not between Claudia and Hartley. She had already accepted that she must let Hartley go.

But he loved Donal. He could provide their son with the security he might never find in this world.

She moved between Claudia and Hartley and spoke to him over her shoulder. "Find our son. Take him where he will be safe."

"That will not be necessary." Claudia gestured toward the door. Eden looked, and gasped.

On the threshold stood a man, a stranger in buckskin and fur. Locked in his grip was Donal.

"Mother!" Donal struggled fiercely in his captor's hold, but the man was far too strong.

"Easy, lad," he said in an accented drawl. He lifted Donal off his feet. Hartley charged the stranger, who pulled up a shotgun one-handed and jammed the muzzle into Hartley's chest.

"Iron shot," he remarked. "You'll die, Wendigo."

Hartley's nostrils flared. "You are the poacher who tried to murder us in the forest."

The man's gray eyes blazed with fanatical light. "It's my calling to rid the world of demons and evil spirits, Wendigo. Lady Claudia told me of the great wickedness you have caused. This innocent child won't be twisted to your shaping." He pressed Donal's head to his shoulder. "I sense your weakness. You'll soon be defeated."

"Lady Eden," Claudia said, "may I present Mr. Blake, of the United States of America."

Eden walked up to the American, jaw set. He refused to meet her gaze. "If you shoot him," she said, "you will also have to shoot me. Give me my son."

"That I can't do, ma'am." But he loosened his hold on Donal and set him down to face Eden.

She smiled brightly at Donal. "I am so glad to see you. Are you all right?"

"Yes, Mother." He stood very still in the stranger's grasp. "Da?"

Hartley reached for him. The American thrust bruisingly hard with the shotgun. Eden knew that Hartley was angry enough to risk a very painful and permanent death.

Why did he not use his magic? Did the iron in the gun prevent it, or was he weakened from the enchanted flight from London?

Lord have mercy.

She placed her hand on Hartley's arm. "What do you want, Claudia?"

Her mother moved for the first time since Hartley's appearance, walking stiffly to the center of the room. "We appear to be at an impasse," she said. "I could have Mr. Blake kill your lover now, but it would harm the boy to witness such violence. However cruel you may think me, I do not relish hurting him." She sighed deeply. "Before your arrival, I had planned to send Donal to America with Mr. Blake, who understands the ways of creatures such as your lover and could properly care for his child. But now . . . I am prepared to offer a bargain."

"Mr. Blake will return your son to you, Daughter, and you may leave Hartsmere, but only if your monstrous lover is willing to sacrifice himself. If he is not . . ."

"I will make whatever sacrifice you demand," Hartley said, never taking his eyes from Donal's captor.

Eden dug her fingers into the rigid muscle of Hartley's arm.

"You cannot do this," Lord Bradwell said, starting for his sister. "I will not —"

"I warned you not to interfere," Claudia said. "Do not mistake my sincerity."

"I beg of you. Stop this."

"You will thank me when it is done. And so will my daughter." She reached inside the her black cloak. A dark, heavy object appeared in her hands.

"I had this made, in case my shot should fail to kill him. It is fortunate that I kept it." She turned it in her hands, and Eden recognized it as a collar — an iron collar, shaped to fit a man.

"Take it, Daughter," Claudia demanded. She signaled to the American, who backed away, Donal still in his grip, and let the muzzle of his shotgun drop. "Your monster must willingly accept this binding, or you shall never see your son again."

Wave upon wave of sickness battered Eden's body. "I will not."

"You must." She felt Hartley's breath on the back of her neck, his warm hand at her waist. "I may die whatever we do, but this way one of us will have him."

"Remove Donal from the room, Mr. Blake," Claudia said. "He need not see this. If I do not come for you within the hour, do as we agreed and take the boy to America."

The hunter backed out of the room. Donal whimpered and struggled, but the sounds receded quickly until Eden could no longer hear him.

You will never see him again.

Like an automaton, Eden took the collar from Claudia. She was not of Faerie blood, yet the metal burned her just the same.

You cannot, her heart cried.

"You have no choice," Claudia said.

Eden let the collar hang from her hand and commanded her feet to carry her back to Hartley. He gazed at her, untroubled, almost serene. He lifted his hand and caressed her chin with his thumb.

"Do not be afraid," he said. "Let me think of others besides myself. Let me know that you and Donal are safe. Let me act . . . as though I have known mortal love."

A prism of tears blurred his face. "She means to kill you."

"I know."

She flung the collar to the ground and embraced him. "Hartley, no."

His lips brushed her forehead. "I know you will care for Donal, my dearest mortal. I understand love well enough for that. Teach him to be proud of what he is, and to survive." He lifted his head and spoke to Claudia, and as he did, he became a magnificent creature once more, proud and otherworldly and untouchable.

"Hear me, woman. You may take my life. But you will first swear to me, upon your God Above All, that you will give Donal to Eden, and that you and your servants will not harm or imprison mother or son for the remainder of your days upon this earth."

His voice hung over them with the weight of power. Eden dared to believe that he might be strong enough to resist his enemy. That he knew something she did not and had a scheme to defeat Claudia.

Claudia was very still, and for once her expression revealed a hint of unease.

Hartley snapped his fingers, and Tod materialized at his shoulder. Claudia stared at the hob with horrified fascination.

"My lord?" Tod said, staring wide-eyed at the mortal company. "Tod has watched the boy. He is not hurt. The cold hunter is clever and hates all Fane, but not my lord's son."

"You have done well. Have you heard this woman's oath?"

The little man became a streak of light and appeared over Claudia's head. "Tod heard, my lord."

"Soon I will be your lord no longer. I have but one task left for you. When I am gone, you will remain to see that Lady Eden and my son leave Hartsmere in safety, using every means necessary to shield them from any who would follow. You will serve the lady and the boy for five mortal years and protect them with your life. Then you are free of all binding forever."

"Free? Home?"

"Home."

Instead of rejoicing, the hob looked at Eden with his bright button eyes. "My lady," he said. He twirled about and vanished.

Hartley set Eden away from him and held her shoulders. "I have done what I can. Now do what you must. Do not be afraid for me."

Love was indeed a miraculous emotion. Hartley saw it moving within Eden's eyes, limitless and mortal, giving her what she needed to bear these final moments.

She would never know that he was afraid. He smiled and lifted her chin with his hand. "Last night will live within me forever."

Her lovely eyes never left his. "As it will within me. Thank you, Hartley. Thank you . . . for my son." She stood on her toes and kissed him, pouring all her passion into that last caress.

"I love you," she whispered.

"I know." He kissed the tears from her cheeks. "Now, Eden. Quickly."

She fell to her knees and picked up the collar. Slowly she rose, holding the iron band tight to her chest.

Hartley bent his head. Her hands shook so badly that the Iron grazed his neck many times before she could fit it around him. Fire encircled his neck, the flames searing through his skin. The cool of her hands was the only relief, and it was nothing.

"Lock it," Claudia commanded.

Through a roar of pain he heard the click of the collar's latch. He thought Eden was weeping, but his vision was gone. All his body's defenses, drained by the swift and magical journey from London, were bent upon fighting death.

"I have done what you asked," Eden said, her voice flat and hard. "Give me my son."

"When this is finished," Claudia said. "I will not break my word."

"I pity you. And I will never call you Mother."

"Someday you will realize that there was one in this world who truly loved you. Let us end this quickly."

"What will you do?"

"We shall go up upon the fell, where he destroyed my Raines. There I will confine him in a cage of iron at the edge of his beloved forest, where he may watch it while he dies." Claudia's voice shifted as if she had turned away. "You will lead our captive to his destination, Cyrus. He has no power to hurt any of us now."

Hartley tried to laugh, but the collar choked off all sound. *Do not fight her, dearest one,* he willed Eden. *Save our son.*

Somehow, he knew that she heard. Someone — Lord Bradwell — took his arm and pulled him away. He staggered and reeled like a drunkard. Pain was his world. All but the most essential parts of his body shut down by the time they left the house.

Yet he still heard Eden's voice. It remained his lifeline as he stumbled over rough gravel and snowbound park, all but blind, unable to summon even the smallest creature to his defense.

"Do not do this. Claudia — Mother — I beg of you. If you only let him go, Hartley will leave this world forever. Let that be enough. . . ."

Her words became an incomprehensible drone. Hartley sensed the change under his feet as they started up the fell. He nearly walked into the escarpment that marked the boundary of pasture and wood.

"I am sorry," Lord Bradwell whispered. "Do not give up hope."

Hartley's response was an animal grunt. On hands and knees he crawled over the rock. Then there was more climbing, and the ground leveled out at the edge of the forest.

Lord Bradwell stopped short. "Good God," he said. "It is barbaric."

Eden sobbed under her breath. Hartley made a great effort, and his vision cleared just enough to reveal what they had seen.

A cage. A cage, big enough for a man to crouch in, barred with iron. A heavy padlock hung from the door. It rested within a few brief yards of the nearest tree — salvation that lay just out of reach of the being it would imprison.

Claudia ran her hand up one of the bars as if she caressed a lover. "I am surprised to hear you say so, Cyrus, considering your facility for the slaughter of all manner of birds and beasts."

Bradwell released Hartley's arm. "I have not . . . killed . . . for many years."

"Then be silent and put the monster in the cage."

"Remember . . . remember your oath," Hartley croaked. "Eden —"

Her warm hand closed around his. "I am here, my love."

"Don't try to stop it. Remember Donal." He released her hand. "Come, Lord Bradwell. You are saving your grandson."

With heavy steps, Eden's father guided him to the open cage door and stopped. "No," he whispered.

Hartley stepped into the cage and fell to his knees. Eden reached the door just as Claudia closed the padlock. Metal clicked home with terrible finality.

"It is done," she said. "At last, it is over."

Darkness enveloped Hartley. There was no portion of his body that did not burn with the touch of Cold Iron. Pain had become so constant, so infinite, that he knew his punishment would not last as long as Claudia wished. He had become insignificant, the least of Nature's creations, soon to be nothing.

Soon it would be over. Eden would be free, their son safe.

"Hartley. Hartley, can you hear me?"

Eden. He stirred, his sprawled limbs untangling as he came back to consciousness. She was the sole point of light in his darkness, true as the golden sun.

"Go," he whispered. "I don't want you . . . to see."

"I will not leave you." She reached through the bars. "Let me give you strength. It worked before —"

"No," he repeated. "Too much Iron. You cannot . . . help me now. If you ever loved me, go. Take our son, and go." He turned his head, blindly searching for his tormentor. "Lady Claudia . . . do not force her . . . to watch. She is your daughter."

He did not expect mercy, but Claudia gave it. "Very well. You have kept your part of the bargain. Cyrus, take Eden away. I will follow soon."

"Come, Eden," Lord Bradwell murmured. "Please."

"Let go of me." The light that was Eden refused to be extinguished. "I love him. Do you know what love is?" Her voice rose in righteous anger. "Do you, Mother?"

"She is like . . . one of us," Hartley said, dragging himself up to the bars. "Perhaps she was born a Fane."

Claudia hissed in rage. "Silence!"

"I . . . do not think I will obey you." He found enough strength to feel through the bars. Molten nerves felt the coolness of flesh he had embraced and caressed and loved. The respite of Eden's tears washed his burning fingers. "Do not weep for me, Eden. Live, as you were meant to live.

"Farewell."

Chapter 23

N*o!"* Eden pressed herself to the bars and tried to hold him. His cheek touched the iron, and he convulsed. His skin was barred with the red mark of burns where his face met metal.

In horror, Eden looked at his hands. Her tears sizzled on his flesh like eggs on a skillet. She pushed him away from the bars.

She could not even hold him. She had failed to stop Claudia, failed to protect her son and the man she loved. She had nothing left.

Nothing but love.

Her existence had been without purpose until the day she'd come to Hartsmere. This was where her life had begun. And this moment was the pinnacle, the fate for which her very being had been aimed since her birth.

"Hartley," she said, stretching her hand into the cage as far as she could reach. "Fight. You will have Donal. You can take him back to your land, where he will be safe. I give you my blessing."

He lay still where he had fallen. Eden pushed harder,

until her shoulder was in danger of leaving its socket. "Hartley. *I love you.*"

Claudia tried to pry her fingers from the bars. Eden acted without thinking. She flung herself about and struck wildly with her fists and feet. Claudia gasped and rolled away. Eden scrambled after her.

"The key!" she demanded, pinning Claudia to the ground.

"Do as she says, Sister."

Eden looked up. Lord Bradwell stood over them, a pistol held loosely in his hand.

"I wished to be absolutely sure that I was not mistaken in my judgment this time," he said. "But it is clear that Eden loves this man by whatever name or shape he chooses, and he would die for her. I am sorry that I waited so long to act." He glanced at the weapon with a grimace of loathing. "I will use this, Claudia, to save my niece and her son."

"You haven't the courage, Cyrus —"

"We have all changed, haven't we, Sister? Do you wish to find out how much?"

Eden wasted no time in surprise. "The key," she repeated.

Claudia lay unresisting, her expression as hard as Lakeland granite. "You will have to kill me, Cyrus. My death is a small price to pay for Eden's freedom."

Choose. Choose, Eden. "Give me the pistol, Papa." She held out her hand, hoping that she could see well enough through her tears to grip the handle.

"Eden."

She heard the hoarse whisper and turned toward the cage. Hartley still lived. His eyes held the only color in his face, but they lit the dusk like torches.

"Forgive her, Eden. Let there be . . . no more hatred."

She dropped her hand. Lord Bradwell bent and pulled Claudia to her feet. Eden crawled toward the cage through the trampled, melting snow, her hair trailing like mourning ribbons.

"No hatred," she whispered. "Only forgiveness."

He smiled and closed his eyes and lay back. Eden bent her face to the ground.

Strange vibrations beat an uneven rhythm under her knees and palms. Behind her, Cyrus Fleming swore. She turned her head and stared down the fell through her veil of hair.

Coming up the fell, seemingly alone, was Donal. He raced swift as a young calf, with leaps and bounds that should have been impossible for a boy of his size. Just over his head, visible only to those with eyes to see, was the trailing, glittering mist of unearthly flight. Tod.

"Mother!" Donal cried. "Da!"

He reached Eden and she caught his wiry body in her arms. "Donal! Donal, my son —"

"The hunter let me go. Tod let Mrs. Byrne out of the house, and she told Mr. Blake that he shouldn't listen to Aunt Claudia. He went away to America." He wriggled free and stared through the bars at Hartley. Before Eden could stop him, he touched the metal. Pain screwed up his features, but he held on.

"Da," he said. "I'll help you." He looked straight up at Claudia, and she leaned back into Cyrus's hold. There was an instant of total silence. And then, from every direction, came the rustling of grass and the patter of little feet and the grunts and snuffles of a hundred animal voices. All converged upon the cage.

Eden watched them with prayers of joy and gratitude. Field mice, voles, foxes, and every sort of creature not asleep for the winter arrived in their varied legions — all accepting the truce that Donal imposed with his call. Claudia shrieked. Donal smiled.

"We will protect you, Da," he said, holding out his hand so that a pair of field mice could run up to perch on his shoulder. Three grumpy badgers, awakened from their sleep, planted themselves at Claudia's feet and glared up at her. The rest formed a large, loose circle about the humans.

Hartley raised his head, and tears fell from his eyes to pool on the cold metal floor of his cage.

"They will not hurt you, Claudia," Eden said. "But they will not leave until you release Hartley."

"So that he may work his evil on some other innocent?" Claudia clenched her hands, shooting glances right and left as if trying to watch all the animals at once. "He will take you away from me, and destroy you, as he destroyed my love!"

"No. He will not take me away. He will go with our son to a place where both of them will be safe from people like you."

"Safe from punishment!" Claudia cried. "I will *not* give him up!"

An unearthly cry silenced them both. Hartley had risen into a crouch within the cage. His chest rose and fell in a deep breath. From his brow sprouted antlers, and from his mouth came another cry that shook the very dale itself.

In the distance came a faint rumbling, like an approaching storm. Eden realized that it was not thunder but the drumming of hooves.

Out of the forest, down the fell, up from the dale dashed the red deer, magnificent stags in full antler and their females in blazing coats. Males that should be fighting each other in rut ran side by side, bellowing challenges as they came.

Cyrus pulled Claudia against him. "Eden, take Donal and run!"

"There is nothing to fear." Eden took Donal's hand as the deer joined the other beasts, towering above them in their magnificence. The air rang with snorts and the tearing of earth.

But among the deer was another red-coated creature, nearly lost in the forest of stamping hooves. It continued to the very edge of the cage when the others had stopped.

A fox. A red fox, crouching and cowering low to the earth. Hartley knelt. He lifted his hand and spread his fingers as if in a benediction.

"Be free," he commanded.

The fox writhed, falling upon its back. Eden was not sure what she saw, for in a single blink the fox was gone, and a man lay there in its place — a man dressed in the fashion of two decades past. He lifted his graying head.

Claudia stood rigid in Cyrus's hold, staring at the man. She spoke a single, croaking word.

"Raines."

And Eden knew. She embraced Donal and thanked Providence for this miracle, and for Hartley's selfless compassion. His freedom would make the miracle complete.

Claudia shook herself free. She took a halting step toward her husband, and then another, and another. The man rose to his knees. He blinked as if he had forgotten how to see with human eyes.

"Claudia?"

Eden turned Donal away. What happened now was a private reunion, and even after all Claudia had done — after all her scheming and hatred — she deserved this promise of redemption.

But when Eden faced the cage, she saw that Hartley lay still.

"No. Not yet." She lifted Donal high and pressed her cheek to his. "Call your father, Donal. Call him!"

"Wake up, Da!" Donal cried. "Wake up!"

Hartley stirred. He whispered something too low for Eden to hear.

"He's trying, Mother," Donal said. "He's so tired."

A large, gentle hand came to rest on Eden's shoulder. "Claudia gave me the keys," Lord Bradwell said. "Take them. I will help you."

Dry-mouthed and shaking, Eden let Donal down and fitted the first key to the padlock. The door opened and she flung the lock aside. She crawled into the cage and grasped the iron collar; using the second key she carefully removed the collar from his neck. She grasped Hartley by the sleeves of his coat, pulling and tugging him to the door.

"Help me," she begged. "Soon you'll be in a place where you can heal. You must try. Damn you, Hartley, try!"

He moved almost infinitesimally. Eden redoubled her efforts. Her father reached in when Hartley was near the door and helped her pull him onto the wet grass. Donal bent beside him, laying his small hand on Hartley's matted hair.

There was no time to let him rest. His only chance at recovery lay in his own land. In Tir-na-nog. But she did not know how to find the way.

"Donal, think very hard. Did your father ever tell you how to get to the land of the Fane?"

"Yes, Mother. I can show the way."

Thank God. "Help me carry him into the forest," she asked Lord Bradwell.

"And Claudia?"

Eden glanced over her shoulder. Two people were locked in a weeping embrace, oblivious to the world around them.

"She is a danger no longer. We must go."

Together, with Donal leading the way, she and Lord Bradwell carried Hartley into the wood, to the heart of the Forest Lord's realm, where the Grandfather Oak spread his limbs in benevolent rule.

Of course, Eden thought. *The gate is here.*

She and Lord Bradwell laid Hartley down. Eden stretched out on the bed of leaves beside him.

"Come, my love," she whispered. "Your gate lies here, but I cannot open it. You must do it. Take our son, and teach him . . . teach him to be happy." She turned his face and kissed him.

His lips moved on hers. He opened his eyes — those unearthly, mysterious eyes like wet summer leaves — and smiled.

"Thank you, Eden," he said. He lifted his hand to stroke her hair. "I . . . cannot repay you. But I . . . I shall never forget you."

She need hold back her tears only a little while longer. "Nor I you. Come." She tugged at his arm. Her father pulled him up. Hartley faced the oak. He murmured words in a language Eden didn't understand, and the air before the vast trunk began to shiver with eldritch light. Lord Bradwell gasped.

"The gate," Hartley said. He looked at Eden. "Once I go . . . I cannot return."

"I know." She smiled for him. "Your life is all that matters now. And Donal's." She pushed Donal gently toward his father. "Donal, you will go with your father to a very special place, where you will be happy and no one can ever hurt you."

"No, Eden," Lord Bradwell whispered.

"Can't you see? It is the only way. I know that now."

Hartley took Donal's hand. "This is a gift I do not deserve. Ah, Eden —"

She covered his lips with her finger. "You must go quickly. Quickly." She turned her face away.

But he caught her face in his hands and turned it again and kissed her. Her tears mingled on their lips.

"You will have love, Eden. You will have it because no mortal . . . was ever more deserving." He bent his head to Donal. "Will you come with me now, my son?"

Donal planted his feet. "Is Mother coming, too?"

"Not . . . now, Donal. We must go first. You will like Tir-na-nog —"

"Mother!" Donal began to cry, as he so seldom did. Eden maintained her composure with the greatest effort of her life.

"I will be along soon," she said, stroking Donal's hair. "Please, go with your father." She nodded to Hartley, and he lifted Donal into his arms, though the effort cost him dearly.

A flash of sparkling light whirled overhead. Tod appeared, circling them joyfully.

"We go!" he cried. "We go home?"

"Yes," Hartley echoed. "Home."

In a heartbeat Tod had flung himself through the shimmering gate and vanished. Hartley cradled the weeping Donal to his shoulder and looked one last time at Eden. "Be happy," he said. He faced the gate again, gathered his strength, and stepped through.

Eden fell to her knees. Lord Bradwell knelt beside her and held her like the true father he had never been before.

"It is my fault," he groaned. "Oh, Eden, this is my doing. I did not believe that love could ever be part of what I started six years ago."

Eden covered his hand with hers. "No, Papa." She tried to smile. "You are not to blame."

"I do not deserve your affection. Oh, my dear, if only I could suffer in your place."

She shook her head. No one else could endure this unbearable loss — and she would endure, for the sake of those who still needed her. For the servants and tenants and beasts of Hartsmere.

"We need not remain here, Eden," her father said. "I am not without resources now. I have friends and connections throughout Europe. We can travel on the continent and forget this place."

Forget. Eden bent forward to touch the bark of the Grandfather Oak. She was obscurely comforted to feel its rough reality, to know that it had sheltered the man she loved. A part of him lived on within that magnificent old gentleman. And in this forest.

For as long as she lived, she would preserve what he had loved. No ax would ever touch these trees, nor hunter invade its borders.

And every time she came to this place, she would know that the two she loved more than life itself were happy and safe on the other side.

That certainty must see her through all the years to come.

"I no longer try to escape what I fear, Papa," she said. "Hartsmere is my home. I will stay."

She settled against the tree and closed her eyes. After a

time, Lord Bradwell left her, and beasts large and small crept from the shrubbery to pay her homage.

Even they did not see her weep.

The Land of the Young was a thousand times more beautiful than Hartley remembered it. He stood at the inner gate with Donal mercifully asleep in his arms and gazed down upon the endless emerald hills, the wildflowers of every hue, the brilliant azure sky. Here it never rained, except for the amusement of its people. Birds more exotic than peacocks fluttered among immense, gold-leaved trees.

In the distance winged Fane performed a complex aerial dance, and then broke apart, laughing. Others feasted at a broad table carved of the rich red heartwood that grew only in Tir-na-nog, heaped with every imaginable delicacy. Crystal palaces dotted the landscape, and fantastic spires pierced the pastel clouds.

It was such a place that mortals called heaven.

It was the home Hartley had been denied for centuries. Now he had earned his way back, and the price of his passage lay quiet against his heart.

But he had surrendered that heart forever.

The bejeweled gate that rose before him was untended, for few Fane had the patience to play guardian. Mortals no longer found their way to the threshold of the Faerie kingdom.

Hartley placed his hand on the diamond-studded silver bars. The intricate metalwork rang with his touch, but the vast doors did not open.

Winged Fane and riders mounted on enchanted white horses began to converge upon the gate, drawn by the novelty of a visitor. Hartley recognized many faces, but he felt no joy. The one he wished to see was not among them and could never be.

He ignored them all and raised his head. "Mother. Father. I have fulfilled your requirements. The child you demanded is here."

An iridescent globe appeared over the gate and hovered there. Even to Fane eyes it was blinding: She had always been proud and imperious, the queen of the Fane, known on earth by a hundred names, first lady of the Sidhe and of the Tuatha de Danaan, rulers of Tir-na-nog.

"My son," a voice spoke from the globe. Human music could not begin to approach such glorious sound. "You have returned."

"Titania." He bent his head in brief homage, and she resolved into a woman of flawless line and form. Her face was unmarred by any hint of emotion.

"This is the child?" she asked.

"My son." He lifted Donal for her inspection, sickened as if he were still subject to the ills of a mortal body. "Donal."

Her long fingered hand descended to touch Donal's face. "He resembles you. Has he the power?"

"He has."

"Then he is suitable to our purposes. Children come less and less often to us. We have need of fresh blood to strengthen our lines." She reached out with both arms. "Give him to me."

Hartley turned his shoulder to her. "You will not have the raising of him, Titania. He remains with me."

One perfect silver brow lifted. "You were my youngest, and always most rebellious. You have changed in the mortal realm. How many of their years have passed since you last entered our land?"

"A thousand, and more."

She shuddered delicately. "It is fortunate you have come, else you would be doomed."

Doomed to remain among mortals, gradually to lose his powers and any hope of return to the Land of the Young. Doomed to "suffer" the love of Lady Eden Winstowe.

Titania made a dismissive gesture. "I grow weary of this. Pass through the gate, and I shall seal it behind you."

The gate swung open. Hartley cradled Donal and bent his head to the boy's brown, sweet-smelling hair.

This was what he had sought for a thousand years. An end to exile. An end to sorrow, and pain, and loneliness. No more unwanted responsibility to the men and beasts of earth.

No more love.

He set one foot over the threshold, and stopped. The watching Fane burst into a flurry of agitated motion. Titania's silver hair lashed about her head.

"What is this?" she demanded. "You cannot enter. You carry a burden that must be abandoned here, else you may not pass."

At first he thought she meant Donal, and he drew back. "My son —"

"Not the child." Titania stared at him in something like horror. "It is what lies in your heart."

Then he understood. It came upon him like sunlight — not this perfect, silvery radiance that filled the Land of the Young, but the warm yellow glow of a very ordinary English afternoon. He looked within himself and saw what Titania feared.

It was love. Love that filled his heart so completely that it could not fit through the Fane gate. Love that was not the game at which the Fane played, but which came from the deepest reaches of a mortal soul.

Love for his son and for Eden.

He could love. He *did*.

And he was not afraid. Not for himself, not for Eden, and not for their son. Donal would become the best of both worlds. He would thrive, because he was loved.

He grinned at Titania. "I cannot pass?"

"No." She drew herself up, merciless queen once more. "We have freed ourselves of mortal savagery and will have no more of it here. Submit yourself to me, and I will cleanse you of this taint, and all memory of the cursed realm of men."

Hartley took a step back. "Thank you, Mother, but that is a gift I do not wish."

A gaping Fane was a remarkable sight. "Have the mortals driven you mad? Come to me at once."

"No." He took another step back, and all the Fane rose up in a whir of wings and amazement.

"Do you know what you do?" Titania demanded. "If you do not submit to me, you will never enter the Blessed Land again. You will be confined forever to the mortal realm, to lose your powers and count your handful of days as the Iron wielders do. You will live among savages who kill each other and everything around them, and tolerate none who wields magic." Her voice boomed like thunder. "Is this what you wish?"

He cast a final look about Tir-na-nog, and the curious, perfect faces filled with astonishment. A few Fane called out to him, urging him to stay. The only sadness he felt was that of leaving behind a once cherished memory.

"You are right, Mother," he said. "I have been tainted by the mortal realm. Its humblest corner is more real and more wonderful than all the Land of the Young. The 'savages' value life because they can so easily lose it. And love"— he kissed Donal's forehead —"love is worth dying for."

The great bejeweled gate slammed shut. Titania blazed to the brilliance of an exploding star.

"You have chosen," she pronounced. "You are forbidden to return to the Blessed Land. Let no Fane open this gate until the end of time!" She pointed at Hartley. "Begone, mortal!"

A great clap of thunder deafened him. He bent himself over Donal and felt the blast strike.

He found himself lying on a bed of leaves, Donal sprawled across his chest, and Grandfather Oak stretching high above. The forest — his forest — was still with that particular silence that comes just before dawn. He breathed air sweet with growth and decay and change, listening to the beat of his very human heart.

Eden lay asleep among Grandfather Oak's twisting roots, an enchanted princess awaiting a kiss.

Hartley set Donal aside and ran his hands over his body, searching for the changes that must inevitably come. Eventually his hair would gray, his bones become fragile, his powers fade. He would be able to touch iron without pain and walk freely among men. Eventually, he would lie beside Eden in a mortal grave.

But not yet. Not nearly yet.

Donal stirred and yawned, rubbing at his eyes. "Da? Are we home?"

Hartley kissed Donal's cheek. "Yes."

"We aren't going to live in that other place?"

"No."

Donal grinned. A whole chorus of birds erupted into song all at once, filling the wood with triumphant music. Eden stirred, flinging one hand across her tearstained face.

"Can I wake Mother?" Donal asked.

"Let us wake her together."

Donal crept on hands and knees to Eden's side. Hartley bent over her, bursting with love, and kissed her.

She opened her eyes. A shaft of new sunlight broke through the trees to illuminate her face. Her beloved, astonished, exultant face.

"My love," Hartley whispered. "We are home."

"Home!" A voice Hartley had never expected to hear again sounded next to his left ear. Tod buzzed between him and Eden, landing with a thump on Donal's head.

Donal gave a whoop of joy and bounded upright. "I'm going to find Mrs. Byrne and tell her what I saw!" He paused with a guilty glance at Eden. "May I, Mother?"

"Claudia will not hurt him now," Hartley said. "Let him go. You will never lose him, dearest one."

"I know." She nodded to Donal. "Tell Mrs. Byrne that we will be coming soon." She smiled at Hartley, while Donal set off at a run toward Hartsmere, Tod clinging to his hair like a tiny jockey.

"Our son," Hartley said tenderly, stroking her cheek.

"He'll learn to live in this world without fear. We'll see to that, you and I."

She rested her forehead in the hollow of his shoulder. "Why do we lose the resilience and faith of children? Where does the magic go, Hartley?"

He enfolded her hand and guided it to her breast. "It is still here, Eden. It never goes away."

She gazed into his eyes. "You have come back? To stay?"

"Forever. With you." Hartley kissed her again. "Will you marry me, Eden?"

"Who asks?" she inquired with a sly smile. "Cornelius Fleming, Hartley Shaw, or the Forest Lord?"

"I will be whatever you desire, love of my life. Whom do you choose?"

"You," she said. "Only you, my dearest husband."

They kissed, and a thousand flowers bloomed in the snow.

Epilogue

Mrs. Byrne packed the last apron into her portmanteau and closed the lid with a sigh. The first of the new year must seem a strange time to leave Hartsmere, and perhaps she would have delayed had she not found so suitable a replacement housekeeper in Mrs. Singleton.

But it was time for her to go. The need that had summoned her here had been fulfilled. She sniffed a little, knowing she would miss these folk more than most.

Best to move on while happiness reigns. And she knew it would reign at Hartsmere for many a year to come.

First there had been the December wedding . . . that of Lady Eden Winstowe and her recently returned cousin, Mr. Cornelius Fleming. Hartley Shaw had mysteriously vanished, and the servants and tenants of Hartsmere insisted that they had no idea where he had gone. Mr. Fleming, they said among themselves, had done the proper thing in marrying the woman he had once abandoned. The dalesmen had never been as ignorant as they at first appeared.

In attendance at the nuptials was their son, Master Donal Fleming. The bride and her husband had decided that they would begin their life together without the pall of any deception. And so it would become known that Donal was what was crudely named a bastard — possibly the most cherished child ever to be born on the wrong side of the blanket. His sixth birthday celebration had followed hard on the heels of the wedding.

A fine solstice child, Mrs. Byrne thought with satisfaction. *He is blessed indeed.*

Donal had gained not only loving parents but a new grandfather in Lord Michael Raines. After Raines's recovery from his transformation, he had spent several weeks in seclusion, cared for by his deeply repentant wife.

Lady Claudia had been quite unable to look Eden, her brother, or Hartley in the eye. She had taken a cottage in another dale and devoted herself exclusively to her husband. But Mrs. Byrne knew she was a changed woman; love had the power to redeem even such as she. And Claudia Raines knew the time was coming when she would have much atoning to do.

Fortunately for her, Lady Eden forgave. Lord Bradwell had remained at Hartsmere to celebrate a joyous Christmas, and then had set about restoring something of the life he had abandoned. He and Cornelius — still Hartley to those who loved him — were well on their way to making a lasting peace. Even Nancy, who had been forced by Lady Claudia into drugging Eden, was excused her lapse. Eden wasn't of a mind to hold a grudge against anyone.

Eden had blossomed in more ways than one, for she was with child again. She continued to share her generous heart with the people of the dale, and everything she touched prospered. Laughter filled Hartsmere. The winter was the mildest the dalesmen could remember, and the snow fell gently upon giggling children and sober farmers alike.

Three times what thou givest returns to thee.

Mrs. Byrne put her hand at the small of her back and arched to stretch her muscles. It would be good to leave behind this elderly shape and resume her own. A little spell away from duty. She glanced in the cracked mirror on her dressing table and smiled at the face framed by its masses of red, curling locks.

"By Dana," she said, "it's glad I'll be to rest, indeed."

"Who do you speak to, Mrs. Byrne?"

She smiled and opened her arms to Donal. He skipped into the room and hugged her about the waist.

"Mother and Da told me you have to go away. Why?"

"It's sorry I am to be leaving you, to be sure, but I have a special job to do, and I must go elsewhere to do it."

He stepped back and frowned up at her. "What job?"

"In some ways, it's not unlike what your Mother and Da have done for the dale — help people when they have great troubles and sorrows."

"I heard Da tell Mother that he may not be able to help the dale anymore. Why?"

"You know your father is special, just like you. Some of the gifts that make him special . . . well, he traded them to be with you and your mother."

"Like talking to animals, and making the snow fall?"

Naturally the child would think of what gave him the most pleasure. He was a boy, after all, no matter how gifted. "Just like that. Only I'm thinking that your Da won't lose as much as he believes."

Donal beamed. "Will I grow up to be like him?"

"I hope so, lad. And like your mother as well. The best of both worlds."

Quiet footsteps crossed the threshold. "I trust my son has not disturbed you, Mrs. Byrne," Eden said with a smile.

"Disturbed! Wisht." She kissed the top of Donal's head. "He's always been a pleasure, my lady."

"Your father is at the stables, Donal," Eden said. "Why don't you go and see your new pony?"

Donal was gone before either woman could draw breath. Eden laughed.

"He will miss you, Mrs. Byrne." She glanced at her feet. "So shall I."

"But not too much, I think. You'll be busy enough, my

lady." She winked, and Eden blushed. "Two bairns with their father's gifts —"

"But Hartley told me that this child would be —"

"Ordinary?" Mrs. Byrne chuckled. "I have my doubts. They —"

"They?" Lady Eden gulped.

"Oh, my runaway tongue. Don't you fret, my lady. They'll be no match for you."

"Mrs. Byrne . . ." Eden hesitated, and then forged ahead. "You have not always been a housekeeper, have you?"

Nuala sighed. She was not to escape with her disguise intact. "Nay, my lady. Not always."

"Are you like my husband?"

Nuala laughed. "One of the Sidhe? Oh, no, my child. But I have known a few in my time."

Eden shook her head. "Hartley told me of the talisman you gave to his servant, Tod, which enabled him to fly to London without suffering harm. You also convinced the American to let my son go. I suspect that there are many more things you did to help us, entirely without our knowledge. I have guessed for a while now that you are not an ordinary woman."

"No more than you, your ladyship."

Eden smiled. "Oh, no. I have found that I really am quite ordinary — and satisfied with very ordinary things."

"Love is never common," Nuala said. "Nor is the making of new life."

"And what new life will you be making for yourself, Mrs. Byrne?"

"I shall go wherever the wind blows me."

"Or wherever others need a little help?"

Nuala chuckled. "No, not ordinary at all." She lifted the portmanteau. "I must be going, my lady."

"Eden."

"Eden," Nuala said with a nod. "My name is Nuala."

"It's a lovely name. Here, let me summon Armstrong to help you carry your luggage."

"No need. It's light enough." Nuala lifted the portmanteau to prove her claim. "And now . . . it's time for me to be on my way."

"Will you not at least allow our coachman to take you wherever you are bound?"

"Ah, but it's on my own two feet that I find the interesting things in the world." She moved toward the door, and Eden gracefully stepped aside. The two women walked to the front entrance, and Eden did Nuala the honor of accompanying her several yards down the drive. The day was sparkling with new-fallen snow, the kind that never seemed to blacken with dirt or crust over. The sun shone brightly. There was not a trace of wind.

Hartley's powers had not yet abandoned him.

"Blessed be," Nuala said, taking Eden's hands. "Give my love to your husband."

Eden leaned forward to kiss her cheek. "Will we ever see you again?"

"I shouldn't be at all surprised." Nuala smiled, and for an instant let the glamor drop.

Eden's eyes widened. "You are —"

"A child of the earth and of the sky." She bowed. "And now farewell, Lady Eden Fleming."

Eden half lifted her hand. "Farewell. God bless you!"

Nuala had gone but a few steps away when the animals came to see her off. Among them were foxes and rabbits, bounding through the snow beside the drive. But towering above all was the stag, crowned by wide branching antlers woven with mistletoe and holly. He bent his great head in salute.

Farewell, Lord of the Sidhe. May you keep the magic alive just a little longer.

She smiled to herself, pulled her cloak about her, and began to whistle an Irish tune as old as the hills.

•   •   •

So it was that the earl found redemption, Lady Eden Fleming discovered the joys of giving, and the Forest Lord learned how to love.

And they all lived happily ever after.

Out of This World